STARFALL

STARFALL

MELISSA LANDERS

HYPERION

LOS ANGELES   NEW YORK

Text copyright © 2017 by Melissa Landers

All rights reserved. Published by Hyperion, an imprint of Disney Book
Group. No part of this book may be reproduced or transmitted in any
form or by any means, electronic or mechanical, including photocopying,
recording, or by any information storage and retrieval system, without
written permission from the publisher. For information address
Hyperion, 125 West End Avenue, New York, New York 10023.

First Hardcover Edition, February 2017
First Paperback Edition, January 2018
10 9 8 7 6 5 4 3 2 1
FAC-025438-17328
Printed in the United States of America

This book is set in 11.125 point Bembo MT Pro/Monotype;
Barkpipe, Nori/Fontspring; Arial Narrow MT Pro, Netraface
Text, Sackers English Script, Sackers Italian Script/Monotype.
Designed by Maria Elias

Library of Congress Cataloging-in-Publication Control
Number for Hardcover Edition: 2016033382
ISBN 978-1-4847-8791-5

Visit www.hyperionteens.com

Once you have tasted flight,
you will walk the earth with your eyes turned skyward,
for there you have been,
and there you would return.

—"I, Leonardo Da Vinci," *Saga of Western Man*

CHAPTER ONE

*L*ight seemed sharper in space. The eyes tended to latch on to anything luminous, starved for a sense of direction in the thick black void. After the first year of living off world, Cassia noticed her sight had adapted to the sensory deprivation. All it had taken then was the glow of a distant star through her bedroom porthole to bring her boots into focus. Now, after her second year in residence on the SS *Banshee*, she moved through the ship like a cat at midnight, her retinas magnifying the barest hint of a spark, so she rarely needed to turn on the overhead bulbs.

She couldn't decide if that was a good thing.

When she'd left her home world of Eturia—or fled, really—it had been with a heavy heart and the intention of returning before the next gathering moon. But that was twenty-six moons ago. She'd counted. Each passing cycle was starting to feel like a defeat, and some days she wondered if she'd ever see home again.

She rotated on her narrow bunk to face one of the pictures taped to the wall, a panorama of her royal ancestral lands unfolding in great, rolling fields that gave way to an even greater lake of vivid indigo. This photograph was one of three items she'd managed to grab during her hasty escape. Since then, she'd spent so much time gazing at it she could trace a fingertip along the lavender-covered hills with her eyes closed. Sometimes in the twilight moments between dreams and awareness, she swore she heard the rustling of leaves on the breeze and smelled the scent of freshly clipped grass. But then she'd blink and find the spell broken, her senses jarred by the throaty snores of her roommate, Kane, and the musky smell of his antiperspirant.

He was snoring now.

She kicked the bunk above her, and he grumbled a curse before shifting on the mattress and dangling one brown arm over the edge. The sight of his blond-dusted knuckles made her smile. Kane was the second "item" she'd brought from home— her childhood best friend since the day he'd rescued her from a goose attack by sacrificing his cookie to the bird, buying her time to get away. Kane talked too much, chewed with his mouth open, and had a tendency to use her laser blade without permission. But without him, these years in exile would've been darker than the south side of hell.

So for that, she put up with him.

"Stop it," he grumbled, his voice rough from sleep.

"Stop what?"

"Pining. You're staring at the picture again."

"No, I'm not."

He didn't bother calling her a liar. "You're thinking about

the good times because we've been away for so long. There's a reason we left, Cassy."

As if she could forget.

She touched the gold disk tucked beneath her shirt. That was the third item to make the journey from home, a royal medallion identifying her as PRINCESS CASSIA ADELAIDE ROSE. But even when she removed the necklace and hid it beneath her mattress, she felt its ghost weight tugging at her shoulders—a constant reminder that she'd abandoned her people during a time of war. All of Eturia hated her. The bounty on her head made that clear.

"It's not your fault," Kane said.

She drew a breath and ran a finger around the edge of her medallion. Logically, she knew he was right. Her marriage to the prince of a rival house would have prevented the war, but she'd discovered the man's true intent was to murder her family and rule both kingdoms. Her parents hadn't believed her when she'd told them. That much *was* her fault. If she hadn't fought so hard against the match and thrown so many tantrums, maybe her word would have counted for something.

"They wouldn't have listened," Kane added.

"Get out of my head."

"But it's so breezy and vacant in there. Plenty of room to stretch out."

Biting back a laugh, she punched his cot.

"Come on." He swung his bare feet into view. "We're going planet-side today. All you need's a little sun to set you right."

At the reminder, she perked up. Real sunlight was such a rare treat that cargo drops seemed more like a vacation than work. And if there was any wiggle room in the schedule, the captain might award them a day of shore leave. "What are we delivering?"

"The grain we picked up on Cargill."

She wrinkled her nose. Stacking crates of grain always left her covered in dust, not to mention whatever eight-legged critters hitched a ride from the last colony. But the prospect of fresh air, firm soil, and warm rays set her legs in motion.

A few minutes later, she was in the washroom for her daily sponge bath, as showers were limited to once a week. She'd just finished pulling on her canvas pants and T-shirt when a flash of auburn fur caught her eye, and she turned to find Acorn, the ship mascot, perched above the doorframe, preparing to launch.

There was a time when Cassia would have ducked and run, but now she cupped both hands and extended them toward the sugar glider. Acorn spread her winglike arms and coasted into Cassia's palms, then scurried up to one shoulder and began seeking her favorite pocket. She found it, the one above Cassia's heart, and burrowed in headfirst.

"At least you love me, girl," Cassia said with a smile. "Though you don't really have a choice, do you?"

Acorn's breed was highly social, to the point where she could die without enough affection. She'd bonded with the previous captain, and after his death, adopted Cassia as a foster mother. Acorn's tiny claws still sent the wrong kind of shivers down Cassia's spine, especially when they were tangled in her hair, but secretly she liked feeling needed.

After handing Acorn a dried lentil, Cassia faced the washroom mirror and unfastened her ponytail. The instant it came loose, she narrowed her eyes at the blond waves brushing her shoulders. She still didn't recognize herself without her waist-long dreadlocks. If she was lucky, the bounty hunters wouldn't recognize her, either.

Kane strolled in, rubbing a hand over his own newly shorn head. The act lifted the hem of his shirt high enough to reveal a trail of golden curls encircling his navel and disappearing below the waistband of his pants. Against her will, Cassia's pulse hitched. She and Kane looked so much alike with their tawny skin and light hair that people often mistook them for siblings, but her body had no such misgivings.

Neither did Kane's. He kept making that clear.

He moved behind her and laced his long fingers through her hair, holding her gaze in the mirror while his lips curved in an appreciative smile. "I like it," he said, low and smooth. "I couldn't do this before."

Chills broke out along her backbone—the *right* kind of shivers. But she shut down the sensation and pulled her waves into a sloppy ponytail before things went too far again. She couldn't afford any more slipups. It wasn't fair to either of them.

Kane's grin fell in a way that said she'd hurt his feelings.

"Breakfast will be late," she reminded him, glancing at her boots because the expression on his face made her insides ache. "I'll get started while you wash up."

Then she backed into the hallway and did what she did best. She left.

CHAPTER TWO

Kane scrubbed himself from head to toe and pulled on his shirt one slow sleeve at a time. He combed his hair until his scalp prickled. Twice, he shaved his face with Cassia's laser blade before checking in the mirror for any spots he'd missed. When he couldn't stall any longer, he set off for the galley and hoped she had finished her breakfast and gone somewhere else. *Anywhere* else, as long as he wouldn't have to spend another awkward meal sitting across from her at the table while the rest of the crew cast sideways glances at them and asked what was the matter.

She'd locked him in the friend zone again. That was the matter.

The instant he crossed the threshold, he scanned the galley and took in three faces, none of which belonged to Cassia. There was no sign of her at all, not even of the jacket she usually left balled up on the counter when working over the burners made her hot. The only proof she'd been there was a vat of porridge left simmering on the stove. He released a breath as the muscles in his shoulders unclenched. He was safe, at least until the next time their paths crossed on this sardine can of a ship.

"Morning," Renny greeted from above the rim of his coffee cup. Steam fogged his glasses, and he scrubbed the lenses with a cloth napkin before scrutinizing Kane more closely. "You feeling okay?" he added, probably worried about transport madness. "Spending enough time under the lamps?"

"I'm fine, Cap'n," Kane said. It felt strange calling the former first mate *captain*, and he wondered if he'd ever get used to it. Renny was a good man and they all loved him, but nobody could replace Phineas Rossi, the crotchety old half-mechanical battle-ax who'd taken them in and made them a family.

"Catch a few watts after breakfast. And soak up all the rays you can when we stop on Vega." Renny nodded at him. "You've lost some pep in your step. I don't like it."

Kane didn't like it, either. He kept his thoughts to himself, but he wondered if a change in sleeping arrangements might help. It wasn't easy bunking three feet above Cassia every night, listening to the little moany noises she made in her dreams and ignoring the floral scent wafting up from her perfume microbes. That was enough to shake any guy's screws loose.

With only three cabins on the *Banshee*, that left him the option of bunking with Renny, or asking Solara to switch rooms. Kane shifted a glance at Solara, who sat on Doran's lap with both arms locked around his neck while he used the end of her long chestnut braid to tickle her nose. Those two were permanently joined at the hips. No way they'd give up their private quarters.

"Hey, Cap'n," Kane said. "Mind if I bunk with you?"

Renny didn't ask why, one of the many reasons why Kane liked him. "Suit yourself. But I snore."

"Me too." At least that was what Cassia claimed.

"It's a deal, then." Renny held up an index finger and dug inside his coat pocket, then produced Kane's watch. It was an antique, passed down from Kane's great-great-grandfather, and the only thing his dad had ever given him besides a tarnished last name. Renny handed it over with an apology in his eyes. "You might want to lock this up. I can't seem to stay away from it."

Kane fastened the metal band around his wrist. "As long as you don't lift the key to my lockbox." Renny had done that before. The man had compulsive sticky fingers, a condition that'd forced him to flee Earth after he'd stolen from the mafia.

Renny grinned. "I make no promises."

Doran tore his gaze away from Solara long enough to ask, "What's our ETA?" But he kept one hand on her thigh and used the other to rub her back with all the dedication of a guy trying to summon a genie from its bottle.

Kane made a face, but the pair didn't notice.

"About noon, Vega time," Renny said. "We'll dock there overnight, so feel free to use the shuttle if you want to meet up with your brother."

That got Kane's attention. Doran's twin brother had invented a super-fuel called Infinium, which was quickly becoming the most valuable substance in the galaxy. The guy was loaded, and he lived below the surface of a nearby planet in a swanky compound that included a beach simulator. "I want in on that."

"But the shuttle only holds two people," Solara pointed out.

"Then I'll curl up in the rear hatch."

"For a two-hour ride?"

"For as long as it takes."

"You must really want out of here."

She had no idea how much.

Renny excused himself to check the autopilot, and Solara leaned forward, resting both elbows on the table. "What's up with you and Cassia?"

Shrugging, Kane told a deceptively simple truth. "Nothing."

"I noticed you two don't fight anymore."

"And that's bad because . . . ?"

"Because bickering is what you guys do," Doran cut in. "Some people write sonnets. Other people draw hearts. You two yell at each other. It's your twisted love language."

The use of the *L* word didn't escape Kane's notice. It hit home like a fist to the chest, forcing him to face the stove to hide whatever emotions were pulling down the corners of his mouth. It was no secret he'd loved Cassia since he was too young to tie his boots—enough to drop everything and follow her out the door two years ago. And she wanted him, too. The way her skin flushed every time he touched her made that obvious. But *wanting* and *loving* were two different things. The real desire of Cassia's heart was to go home and rule their colony, which she couldn't do with the bastard son of a merchant by her side.

Kane stirred a pinch of cinnamon into the porridge. "We're friends. That's all."

His tone warned them to drop it, and they did. But when breakfast was over and the crew left him to clean up the mess, their words replayed inside his head. They were right. The dynamic on the ship had shifted, and a knot was building inside his chest, pulling a little tighter each day. Something had to change before that knot snapped him in half.

He decided to forgo the sunlamps and returned to his room, where he stuffed everything he owned inside a spare storage box. He'd just grabbed his pillow when Cassia walked in and stopped short at the doorway.

Her honey-brown eyes flew wide, darting from the box in his hands to his now empty bunk. "What's going on?"

Kane knew he hadn't done anything wrong, but that didn't stop his stomach from sinking. The sensation reminded him of the time his mother had caught him hiding a broken figurine under the sofa. He fixed his gaze over Cassia's head and into the hallway. "The room's all yours. Now you don't have to listen to me snore."

"But where are you—"

"With Renny. I think it's best."

For a long time she said nothing. Then her mouth pressed into a hard line while her eyes flashed with anger. "Perfect," she spat, reaching behind her neck to unfasten the Eturian prayer necklace he'd bought for her—the one that had cost him two months' wages. She stood on tiptoe and shoved the necklace into the box, right beside his pillow. "Don't forget this."

Before he could tell her to keep it, she spun on her heel and took off toward the common room. The clang of her boots on the stairs soon followed.

Ignoring the heaviness in his gut, Kane left his old room and kicked the door shut. His brain understood this distance was long overdue. Now he needed the rest of him to get the message.

CHAPTER THREE

*E*ven if Cassia hadn't known Vega was a brand-new terra-form, the silence would have clued her in. Planets in solar systems like these were settled by the poor—refugees from the overcrowded slums of Earth who wanted a fresh start and plenty of room to grow their families. Not the kind of people who could afford to import sparrows or bullfrogs. Settlers brought only useful stock with them. If you couldn't ride it, wear it, or eat it, you weren't likely to find it in the outer realm.

Shielding her eyes from the sun, she stood at the base of the ship's cargo ramp and gazed past a verdant field to the budding town in the distance, where a dozen prefabricated buildings lined a single paved street. The saltbox structures looked the same on all these fringe settlements, like they'd been ordered from a clearance catalog.

They probably had been.

"Let's get on with it," Kane called from inside the cargo

hold. "The sooner we make this delivery, the sooner we can go."

"Fine by me," Doran agreed.

Cassia's jaw tightened. She'd heard about the trip to Gage Spaulding's underground mansion, but no one had bothered to invite her. Not that she cared. She didn't want to spend her shore leave with Kane anyway.

Still facing away, she told them, "Let's make a deal. You guys stack the crates, and then you can leave. I'll see the pallet to town and collect payment."

"But don't you need the shuttle for that?" Solara asked.

"No. The warehouse is sending a hovercraft to tow everything in. I'll ride with them and walk back here when I'm done. It's not far."

There was a long beat of silence. Then Kane said, "I don't know. Maybe we should stay together."

For some strange reason, his words caused a sharp ache in the spot directly behind Cassia's breastbone. She whirled on him, seeing nothing but a blond blur through the moisture welling in her eyes. She didn't know what had possessed her, but she'd roll naked in a thorn bush before letting Kane see her cry.

"It's just a cargo drop," she snapped, charging into the hold and skirting around him. "I don't need you for that." As she continued up the stairs, she called over her shoulder, "I don't need you for anything."

* * *

An hour later, she was sitting on the edge of a wheeled pallet, watching the *Banshee*'s shuttle fade into the atmosphere. Once the shuttle vanished from sight, she sighed and rested her head against a crate of grain as a wheezing hovercraft towed her across the field toward Main Street.

"Sure you don't want to ride up here?" shouted the hovercraft pilot, a smiling boy who filled out his coveralls with the broad shoulders of a grown man. There was a hint of mischief in his eyes, the kind that promised a good time with no strings attached. But she wasn't in the mood for company.

"No thanks."

Once they reached the warehouse, Cassia hopped down and went in search of the foreman, who pointed her in the direction of the finance officer. A few electronic signatures later, full payment was transferred to the *Banshee*'s account, and Cassia found herself with twenty-four hours of shore leave on her hands— usually a good problem to have. This time she didn't know what to do with herself.

She turned her gaze to the open warehouse doorway, where the hovercraft pilot caught her eye. He stood outside, tipping his head toward the heart of town in an unspoken invitation. When she didn't answer, he said, "Have a drink with me." He held up both hands. "I promise I'll keep these to myself . . . unless you beg me to reconsider."

She laughed, but she still wasn't interested. "You seem nice, but—"

"I heard the pub just got a shipment of hellberry wine."

Her brows jumped. "From Pesirus?"

"Yep. The real deal."

That was it. He'd found the chink in her armor. There was nothing in the galaxy Cassia loved more than hellberry wine.

Everyone on the *Banshee* knew she lived for their yearly delivery to Pesirus, the only place where hellberries grew. The wine was spicy and sweet, served warm with a shot of cane syrup that made her feel like she was bathing in bliss.

"All right," she decided, jogging outside to meet him. "But only one glass. Any more and I'll wind up naked in the town churchyard." She knew from experience.

The boy winked. "One extra-large glass, coming right up."

After closing the warehouse doors, he led the way to the pub. They strode together down the center of the road through town, which seemed deserted now that Cassia had a chance to pay attention. While her new friend tried to impress her by prattling on about the farmland he was about to buy, she peered through store windows and in between buildings for the settlers she'd seen shopping a few minutes earlier. She noticed movement inside the general depot, but aside from that, it seemed everyone had taken a simultaneous lunch break.

That struck her as odd.

She turned to the boy to ask for an explanation, only he wasn't there anymore. She spotted his retreating form just before he ducked out of sight behind the washhouse.

Her senses fired a red alert.

She halted her steps, darting glances in every direction. Ahead of her, three men stepped out of the pub and ambled onto the street. Her eyes took in the restraints hanging from their utility belts, and she instantly pegged them as bounty hunters. Fear gripped her, but then sunlight glinted off a metal disk embedded in one man's temple—a prefrontal cortex blocker— and the bottom fell out of her stomach.

These weren't ordinary bounty hunters.

In a flash, she whirled around and sprinted between two buildings, heading toward a nearby soy field. The short, leafy stalks wouldn't hide her, but she had to lead the men away from her ship before they tortured the captain into telling them where Kane had gone. The Daeva had found her, and these hunters had no limits. Kane's name was on the contract, too, but unlike her, he was marked for death.

The worst kind.

When you want someone dead, you hire a hit man. When you want someone to scream until his vocal cords rupture, you call the Daeva. Cassia's former captain had said that, and she'd never been able to get the image out of her head. She wouldn't let that happen to Kane, not while she still had breath in her body.

She ignored the burning in her muscles and sprinted faster through the field. A sudden whizzing noise rose above the sound of boots pounding on soil, and before she had a chance to glance over her shoulder, something tangled around her ankles and sent her pitching forward.

She landed hard on her stomach with a grunt that knocked the wind from her lungs. Rolling aside, she tugged in vain at the bindings that had hobbled her. The ropes were metal, fixed in place by two interlocking spheres that wouldn't release without a key.

Her chest filled with enough air to allow her a single sob of panic. She dragged herself into a cluster of plants and curled up beneath the leaves. Judging by the snap of breaking stalks nearby, she didn't have much time. With trembling fingers, she unfastened the com-link from her shirt and relayed a final message to the *Banshee*.

"Renny, the Daeva caught me," she whispered. "Collect everyone and get as far away as you can. I'm dumping my tracker so you can't follow me. Please take care of Kane."

"The tracks lead this way," said a man. "I see her now."

She shut down the link and buried it in the soil.

A moment later, strong hands gripped her ankles and tugged her into the open. She squinted against the sun and met her captor's bloodshot gaze before she scanned his utility belt for anything she could use against him. She spotted a pulse pistol hanging loosely in its holster. When the man bent down to taunt her, she snatched the weapon and shot him in the chest.

His body collapsed beside her, and she heaved him onto his back to search for the key to her ankle restraints. She'd just dug into his shirt pocket when a new hand appeared from her periphery and struck her across the face. Pain exploded behind her cheekbone while the force of the blow sent her slamming into the dirt.

"Careful," a third man warned from behind them. "She's a return, not a kill. You break her, you buy her."

The Daeva towering over her released a snort. "Might be worth it."

Cassia spat blood onto the soil and laughed, despite the pressure of tears building behind her eyes. "As if you could afford me."

That earned her another slap, but only half as hard as the first.

"Where's the boy?"

As she lay on the ground, she resisted the urge to ask which boy the Daeva was talking about. Provoking him any further might hurt her odds of saving Kane. "He's not here. He flew off world for shore leave."

"Don't lie to me," the man said, and kicked her in the stomach. Her lungs emptied again as her mouth gaped to take in air that wouldn't come. She curled into a ball, racked by dry heaves, until a trickle of breath made its way past her throat. Gasping, she told the Daeva, "I swear! He already left."

The second man knelt by her side, then roughly yanked back her hair to peer at her with eyes colder than the grave. Finally, he gave a satisfied nod and released her. "Her story matches what her captain told me."

At the mention of Renny, her head snapped up. "What did you do to him?"

"The boy's on New Haven," the Daeva said, ignoring her. "Let's dispatch a recovery team for him and set our course for Eturia. There's a bonus for returning the princess before the next gathering moon. I don't want to wait."

CHAPTER FOUR

When Kane arrived at Planet X, he had to do a double take.

A lot had happened in the months since his last visit—enough that the barren, moon-size planet now boasted an impenetrable shield and the foundations of a manufacturing plant unfolding across its frozen landscape, all provided by the Solar League in the interest of quickening Infinium production.

Kane had no burning love for the government, but he couldn't blame the League for wanting to get its hands on another shipment of super-fuel. One chunk of Infinium had been powering the *Banshee* for weeks, allowing the captain to make ten times the deliveries at half the cost. Colonization in the fringe was expected to triple as soon as Infinium reached the open market. With his invention, Gage Spaulding had single-handedly transformed the fringe from a desolate hellhole to a promised land for the poor.

Not bad for a homeschooled eighteen-year-old.

Once Kane made his way inside the underground compound, he hardly recognized that, either. The typically silent bunker hallways now bustled with activity as engineers and construction foremen scurried from one makeshift conference room to another, having been forced to seek shelter from the icy winds aboveground.

Kane and the others eventually found Gage standing behind the sofa in the living room, which was being used as a command center. Surrounded on all sides by advisors, Gage pinched his temples and blew a lock of dark hair away from his face, probably wishing he could retreat to his lab and leave the business details to someone else.

As soon as Gage glanced up and locked eyes with Doran, his expression brightened. He lifted a hand to silence the chatter around him and strode toward his brother wearing the broadest smile Kane had ever seen on him. Gage and Doran were twins, identical except for the scar tissue that marred Gage's face. They'd recently found each other after a decade apart, and they were still navigating the uncharted waters of their relationship.

With a prickle of envy, Kane stood back to give them some space, thinking about the half brothers he'd never met and probably never would. There were three of them, or so he'd heard. For all he knew, his dad had a bastard at every port.

"I'm glad you're here," Gage said to his twin while extending a hand. The two clasped palms and moved in for a hug, but must have thought better of it because they pulled back at the last second and gave each other an awkward pat on the shoulder. "You were the business intern, not me. I'm in over my head."

"Is Mom here?" asked Doran while sweeping a cautious gaze around the room. It was clear he didn't want to see her. Understandable, as she'd faked Gage's death and kept the twins apart for years. Their dad was a real prize, too. He was serving ten years on a penal colony for trying to steal Gage's invention. Maybe Kane didn't have it so bad in the family department.

"No," Gage said. "She's on Earth negotiating taxes with the Solar League."

Doran released a long breath. "I'll see what I can do while I'm here."

"Excuse me, Mr. Spaulding," interrupted a tall, middle-aged man in a colorful patchwork tunic Kane recognized as Calypsian. "I need an answer to take back to my council. We're willing to invest, but only if you give us exclusive distribution rights inside the tourist circle."

Kane suppressed an eye roll. He'd dealt with merchants from Calypso during his clerk's apprenticeship. They always acted like a bunch of marriage-hungry debutantes—obsessed with monogamy. But exclusive trade was rarely a good idea, so he'd learned how to keep the figurative ring off his finger. With a lazy smile, Kane sauntered up to the man and slung an arm around his shoulder. It wasn't a move he'd make with just anyone. Casual touch was common on Calypso.

"You'll have to forgive our young genius here," Kane said to the man while flourishing a hand at Gage. "He's a visionary, not a businessman. Guys like him value change over profit." Leaning in like they were old friends, Kane quietly added, "Frustrating for men like us, huh?"

The man grunted in agreement.

"You won't get an exclusive out of him," Kane went on, "but I wouldn't let that stop you. If you don't get in on the ground floor, someone else will. Maybe the Obsidians," he said, recalling there was a heated rivalry between the two colonies.

That was all it took to convince the man. He left to draw up a contract, and Gage spun on Kane with a smile so wide it tested the boundaries of his cheeks. "I want you on my team. Whatever they're paying you on the *Banshee*, I'll quadruple it."

"Hey," Solara laughed, gripping her hips. "You've got some nerve, trying to poach him while we're standing right here."

"Oh, come on," Gage told her, still peering at Kane in wonderment. "Talent like his is wasted on a ship hand. He shouldn't be scrubbing floors and washing dishes. He belongs on my sales crew with Shanna. That girl could charm the gills off a shark. Together, they'd be unstoppable."

Kane appreciated the praise, but tempting as the offer was, he couldn't accept it. The bounty on his head had forced him to lie low, and besides, he'd left that life behind to watch over Cassia.

Cassia.

An invisible blade jabbed at his sternum. He'd managed to forget, for one moment, her final words to him: *I don't need you for anything.* She'd hurtled plenty of colorful barbs at him over the years—*scatweed, wharf-licker,* and his all-time favorite, *scum-eating son of a crotch smuggler*—but this was different. This time it was personal. She'd taken extra care to aim for his soft spot before plunging in the knife, and he didn't deserve that, especially after everything he'd sacrificed for her. What he deserved was someone who didn't run hot and cold all the time, who wouldn't play with his feelings and hurt him just because she could.

Maybe he should do something about it.

He studied Gage and tried to picture working for him. It was surprisingly easy to imagine. He liked Gage, and more than that, he admired what Infinium had done for the outer realm. The pay raise wouldn't hurt, either, or the beach simulator. The more Kane thought about it, the more he could see himself making a life here. He'd even be able to stay in touch with the *Banshee* crew when Doran came to visit his brother.

This job might be a dream come true.

Kane tempered his excitement, not wanting to seem too eager and hurt his negotiating power. He was about to ask for more information when a new voice called, "I heard my name." A young brunette strode into view, curvier than the Volcanus mountains and twice as hot. But gorgeous as she was, that wasn't what held his attention. What struck him was the way she moved—with an easy sort of confidence that was rare for someone her age.

"Shanna"—Gage waved her over—"I want you to meet Kane Arric. I'm trying to steal him away from his ship."

She stopped in front of Kane, standing close enough to share the sweet scent of her perfume. He noticed her eyes were violet, cosmetically enhanced, and even more striking when contrasted against the long chestnut hair tumbling over her shoulders. She unleashed a brilliant grin and slid her palm into his grasp. Kane was so caught up in her smile that he held on for longer than a friendly shake. She didn't seem to mind. Instead, she gripped him harder while her gaze brightened with interest. It'd been a long time since a girl had given him that look, but he recognized it. She liked him.

He returned her smile. Yeah, he could definitely see himself fitting in here.

"Kane," she repeated, drawing out his name as she continued to hold his hand. "I hope you'll join us. We're changing the galaxy out here. Plus"—she gave a teasing wink—"there's talk of a dental plan. If that won't sway you, I don't know what will."

Gage chuckled. "He just sealed the Calypso deal."

"Really?" Her brows lifted. "Without an exclusive?"

"It didn't take much," Kane admitted. "I just pitted him against the Obsidians."

"That's ingenious," she said, and Kane couldn't help standing a bit taller. "Now you *really* have to come work with us. At least think it over."

A few minutes ago, he would have told her no. But now his heartbeat quickened with the excitement of new possibilities—of starting over in a place where he was appreciated, where he could excel instead of simply exist. He still didn't want to tip his hand by seeming too eager, but he already knew what his answer would be.

"I'm willing to talk about it . . . maybe on the beach?" Giving her palm a light squeeze before releasing it, he added, "I want to hear about this dental plan."

Her face lit up as she pointed toward the simulator room. "You go ahead. I'll slip into my swimsuit and meet you there."

He tried not to watch her as she walked away, but he didn't quite succeed. "Best shore leave ever," he muttered under his breath.

Solara elbowed him. "You're not really considering this, are you?"

"Why wouldn't I?"

"What about Cassia?"

At the mention of her name, Gage perked up and began peering around the room for her. "Yeah, she's cute. Did she come with you?"

Kane snapped his gaze to Gage's.

"Whoa." Gage flashed both palms. "Never mind."

"Oh, they're just friends," Doran said in a sarcastic tone that was going to get his ass kicked if he didn't knock it off. "So you've totally got a shot with her."

Kane refused to lose his temper. This job offer was the first decent thing to happen to him in two years, and he wouldn't ruin it by thinking about Cassia. Anyway, she'd made her feelings clear—she didn't need him. So he put her out of his mind and strode to the beach simulator, calling over his shoulder, "You know where to find me. And by the way, yes. I'm really considering it."

* * *

Half an hour later, he and Shanna were kicked back in the sand, wearing next to nothing and doing their best to manufacture sunburns. His mood had lifted, and he had her to thank for it. Her smile was infectious, she laughed at his jokes, and although he made a concerted effort to keep his eyes on her face, he couldn't help noticing she rocked a bikini like nobody's business.

But mostly he enjoyed talking to her. He hadn't expected the conversation to flow so easily, or to learn they had so much in common. It turned out her father had cut and run before she was born, exactly as Kane's dad had done. She'd grown up poor, too, and just like him, she'd learned at an early age to charm her way out of trouble. Her apprenticeship with a textile corporation had taken her to settlements he'd never heard of, and listening to her stories confirmed how much he could learn from her.

When the conversation began winding down, he traced a finger through the warm sand between their beach towels and told her, "Thank you for this. I almost forgot what it felt like to have fun."

She watched him for a long moment, then settled a hand on top of his. "It sounds like you need a change."

"I think I do."

"So what's holding you back? I can tell there's something."

More like some*one*. But he didn't want to think about her.

"I know we just met," Shanna told him, "but I'm a pretty good judge of character. I know you have a lot to offer, and I think we'd make a great team."

He nodded. Gage was right. The two of them would be unstoppable.

"I also think we have a connection." She turned toward him, propping herself on one elbow to bring her face closer to his. "I'm not imagining that, am I?"

Kane's pulse hitched at her nearness. He found himself angling his body toward hers. "No, it's not your imagination."

The air between them seemed to thicken.

Time slowed down.

Neither of them moved or breathed until he reached out and took her cheek in one hand. He didn't know what had prompted him to do it—he barely knew this girl. Maybe he was caught up in the moment, or maybe some small part of him wanted to get back at Cassia for hurting him. Either way, Shanna didn't tell him no. She didn't reject him or recite a list of reasons why they couldn't be together. There was no regret in her eyes, only encouragement. And when her gaze dipped to his mouth, he knew what she wanted him to do. More important, he knew that whatever happened next, she wouldn't call it a "slipup."

So he went for it. He kissed her.

The moment their lips met, he released a sigh as a thrill passed through him. Her mouth was soft and warm, and she knew how to use it. But when he angled his face to deepen the kiss, his gut twisted, and not in a good way. She tasted wrong. She smelled too sweet. He could feel his body rejecting her.

He forced himself to keep going, hoping the kiss would eventually feel right if he gave it a chance. But a few beats later, he knew deep down that he'd made a mistake. He had just decided to pull away when the door behind them banged open, and they flinched apart, bumping each other's faces.

Kane glanced at the doorway to find Doran and Solara staring at him. His breath caught, and he had to remind himself he hadn't done anything wrong. He and Cassia weren't a couple; this wasn't cheating.

But one look at their pale faces and he knew that wasn't the problem.

"Something's wrong," he said as his body tensed.

"It's Renny," Solara told him in a hollow voice.

"What happened?"

"He just radioed from the *Banshee*. He's hurt pretty badly and . . ."

"And?"

"Cassia's gone. The Daeva took her."

Kane didn't remember standing up, and he didn't remember running across the sand or leaving the beach simulator. But the next thing he knew, he was within arm's reach of the compound air-lock, trying to claw his way half-naked toward the shuttle docking station while Doran and Gage wrestled him to the floor.

"Let me go," he growled, shaking them off. As he pushed onto all fours, he realized he needed a suit and an oxygen helmet to make it aboveground, and he began looking around for the set he'd worn earlier.

Solara ran in front of him, blocking his path to the air-lock. "Kane, you have to stay here. The Daeva are still hunting you. Renny lied and told them you're on New Haven, but they have a team watching the *Banshee* in case you come back. If they catch you, it means Cassia gave herself up for nothing. She wouldn't want that. You need to slow down and think about this. One of us has to go instead of you."

Kane snatched a suit from the wall. "Get out of my way."

"No, this is suicide," Doran said. "You're staying here until we know it's safe. Then we'll do whatever it takes to find Cassia—I promise."

"I'm not asking for your permission. Get out of my way."

"And I'm not asking for yours. You're staying put."

For a charged moment, they stared each other down. Then Doran grabbed Kane's wrists and tried twisting his arms behind his back. Kane was stronger. With one downward jerk, he freed himself and delivered a right hook to the nearest jaw. His knuckles collided with bone, but he felt no pain, only panic. Nothing mattered except finding Cassia. He never should've left her alone. While he was here, tangled up on the sand with another girl, she was scared and suffering, and that knowledge drove him to the brink of delirium.

She needed him. He had to go to her.

He barely managed one step before Doran and Gage ganged up on him again. They each took one of his arms and dragged him backward while he thrashed like an animal. Then Solara advanced on him, pulling a small button from her pocket.

Except it wasn't a button. It was a handheld stunner.

"No!"

"I don't want to do this," she said. "I'm so sorry, Kane."

He lurched back, desperate to get away from her. He couldn't let the stunner touch his skin. Once it did, it would flood his system with enough neuro-inhibitors to knock him out cold, and even after he woke up, his memory wouldn't return for a full day. The Daeva would be in the next sector by then. He'd never catch them in time.

"Please don't! I'll stand down, I swear!"

But Solara didn't listen. She slapped the device against his bare chest, and at once, he felt a rush of drugs careening through his nervous system, deadening his muscles until his head hung limp and his body went slack.

He had just enough strength to whisper, "She needs me," before his eyes slammed shut and darkness swallowed him.

CHAPTER FIVE

Cassia didn't know how long the voyage lasted. Tracking time was impossible when every moment inside her filthy metal cage felt like an eternity. It didn't help that there was no sunrise or sunset in space, only darkness. And without any live company in the cargo hold, she had no one to ask what day it was.

The Daeva didn't retrieve many breathing targets, so hers was the only cage on board the ship. On either side of her cell, coffins were stacked high and strapped to the floor, proof of a job well done for the contract holders. Cassia kept her eyes fixed in front of her and tried not to picture what remained of the people inside those caskets. It chilled her to think one of them might've been Kane.

At least she'd spared him from that fate.

She missed him so much it hurt. She'd lost count of the number of times she'd reached toward her throat to touch the Eturian prayer necklace he'd given her, only to find it wasn't there. She should've kept it. She needed all the comfort she could get.

There was no royal welcome waiting for her on Eturia. The title of princess meant nothing without the backing of her family's military, which wouldn't come riding to the rescue of a disgraced girl who'd broken her marriage contract and started a war. She'd be lucky if the Daeva bothered to hose her off before presenting her to Marius. After that, it would be a toss-up between execution and a chemical lobotomy—one of the many sadistic procedures his family had engineered.

Either way, her life was over.

The only bright side to her hopelessness was that it gave her a perverse sort of freedom. She had nothing to live for, so there was no reason to play nice. She'd learned which behaviors would make the Daeva sedate her. (Kicking the bars produced a noise they especially hated.) And because a punch to the face was worth the reward of passing her days in a dreamless coma, she kept kicking those bars.

By the time the ship landed, her face was one throbbing bruise.

On the morning of delivery, the Daeva hauled her out of the cage and shackled her wrists and ankles with lightweight restraints that delivered an electric shock if pulled too far apart. Her legs had grown frail from weeks of disuse, and her knees wobbled when the men dragged her into the blazing light of day.

She winced, blinded by the sun. Her boots met the crunch of dried grass, but she couldn't see or hear anything to indicate where she'd landed. From somewhere in the distance, a crow gave an eerie caw, and then a light breeze stirred her hair, smelling faintly of smoke. Slowly, she blinked until her surroundings came into focus.

It was obvious there'd been a fire here, which explained the charred scent in the air. Blackness covered the gently rolling hills, stretching all the way to the horizon. A few jagged tree trunks pushed up from the ground at awkward angles, like corpses rising from their graves. For miles around, there was only death.

She didn't recognize this place. Had they landed on the wrong planet?

One of the men shoved her forward and pointed at a shuttle bearing the Durango crest, the house seal of Marius's family. "Marius wants you to take a homecoming tour before your delivery."

The breath caught at the top of Cassia's lungs. She jerked her gaze back to the landscape, this time picturing the hills covered in lavender wildflowers and graceful willows spilling leaves onto the breeze. She spun in a clumsy circle until her eyes found a lake in the distance, and then her vision flooded with tears. Because she did know this place, knew it by heart from the years she'd spent gazing at its likeness taped to her bedroom wall. She was standing on her royal ancestral land.

Ravaged by the war she'd caused.

"Move," the man said, shoving her again.

Cassia lumbered onto the shuttle and took a window seat, then watched as the devastation unfolded below. Nothing could have prepared her for what two years of battle had done to her city. Most of the streets were impassable, pockmarked by shock wave mortar, and the Rose Academy at the heart of the scholastic district was reduced to rubble. Fields were ruined and warehouses torched. Not even the hospital was spared. Half its roof had melted off, revealing heaps of twisted metal and piles of scorched beds that likely hadn't been vacant during the attack.

Her eyes couldn't process the devastation. She wasn't naive—she'd seen images of war on other planets—but weapons of mass destruction didn't exist here. The four founding dynasties had agreed to that in the colony charter when they'd terraformed Eturia hundreds of years ago. Obedience to the charter was their most sacred tenet, and the Solar League was supposed to help enforce it. That was why colonies paid taxes. So why hadn't the League stepped in?

She continued scanning the city and noticed her family's palace was still standing, though a portion of the east wing had crumbled, and the walls around the front entrance were defaced with symbols painted in red. Squinting, she was able to identify them as basic squares with an *X* marked through each one, but she didn't know what they meant.

As the shuttle jettisoned away from her family's territory, she peered into the distance and noticed similar devastation in the neighboring kingdoms. Only the Durango lands seemed unaffected, which told her it was Marius's family who'd betrayed the charter. That didn't surprise her, but she couldn't understand how they'd funded the war. Weapons didn't come cheap, and the Durangos possessed the least amount of wealth. That was why they'd agreed to a marriage between Cassia and Marius in the first place.

The question moved to the back of her mind as the shuttle touched down behind the Durango palace. She steeled herself, using both shirtsleeves to scrub the wetness from her eyes. Her enemies had already taken too much. She wouldn't give them her tears, too. When she exited the shuttle, it was with her matted head raised to the sky.

She'd assumed she would end up in a jail cell, and she was right. But instead of taking the most direct route to the basement, the Daeva led her slowly along every corridor in the main house so the servants and visitors could see how the once-regal Cassia Adelaide Rose had been reduced to a stinking prisoner in bloodstained rags. Refusing to acknowledge any of them, she stared blankly in front of her as she made her way through the mansion and eventually down the staircase to the brig.

She'd never had an occasion to visit a dungeon before, not even inside her own palace, but this was how she'd imagined one would look. Half a dozen long cells stretched opposite a security station, which was manned by two gray-uniformed guards. By habit, she made note of the weapons at their hips—an electric prod and a pulse pistol, each hanging on an unsecured holster loop. She estimated how quickly she could grab a weapon with her wrists bound, but as if sensing her awareness, both guards stood out of reach while they pulled aside the cell door of fiberglass bars.

The cell was dim and cool, smelling slightly of mold, and the floor tilted on a decline that led to a round drainage grate near the back wall. She tried not to dwell on what fluids had once flowed there, but the burgundy-colored stains around the catch basin painted a vivid enough picture. The door slammed shut behind her, making her jump.

"Unshackle the prisoner," one guard told the Daeva, his

voice thick with disgust for the bounty hunters. Among lawmen, the Daeva commanded fear, but never respect.

Cassia stood flush with the bars, holding still while the Daeva who'd taken the most delight in abusing her reached through and unfastened her wrists and ankles.

"I'm gonna miss this one," he said while leering at her. "She has a nice scream. Wish I had the credits to buy her so I could hear more of it."

Each time his skin brushed hers, she had to clench her teeth to keep from flinching. His cuticles were crusted in her blood. The sight of his hands brought back a flood of memories the sedatives had dulled. When the Daeva slid the chains free and turned to leave, Cassia drew a furious breath.

"You forgot something," she said.

The instant he glanced over his shoulder, she moved like lightning, jabbing her fist between the bars. Her knuckles connected with his nose, and a light crack sounded as his bones splintered beneath her hand. Before he could react, she darted out of his reach into the cell. She tripped over her own boots and landed hard on the concrete floor, but the fury in the man's eyes was worth a bruised tailbone.

He gripped the bars and rattled them in a violent clatter, sputtering curses through the blood flowing over his lips. One of the Durango guards prodded the Daeva with an electric wand and warned, "Any more damage to Marius's prize and it'll come out of your bounty. I suggest you see the clerk and then return to whatever hole you crawled out of."

The Daeva growled and snorted for a full minute, but he eventually gave up the fight and stalked out the door. Once the clatter of his footsteps faded up the stairs, the guard turned to his partner and issued an order. "Take an extra set of restraints to the maids and tell them to put down a vermin-resistant tarp before they begin." He thumbed at Cassia. "God knows what kind of mutated lice she's tracked in here."

The other man nodded and nervously scratched his scalp.

As soon as he left the room, the first guard leaned against the wall and folded both arms, studying Cassia as if she were a riddle that needed solving.

"You've changed," he said. "For the better, I think."

He spoke as if they knew each other, which prompted her to examine him more closely. Now that she studied the contours of his face, he did seem familiar. He was in his early twenties, tall and slim with sandy hair and a crooked nose that indicated he'd broken it more than once. Something prickled at the edges of her memory, but she couldn't place him.

"You don't remember me," he said flatly, like he'd expected as much. "Let me help. I was the cadet charged with supervising your shopping trips in the city. You always gave me the slip, and then I had to pull extra detail as punishment for losing you."

The missing pieces connected, and she gave a small gasp of realization. He was one of her family's soldiers wearing an enemy disguise. She would've recognized him sooner if he hadn't changed, too. His gaze had grown hard and cold, as if the last two years had drained all the youth out of him. "Private Jordan?"

"It's General Jordan now."

"General? That's a high rank for someone so young."

"Consider it a side effect of war," he said, eyes narrowed. "Promotions come quickly when your superior officers are dead."

Cassia's cheeks grew hot. Her first instinct was to hang her head, but she kept her gaze firmly fixed on his. "I didn't want any of this to happen. I had to leave."

"I know. If you'd married into the Durango family, Marius would have killed your parents. And maybe you, too, once he secured the Rose title."

Her brows lifted. "Who told you?"

"I have my sources."

"So is that why you're here?" Her heart swelled with hope, filling her with the first real warmth she'd felt in ages. "To take me home? Do my parents believe me now?"

Jordan watched her for a long moment before shaking his head. "You're even more out of touch than I thought."

"What do you mean?"

"Your parents are gone. They escaped off world months ago."

"Escaped? To bring back reinforcements?"

He laughed without humor. "More like to save themselves. They turned tail and ran in the middle of the night. We haven't heard a word from them since. As an added bonus, they emptied the coffers before they left. So I think you'll agree that whether or not they believe you is irrelevant."

All that hope sank to the bottom of Cassia's stomach and turned to ice. She couldn't believe her parents had left the kingdom defenseless, especially after all the years they'd lectured her on the merits of duty to the throne. Her people must hate the Rose name now more than ever. She pushed past the ball of shame in her throat and asked, "What else have I missed?"

"Well," Jordan began with a hitched brow, "after you left,

the Durangos started making empty threats. No one believed they would invade; everyone knew they didn't have the money for a war. I figured they'd accept a payout for the broken marriage contract, and that would be the end of it. But then the king and queen died in a shuttle 'accident' "—he used his fingers to make air quotes—"and Marius took control."

"Marius is king?"

"Of three thrones—every dynasty except for yours. He's the one who attacked, and not only us. He hit the other two kingdoms so fast there wasn't time for an alliance. They fell in a matter of days. Now he owns those lands, and the former title holders are probably waiting for their own 'accidents' to happen."

"But wait," Cassia said. "That doesn't make sense." According to the charter, Marius was within his rights to invade her kingdom because she'd broken their marriage contract. But that privilege didn't extend to the other two dynasties. He had no cause for aggression there, and certainly no right to assassinate royals. The Solar League should've intervened and sent a legion of Enforcers to stop him. "Who's allowing this?"

Jordan delivered the kind of amused look one might give a child who'd asked where babies came from. "I imagine the same person who paid for his missiles."

"You think he has a financial backer?"

"I know he does. And it's someone with connections powerful enough to make the Solar League look the other way."

"What about my kingdom? Who's in charge?"

"That depends on who you ask."

"No one?"

He answered with a shrug. "Or everyone. Either way, it's a mess."

"So how have you fought off the Durango army for this long?"

"The citizens took up arms. Which seemed like a good thing, at first. . . ."

"Until?" she prompted.

"Until they stopped taking orders and formed a rebellion. They want the charter amended to form a republic."

"Oh god." Cassia gripped her temples and thought back to the symbol she'd seen defacing the palace. That must be the mark of rebels. But an uprising was the least of her problems. Without a leader, the Rose kingdom would continue its downward spiral until it tumbled right into Marius's hands. Her people needed a queen, and no matter how tarnished her reputation, she was the rightful heir to the throne. She nodded at the cell door. "Let me out of here and take me home."

To her great surprise, Jordan told her, "No."

"Excuse me?"

"This isn't a rescue mission."

"Enough games," she snapped. "Unlock this door right now."

"Let's say that I do," Jordan countered, "and that we actually make it out of here alive. Do you think Marius will just shrug it off and let you go?"

Cassia tightened her jaw. She knew the answer.

"He won't," Jordan said. "He'll burn down every house in the kingdom until he finds you. This is personal for him—he's been the colony joke ever since you left him at the altar. I think the reason he hasn't completely crushed us is because he wanted you to be here to watch it happen. When I heard you were captured, I infiltrated his guard detail so I could see you. But I didn't tell anyone. Not even my next-in-command knows I'm here."

"Then what's the point? Did you come here to taunt me?"

"No. I came to see if you grew a backbone. To see if there's any fight left in the Rose bloodline." He delivered a pointed look. "And to see if you can help me take down Marius from the inside."

That shocked a laugh out of her. "And what've you decided?"

"That I think you have it in you."

"Well, I think you're unhinged."

"Maybe we're both right," he said. A click of footsteps from overhead warned their conversation would be cut short. He moved closer and spoke in a whisper. "Running away won't solve anything, and neither will assassinating Marius. We have to take him alive so he can tell us who's supplying his missiles *and* where he's hiding them, because they're not in his armory. Once we have his missiles, his army will have to stand down. If you find a way to neutralize Marius, I'll come back for you. And when I do, you'll have the full support of the military to reclaim what's yours."

His idea set Cassia's inner wheels in motion, but she still didn't see how it was possible. "I can't do anything from in here."

"Then you're not as cunning as I remember."

"But I don't have so much as a hairpin on me."

Jordan's shrug said that didn't worry him. "If you play this right, you won't need one. I heard the ladies' maids talking before you arrived. They're supposed to clean you up and present you to Marius's court at supper. Maybe you can persuade him to honor your marriage contract."

"Now I *know* you're unhinged."

"Planning a royal wedding takes a lot of work. Creates distractions that make a man vulnerable. Whatever you decide, I suggest you use that famous charm of yours." As the general backed away, he frowned at her stained clothes. "I'm sure it's buried under there somewhere."

"How do I contact you?"

"You don't."

"But we need a plan. How will you know when to come for me?"

All he told her was, "Don't worry. I'll know."

Then he ducked out the side door, leaving her head spinning.

*   *   *

An hour later, a team of guards arrived to bind her wrists and usher her to the servants' wing, where a trio of scissor-wielding maids awaited on a tarp that protected the floor from a scourge of "mutated lice." With pinched faces, the maids cut away her clothes and tossed the soiled rags into the fireplace, all the while remarking that poor Marius should never have been contracted to wed such a disgusting girl.

Over the next several hours, they scrubbed Cassia raw, washed her hair until her scalp burned, and then erased her bruises using medical cosmetics she hadn't seen since her days in the palace. When the pain was gone and the real makeover began, she pretended to enjoy the tickle of shimmer being dusted on her cheekbones, but her focus was on Jordan's offer. There had to be a way to make it work.

She considered every angle, no matter how wild, as the maids styled her hair in a twist and secured it in place. The light scrape of metal against her scalp told her she now had access to hairpins, but she wouldn't win this battle with lockpicks and pulse pistols. For Marius, tonight was about settling a vendetta. She would have to placate him, and her instincts told her humility was the key.

For that reason, she didn't object when the maids zipped her into a strapless minidress more fitting for an escort than a princess. Nor did she complain when the guards left her feet bare and her wrists bound as they escorted her to the banquet hall. If Marius wanted her humbled before his court, she would give him that.

Once the banquet doors parted and she stepped across the threshold, she took care to shorten her stride into the steps of a girl ashamed. She dropped her gaze to the glittering quartz tiles beneath her feet and didn't look up until she heard a familiar baritone that turned her blood cold.

"My god, is that you, dear Cassy? You're nothing but skin and bones."

The intimate use of her nickname grated her nerves. Nobody except Kane called her that. But she peeked shyly through her lashes at Marius, making sure to bite her quivering lower lip for effect.

From his seat at the head of the long dining room table, Marius looked the same as she remembered: like he belonged on a billboard. He'd always been beautiful, both by genetics and design, and tonight was no exception. There wasn't a blemish on him, from the copper waves curling gently against his collar to the tips of his perfectly manicured fingers. He seemed as sculpted as ever, with a body that was literally known to stop traffic. (His exposed chest had once caused a three-hovercraft pileup.) But beneath the facade of perfection simmered a cruelty that all the enhancements in the galaxy couldn't hide.

That was why she'd refused him.

The half dozen girls hovering around his chair didn't seem to mind. Especially not the one sitting on his lap, stroking his well-trimmed beard with her fingernails. She looked content enough to purr, barely flicking a glance in Cassia's direction before gazing in wonder at Marius's face.

He lifted a chiding hand toward his guards. "Shackles? Our guest is a sovereign, not a soldier. Free her so we can dine like civilized human beings."

The guards obeyed, but they lingered within arm's reach, keeping their eyes fixed on her hands. They must have heard what she'd done to the Daeva. In retrospect, maybe punching the bounty hunter had been a bad idea.

"Come." Marius indicated the upholstered chair adjacent to him at the table. Every head in the room turned toward the seat. "I ordered my chef to prepare your favorite: braised pheasant with asparagus spears, hold the truffles." With a grin that didn't reach beyond his lips, he added, "I remembered you hate mushrooms."

He snapped his fingers, and a dozen platter covers simultaneously retracted, filling the room with the steamy scents of roasted meat and decadent spice. Cassia's stomach grumbled as she settled in her chair.

Marius laughed at the sound of her hunger. "Had I known the Daeva would starve you, I would have sent someone else to bring you home."

"Would you have?" She unfolded her napkin. "Even knowing why I left?"

His arrogant smile slipped. When he recovered, his lips were noticeably thinner than before. "I won't pretend I was happy to learn you'd run off with a bastard, but if what I've heard is true, you're not the first girl he's seduced for money. I can't blame you for falling victim to his charms. You were only sixteen."

The terseness of his response caught her off guard. She scanned his face for a hint of subtext—a sardonic twist of his mouth to show they both knew the *real* reason she'd left. But if the bloom of color on his cheeks was any indication, he actually believed she'd run away with Kane out of love. And if that was the case, it meant her parents hadn't told anyone about her accusations.

She saw a way to make Jordan's idea work.

"You're more forgiving than I deserve," she murmured, staring into her lap but speaking loud enough for all to hear. She peeked up at Marius and then back down again. "I knew it was a mistake as soon as I left, but I was too afraid to come home and face you. Now there's been so much suffering, and it's all my fault."

"Mmm," he agreed. "Things could have been different if you'd stayed."

"Maybe it's not too late to fix this. We can join our thrones and stop the fighting."

He turned his attention to the girl on his lap, grinning as he ran a lazy finger down the length of her spine. Despite his attempt at uninterest, clearly this was what he'd wanted—for Cassia to publicly ask him to take her back. "Why would I agree to that when I'm about to capture your throne? There's no need for a marriage alliance now. The fighting will end in days with your surrender."

"But there are insurgents in my city," she warned. "A rebellion to destroy the monarchy, all because of the war you waged against them. They'll never follow you unless I show them there's nothing to fear."

Marius lifted a shoulder. "Rebels can be destroyed easily enough."

"True," she conceded. "But if you keep using your weapons, soon there'll be no one left to rule."

That must have resonated with him, because he hesitated and wrinkled his forehead in consideration. She knew she almost had him. She thought hard of a way to sweeten the deal, to give him whatever he needed to save face with his people.

Above all else, what did he need?

One humiliation for another, she decided as she pushed up from her chair and sank to her knees, right there in front of Marius, his entire court, his romantic playthings, and every servant in the room.

"Please," she begged, clasping both hands together. "Withdraw your troops and join our families. Help me make this right." When he didn't seem convinced, she swallowed her pride and took her submission to the next level. She bent down and rested her forehead on the tip of his boot. She could sink no lower than this. "If you'll have me, I'll marry you. I'll do whatever you ask me to do. Just say you'll have me."

When she glanced up, Marius wore a smile so broad it threatened to split his face in half like an overboiled egg. He didn't favor her with a reply—naturally, he would draw out the suspense—but his expression told her everything she needed to know.

Yes, he would marry her.

And he'd make sure she didn't enjoy one moment of it.

CHAPTER SIX

*I*n the days that followed, Marius made good on his unspoken promise to punish her. When he announced their engagement from the palace balcony, it was with a girlfriend under each arm and Cassia standing off to the side like a used-up handkerchief. Her display as the spoils of war elicited cheers from the crowd, just as Marius had intended, but she ignored their taunts and kept her gaze turned down, scanning the crowd for a familiar broken nose and a squadron of soldiers in disguise.

No one had come for her yet.

She expected to see General Jordan later in the week, escorting the royal cleric during marriage contract negotiations, but he didn't appear then, either. Nor did he send a message or convey any type of instructions for what she should do next. She signed the contract and slammed down the pen in frustration.

Why wouldn't Jordan communicate with her? What did he

expect her to do? And just how far was she supposed to take this marriage act—all the way to the altar? She hoped not, because at this rate Marius would make her crawl down the aisle with an apple between her teeth. She didn't even want to think about the wedding night, not that she had any intention of following through on that part of the ruse.

But when two more days passed without word, she was forced to do a lot more than think about it. The morning of her wedding arrived, along with an ivory satin gown, slightly yellowed at the hem, and a handwritten note from Marius.

My mother wore this on her wedding day.
May it bring you the same luck, dear Cassy!

"Cassy," she hissed through clenched teeth. He needed to stop calling her that. And considering the fact that he'd killed his own mother, she had no interest in duplicating the woman's "luck."

She crumpled the note and threw it into the fireplace as her cheeks burned with anger. Where was her support? Where were the troops to help her with this mission? She'd never felt so alone. Every single person in her life had abandoned her, even her parents and her closest friends. Why wasn't anyone trying to find her—and where was Kane when she needed him?

Kane.

An imaginary band squeezed her chest. Just when she thought she couldn't miss him more, she pictured his face and lost another piece of her soul. She hadn't meant to blame him for staying away. That was what she'd wanted, for him to disappear and be safe. But she would give anything to have him with her, to feel his long fingers in her hair and to listen to the low murmur of his voice in her ear.

If he were here, this time she wouldn't pull away or make him stop. She would give him what he'd always wanted, what she'd secretly wanted him to have: her whole heart, all in. She wouldn't care about political marriages or royal bloodlines. She would be brave and let herself love him.

But it was too late; she was out of time.

Tears blurred her vision as she drifted into the washroom. If Kane could see her now, he would tell her to stop brooding and rescue herself, then add a teasing insult to get a rise out of her. She would yell at him for some silly reason or another, and then they would bicker until one of them kissed the other one silent. She couldn't believe those days were gone.

She was still smiling through her tears when she glanced at the sink basin and noticed something she'd overlooked before. There beside the soap rested a shiny new laser blade, much like the one she'd left on the *Banshee*, the one Kane was probably using right now.

A possibility occurred to her.

The idea seemed far-fetched at first, but by gradual degrees it bloomed into a plan, and in the span of a few minutes she knew what she had to do.

"Thank you, Kane," she whispered to herself.

Then she put him out of her mind and set to work.

*   *   *

"Do you swear to honor His Royal Colonial Highness, Marius Edwin Durango, in your thoughts, words, and deeds?" the cleric asked Cassia through a long gray beard that puffed at the lips when he spoke.

"Yes." She held her hand, palm up, toward the man. "I swear it."

He pricked her index finger with a ceremonial knife and squeezed the wound until a fat droplet of blood rose to the surface. He guided her finger to a glass disk about the size of a walnut, etched with interlocking swirls, half of which already ran red with Marius's blood. With one touch of her finger, the glass absorbed her life force and sent it rushing through the empty channels, where it completed the pattern and marked the joining of two families.

It was official. They were wed.

In a rare display of decorum, Marius cupped her chin and tipped her face toward his for a kiss. Cassia closed her eyes and held her breath. She felt a brush of contact at her lips, warm and soft, but beneath it lurked a wicked smile, one that promised he would make her pay once they left the sanctuary of the temple.

From behind, a row of girls sighed dreamily. They knelt on the floor, seeing only what they wanted to see—a blindingly gorgeous young king offering a second chance to the princess who had jilted him. None of them knew what awaited her later in his chambers. None of them knew what their king was capable of.

But she knew.

So she kept her head down during the wedding feast, lifting

her gaze and her cup only when a toast called for it. She didn't bother looking for a friendly face in the banquet hall. She had no friends here. While the court laughed and chattered among themselves, she sat obediently by her husband's side until the sun's last rays sliced through the windows and announced it was time to go wait in his suite. Then she stood and exited the room to the sound of whistles, leaving her dignity somewhere behind.

Marius had already delivered a flimsy excuse for a nightdress to her quarters, along with a note explaining how she should present herself to him. Numbly, she changed into the outfit before wrapping herself in a robe and making her way to the royal suite. Two guards flanked the entrance. One of them opened the door for her while muttering something to his partner that made the other man laugh. She didn't hear the remark, or particularly care. As the door shut behind her, she scanned past the oversize bed and the lavish wood furnishings to the balcony at the far end of the room—a possible exit point if things got out of hand.

On bare feet, she padded to the balcony doors and opened them a crack, peeking outside as the cool night breeze tickled her cheeks. The drop from the second-story suite didn't seem too far, especially with a thick carpet of grass to cushion her fall. With that in mind, she backed away and prepared for her husband's arrival.

She shed her robe and knelt on the cold tile at the foot of his bed, just as he'd ordered her to do. She didn't know how long he kept her waiting there, but by the time she heard his voice in the hallway, she'd lost some of the feeling in her knees.

The bedroom door opened and shut again. Soft footsteps

clicked across the floor, soon stopping to the left of her, where the rustle of fabric punctuated the silence. When she glanced to the side, she saw Marius shrug out of his suit jacket and toss it onto a nearby ottoman. Under the glow of a single moonbeam, he watched her the way a spider might regard a ladybug caught in its web, his lips curving up as he unknotted his tie and flicked open the buttons of his shirt. After peeling it off, he stood over her wearing a linen undershirt and trousers—much more than the lacy fabric that barely covered her thighs. It was another way of flaunting his power.

"Stand up," he commanded.

She obeyed, clasping both hands behind her back.

He took his time as he inspected her, pacing while his grin widened. "I didn't think I had any use for you, Cassy, but maybe I was wrong. You seem to have found the quickest way to my heart."

When he touched the strap at her shoulder and began to push it down, Cassia curled her fingers around the slim device she had tucked beneath her thong. In a smooth motion she'd rehearsed a hundred times in her mind, she whirled behind him and hooked an arm around his neck. Less than a heartbeat later, she stood with one hand clasped over his mouth and the other holding a laser blade to his throat.

His pulse throbbed against her fingertips as he froze in place, bent backward and breathing hard through his nose. He didn't move or speak, and to keep it that way, Cassia made sure he knew she wasn't the delicate princess he remembered. Starting with his undershirt collar, she dragged the laser blade in a slow trail leading to his navel. The fabric sizzled as it flayed apart, filling the air with the stench of burnt linen and exposing the famed contours of his abdominal muscles.

"I do know the quickest way to your heart," she murmured in his ear. "It's through your chest with this laser blade. And unless you'd like a demonstration, you're going to keep that pretty mouth shut. Nod if you understand."

His chin dipped.

"Good," she said. "We're going to the washroom, nice and slow." She tapped the blade against his jaw, barely nicking him. "Don't move too fast, or you'll slit your own throat."

Together they shuffled toward the adjoining bathroom. Her intention was to knock him unconscious, then scale down the balcony and steal a shuttle in hopes of returning before he woke up. With any luck, she might be able to drag his body into the craft and hold him hostage until he surrendered his missiles.

She was halfway to her destination when a tall, shadowy figure pushed open the balcony doors and nearly gave her a heart attack. But then the man turned his face to the moonlight, illuminating a familiar crooked nose, and Cassia released a breath.

"It's about damned time," she hissed, lowering her laser blade as General Jordan raised his pistol at Marius.

Jordan remained as stoic as ever. "There were a few complications. Besides, I figured you wouldn't be able to get him alone until now." When Cassia stepped out from behind Marius, the general caught a glimpse of her flimsy nightdress and did a double take. At once, he looked away, shifting his gaze all over the room as if torn between averting his eyes and keeping the prisoner within sight.

Cassia strode to the bed to retrieve her robe. "I hope you brought some friends this time."

Jordan cleared his throat. "Our ride will be here soon."

"Let's make a quiet exit." She pulled the lapels tightly over her chest and knotted the belt tie. "I don't want anyone to notice he's gone until morning."

Marius finally spoke then, looking ridiculous with his palms raised and the edges of his scorched shirt flapping in the breeze from the balcony—quite the contrast from the king who'd made her kneel on the floor a few minutes earlier. "Where are you taking me?"

Cassia approached him in slow steps, warning him with her gaze that she wouldn't sink to her knees again, not for him or any man. "We're going someplace where no one can hear you scream. If you value your body parts, you're going to tell me where your missiles are, and who's been funding this war." She stood close enough to smell the fear that mingled with his sweet cologne. She inhaled the scent, savoring it for a moment, before she added, "And you will address me as 'Your Royal Colonial Highness.' If you call me Cassy again, it'll be the last word you ever speak."

CHAPTER SEVEN

Cassia awoke to total darkness, gasping and throwing punches until she sobered up enough to realize she wasn't paralyzed on the floor of the Daeva ship while Marius slid down the shoulder straps of her nightdress.

It was only a dream.

Instant relief washed over her, but even as she sank back against her pillow, she tapped the security link on her bedside table and waited for the officer on duty to answer.

"Status report," she told him.

"Everything's quiet, Your Highness."

"And the prisoner?"

"Asleep in his cell."

"Thank you. Carry on."

She blew out a long breath and reminded herself that no one could hurt her. Marius was behind bars, and the Daeva were probably in the next quadrant by now. As for her nightmares, they were a normal reaction to stress—General Jordan had told her so, and he knew a thing or two about posttraumatic stress disorders.

He'd recognized the signs a couple of days ago, the morning after her escape, when he'd tapped her on the shoulder and she'd jumped halfway out of her skin. He'd said that dealing with trauma was like jumping from a roof: terrifying as the descent may be, the fall only hurt when it was over. Now that she'd slowed down, safe and secure inside the Rose palace, it was natural to feel the impact of her kidnapping.

And she did.

In addition to nightmares, noises and scents bothered her, too. The sound of rustling plant stalks took her back to the soybean fields on Vega. The smell of roasted beef reminded her of the Durango palace, which was unfortunate because she'd seized every head of Durango cattle to feed her people, and now beef was everywhere.

She dealt with the changes the only way she knew how—by staying busy, a strategy made easy by Eturia's never-ending list of crises. In fact, she should probably get out of bed. The sun hadn't risen, but she knew she wouldn't be able to go back to sleep.

She dressed in simple clothes and made her way down two flights of stairs to the basement tunnel leading to the security building, where the command center and the holding cells for high-profile prisoners were located. At this early hour, the station was quiet with only a skeleton crew of guards on duty. Clearly exhausted, her men suppressed yawns as she walked by. When she pushed open the door to the communication room, the attendant jerked upright in his chair, having nodded off.

"Your Majesty . . ." he stammered. "I'm—"

"It's all right." She lifted a palm to halt his apology. She envied sleep too much to fault him for it. "I need you to do something for me."

"Of course, Highness."

"Find a way to send a message to this ship." She wrote down the *Banshee*'s radio frequency and handed it to him. Her first act after imprisoning Marius had been to block all interplanetary transmissions so the Durango army couldn't contact his financial backer for help. It had worked, but it'd also left her unable to tell her friends that she was safe, or to ask if Renny was all right. "You'll need to pilot a shuttle beyond the shield to do it, but I don't know how far."

"At least a day's ride, Majesty."

"Then make it a priority." She noticed the drowsiness in his eyes and added, "Bring someone with you to take first shift. I don't want you falling asleep at the wheel."

"Yes, ma'am."

She left him to his work and strode to the data screen at the other end of the room, where she accessed the judicial operations network and selected the file of arrests made in the last twenty-four hours. During the war, the military had used all of its resources defending the borders, which left no one to enforce the law. Now gangs roamed the city, looting businesses and terrorizing the weak. Some of the rebels had taken up arms to police the streets, but while their efforts had helped, she couldn't allow them to continue. Vigilante justice was never a good idea, and besides, she wanted the rebels disarmed. So for those reasons, she'd orchestrated a mass sting operation, using new imports as bait to lure in the gangs and catch them in the act.

She grinned at the lengthy list of arrests. The sting had worked.

A set of booted footsteps entered the room, bearing an exaggerated heaviness that told her they belonged to Jordan. He'd been careful to make his presence known so as not to startle her from behind. Still facing the screen, she asked him, "Why are you up so early?"

"Same as you." When he joined her, one corner of his lips twitched up. "Too excited for troop inspections to sleep."

"Why, General Jordan," she said, feigning shock. "Was that a smile—*and* a joke?"

He made a show of rubbing his freshly shaven face. "Involuntary muscle spasm. I never joke about troop inspections."

"Of course you don't." Her grin widened at the gleam in his eyes. He seemed a little lighter today, and she enjoyed this side of him. "Mind if I join you? It sounds thrilling."

By way of answer, he swept a hand toward the compound's military wing, and together they made their way to the barracks for morning assembly. As they walked along the network of hallways, she broached the topic of the rebellion.

"This isn't going to win me any popularity contests, but I want weapons out of civilian hands." Her colony was in a delicate place, and it wouldn't take much to send them backsliding into chaos. "I don't have the resources to fight my own people."

"You won't hear any arguments from me," Jordan said. "Last month, I lost eleven men to friendly fire during a special op gone sideways. We were trying to cross the border in the Durango uniforms I stole."

"And the rebels thought you were the enemy?"

"Idiots tore right through us. I'm done letting civilians play soldier."

"Did the military keep a record of the arms they issued to volunteers?"

Jordan nodded. "Collecting them won't be easy, though. A lot of munitions were reported lost or stolen during the war. Whether they really *were* stolen is impossible to prove. More likely they're being stashed in basements or under beds."

"Then we'll conduct a search if we have to. Let's hold a weapons collection in the city market. Make it known that every colonist who volunteered for duty will be held accountable for the arms they were issued."

"I'll set it up today."

"And I'd like to thank the colonists for their service," she added. "Maybe offer some extra rations when they turn in their weapons. I don't want them to think I'm ungrateful. They hate me enough as it is."

Jordan fell silent—conspicuously so.

"What?" she prompted.

"Nothing. It's not my place to question you."

"But you already are. You're just not vocalizing it."

"Are you asking for my opinion?"

She nudged his arm. "As your queen, I demand it."

"All right, so the colonists dislike you," he told her. "So what? The rebels want a republic because they think the monarchs are and weak and corrupt—your parents proved that when they left. But now everyone's talking about how you turned the war on its ear with nothing but a laser blade. Your strength is your greatest asset. Hold on to that."

"You think extra rations will make me look weak?"

"I think the people aren't owed anything for doing what's required of them. If their queen orders them to turn in their weapons, they should obey." He went quiet again, as if hesitating to say something more, then added in a softer tone, "I know you think you're responsible for this war, but you're not. Don't let guilt cloud your vision."

His words resonated with her. For the last two years, she had carried around so much guilt and shame that it trailed her like a second shadow. "I'll think about it. Thank you for being honest with me."

"Thank you for listening."

When they arrived at the barracks and strode onto the lawn, the troops had already assembled for inspection: endless rows of soldiers standing at attention in the glow of the rising sun. Jordan's officers strode among the men, occasionally straightening a sleeve or smoothing a wrinkled lapel. Their scrutiny brought a smile to Cassia's lips because it reflected how far they'd come. Less than a week ago, these men had been too focused on survival to worry about polishing their boots.

Jordan addressed the troops after the inspection, both praising them for outlasting the enemy and encouraging them to stay vigilant. "The war isn't over," he bellowed in the commanding voice of a man twice his age. "Our queen has captured the Durango king along with his missiles, and bought us a much-needed cease-fire. But his supporters won't give up so easily.

Right now they're out there conspiring against us, and we must not allow them an inch. Look at what we've accomplished in such a short time: order is restored, your families are fed—even the market is up and running again."

As Cassia listened to him describe the progress they'd made, she felt a fierce swelling of pride. She had always wondered if she would make a good queen, and now she knew. Her only wish was that her parents could see her now, so they could know it, too. After all the times they'd criticized her lack of commitment to the throne, *she* was the one rebuilding Eturia while they cowered on another planet. On second thought, she was glad they weren't here. She was stronger without them tearing her down.

"Don't let the enemy take that away from us," Jordan concluded, and then he dismissed the troops for duty.

"Very inspiring," Cassia told him as they strode back to the command center. "You're a natural."

"I only told them the truth."

"But the delivery makes a difference." She knew firsthand. Maybe if her parents had spent more time telling her what she'd done right instead of magnifying each one of her mistakes, she wouldn't have doubted herself for so long. "Motivating people is a skill."

Jordan drew a breath to respond but released a groan instead, prompting Cassia to follow his gaze to the other end of the hallway. Then she groaned, too. Her parents' chief advisor, Councilor Markham, charged toward her in hurried steps that caused his trousers to swish between his thighs.

She forced a smile, reminding herself that Markham was

a gifted political strategist. She only disliked him because he'd facilitated her match with Marius. That wasn't his fault.

"There you are," Markham said, his gray hair tousled by exertion. "I've been all over the palace looking for you." He glanced at the electronic button tacked to her tunic. "Is your link turned on?"

She sensed Jordan stiffen in offense. He had his own issues with Markham, mostly stemming from the power struggle between the military and the council of advisors after her parents had left. "Remember who you're talking to," Jordan warned.

Markham narrowed his eyes as if to argue, but he must have thought better of it. "My apologies, Your Highness. I meant no disrespect."

"It's all right," she said while activating her link. In truth, she'd forgotten to turn it on. "What do we need to discuss?"

"An offer of marriage."

Jordan's brows jumped in perfect time with hers. "Has it escaped your notice that the queen already has a husband?"

"And I don't even want *him*," she added. "What's the meaning of this?"

Markham held both palms forward. "Please let me explain. I know it may seem premature, but these discussions are critical to the colony. You can't imprison Marius forever. At some point, you'll have to prosecute him for his crimes against the charter, otherwise you'll be in violation of the law."

"That's true," she conceded. "And when the time comes, I'll divorce him and consider a new match."

"That time is now, Majesty. The fallen kingdoms want their titles restored."

"Well, of course they do," Jordan said. "But it's too late. They officially relinquished their holdings to Marius in accordance with the law."

Markham held up an index finger. "Under duress."

"All wartime choices are made under duress," Cassia argued. "My rule is perfectly legal. I'm not giving Eturia back to the same people who allowed it to be destroyed. The old system was broken. It's time for a change."

That piqued Jordan's interest. "What kind of change?"

"I don't know," she admitted. "But whatever I decide, the transition will happen under my leadership. I've seen the damage a power vacuum can cause." She shook her head. "Never again."

"I don't dispute any of that, Highness," Markham said. "But the planet has never been ruled by a single monarch before. The other houses believe that's too much power for one person. If you refuse to restore their holdings, they may form an alliance against us and attack."

Jordan huffed a dry laugh. "With what? Rocks and sticks from their crumbling palaces? I'd love to see them try."

"So would I," Cassia said, because he was right. The war had left the other kingdoms just as broken as hers, but as Marius's queen, she had access to the Durango coffers, as well as to their weapons. No one would make a move against her. However, she needed to handle the situation with care or she might have multiple rebellions on her hands. Rocks and sticks could win battles if wielded by a large enough group.

"Stall them," she decided. "Convey my gratitude for the offers of marriage, but tell them my first priority is to stabilize our lands. Once that's done, I'll consider each offer carefully and ensure that everyone's needs are met."

"But—"

"I've made my decision," she told Markham. "I trust you'll find a way to convey my request in a manner that placates the nobles."

He released an audible breath through his nose. "As Her Majesty wishes."

After Markham strode away, she glanced at Jordan and found him watching her. He didn't say anything, but a corner of his mouth curved up again.

"Two smiles in one day?" she said. "Careful or you might hurt yourself."

"I like the way you stood up to him."

"Excuse me, General," interrupted a voice through his com-link. "We have a potential security breach."

Jordan tapped his link. "Where?"

"Outside the planetary shield. There's a ship approaching with a speed and trajectory that indicates they mean to force entry."

He muttered a swear. "What class vessel?"

"Looks like a small cargo ship, sir. Permission to engage?"

"Permission granted. I'm on my way."

CHAPTER EIGHT

When the *Banshee* reached Eturia's planetary shield, Kane didn't try to make contact with anyone on the ground. One look at the scorched landscape told him the Rose army was no longer in control of the security station. His mind flashed to Cassia and then to his mother as a lump of panic lodged in his throat. But he swallowed hard and poised his finger above the Launch button. He couldn't help either of them until he'd breached the shield.

"Get ready," he told Renny, who sat beside him in the pilot's seat. "Whoever's in charge down there isn't going to like this."

Renny tightened his grip on the wheel and gave a tight nod, peering intently through broken glasses held together at the bridge with medical tape. The scars on Renny's face had lightened to a pale pink, but the rigid set of his jaw said he hadn't forgotten the Daeva who'd put them there.

None of them had.

With the punch of a button, Kane launched the surge bomb Gage had made for them using an Infinium core, guaranteed to short out any electrical field. The instant the sphere drifted into contact with the shield, its waves of distortion vanished and Renny rocketed the ship into the atmosphere.

"We're away," Doran called from the two-man shuttle, and he and Solara detached. The pilothouse control screen lit up to indicate the shuttle veering east toward the Rose palace while the *Banshee* zoomed toward the Durango lands, where Cassia was probably being held. But they didn't know for sure, so they'd agreed to cover both bases.

"Copy that," Renny said. "Be careful and keep your tracking beacon—"

A crackle of static interrupted him, followed by a man's voice barking through the radio speakers. "Cargo craft, model FD247, identify yourself and land your ship at the following coordinates. If you fail to comply, we will open fire."

Kane scanned the coordinates and recognized the location as the security base outside the Rose palace. He answered the summons but waved a hand to indicate that Renny should stay on course. "This is the vessel *Banshee*," Kane said. "We're unarmed and en route to deliver cargo in the neighboring kingdom. No aggression is warranted."

"I repeat," the man said. "Land your ship at—" He cut off with a loud rustle, as if someone had snatched the microphone away from him. Then a new voice rang through the speakers.

"Kane!" Cassia's familiar screech lifted Kane's heart in tandem with his lips. "I'm fine, you idiot son of a two-assed mule! You just blew my shield to hell! I'll have your hide for this!"

Kane and Renny turned to each other and shared a look of pure joy, right before they broke into rib-shaking laughter. It'd been so long since Kane had laughed that his muscles seemed to have forgotten the act. He didn't mind the stomach cramps. It was the most glorious pain he'd ever felt.

"My skin's all yours," he told her. "You can use me like a blanket to keep you warm at night. Isn't that the root of all your fantasies?"

She didn't respond to his teasing, but he knew her well enough to picture her standing in the com center, her tiny body rigid with rage and her cheeks flushed crimson. The mental image thrilled him. Her combustive temper meant she was safe. That was all he needed to make his spirit soar.

His feet barely touched the ground when he and Renny descended the *Banshee*'s cargo ramp, never mind the squadron of armed Booters waiting for him. Kane gave them a jaunty wave and practically bounced on his heels all the way to the security station. He found Doran and Solara inside, sitting on a bench and handcuffed to each other. They must've heard Cassia's voice on the radio transmission, because they glanced up at him and grinned.

"Looks like we're in trouble with the princess," Doran said.

Kane wanted to return their smiles, but his mouth wouldn't cooperate. He couldn't shake the feeling that Doran and Solara had robbed him. While they'd returned to Renny on Vega, he'd spent two groggy days in the underground compound before his memory had returned, and that was two days he could've used to track Cassia. He knew he'd forgive his friends eventually, but today wasn't that day.

He gestured at Doran's wrist. "More like your dream just came true. Now you have a legit reason for never leaving her side."

"Hey," Solara objected, but then the synchronized click of a dozen boots sounded from the other end of the hall, and they turned to find another squadron approaching, wearing uniforms Kane recognized as belonging to the royal guard.

The guards came to a halt in the lobby and parted to reveal Cassia, who was dressed like royalty from the waist up and a soldier from the hips down, in a red satin tunic above black leggings and knee-high boots that matched those of her men. Kane's heart leaped at the sight of her . . . until he scanned her face and his insides sank to the floor.

Oh, Cassy, he mouthed.

The furious girl from his imagination was gone, replaced by a shadow version of herself with sunken cheeks, hollowed from weight loss, and weary, bloodshot eyes that told him she hadn't slept well in days, maybe weeks.

She had survived, but at a terrible cost.

He could only imagine the things the Daeva had done to her. A fresh surge of guilt erupted within his ribs. He should've listened to his instincts on Vega and stayed with her instead of running away like an injured dog . . . and then letting another girl lick his wounds. He'd failed Cassia in the worst possible way, because he hadn't simply been absent when she'd needed him; he'd pushed her out of his mind.

Did she hate him as much as he hated himself?

Glancing at her, it was hard to tell. Her gaze sparked when it met his, and for an instant he thought he saw a hint of a smile, but he blinked once and it was gone. She kept looking down and fidgeting with her hands as though she couldn't decide what to do. He wanted to close the distance between them and gather her in a hug, but something in her expression warned him not to. He didn't deserve to touch her anyway.

Finally, he told her, "I'm sorry."

"It's my fault. I should've sent word to you sooner." She nervously tucked a lock of hair behind her ear. "We'll have the grid up and running again soon."

"I'm not talking about the shield."

Her cheeks colored.

"Are you okay?" he said, and immediately cursed himself for asking such an idiotic question. Of course she wasn't okay. "What happened? Did Marius let you go?"

She answered with a dry laugh, then lifted her right hand to reveal a scab bisecting the pad of her index finger. "No. I gave him what he wanted." A tiny smirk played on her lips. "Or what he thought he wanted. I'm sure he's regretting that decision now."

It took a moment for Kane to absorb the meaning. He'd been away from Eturia for so long he'd forgotten the royal custom of joining bloodlines. Then realization hit with the force of ten solar flares and nearly knocked him off his feet.

"You married him?"

He wasn't sure if he'd asked the question out loud. The choking sensation in his chest felt like the time he'd accidentally inhaled a sip of Crystalline. His lungs had burned and refused to draw air until he'd coughed himself raw. He felt that way now, like he needed to cough in order to breathe.

"A few days ago," she said. "He's honeymooning in a jail cell down the hall."

A few days. That was nearly how long Kane had spent dazed and useless in the underground compound. He should've tried harder, reached her sooner. After all the years she'd spent running from Marius, she'd had to marry him anyway. She'd had to stand in the temple and kiss him . . . and then do a lot more than kissing after the ceremony ended.

No. He couldn't think about that.

Instead, he peered into the eyes of his closest friend, wishing more than anything he could rewind time. "I should have been here." He knew he'd spoken aloud, because he heard the subtle shift of his voice breaking. "I'm so sorry, Cassy."

As soon as he spoke her name, the guard standing beside her went rigid and growled, "You will address your queen as Her Royal Colonial Highness."

Kane blinked at the man and noticed he was a Booter, not a royal guard, and a high-ranking one if the colorful bars tacked to his shoulders were any indication. He seemed young, no more than twenty-five, but with an arrogant, dour attitude that made Kane want to rebreak his crooked nose.

Cassia waved him off. "It's fine. These are friends, and we're not in public."

"Wait a minute," Kane said as the Booter's words finally sank in. He wrenched his gaze back to Cassia. *"Queen?"* Did that mean her parents had died during the war? Panic gripped him. He still didn't know if his own mother had survived the bombings.

"Yes." She lifted her chin with pride, and in doing so, she

gave him a glimpse of the girl he remembered. "My parents flew off world when the war began and never came back. Can you believe that?"

He could, easily. He'd watched Cassia's parents abuse and neglect her for so long it seemed fitting that they would neglect the colony, too. But he didn't want to discuss them, not until he knew his mother was safe.

"My mom," he began, and trailed off to read Cassia's reaction. When her lips parted in the classic look of having forgotten something important, he knew she hadn't tried contacting his mother. "It's all right," he assured her before she could apologize. "I'll find her. Are you okay if I . . ." *Leave again?* He let his gaze ask the question.

Nodding, she reached out as if to touch him but quickly pulled back her hand and folded both arms across her chest. "Of course. Go. We'll talk later."

*   *   *

The city was a virtual wasteland, with half its inhabitants living in a tent camp near the farmers' market, but not even war could stop the rumor mill from churning. The allure of fresh gossip was more indestructible than any breed of cockroach known to man. No matter how far down life knocked a community, they could always take pleasure in the scandals of others.

That was universal.

According to rumor, a guard at the security station who'd witnessed Kane's reunion with Cassia had told the story to a friend. That friend, who was in charge of distributing rations outside the palace gates, had told the butcher's wife, who, in turn, told her prayer group. From there, the story spread like a fever, passed from one eager mouth to the next in excited whispers. *Kane Arric is back, the queen's ex-lover. She didn't seem happy to see him. I heard he only came home so he could join the rebellion.*

None of it was true—not the "lover" part and certainly not his interest in overthrowing the crown—but news of his return helped him find his mother. When he'd landed the *Banshee*'s shuttle at his childhood home and found it abandoned, a stranger scavenging nearby had recognized Kane and mentioned that his mother was living at a farmhouse on the outskirts of town. After thanking the man, Kane flew to the farm, where his mother greeted him in a flurry of hugs and tears.

An hour had passed, and he still hadn't let go of her.

"I'm sorry I didn't call," he said for the tenth time. "I wanted to, but I was afraid the Daeva might find you."

She patted his cheek. "You're safe. That's all I care about."

While they sat side by side at a rustic kitchen table, he smoothed a thumb over the back of her hand. It was the only part of her that had aged. Her once-clear skin was now covered in dark spots and a road map of bluish veins. Those small changes, along with the dirt stains beneath her nails and a slight trembling of her fingers, hinted that she hadn't simply lived on this farm. She'd worked on it, too. He figured she'd lost her job as a dressmaker in the palace—luxuries were always the first casualty of war—but he didn't like her doing manual labor.

"Are they good to you here?" he whispered, nodding toward the middle-aged farmer scrubbing root vegetables in the sink. The man housed a lot of transients under his roof, most of them women who slept six to a room on blanket pallets. The farmer kept glancing over his shoulder as if to check on her, like she needed protection from her own son. Kane scowled and scooted his chair to block the man's view. "Be honest. If you don't feel safe, I'll move you into the palace."

"The palace," she spat as if it were a dirty word. "They turned me out the morning after you left."

"Before the war?"

Instead of answering, his mother paused to let him figure it out.

"Oh." He hung his head. "Because it was your dastardly son who ran away with the princess and ruined her for all other men."

"It worked out for the best," she said, and used a kerchief to blot her dewy cheeks. "I'm happy here, and they need me. I like making a difference. I network with other farms to trade food for labor. I place orphans in safe homes. I even created a medicine swap."

"You've been busy."

"It's about survival now. We need food and shelter more than we need dresses."

"I'm sorry I wasn't here for you," he told her. "If it makes any difference, the rumors aren't true. We left because Cassia was in trouble."

"That's why *she* left," his mom said with a knowing smile. "But it's not the reason you followed her, Doodlebug."

He whipped his gaze over both shoulders to ensure no one except the farmer was within earshot. If his nickname made it back to the crew, he'd never hear the end of it. *"Mom,"* he whispered, drawing out the word. "You can't call me that anymore."

She gave him a watery sort of grin that tugged at his heart. "All little boys grow up and leave home, but for a mother, nothing changes. You'll always be my Doodlebug."

He squeezed her hand and looked down at her fingers. Was it his imagination, or were they trembling harder than before? He was about to brush it off as nerves when she blotted her cheeks again. That was the second time she'd grown sweaty, but the kitchen didn't feel hot. If anything, he could use a sweater.

"Are you all right?" he asked while inspecting her complexion. Her color seemed fine, the same shade as his with a rosy undertone in her cheeks. "You look jittery."

She flapped a dismissive hand. "We finally got a ration of coffee this morning. I haven't had any since the war began. There's too much giddyup in my blood. That's all."

"You wouldn't lie to me, would you?"

Before she could answer, someone knocked on the kitchen window. He glanced at the back porch, where a young Booter waved at him through the glass. Kane didn't recognize the soldier at first, but then the boy pulled off his hat, revealing an enormous pair of ears that lifted when he smiled.

"Badger!" Kane called.

He crossed to the back door and greeted his friend with a one-armed hug that was more of a mutual slapping of backs. The guy's real name was Norton, but even in his stately military uniform, he was the same goofy kid who used to ditch class and flush sonic bombs down the toilets in the boys' room.

"You're a Booter?" Kane asked. "I don't know whether to laugh or cry."

Badger brushed the dust from his sleeves. "Hey, the ladies love a guy in uniform. Plus I get first dibs on rations." He tipped his hat at Kane's mom. "Isn't that right, ma'am?"

"It's true," she said. "Thanks again for the coffee." The affection in her eyes indicated Badger was a regular here. Kane made a mental note to thank his friend for checking in on her.

"Hey," Badger said to him. "Is there someplace quiet we can talk?"

The farmer was obviously eavesdropping, because he'd been washing the same potato for five minutes. He wiped both hands on his pants and thumbed at the kitchen table. "You two can stay here. Rena and I have to tend to the hatchlings."

Kane frowned. He didn't like the farmer calling his mom by her first name, and he especially didn't like the man settling a hand on her lower back when they walked into the backyard. Leaning out the open doorway, he squinted at them until they disappeared inside the barn. Something was up with those two.

"Is it just me," Kane asked, "or is he putting the moves on her?"

"Sorry, man. I'm not here to discuss your mom's love life."

The abrupt change in Badger's tone prompted Kane to turn around. The smile had left his friend's face, and in its place was a sober expression that didn't fit with the wide ears protruding through his boyish mop of hair. There was a sternness in Badger's eyes that aged him beyond his years. It seemed he'd grown up, and he hadn't come over to relive old times.

"Then why are you here?"

Badger sank into a chair at the table and indicated the seat beside him. "My squad leader sent me to talk to you. But the original order came from the junior commander."

Kane thought back to the high-ranking Booter at the security station. "That twentysomething asshole with the broken nose?"

Badger shook his head, leaning back and crossing his long legs at the ankles. "No, that's General Jordan. I meant my other commander." He lifted one sleeve to reveal the inside of his wrist. He clenched his fist tightly, and a faint tattoo came into view—a red rectangle with an *X* marked through the center.

Kane recognized that symbol. He'd seen it all over the city. "You're part of the rebellion I keep hearing about." He lifted a brow at his friend. "I'm surprised you told me."

"I don't think you'll turn me in. You wouldn't believe how many members we have . . . some of them right in this backyard."

"The farmer?" Kane asked, then sat bolt upright when he realized Badger had said *them*. "My mom?"

"Can you blame her? The monarchy blackballed her when you ran off, and then they left the rest of us to fend for ourselves after the war started. Now anyone with a house still standing shares it with five families. Everyone else squats in a tent, if they're lucky."

"But Cassia's in charge now," Kane said. He'd heard stories of how she'd dismantled Marius's missiles and brought in food and supplies from his kingdom. "Look at what she's already done."

"She's got Marius by the stones. I'll give her that. But why should I break my back rebuilding this colony for her? I work the land, and she owns it. My great-great-grandfather agreed to serve the Rose dynasty for a new life here, but I shouldn't be bound by his choice. It wasn't his to make."

"I get it," Kane said, and he truly did. Two years of space travel had opened his eyes to all sorts of political systems, some of them better than others. "You don't owe the royals anything, but life's not perfect on the other settlements, either. I've been to places so broke your own neighbors will sell you into slavery."

"So I should be grateful to the royals?"

"I didn't say that. Give Cassia a chance. She might surprise you."

"Let's assume she does," Badger said. "Even if she's the best damn monarch in Eturian history, that doesn't mean her kids will be, or whatever husband she takes next. But they'll rule over us for generations to come based on their last name."

Kane didn't want to think about Cassia with children because it forced him to question which blue blood would put them in her. What he wanted to do was to shut down this conversation. "Look, if your commander thinks I can persuade Cassia to walk away from the throne, he's delusional. She's wanted this ever since we were kids."

"We're not asking that."

"Then what do you want?"

"No one's closer to the queen than you are. She even bought out your Daeva contract."

"She did?"

"Yeah, and from what I heard, it wasn't cheap."

"You heard right," Kane muttered. The price Marius had put on his head was enough to tempt a saint, not that the Daeva had any morals to speak of. By buying out the contract, Cassia had freed him for a whole new kind of life. Now he could show his face in public, anywhere he wanted, without looking over his shoulder.

"My point is," Badger continued, "she'll confide in you. What we need is for you to tell us what she's planning. That's how you can help the cause."

"You want me to spy on my best friend—the one who bought my contract?"

"Not *spy*, really. Just keep your ears open and report . . ." Badger nodded and threw a hand in the air. "All right, yeah, I want you to spy on her."

"Not happening."

"Listen, man, we're taking over this colony, with or without you. Your help might make the difference between a quick transition and a long, bloody battle. The war was bad enough. I don't want to see anyone else get hurt." Badger's gaze shifted toward the barn in the backyard. "Do you?"

"I liked you better when you were blowing up toilets."

"And I liked you better when you weren't wrapped around Cassia's pinkie finger." Badger's ears lifted as he grinned. "Oh wait. Never mind. That finger's always had your name on it."

Kane chuckled darkly and flashed a hand gesture recognizable to anyone within the Solar Territories. "Here's a special finger just for you."

"Seriously, though. Will you at least think about it?"

"There's nothing to think about." There were some lines Kane wouldn't cross, and betraying Cassia was one of them. "I'll keep your secret, but that's all I can promise."

"If you change your mind, you can reach me here most days."

"I won't change my mind," Kane said.

CHAPTER NINE

*T*he morning dew transformed into a glittering mist beneath the sun's warmth, clouding the docking field and curling its tendrils around the *Banshee* where it slumbered. Cassia approached the landing gear and tilted her ear toward the ship's belly to listen for clunking footsteps or tinny voices. She heard nothing. The crew was probably asleep. She reached for the boarding ramp keypad and then pulled back her hand. She knew the code, but it didn't seem right boarding the ship without permission.

She didn't live there anymore.

Standing on the outside looking in, she couldn't deny feeling a little wistful. The ship had been more than a home; it'd been her lens to the galaxy. Within its walls, she'd traveled from bustling tourist planets to systems so remote they didn't have names. She'd witnessed the birth and collapse of stars—miracles most people would never see.

"What's the problem?" Jordan asked. He pounded the side of his fist against the hull and shouted, "Lower your gear for the queen!"

Cassia cringed. "This is why I wanted to come alone. These people aren't my subjects. They're my friends."

"Then why didn't they spend the night in the palace?"

"Because they didn't want to impose."

The lie slid smoothly off her tongue. Kane had called last night from the ship, claiming that he didn't want to take a bed away from a refugee when he could sleep in his bunk. But she sensed there was more to it than that.

Jordan didn't look convinced. "How considerate of them."

The speaker box above their heads crackled to life, and Kane greeted them in a gravelly voice that oozed annoyance. He was always cranky when startled awake. "If the queen wants to use my gear, she'll have to buy me a drink first. Preferably hellberry wine, but Crystalline will do. I'm not picky."

Jordan pinched the bridge of his nose and grimaced as if he'd sucked a lemon. He made an obvious effort to keep his opinion to himself, though it didn't escape Cassia's notice that he settled one hand on his pistol.

She lifted her face toward the speaker. "Kane, let me in. I want to talk to you."

"Let yourself in. You know the code."

"But I didn't think . . ." She trailed off with a groan and punched in the code. "Never mind. I'll meet you in the galley."

The boarding ramp descended with a mechanical whine.

"Stay here," she told Jordan. He and Kane were in rare form

this morning, and she didn't have the patience to deal with both of them.

"Gladly," he answered.

Once the ramp touched down, she jogged into the cargo hold and then climbed the stairs leading to the galley. Her feet automatically knew to skip the middlemost step, the creaky one, and she caught herself smiling at the mingled scents of engine grease, rust, and day-old chili. She never thought she'd miss that smell. The aroma of ground coffee beans soon followed, and she crossed the threshold into the galley to find Kane standing with his back to her, setting an enormous pot of water on the stove for the morning's porridge. He must have grabbed yesterday's clothes off the floor, because he wore a wrinkled pair of canvas pants.

And nothing else.

She slowed to a halt and watched the play of his back muscles bunching and flexing beneath his skin as he tended to break-fast. She'd always enjoyed the sight of him shirtless, but until now she hadn't realized how strong his work as a ship hand had made him. The work had made her strong, too, but his body showed more evidence of it in the form of hard contours that made it difficult not to stare. When he turned around and leaned a hip against the counter, crossing both arms over his bare chest, it took all her strength to level her gaze on his eyes instead of someplace lower.

"Would the queen like some porridge?" he asked with a grin, but then his expression shifted. He studied her face while inching closer. "Did you sleep at all last night?"

And that was when she saw it—pity. The same pity that had tainted his gaze yesterday when she'd met him in the security station. She hadn't appreciated it then, and she sure as hell didn't like it now. "Stop it. Don't do that."

He stopped in the literal sense, frozen in place.

"Not *that*, you idiot," she said, and pointed at his face. "I mean that thing you're doing with your eyes. Stop feeling sorry for me." When he opened his mouth to argue, she cut him off with a threatening glare. "Don't you dare deny it. I can see it all over your face, and it's insulting. There's no reason to pity me. I did more than just survive. I went from the dungeon to the throne, and I did it all by myself."

His posture sank. "I know you did."

"You should be proud of me."

"I am proud of you, Cassy," he said, splaying both hands. "The happiest moment of my life was when you called me an idiot son of a two-assed mule and I knew you were all right. But you shouldn't have had to do it alone."

"So that's the problem? You blame yourself?"

"I wasn't there for you."

"That's a *good* thing," she stressed. "Do you think it was an accident that I bumped into the Daeva? Because it wasn't. They knew we were coming. It was a trap—half the town was in on it. If you had been there, they would've taken us both."

"You don't know that."

"Damn it, Kane, I *do* know that. And let me tell you what else I know: your safety was the only thing I had to hold on to. If they had tortured you to death while I listened, I wouldn't have survived it."

That seemed to get through to him, because he stood an inch taller.

"It's a miracle you weren't there. It saved us both." She moved close enough to deliver a light shove to his chest. "So stop acting like I'm broken. I'm not."

"Ouch," he said, teasingly rubbing the spot on his chest. "Don't I know it."

"So you'll treat me the same as before?"

Mischief flickered in his gaze. He turned to face the stove and told her, "Quit jabbering and set the table, Your Royal Colonial Highness. Breakfast isn't going to serve itself."

Smiling, she strode to the cabinet and pulled out five bowls. Now that she and Kane had cleared the air, she searched for a safe topic.

"How's your mom?"

"You mean aside from losing her job and everything she owns?"

"Aside from that," Cassia said tersely, plunking down a bowl with extra force. "I already promised to reinstate her as soon as I can afford to."

"She's fine." He stirred the porridge and lowered the heat to let it simmer. "Or that's what she told me. There was something off about her yesterday. She seemed jumpy."

"That's understandable." Cassia found her favorite mug and peered around Kane to see if the coffee carafe was full. "It was probably an emotional day for her, seeing you for the first time in so long."

"I guess," he mumbled, taking the mug from her. He filled it with coffee and added three squirts of vanilla syrup and a pinch of cinnamon, just the way she liked it. "Maybe it's a good thing I didn't tell her too much." As he handed back the mug, he peered at her with a cautious expression that tripped her internal alarm. "By the way, I have to talk to you about something."

"That doesn't sound good."

"But first you have to promise not to freak out."

"Has that ever saved you in the past?"

"Point taken." He took a deep breath and blurted, "Gage Spaulding offered me a job."

An instant smile sprang to her lips. "That's great!"

"Really?" He looked as though he didn't believe her. "You're not angry?"

"Why would I be angry? This is perfect! There's not a clerk in the kingdom who negotiates like you do. If you're Gage's liaison, you can get us a discount on Infinium. We're going to need a lot of it to power the construction equipment if we want to rebuild."

For a moment, he just watched her. "It's not that kind of job, Cassy."

"What kind, then?"

"He wants me on his sales team. He's building a barracks near his compound as a sort of home base, but I'd be doing a lot of traveling, mostly in the third sector."

"So you wouldn't live here at all?"

"I could visit. But, no, I wouldn't live here."

"You turned him down, right?"

He cocked his head in offense. "Excuse me?"

"Oh, come on. You can't possibly take this job."

"Actually, I can," he said, gripping his hips. "And I plan to, as soon as . . ." He looked down at his bare feet. "As soon as things calm down around here." Before she could ask what *things* he was referring to, guilt flitted across his face and he delivered the same pity-filled glance as before. "I want to make sure you're okay first. You've been through a lot. I'll be here for you for as long as you need me."

It was a good thing she felt too stunned for anger, otherwise he would've been wearing her coffee. "None of this makes sense. Why would you take an off-world job? We're home now. It's what we always wanted."

"It's what *you* always wanted. Did it ever occur to you that I was happier on this ship? The *Banshee*'s no palace, but at least here we were equals."

"We're equals now."

He barked a laugh. "Sure we are, Your Majesty."

"I never treated you like a subject," she insisted as she set down her mug. "Not one time in all the years we've been friends. My title didn't bother you before we ran away, so it shouldn't bother you now. Nothing's changed."

Kane seemed somber, almost sad, when he said, "Everything's changed."

Suddenly, she detected movement in her periphery, and she glanced at the top of the doorway to find a ball of auburn fur perched there. It was Acorn. Cassia had forgotten all about her. With a gleeful chirp, the sugar glider launched into the air, spreading her tiny arms wide to sail toward Cassia's waiting hands.

"Oh, sweet girl, I went off and left you." As she nuzzled a patch of soft fur, she imagined how terrified Acorn must've felt when her "mother" disappeared. "I'm so sorry, baby."

"She was a basket case that first week," Kane said. "Then Solara started wearing your coat and that helped. Acorn likes having your scent."

Cassia dusted kisses on Acorn's head. "I'm the worst mama ever."

"Cut yourself some slack." Kane turned his gaze to the floor, his voice darkening. "You had to focus on something else for a while. Doesn't mean you love her any less."

Acorn began rooting around for her favorite pocket above Cassia's heart, but it didn't exist on the royal silken tunic.

"I think she should stay with you when the *Banshee* leaves," Kane added. "It makes sense. You're the one she's bonded to."

Something heavy tugged on Cassia's stomach. Logically, she knew the crew wouldn't stay here forever, but at the same time, she couldn't picture them moving on without her. Especially not Kane. "Whatever Gage promised you, I'll make sure the clerk's office matches it."

"I don't care about the money."

"Then what?"

"You *know* what."

She opened her mouth to deny it, but she couldn't. She did know what he wanted: a commitment, which was the last thing she could give him right now. She thought back to the morning of her wedding, when she'd wished for a second chance with Kane. That chance had come at the worst possible time. The colony was more fragile than spun sugar. Eturia's needs had to come first. It would take months, maybe years, before she had time to devote to a relationship.

"Your mother is here," she reminded him. "All your friends are here." *And me,* she added silently. *I'm here.* "This is the life you wanted before. Why not now?"

"Because I'm different than I was at sixteen, and so are you." He spoke his next words carefully, as if afraid they might detonate inside his mouth. "You're a queen, Cassy—a *married* queen—and not just of the Rose kingdom. You own the entire planet." He spread both arms wide, gaping in shock. "I can't wrap my head around that much power, and to be honest, I can't believe you're okay with it."

If she hadn't been so caught up in the conversation, she might've heard General Jordan enter from the lower stairs. As it was, he made his presence known by announcing, "The rebels can't believe it, either. Makes me wonder if the rumors about you are true."

It was then that Renny stepped inside the galley from the opposite doorway. He blinked sleepily through his glasses, but there was nothing gentle about his voice. "If you have an issue with one of my crew, take it up with me. Otherwise, get off my ship."

"Everyone, calm down." Cassia narrowed her eyes at Jordan. "I'm sure no one's accusing Kane of being a rebel."

"Of course not," Jordan droned. "Must've gotten my rumors confused."

"I asked you to wait outside."

"Believe me, I wanted to. There's an emergency."

"What kind?"

Jordan hesitated, darting glances around the room as if gauging whether to trust its occupants. "Biological warfare from the sound of it. A third of the city's sick with the same symptoms, but the royal physician says it's not viral or bacterial."

Kane pushed off the counter. "What are the symptoms?"

"Nausea and vomiting." Jordan paused in thought and then continued ticking items on his fingers. "Fatigue, headaches, loss of appetite . . ."

"What about sweating?" Kane asked. "And trembling hands?"

"How'd you know?"

"My mom. I knew something was wrong yesterday. She blamed it on the coffee, but that didn't—" Suddenly, Kane stiffened. "The coffee! That's a new ration, right? If you imported it from the Durango stock, maybe it was poisoned."

"I drank the coffee, and I feel fine," Jordan said. "But I'll have my men survey the victims to see if they can find a common denominator. If so, we should be able to analyze a sample and identify the contaminant."

"While you do that, I want five minutes alone with Marius," Kane muttered darkly. "If there's an antidote for whatever his army used, I'll get it out of him."

Cassia shook her head. "No way. If anything happens to him, his army has no reason to observe the cease-fire. I hate him as much as anyone, but he's under my protection, at least until we figure out who his off-world backer is. I have to sever that relationship to make sure his supplier can't send more weapons, otherwise the war will start all over again."

"Wait a minute," Renny interjected while shuffling toward

the sink to fill a glass with water. "You told me the Durangos specialize in neurological advancements. Didn't they invent some kind of truth extractor?"

"Yes, and we already used it," Cassia said. "Marius doesn't know who his backer is. His father arranged the deal and kept the details to himself. Now the old king is dead, and all Marius has is a transmission code to reach his supplier through a third party in the outer realm."

"We haven't questioned Marius about the outbreak yet," Jordan told her.

"All right. I'll handle it."

"*We'll* handle it," Kane corrected.

"Fine." She waved him toward the stairs. "Go get dressed. We'll handle it."

*　*　*

Even though the palace was within walking distance, they took the *Banshee*'s shuttle to give Cassia an aerial view of the refugee tent camp, where the outbreak was believed to have originated. On a usual day, half the displaced colonists wandered into the city to look for work or to scavenge for anything they could repair and sell. The other half milled about the market or stood in lines for rations.

But that wasn't the case today.

"My god," she breathed as she pressed her forehead to the windshield and stared at the listless masses slumped over on the ground outside their tents. There were thousands and thousands of them, all too tired to walk. Nearly every pair of shoulders shook from either coughing or retching, maybe both. That was why they chose not to rest inside their tents. They didn't want to fill their homes with the stink of vomit. "Look at this, Kane."

His fingers squeaked from tightening around the pilot's wheel. "I see it."

"There are so many of them." She prayed the illness wasn't contagious, otherwise the neighboring kingdoms wouldn't need sticks and rocks to lay waste to her people. "Is your mom this bad?"

"Not quite, but I just called her a few minutes ago. Who knows what kind of shape she'll be in by tonight."

"All right, I've seen enough," she said. "Take us to Marius."

By the time they walked through the security station door, Jordan had left a message saying he and his men found a common link among the sick. They all appeared to spend most of their days outside, which was consistent with Rena's work as a farmhand.

"Something in the soil, maybe?" Kane guessed as they crossed the lobby. "It can't be in the water supply or we'd all have symptoms."

Cassia nodded absently while making a mental note to talk to Councilor Markham. She wanted him to find out whether colonists in the other kingdoms were sick as well, but to do so in a way that didn't reveal how dire the problem was at home. She had to maintain a strong front. At the first sign of weakness, the other houses might unite against her.

"Hey, are you listening to me?"

"Sorry." She refocused on Kane, who stood with one hand

on the door leading to the cell block. "Before we go inside," she said, "I should warn you about Marius."

"He's locked up, right?"

"Yes, but if you thought he was awful before, that's nothing compared with what he's like on the truth extractor. He won't hold back. So brace yourself and don't lose your head."

The impish grin on Kane's lips reminded her of old times, when he treated her like a friend instead of a wounded bird. "He'll have to step up his game if he wants to provoke me. I lived with you for two years."

"And you never lost your head." She smiled sweetly and knocked on his skull. "Not that there's anything in there to lose."

"Nice one."

"I know. Come on."

After keying open the door, she led the way to the maximum-security cell at the heart of the block. There she found Marius behind fiberglass bars, reclining on his cot and reading from a data tablet. He glanced up from his device and greeted her with an arrogant grin that fell when he noticed Kane.

"I see you reunited with your boyfriend." Marius raked his gaze over Kane's rumpled clothing. "You do have a taste for the fouler things in life."

"Guards, administer the truth extractor." She kept her eyes fixed on Marius so she wouldn't miss his reaction. He bolted upright and dropped his tablet. "I want to question our guest."

It gave her a tingle of satisfaction to know how much he hated the extraction process. The electrodes always made him confess embarrassing secrets unrelated to her line of questioning.

He'd once announced a fetish for body hair, and ever since then the guards had way too much fun at his expense when they came on duty, lifting a pant leg to show off their furry calves. She disdained the invention itself and wouldn't allow its use on the colonists, but she was all too happy to make an exception for her husband.

The guards followed her orders, and twenty minutes later, Marius was cuffed to a chair in his cell, under the influence of his own family's invention.

"Perfect," Cassia said through the bars. "Now we can begin."

Marius clenched his fists in fury, wrenching uselessly against his restraints. "I'm going to find a way out of here, and when I do, I'll have your eyes gouged out and every inch of your skin flayed from your bones." He glared at Kane. "You *and* your filthy bastard of a lover."

Kane snickered. "It's working. That's unfiltered honesty, right there."

"My people are sick," Cassia told Marius. "Thousands of them."

"Good. I'm glad."

She kept her voice calm as a vein throbbed at her temple. "It's not viral or bacterial. We think your army launched a biological contaminant on us. Do you have a weapon like that?"

He growled through clenched teeth. "Yes."

"Have you ever deployed it?"

"No."

"Tell me how the weapon works."

"If we wanted to poison you, we would drop tablets down-river. Or launch them into your lakes."

"My turn," Kane said. "What are the symptoms?"

The loathing on Marius's face was nearly tangible. Spittle frothed at the corners of his mouth, but he was incapable of remaining silent. "Skin sores and shortness of breath. Loss of consciousness. Your people would faint on the streets. It would make an invasion effortless. I'm going to use it on you the first chance I get."

Cassia frowned. Those symptoms didn't match. "What about your weapons supplier? Could he have launched some-thing different without telling you?"

"Of course," Marius spat. "It sounds like something he would do. My father said he was the most twisted man he'd ever met." Marius tried to hold back his next words, clenching his jaw so tightly his eyes watered. Finally, he gasped and said, "There's more."

Kane chuckled and made a mock sympathetic face. "Go ahead, buddy. Get it all out."

"I hate you!"

"Enough games." Cassia landed an elbow in Kane's ribs. "Tell me the rest."

"A shipment arrived on our wedding day," Marius grunted through his teeth.

"What kind?"

"I don't know. I didn't have time to inspect it."

"But it might've been a biological weapon?"

"Maybe," he howled with fury. "I had it delivered to the

armory. One of my men might've deployed it after you took me."

Cassia tapped the com-button at her collar and told the answering attendant, "Send a message to General Jordan at once. He should inspect the Durango armory for the presence of a biological weapon."

"Yes, Highness."

Marius smiled, forcing her to suppress a shiver. "Search all you want. If my supplier created a poison, he's the only one with the cure."

"What's his name?" Kane asked.

"I don't know."

"But you must have a theory."

"His operation is in the outer realm, isn't it?" Marius hurled back. "Even someone as stupid and low-born as you should be able to figure out that he's a fugitive. Beyond that I have no damned idea."

Cassia asked one last question. "Is there anything else you're not telling us?"

"Yes." Marius's lips curled into the same sick leer he used in her nightmares. Suddenly, the memories of her latest dream came rushing back and stole her breath. "I'll see you dead, my dear Cassy. I promise you that."

She turned on her heel and signaled for the guards to remove the electrodes, then strode briskly out of the cell block so no one would notice the cold sweat breaking out on her face. Even as her chest constricted, she reminded herself there was nothing to fear. Marius couldn't hurt her.

"I'm in control now," she chanted under her breath.

When Kane caught up, he settled a hand on her shoulder.

She flinched at first, but then she relaxed into his touch and let him rub circles on her lower back. The contact felt better than she cared to admit.

"Want to talk about it?" he murmured.

She shook her head. The only thing she wanted to talk about was finding Marius's supplier, which she had to do before the entire city fell ill and the other noble houses grew tired of her stalling. She hated to leave Eturia so soon after her parents' defection, but without a cure, all the progress she'd made would unravel. There was too much at stake to delegate this task to anyone else.

"My tech team pinged Marius's transmission code and tracked the signal to a moving satellite station in the fringe." She turned to face Kane. "There's not much money in my coffers right now, but if Renny won't mind taking a partial payment, I'd like to hire the *Banshee* to take me there."

"You and me both," Kane said, and paused for a moment. "I don't want to leave my mom, but the fastest way to help her is to find whoever made her sick. If money's a problem, I'll ask Gage for the signing bonus he promised me."

The reminder of his job offer made her stomach clench. "Talk to Renny first. I'd like to handle the bill. While you do that, I'll tie up loose ends and pack a bag."

"Your clothes are still on board," he reminded her.

"Oh. Right." She had forgotten. "Then I'll pack light. Meet you at the *Banshee* in an hour."

CHAPTER TEN

S tanding inside her former quarters for the first time in over a month gave Cassia an odd sense of déjà vu, almost as though she'd dreamed the two years she'd spent on board this ship instead of living them.

Looking around, she found cold steel panels surrounding her on all sides, quite the contrast to the artfully papered walls of her palace bedroom. Instead of royal silk, she wore canvas pants, a T-shirt, and the jacket she'd inherited from her old captain. There was even a sugar glider snoring inside her left breast pocket. But strangest of all was the sudden absence of activity she'd grown accustomed to as queen. On the *Banshee*, there were no advisory sessions, troop inspections, supply raids, or rallies for volunteers. Those tasks belonged to General Jordan now, and that left her with idle hands . . . and an idle mind.

A breeding ground for dark thoughts.

She needed something to do. Since boarding the ship, she'd

double-checked the air-lock seals, swept and mopped the decks, flushed the garbage chutes, and logged the contents of the supply closet. She'd even stopped by the engine room to see if Solara needed help with repairs, but Doran was already on the job. That left Kane. He could probably use her help with dinner, but something awkward had hung between them all day and she didn't know why. Maybe it was because she'd fallen out of step with her old routine. Or maybe it was the way he coddled her, offering extra servings at lunch and then suggesting she take a nap afterward. Either way, he was right when he'd said their dynamic had changed. They were out of sync now, so she tried to avoid him.

Which left her no choice but to confront this empty bedroom, particularly the naked top bunk. She didn't know how she felt about that. Nearly every night for the last two years, she'd fallen asleep to the sound of Kane's breathing. His presence had been her only constant on board this ship, and despite the strangeness between them, it didn't seem right sleeping here alone. Even standing in the empty quarters felt unnatural.

Maybe Renny needed help in the pilothouse.

She jogged up to the top level and found him relaxed in his seat at the helm, letting the autopilot fly the ship while he studied his data tablet.

"Permission to come aboard?" she teased.

He glanced up at her and smiled. "Hey, there. I thought you were resting."

"I'm not tired."

"Anything on your mind?"

"No. Just wanted to say hello."

He patted the copilot's seat. "Then you can keep me company while I review these job orders." While she sat down, he watched her with an expression she didn't recognize, pride mingled with something deeper. "Have I told you how good it is to have you home?"

Home.

That wasn't the word she would've used, but she didn't correct her captain. Seeing him grinning at her through his broken glasses, his sweet face marred by scars—it was all she could do to keep her eyes dry. She knew the Daeva wouldn't have touched him if it hadn't been for her.

"Only twice."

"Well, one more time won't hurt. I missed you. We all did."

"I missed you, too. It's good to be back."

His grin slipped, warning her the conversation was about to turn heavy. "Listen, I don't want to dredge up bad memories—"

"Then don't," she said with a laugh that didn't fool either of them.

"—but I need you to know why it took so long to reach you." He removed his glasses and rubbed both eyes in a nervous tic she'd seen him do a hundred times. "The Daeva really worked me over. I was unconscious for hours after they finished with me. I think the only reason they left me alive was so I would lead them to Kane, but I couldn't—"

"Renny, please." It didn't make her feel better to imagine her captain lying on the floor, bloodied and beaten. "I was already gone. You did the right thing and protected Kane. I'm just sorry we put you in that position."

"Don't be sorry." He was still fidgeting with his glasses.

"There's nothing I wouldn't do for you. I hope you know that."

She nodded while studying a crack in the leather of her seat. She knew how much Renny cared for her. She cared for him, too, more than she loved her own father. But the pilothouse seemed to have shrunk three sizes since the conversation began, and now she couldn't get enough air.

"I should go," she said, and stood up. "I forgot that I promised to help with dinner."

"Oh. Okay. See you at supper."

She dropped a kiss on his shaggy head and then jogged down the stairs, pausing at the landing to catch her breath. Her relief was only temporary because now she had to help Kane in the galley, otherwise Renny would know she'd lied. She mentally groaned. She should've come up with a better exit strategy.

Her boots dragged as she continued down another flight of steps to the galley. When she strode through the doorway, Kane glanced up from a fish-shaped wooden cutting board piled high with the onions they'd bought from the farmers' market on Eturia.

He used the back of one hand to blot his watery eyes. "Hey, I thought you were—"

"Not tired," she interrupted, and gestured at the cutting board. She knew how much he hated dicing onions. "Want me to do that?"

"God, yes." He immediately tossed down the knife and spun toward the sink, then washed his face and dried it with a dishtowel. "I hate those things. If it were up to me, we'd use dehydrated. They taste just as good."

"No, they don't." She carried the cutting board to the sink

and positioned it below the flowing faucet. That was the trick to tear-free onion dicing—cutting them under running water. Kane didn't know that because she'd never told him. She liked being able to do something he couldn't. It made her feel needed.

"Good thing you've got me to do it for you."

He snickered while sorting dried lentils in a bowl. "You missed your calling, Majesty. Forget the throne. You can come with me and be my personal onion cutter."

Come with me. To the Infinium compound—that was what he meant. Because apparently he couldn't go five minutes without dropping a reference to his job offer. Just today she'd had to listen to him brag about how Gage had told him to name his own salary and choose his own territory and order all the custom upgrades he wanted for his company ship.

She wished he'd shut up about it.

Gripping her knife, she bore down hard on the onions with a satisfying *thunk.* It felt so good that she did it again, and soon the only sound in the galley was of her blade against the cutting board.

"Whoa, take it easy," Kane said, pointing at an onion. "Does it owe you money?"

She snapped her gaze to his. "Would you rather do it?"

He flashed both palms in surrender. "Never mind. Hack away."

For the next several minutes, they worked side by side at the counter, neither of them saying a word as she finished dicing the onions and Kane rinsed the lentils and set them on the stove to cook. She could tell he was working up the nerve to speak by the way he kept tapping one foot and sneaking glances at her. Finally, he propped an elbow on the counter and came out with it.

"So, uh, did you get any sleep after lunch?"

"No."

"Why not?"

"Because I had chores to do, and I wasn't tired."

"I would've done your chores."

"I. Wasn't. Tired."

"Well, you, um," he began while nervously scratching the back of his neck, "you didn't eat your leftovers from lunch."

"So what?"

"So you've lost a lot of weight—that's all."

"I'll gain it back."

"And at some point we have to talk about what happened." He hesitated once and then took her hand, still wet from the sink. "You've been through a lot. You can't hold that pain inside or it'll spread like an infection. The sooner you open up, the faster you'll—"

"I'm aware of what I've been through," she said, taking back her hand. Did he think she needed a reminder? Or, rather, *two* reminders, as he'd already told her this earlier in the day, when he'd promised to stay with her until she was "okay." Maybe that was the problem. Maybe he'd spoken too soon and now he was starting to realize how long "okay" might take. "Is that what this is about? Are you trying to hurry up and fix me so you can run off to your new job without feeling guilty?"

"*What?*"

"Is that why you're pushing me to take naps and eat more?" She wiped her damp hands on her pants, backing away from him. "And nagging me to talk? Because you can't move on until you fix what you think is broken?"

For a beat, he went quiet—angry quiet. Then he exhaled an audible breath and said, "Yeah, you nailed it. I want to help you bounce back so I can leave sooner. Not because you're my best friend and you mean everything to me. Not because I care about you so much that I left my mother behind and spent two years slinging grease inside this galley just so I could be near you. No, that's not the reason."

She folded both arms and looked down, her face heating.

"I'm only thinking of myself because I'm selfish, right?" he went on. "I never, *ever* put your needs first, do I, Cassia?"

She winced at the use of her real name. She could count on one hand the number of times he'd called her that. "Okay, I get it. I was wrong."

He jabbed a finger toward the doorway. "Just go—take a nap, don't take a nap—I don't give a damn what you do."

She knew he didn't mean it, but the words still pricked at her heart. Before she walked away, she paused at the threshold. "The secret to cutting onions is to do it under running water. I thought you should know."

* * *

The mood at dinner was tense, to say the least.

She and Renny shared the bench on one side of the table while Kane sat in between Doran and Solara on the other. The lentils were too hot to eat, so each of them stared into their bowls as if the wafting steam might show them the future.

When the lack of conversation grew nearly unbearable, Renny summoned a smile and rubbed his palms together. "I don't have to ask whose turn it is. Make it good, Cassia. You've missed a lot of suppers."

All eyes shifted to her. It took a moment for her to catch on and remember their nightly ritual of playing "would you rather." "Oh, right. Give me a second."

"Take your time."

She tried to think of a question no one had asked before. At first, nothing came, but then she thought back to the rebels on Eturia and their hatred of the throne. It seemed she couldn't do anything right in their eyes. They didn't care that she'd ended the war or given them food and rations. They wanted her gone because her last name was Rose. They'd forgotten that the founding houses had spent their entire fortunes terraforming Eturia. If not for the Rose family, the rebels would be living in slums on Earth.

"I have a question," she announced. "Would you rather be a servant in someone's home and have all your needs provided for, or serve no one and exist in total poverty?"

The crew pursed their lips in consideration, all except for Kane, who watched her while blowing on a spoonful of lentils. She could tell from the guarded look in his eyes that he knew exactly what she was referring to.

"There's no shame in being anyone's servant," he said. "But a man should be able to choose who he serves. He shouldn't be born into it."

Renny pointed out, "You didn't answer the question."

"The second one, I guess."

"Not me," Solara said. "I've had a peek behind door number two, so I'd pick the first one."

"Ditto," Doran answered. "I'm too pretty to be poor."

Renny chuckled and pulled a napkin across his mouth. "I guess it boils down to what I value more: freedom or comfort." He pondered in silence for a few seconds. "Freedom, I think. So I'd pick the second one."

Kane leaned across the table and fist-bumped the captain.

"What about you?" Solara asked Cassia. "You didn't answer your own question."

"She'd pick door number one," Kane mumbled with one cheek full.

Cassia nodded. "As long as I was treated fairly, yes."

"Now it's my turn," Kane said, and leveled a challenging gaze at her. "Would you rather leave your home world forever, or stay on your home world and never leave?"

All around the table, the crew gave a collective "*Oooh*" and fired off the same response. They chose wanderlust over home and said the question was too easy. They didn't realize what Kane was trying to do: force her to admit how much she'd miss space travel once she settled down as queen.

"I don't know," she said, and meant it. Neither option appealed to her. She wanted both—to have her world and leave it, too. As much as she loved Eturia, she couldn't deny that staying there forever would feel suffocating. She'd barely scratched the surface of what the universe had to offer. But she supposed she'd already made her choice when she'd taken the throne, so she answered, "The second one."

Doran drew back an inch. "Really?"

"But . . . but . . ." Solara sputtered, tongue-tied from shock. "You'd never leave home. That means you'd never visit the Obsidian Beaches or see the quantum nebulae fields."

"Or drink hellberry wine," Kane added.

"I could have it imported," Cassia said.

"Wouldn't taste the same as drinking it fresh on Pesirus."

She used a spoon to stab at her lentils. Everyone was taking this game too seriously. She was about to tell them so when her com-bracelet beeped a transmission request from General Jordan. "Start the next question without me," she said, and stood from the table. "I'll be right back."

She jogged up the stairs to the landing and tapped the Accept button. There was a flicker of light, and Jordan's hologram appeared—all six feet of him, practically on top of her. She took a backward step and bumped into the wall. The added space didn't help much. She was still close enough to waltz with his image.

The color in his cheeks said he'd noticed it, too.

"Wait, let me find a better place to talk." She strode into the lounge, where the crew usually spent the hours after dinner playing billiards or sitting around the holographic fire pit. "Better?"

Jordan took in the surroundings, peering at the wall mural behind her.

"It's the Black Forest," she told him. "My captain, the previous one, had it commissioned to remind him of home."

"*Your* captain. He must have meant a lot to you."

"He did. I loved him like a father."

Jordan nodded, though his face was impossible to read. "So how is it, being back on the ship again?"

"I won't lie; it's strange," she said while lowering herself into one of the cushioned chairs around the fire. "It feels like I'm wearing a pair of boots that don't fit anymore. It's a good thing you called when you did. You saved me from death by awkward dinner conversation."

He gave her one of his rare smiles, and with no warning whatsoever, a flutter broke out inside her stomach. "I live to serve."

She rubbed a hand over her abdomen. Maybe she was hungrier than she'd thought. "Did you find anything at the armory?"

"Yes and no," he said, tucking both hands in his pockets. "The shipment from your wedding day contained a supply of shock wave grenades."

"No biological weapons?"

"None that we could find."

"What about Markham?" she asked. "Any word from the other kingdoms?"

"Yes. They haven't reported any outbreaks."

She swore under her breath. "That can't be a coincidence."

"It's not," he agreed. "Someone's trying to weaken us."

"Until we find out who, we need to keep this quiet. I want a gag order issued."

"Already done," he said. "We also quarantined infected colonists to their homes."

"Good, thank you."

They exchanged a few silent glances after that. There didn't seem to be anything more to say. Just when she assumed Jordan would sign off, he grinned in an almost sheepish way and told her, "Troop inspections aren't the same without you."

That made her smile.

"Stay safe," he murmured, and then disconnected.

She released a breath when his image disappeared and found herself wishing she'd kept the conversation going a little longer. She sat alone in the quiet room, listening to the scrape of utensils and muffled conversations from the galley until her rumbling stomach forced her back downstairs to finish her dinner.

Her bowl sat alone on the table when she returned. Doran and Solara were gone, probably to the engine room, and Kane stood at the counter drying the last of the crew's dishes. Renny had already filled his favorite mug with Crystalline. As he headed for the doorway, no doubt to occupy the same cushioned chair she'd just vacated, he pointed at her bowl and asked, "Want me to heat that up for you?"

"No thanks." She patted his shoulder. "You go ahead."

She picked up her bowl and leaned against the wall, watching Kane stow the clean dishes inside the cabinets. She waited for him to ask about the transmission. When he didn't, she volunteered, "That was Jordan."

"Figured as much."

"He didn't find anything at the armory."

Kane nodded in acknowledgment but didn't offer his opinion. He finished putting away the dishes and latched the cabinet doors. Then he stood in front of her and dug inside his pants pocket. "I keep meaning to give you this."

He placed something light and warm into her hand. She

knew without looking that it was the Eturian prayer necklace he'd bought for her. She'd memorized its weight like a favorite song.

"You accidentally left it in a box of my stuff," he added.

They both knew that wasn't true. She gripped the stone pendant and drew it to her breast. "I'll be more careful with it from now on."

She wanted to say something more, to thank him for the peace offering and apologize for what she'd said to him earlier. But before she could shake the words off her tongue, she found him with his back turned, disappearing down the stairs to the cargo hold.

CHAPTER ELEVEN

Weeks later, when they reached the outer realm, Kane and the crew met in the bridge to pinpoint the exact location of their moving target. Stooping to avoid hitting his head on the low ceiling, he approached the navigation table and studied the star charts spread out across its surface.

Earth wasn't the center of the galaxy—not by a long shot—but the Solar League liked to pretend it was. They'd divided the Milky Way into four sectors and five rings, similar to a dartboard with their planet as the bull's-eye. If the League ever moved headquarters, they'd probably recalibrate the whole star chart to reflect it, but for now, the first ring in the Solar Territories was the tourist circle, a playground for the wealthy. Next came the colony planets, including Eturia, followed by the ore mines and the prison settlements. The fifth ring was known as the outer realm, or the fringe, a lawless collection of planets the League hadn't annexed because of the lack of taxable income.

Money—it made all worlds go around.

And because Kane understood that simple fact, he also knew money was at the root of whatever deal Marius's father had struck with his backer. People didn't invest in foreign wars for fun. There was something to be gained by helping the Durango kingdom defeat the other three houses. All Kane had to do was figure out what, and it would lead him to the man who'd poisoned his mother.

He leaned closer to the table. "Where's our target?"

Renny tapped their location with an index finger. "About an hour away. Cassia's theory was right. The coordinates keep moving because they're in orbit around a planet that's not even terraformed. It's a satellite station."

"Of course I was right," Cassia said. "It's a black market hub. Why else would it be out here in the . . ." She paused to yawn, and while doing so, shot Kane a glare that warned him not to suggest that she go lie down. ". . . middle of nowhere?"

He patiently held his tongue, but he was getting tired of pretending not to care that she was the last to go to bed at night and the first to wake up in the morning. Or that she spent the hours after dinner holed up in her bedroom. At least her face had filled out and her pants no longer hung from her hip bones. If nothing else, that was progress.

He turned his focus to Doran. "If it's a black market satellite, we might need Daro the Red to come out of hiding."

Doran frowned at the tattoo on his wrist: four curved sabers forming a figure eight. It was the logo for the Brethren of Outcasts, pirates who ran roughshod over the fringe. A few months ago, Doran had accidentally inherited one of their territories when he'd killed a pirate lord named Demarkus Hahn. And because no self-respecting criminal would swear allegiance to the preppy son of a fuel mogul, Doran had donned a costume and taken a fake name during the fealty rite. Since then, he'd delegated most of his authority, but he still had to dress up and make appearances once in a while.

It was a long story.

"Fine," Doran said. He raked a hand through his dark hair, which he would have to color red. "But we're almost out of dye. I should've called myself Daro the Black."

Solara stood on tiptoe and whispered to Doran. Whatever she said made the tips of his ears turn pink. He whispered something back and then kissed the tattoo on the inside of her wrist, which matched his, because she was his fake pirate wife.

A *very* long story.

Renny told everyone, "This time we stay together. All of us, no matter what. I suggest you use the bathroom before we leave, because any pit stop you make on that satellite will be a team effort." He pushed his glasses higher up his nose. "Understood?"

"Yes, Cap'n," they echoed.

"And remember to keep your heads down. Stay away from large crowds, and don't advertise who we are once we're inside. I crossed the Zhang mafia once, and they never forget a name."

"But they operate on Earth," Doran said. "The fringe is Brethren territory."

"Tell that to my pistol wounds." Renny pointed at Doran. "And don't go throwing your name around, either, *Daro the Red.* All anyone has to do to claim your territory is challenge you to a fight."

"Or kill you," Kane added with a grin and a hearty slap on his friend's back. "I heard the pirate lord in sector three was garroted last week."

"Thanks for the reminder."

"Anytime, buddy."

"Let's keep it simple—in and out," Renny said. "We'll only use Doran's alter ego as a last resort. Got it?"

Everyone nodded.

"Good. You have one hour until we dock. Crew dismissed."

* * *

Kane had never visited a black market satellite until now. The satellites tended to move to locations that were kept secret—one day here, another day there—and they drew the kind of people a guy tried to avoid if he had a bounty on his head. Still, the hub looked similar to how he'd always imagined it: like a common trading post, only sketchier.

Artificial light flickered overhead, casting a jaundiced glow over the faces of shoppers as they browsed the long rows of booths erected near the pub. A variety of items were on display, everything from weapons that were probably stolen to prescription drugs that had likely expired. Other goods were advertised on signs, services rendered by escorts and hit men. Half the booths stood empty, and the other half were manned by vendors with their feet kicked up and their hats pulled down. Once every few minutes, a peddler would spot an easy target and try to wave him over, but otherwise most folks avoided eye contact and kept to themselves. None of that surprised Kane.

What he hadn't predicted was the smell.

"Hot damn," he said, pulling his shirt collar over his nose and mouth. "It smells like a skunk threw up on a dead body in here."

"Add a hundred sweaty jockstraps, and you nailed it." Doran waved a hand to dispel the stench. "It's making my eyes water."

"What *is* that?" Cassia asked.

Renny pointed ahead toward the mouth of an open doorway. The entrance was too dark to reveal anything inside, but a sign affixed to the wall promised CHEAP LABOR!

"Low-end slave traders," Renny said. "Their product doesn't have a long shelf life, so they don't bother with basic hygiene."

Everyone quit complaining after that.

Kane lowered his shirt collar out of respect as he passed. There was nothing like slavery to put his problems into perspective.

The crew continued in silence for a while, following Renny as he led them out of the marketplace, past a stretch of storage units, and toward what looked like an office door with a single word stenciled above it: INQUIRIES.

"What are we doing?" Cassia whispered.

"We can't go around asking questions," Renny told her, "or it'll draw too much attention." He nodded toward the door. "We'll hire someone to do our digging for us."

"A ferret," Kane said. He'd heard of that service. For a fee, a local with the right connections would find the information they wanted while protecting their identity.

"Exactly. Now, let's see what we can afford to bid."

Renny dug in his pocket and pulled out a handful of fuel

chips. Cupping his palm, he used a finger to push aside the random junk he'd stolen—a pillbox, two disk batteries, the tip of a broken grease pencil, and Cassia's pink laser blade. Kane had borrowed it enough times to know.

"Hey!" Cassia objected.

Renny ducked his head. "Sorry. I can't—"

"Help it," she finished, snatching the object from him.

"Yeah, I know."

"Thirty chips," Renny said. "It'll have to do. Wait here while I put in our bid."

He returned five minutes later, followed by a young bearded guy whose bouncing steps reminded Kane of a grasshopper. The ferret couldn't stand still, even when he reached them. He shifted his weight back and forth, compulsively scratching his beard while peering around the group for instructions. Whatever money they paid him was going up his nose tonight.

"Whatcha want me to find?" he asked Renny.

Cassia spoke first, lifting her chin in that haughty way of hers. "I'm here representing my husband, Marius Durango."

Kane felt a pinch in his gut. He kept forgetting that Cassia was married. The union was in name only, but that didn't mean he liked it.

"He gave me this transmission code." She handed the ferret a slip of paper. "He's been using it to talk to someone on this hub. I'd like to set up a meeting with that person. Whoever it is, tell them it's regarding our partnership on Eturia. They'll know what that means."

The ferret glanced at the paper while bouncing one heel on

the floor. He'd fidgeted so much his forehead was glistening. "Okay. Gimme a day or two. I'll get it done."

Cassia wrote down the *Banshee*'s radio frequency so he could contact her when he'd finished the job. The ferret bounded away, and the rest of them agreed there was nothing they wanted from the marketplace except to put it behind them. So they returned to the ship, where they took extra precautions to lock themselves securely inside.

∗ ∗ ∗

When three days passed without word, they were forced to revisit the hub.

Again, Renny led the way through the fetid marketplace, past the storage units, and to the inquiries station, but this time with the rapid stride of a man who'd been cheated out of his last thirty fuel chips. Kane almost felt sorry for the ferret. Renny was a gentle captain, but he knew how to bring the pain when a situation called for it.

Renny rapped on the office door, and it opened a crack. "I'm looking for my rep. Tall kid. Brown hair, short beard. Jumpier than a caffeinated squirrel."

"That's Gill," came a man's voice. "Haven't seen him since yesterday."

"Where does he live?"

A knobby finger extended from the crack, pointing behind them. "Check the bordello. The girls let him sleep there when he brings new clients around."

Kane snickered and elbowed Doran. "Our ferret's a genius." When Solara and Cassia burned their glares into him, he clarified, "I mean, if you're into hired ladies. Which I'm not."

"Let's go," Renny told them.

The crew followed as he charged down the side corridor to a two-story building with a glowing red rooftop. No matter how far you traveled, that was the mark of a flesh house. At this early hour, they didn't pass any travelers except for a drunkard or two curled up on the floor in a Crystalline coma. If there was ever a time to go nosing around a black market hub, it was now.

Renny pushed open the brothel's front door and met a bouncer the size of a whale. The giant didn't bother standing up from his stool. Renny told him, "We're looking for Gill. Did he stay here last night?"

The bouncer grunted. "Up the stairs. Room thirteen."

One by one, they skirted around the man and crossed the lobby to the staircase. Renny held a finger to his lips in warning, then led the way quietly up the steps and down the hall to room 13. When they reached the door, he pressed an ear to it, listening for movement from the other side. Instead of using the touch-sensor keypad on the wall, he hooked a finger around the door's manual latch and gave a sideways tug.

It was locked.

He moved aside and pointed from Solara to the keypad. She nodded and pulled a small tool kit from her inside jacket pocket. In less than a minute, she'd overridden the lock, and the crew filed inside the room. Kane spotted Gill at once, sprawled faceup on a stained mattress in the corner with his jaw askew and his eyes half-open.

Dead as a stone.

Kane froze. From behind, someone shut the door, probably Renny because he was the only one to have broken out of the paralysis of shock. While the captain crouched down and inspected Gill's bloated face, Kane reached out and linked his hand with Cassia's. The act was reflexive, like breathing.

Renny puffed a sigh and stood up. "Poor kid."

"An overdose, you think?" Kane asked. "I could tell he was on something."

"Oh, he was definitely using," Renny said. "But I don't think that's what killed him. I imagine this was an occupational hazard."

Nobody spoke for a while. They let the implication hang in the air, unwilling to acknowledge that a young man had died because they'd paid him to dig in a land mine.

"But it had to be drugs," Solara said. "The door was locked from the inside."

"And there's no sign of a struggle," Doran pointed out. "He's not bruised or stabbed or shot. Probably he died in his sleep." Doran sounded confident, but he looked away from the body and began chewing his thumbnail.

"Check his pockets," Cassia told Renny.

"Already did. They're empty."

"Then look under the mattress." She pulled her hand free from Kane's and crossed both arms across her chest. "No matter how he died, addicts always hide their stash. If he found any information, maybe he put it there."

While Renny knelt on the floor to lift a mattress corner, Kane glanced around the room for a place to hide money or drugs. There was no furniture other than the bed, and anyone smart enough to reset the keypad after killing a man was also smart enough to check for loose floorboards or removable heat registers. If there was anything to find, the killer had probably beaten them to it. On a whim, he reached up and skimmed his fingers along the ledge over the door. At first he felt only dust, but then his hand brushed something, and a folded piece of paper fell to the floor.

He unfolded the scrap and recognized Cassia's meticulous handwriting. It was the paper she'd given the ferret, the one with Marius's transmission code on it. Kane turned the slip over and squinted at the messy scrawl on the back. In letters so jumbled he could barely make them out, it read, *adelvice*.

He handed the paper to Renny, who spoke the word aloud. "It sounds like 'edelweiss,' the little white flower that grows on Earth."

"Maybe he misspelled it," Kane said.

"Could be. Whatever it means, if someone killed this kid for finding it, there's a good chance he gave up our names before he died. We should go. Preferably out the back door."

"But what about Gill?" Solara asked, casting a sideways glance at the mattress. "Shouldn't we tell someone what happened?"

Renny placed a comforting hand on her shoulder. "It's best if they don't find him until we're gone."

She nodded, and together they all made their way out of the room as silently as they'd come, but using the emergency exit at the other end of the building instead of the main stairs. Minutes later, they were back at the marketplace, which was beginning to bustle with morning activity.

Steam rose from food carts, heating the air and sending up the scents of bread and sausage. Ordinarily, the combination would make Kane's mouth water, but here it mingled with the stench of unwashed bodies and turned his stomach. He kept pace with Renny, eager to return to the docking station and put some distance between himself and this hellhole.

They were nearly out of the market when a woman called, "Popovers! Hot popovers!" Renny stopped so quickly that Kane collided into him from behind. The pileup continued as Cassia stumbled into him, and then Doran and Solara into her.

The crew righted themselves while grumbling complaints, but Renny didn't seem to notice. He stood there, stiff as titanium, staring at the woman selling breakfast from a food cart five yards away. Kane glanced at the vendor. She was about thirty years old with owlish blue eyes and a round, freckled face framed by scarlet curls. She was cute in a motherly sort of way, but he didn't see what the big deal was.

Until Renny opened his mouth and said, "Arabelle?"

Kane almost sprained his neck craning for a better look. He stared at the woman through the fresh eyes of someone who'd heard stories about her—plenty of stories, none of them ending well. Arabelle was the love of Renny's life, the girl he'd left behind years ago when he'd made an enemy of the mob. But what was she doing in the outer realm? She was supposed to be on Earth, leading a safe, normal life.

When the captain didn't budge, Solara moved up from behind. "Who's that?"

Kane was almost afraid to say. Losing Arabelle had wrecked Renny. He still talked about her in his sleep. The whole crew knew better than to mention her name unless he broached the subject, which only happened when he overindulged in Crystalline.

"It's her," Kane whispered. "Arabelle."

Solara clutched Kane's left arm while Cassia grabbed the right. At the same time, they hissed, "Are you sure?"

Kane watched the woman's gaze meet Renny's and hold there. The whites of her eyes grew while her lips parted. She went every bit as still and pale as the captain. Soon her fingers slackened, and she dropped a pastry to the ground.

"Yeah," Kane said. "I'm sure."

"What's she doing here?"

That was what Kane wanted to know. It seemed a little too convenient that after years of no contact she happened to cross Renny's path at this exact moment. The captain finally sobered up enough to process the questions buzzing around him. He kept his eyes glued on Arabelle when he spoke, as if afraid she might vanish if he looked away. "She's wearing a collar. She belongs to someone here. Probably the owner of that restaurant."

Kane took notice of the slim silvery choker around Arabelle's neck. It was a device programmed to deliver pain injections if a slave or an indentured servant strayed too far from home.

"I have to buy her contract," Renny said.

Kane nodded. "Of course. We'll help you."

"I hate to bring this up," Doran cut in, "but what if she doesn't want to come with us? She could have a husband, or someone she doesn't want to leave behind."

"I don't care," Renny told him. "I'll buy her freedom

anyway. And her husband's or friend's or boyfriend's, too, if that's what she wants."

It was then that Kane saw two major snags in their plan. The first was Renny. "You can't be here. You have to go to the ship and let us handle the deal. If Arabelle's contract holder sees the look on your face, he'll ask for the moon . . . and you'll give it to him." Which led to their second problem. "We don't have much to spend."

"I have the *Banshee*," Renny said, confirming Kane's worst fear.

The crew traded nervous glances.

"Renny, listen to me." Cassia touched the captain's elbow. When that didn't get his attention, she cupped his cheeks and turned his face until it met hers. "Come back to the ship with me. Let the others do the negotiating."

"But what if—"

"They won't let you down," she told him. "Kane could sweet-talk water from the desert, and Doran and Solara have more street cred than anyone in this hub."

Doran cracked his knuckles menacingly. "It doesn't matter who owns her contract. I promise he won't say no to Daro the Red."

Renny still didn't look convinced.

"Do you trust me?" Kane asked.

Renny's gaze wandered back to Arabelle. "Yes, but—"

"Then let Cassy take you to the ship."

"But I have to talk to her first, to tell her I'm not really leaving."

"No. She could belong to anyone. Maybe he's watching right now."

"You don't understand," Renny said in a small, broken voice that plucked at Kane's heartstrings. "I walked away from her once, and it almost killed me."

"I do understand," Kane promised. "And I won't come back without her."

After a long pause, Renny took one backward step and then another. Each pace toward the docking lot seemed to cause him physical pain, but he kept his boots moving. A group of men passed in front of him, breaking his view of the food cart. That seemed to help because he turned around, paused for another moment, and strode away.

Right before Cassia followed him, she crooked an index finger at Kane and waited for him to lower his ear to her lips. "Don't bring that woman on board until you scan her for weapons," she whispered. "Com devices, too."

For once, they were on the same page. "Already planned to."

CHAPTER TWELVE

Cassia had a feeling Kane might not follow her instructions to the letter, but she never expected him to come
barreling into the docking lot with Arabelle hoisted over
one shoulder, shielding his head with his free arm and yelling
like his pants were on fire. Behind him, Doran and Solara ran
through the open doorway, each armed with a stolen pulse pistol
and firing indiscriminately at someone out of view.

So much for smooth negotiating.

Cassia darted up the boarding ramp while tapping her com-
link. "Fire it up, Renny. We've got Arabelle, but it looks like we
wore out our welcome."

"Copy that," Renny said from the pilothouse. The engine
rumbled to life, followed by the low whine of the thrusters
warming for takeoff. He asked in a tentative voice, "You're sure
they have her?"

Standing out of the way, Cassia glanced down the ramp and

watched Arabelle's skirt-clad rear end bounce atop Kane's shoulder as he hauled ass—literally—onto the ship. "Yep, I'm looking at her right now." Once Doran and Solara made it up the ramp into the cargo hold, Cassia punched the Retract button and told Renny, "Go!"

The floor lurched, sending Cassia to her knees. She met the metal grating with a jolt of pain and scrambled toward the stairs for something to hold on to. As soon as she gripped the bottom step, she hollered to Kane over one shoulder. "Did you scan her?"

He didn't answer right away. He was too busy belly-crawling toward a stabilizing strap bolted to the floor. "Sure!" He wrapped one fist around the belt while hooking his opposite arm around Arabelle's waist. "There was plenty of time for that in between holding her boss at gunpoint and running for our lives from the mob!"

The mob?

A burst of energy struck the hull near enough to travel through the floor and rattle Cassia's bones. As the ship rolled in an evasive maneuver, she hung on tightly while her body skidded sideways. Screams filled the cargo hold, mostly coming from their new guest.

If Arabelle belonged to the Zhang mafia, that explained why Doran's reputation as Daro the Red had backfired. Pirates weren't exactly at war with the mob, but both groups were territorial. Every once in a while someone would sneak a toe over the line, and the other side would bring down the hammer. That meant the Zhang operative they'd just busted had two choices:

close up shop and return to Earth, or kill the witnesses before word got out.

Cassia swore to herself. "We have to scan her," she shouted. "We can't hide if they're tracking us."

"Be my guest," Kane shouted back, clearly in no position to help. He resembled a man stretched on a torture rack, both arms spread wide between Arabelle and the floor strap.

Arabelle's red brows formed a slash over her eyes. "I'm not bugged! And I didn't ask to come here with you people!"

Cassia fought to maintain her sweaty grip on the stairs. Before she could give the matter any more thought, the *Banshee's* signature shriek pierced her eardrums, and the ship rocketed forward with enough velocity to pry her fingers loose. She slid across the floor until her back hit the wall, knocking the wind out of her.

For what felt like an hour, she stayed pressed there by acceleration. Then the ship slowed and lurched to a stop, sending her into a roll in the opposite direction.

She landed on her back, blinking at the dancing ceiling lights. All motion had ceased, but it took a few seconds for her body to get the message. Soon the engines powered down, and her ears detected a harmony of high-pitched ringing and low groans of pain. She pushed to her elbows and instantly regretted it. They were bruised, much like the rest of her.

Peering across the hold, she found Kane sitting up, massaging one shoulder and frowning at Arabelle, whose arms were still locked around his waist. Solara crouched near the opposite wall, one of her eyes swollen half shut. She rubbed Doran's back while he pressed a palm over his lips in an obvious effort to keep from vomiting.

The whole crew was battered and shaken, but Renny only had eyes for Arabelle when he appeared at the upper landing. His boots formed a blur as he flew down the stairs. In the time it took Cassia to blink, the captain was kneeling by Arabelle's side, delicately brushing the curls back from her face.

"Belle," he crooned in the gentle voice of a parent rousing a child from sleep. "Baby, are you all right?"

The redhead smacked away his hand and tried to sit up, without success. "Don't touch me. And don't call me baby"—she thrust a finger at him—"*ever* again."

Renny cradled her shoulder long enough to help her into a sitting position, then released her and flashed both palms like a robbery victim. "Belle, I know you're upset."

"Upset?" she screeched.

Cassia raised a hand. "The rest of us are fine, thanks for asking."

"I feel upset when I stub my toe," Arabelle raged on. "Or when someone tries to steal my shoes while I'm sleeping. *Upset* doesn't describe how it feels when a man says he loves me and then leaves me behind to cover his debt!"

"Debt?" Renny's mouth dropped open. "What debt? I only left—"

"Because you picked Ari Zhang's pocket," she finished. "I know. You told me in your letter. But when Zhang couldn't find you, he sold *me* to pay for what you took."

"Sold you?"

"To Reegan Fleece, of all people."

The news knocked Renny off his feet. From where he knelt, his legs gave out until he was sitting on the floor. Cassia could almost feel his pain. She didn't know whether to hug him or make a quiet exit. When Kane caught her eye and thumbed toward the stairs, she knew they were both on the same wavelength.

But first they had to take care of something. She crossed to the supply closet and pulled out the scanning rod. "Arabelle, I need you to stand up for a minute."

"If you're dizzy," Kane said, "I can help you."

Renny started to object, but Arabelle silenced him with a glare. She pushed to her feet and stumbled a few times, refusing Kane's arm when he offered it. Finally she was able to stand upright. She extended both arms to the side and clenched her jaw while Cassia passed the scanner over every curve of her body—twice.

The machine detected no devices. She was clean.

Arabelle propped one hand on her hip. "Happy now?"

"Yes, I am," Cassia said, and pulled back her shoulders to stand taller. "You know why? Because you're safe, and that's what my captain needs to be happy. He loves you, and I love him. That's how it works on this ship."

Kane settled a hand on her waist, nudging her toward the stairs. "Come on. I'm sure they have a lot to talk about."

"Buzz us if you need anything," she told Renny, but he wouldn't look up from the floor. She turned and made her way on jelly legs up the stairs to the galley, where Acorn was already helping herself to a box of raisins that had spilled during the turbulence.

Kane rushed to scoop up the fruit. "Stop her. The last time

this happened, she ate too much and upchucked on my laundry."

Cassia sniffed a laugh. She picked up Acorn but handed her another raisin while Kane's back was turned. "That's what you get for leaving your dirty clothes on the floor."

"My *clean* laundry."

Doran slogged to the cooler, still green in the face as he filled a bag of ice for Solara's swollen eye.

"Here, let me do that," Cassia said. She tucked Acorn in her breast pocket and reached for the bag. This was her job as ship medic. Besides, Doran was going about it all wrong. The best cure for swelling was a cool gel mask, not ice, followed by an application of camelback leeches. "You sit down," she told Doran. "And you," she added to Solara, who was probing her puffy eyelid, "hands off. You're making it worse."

"Yes, ma'am," Solara teased. Doran added a fake salute.

Cassia set a smile free as she left to find her med-kit. She enjoyed falling into her old routine. This was the most normal she'd felt in ages.

A while later, after she'd treated one black eye, a sour stomach, and dozens of abrasions, she sat beside Kane on the bench and cocked an ear toward the cargo level to listen to the murmur of voices. She couldn't make out any words, but Arabelle had stopped shouting. That had to be a good sign.

Renny had docked them inside an asteroid crevasse, but they couldn't hide forever. Cassia's people needed a cure, and she wouldn't find it in a cave. Maybe her tech team on Eturia could run a search on the term *adelvice* and point her in the right direction. She should probably contact General Jordan, too.

"The hub wasn't a total bust," she whispered, leaning in to

form a huddle. "We found a puzzle piece or two. We know that Marius's financial backer is somehow tied to adelvice, and whatever that is, it's important enough to kill for."

"Don't forget the Zhang mafia," Solara said around her gel mask. "They belong on Earth, not in the fringe. I doubt it's a coincidence that they were operating out of the same hub as Marius's contact. Your husband's probably in bed with the mob."

Cassia agreed. It made sense. The financial backer had powerful connections within the Solar League, not to mention access to illegal weapons. Plus Marius's father had described the backer as "the most twisted" man he'd ever met. That certainly fit Ari Zhang's profile. What she didn't understand was what Zhang would stand to gain from the deal.

Doran shifted nervously in his seat. "Did you notice who bought Arabelle?" When they shook their heads, he told them, "Reegan Fleece. I've heard of that guy. He's kind of an urban legend on Earth. They call him Necktie Fleece because he has a thick scar across his throat and he likes to use a garrote for his kills."

"A garrote?" Kane repeated. "That's how the pirate lord of sector three died."

Doran lifted a shoulder. "I don't know if Necktie did it, but I'm glad we didn't run into him at the restaurant. Arabelle's boss was a puppy dog compared with him."

That raised an interesting question for Cassia. Renny had once bragged that Arabelle was an electrical engineer on Earth, and a successful one. So why would a mafia hit man buy her and then outsource her to a restaurant to sell food from a cart—a job anyone could do? It seemed like a waste of human resources.

"Tell me about her boss," she said. "You held him at gunpoint, right? Was that before or after he met Daro the Red?" At the confused looks the crew gave her, she clarified, "Did the deal go sideways because you didn't have enough money, or because the mob met a pirate lord and panicked?"

Solara shared a glance with Doran and Kane. "Both, I guess."

"It happened so fast that it's hard to tell," Kane said. "Why?"

"Because at first I was afraid Arabelle might be a spy," Cassia explained. "That's why I wanted her scanned before you brought her on board. But if she was a plant, the mob would *want* you to have her. They would've made the deal easy."

"Not necessarily," Kane argued.

Doran nodded. "Yeah, it would've been suspicious if they'd let her go without a fight."

"But the scan came up clean," Cassia said.

"And she didn't come with us willingly," Solara pointed out. "Kane grabbed her and ran. It's not like she had time to stuff a wire down her bra."

Kane tipped his head in concession. "Still, something about this doesn't feel right. What we need is a place to lie low while we figure out how it all fits together."

"Very low," Solara said. "Just because we're out of sight doesn't mean we're hidden. The mafia ship can pick up our current if they have an electrical scanner. We should probably shut down all the systems and disconnect the batteries."

"What about oxygen?" Kane asked.

"There's an emergency hand crank in the engine room,"

Doran said, earning him a proud smile from his mechanic girl-friend. "We can take shifts turning it."

That was true, but manually cranking air through the ship would get old fast. And until Cassia could radio Eturia, she had no access to her team of technical wizards. "The sooner we leave, the better."

"The obvious choice is Gage's place," Kane said. "Even if the Zhangs look for us there, they won't be able to touch us. The whole planet's shielded."

Doran lifted his mug of seltzer. "Plus my brother can hook us up with a crate of Infinium. It comes in handy for trading." He stood from the table and strode to the upper stairwell. "I'll call him now."

"And I'll start shutting down the systems," Solara said while heading for the lower stairs.

Once they'd left, Kane released a long breath. "We need currency, too. Credits and fuel chips to replace what we lost. I'll ask Gage for the advance he promised me."

The ship didn't move, but Cassia felt a sudden dropping sensation, followed by the urge to grab on to something sturdy. She gripped the bench ledge near her thighs and stared into her lap. She didn't mean to speak, but some unknown force hijacked her voice and said, "Don't take the advance."

For a long beat, there was only silence.

"Why not?" Kane asked.

She sensed him watching her, but she couldn't meet his eyes. She knew the answer, and she suspected he knew it, too. Until he accepted payment, she could pretend his job offer was hypothetical, that he might change his mind. But a signing bonus would make it real, and she wasn't ready for that. She wanted to tell him, to be transparent for once, but her throat tightened and she could barely get three words out. "Just don't, okay?"

He pried one of her hands from the bench and laced their fingers together while wrapping an arm around her shoulders. She let him draw her in until her cheek rested against his chest. Usually, she discouraged cuddling because it led to more, but this time she couldn't pull away. She nestled against him and closed her eyes, inhaling a blend of soap and sweat and warmth that reminded her of the best parts of her childhood. Holding on to Kane made her feel rooted to the ground, and she needed that today.

She needed her best friend.

He rested his chin on her head and told her, "Okay."

*　*　*

Shield or no shield, Cassia couldn't shake off the prickles of anxiety that skittered over her when the *Banshee* reached Planet X. She sat beside Renny in the pilothouse, peering out the windshield at a long, jagged tear in the frozen landscape where Kane had crash-landed the shuttle many months ago. This was the first time she'd revisited the crash site, and seeing it brought back the panic she'd felt when she found him unconscious in the cockpit. The moments before rousing him had been the longest of her life.

She didn't like this place. Nothing good ever happened here.

She shifted her focus to Renny, who'd been unusually quiet in the two days since Arabelle had come on board. "Any progress?" she asked, figuring he would know what that meant.

He slouched in the pilot's seat. "She won't talk to me."

"Try not to take it personally. She won't talk to me, either, and I bunk with her."

What Cassia didn't mention was how uncomfortable she was sharing her quarters with Arabelle. The woman didn't make a sound. And even though the entire crew had been on their best behavior, she rebuffed their every act of kindness. The toiletries and changes of clothes Cassia had left on the top bunk ended up in the hallway, neatly folded.

It was like rooming with a passive-aggressive ghost.

The only benefit of the arrangement was that Cassia found she slept better with someone occupying the top bunk. She didn't know why her nightmares had suddenly quieted, but it reminded her that trauma did strange things to people.

People like her roommate.

In all fairness, she could only imagine how awful the last two years had been for Arabelle. After spending so much time enslaved by the mafia, freedom probably felt a little jarring. Almost as jarring as a ship full of strangers feeling sorry for her. Maybe Arabelle had mistaken their kindness for pity, and that was why she kept giving them the cold shoulder.

Like I did to Kane.

Renny drew her from her thoughts with a weary sigh. "I thought I was protecting her by staying away, but all I did was abandon her when she needed me." He docked the ship on the landing pad, then cut the engines and pushed his glasses atop his head so he could rub his eyes. "No matter how much she hates me, it can't be more than I hate myself."

"Hey, now. Nobody hates on my captain."

"Not even your captain?"

"Especially not him." Cassia stood from her seat and perched on Renny's armrest. "You've got the biggest heart of anyone I've ever met. No one could hate you, not if they knew you like I do. And I'm pretty sure Arabelle knows you. Give her time. She'll come around."

Renny patted her knee. "I hope you're right."

"When am I ever wrong?"

That earned a small laugh from him, which lifted her spirits, too.

When they met the crew at the boarding ramp, everyone was suited up and ready for the brief-but-frigid walk to the compound air-lock, everyone except for Arabelle, who was nowhere in sight.

Renny peered around the cargo hold for her. Before he could ask, Kane raised his helmet shield and delivered a pointed look. "She wants to stay here."

"But we could be gone for hours," Renny said.

"Yeah, I know. Unsupervised hours."

Renny gripped one hip. "What are you implying?"

"Just that she shouldn't have free run of the ship." Kane glanced at Doran and Solara for backup. "At least until we know her better, right?"

Doran shrugged and said in a helmet-muffled voice, "A lot can change in two years. Wouldn't hurt to take precautions."

"I trust her," Renny said. "As much as any of you."

Cassia touched Renny's arm. "I'm with you, Captain. I don't think she'll do anything to sabotage the ship." When Kane frowned at her, she added, "But let me talk to her and see if I can convince her to come. Some time under the sun lamps would do her good."

Renny made a *go ahead* motion, so she jogged to her quarters and knocked once on the door before opening it. She found Arabelle in the same position she'd expected: curled up on the top bunk, withdrawn, and facing the wall. Cassia batted down her feelings of sympathy and spoke the way she would want to be spoken to—with respect instead of pity.

"Hey, I know you want to stay here, but you can't. This place is a frozen hellhole. You won't survive an hour on board without the engines running." It wasn't exactly the truth, but close enough to fool an electrical engineer. "But there's a beach simulator in the compound . . ."

Arabelle's curly head lifted in interest.

". . . and because the crew's here on business," Cassia continued, "you'll probably have the whole thing to yourself."

That was all it took.

Ten minutes later, all six of them trudged down the boarding ramp to the external air-lock chamber, where they crowded inside and waited for the room to fill with pressurized oxygen. A green light flashed and the interior door unlocked, admitting them into the heated compound. They'd just shed their thermal suits and hooked their oxygen helmets to the wall when Gage strode to meet them.

He was dressed in a white lab coat over singed coveralls that had obviously seen a few brushes with the lab furnace. He must've left the lab in a hurry to greet his brother, because a pair of safety goggles hung half around his neck, still snagged on one ear. He shook Doran's hand and gave the rest of them a detached wave.

"Cassia," he said when he noticed her. His grin confirmed her suspicion that he had a crush on her. If he weren't trying to steal her best friend, she might've returned his smile. "Glad to see you're okay."

She lifted a shoulder. She was about to tell him that it took more than a few bounty hunters to bring her down when the distinct clicking of high heels drew her attention to the other end of the hallway, where a young woman about her age was walking toward them, scanning the group as if expecting to find someone she knew. She was beyond beautiful, with long, glossy chestnut hair and the kind of face that made you keep looking. But even more attractive was the way she carried herself, with a confidence so bold she almost glowed.

Cassia liked her at once.

Until the girl moved into Kane's personal space and curled one hand around his biceps while settling the other possessively atop his chest. Then Cassia stopped admiring the girl and wondered why she was feeling up a total stranger. The answer came when Kane freed himself and immediately glanced at Cassia like she'd caught him doing something wrong. It was the same look he'd given her at age fifteen when she'd walked in on him in the boathouse with one of the palace maids.

"Oh," she said dumbly as the pieces clicked into place. He was no stranger to this girl. They must have met during shore leave and . . . really hit it off.

"Cassy . . ." he began.

"Oh," she said again, louder this time, because full realization struck her, and now she understood why he couldn't wait to take a job here. It seemed his benefits package included more than a generous salary and a company ship.

Cassia felt sick.

"This is Shanna," Kane mumbled. "She works on the sales team."

The weight of half a dozen gazes settled on Cassia's face. She feared looking at the crew because she knew she would find pity on their faces. She chanced a glance at them and found something far worse—proof that she was the last to know.

"Nice to meet you, Shanna," she heard herself say. "I like your shoes."

She didn't wait for a response. Instead, she faced Gage and focused on the safety goggles around his neck. "Kane told me you offered him a signing bonus. Would you give it to him now so we can get airborne again? We're in a hurry." She held up her com-bracelet, then noticed her hand was shaking and quickly lowered it. "I need to make a call. Is there someplace quiet I can go?"

When he didn't answer fast enough, she bored her gaze into his and silently begged him to take her away. Something hot and sharp was stabbing the organs behind her navel, and she couldn't hold it off for much longer.

"Of course. I'll show you to my mother's room."

He cupped her elbow and led her down the corridor in smooth, casual strides that turned hasty as soon as her breath began to hitch and her lower lip started quivering. They picked up the pace to a jog. Seconds later, he ushered her through an open doorway into an enormous, blurry bedroom.

"Thanks," she said, reaching for the keypad. "I owe you one."

Gage stood on the other side of the threshold, fidgeting with his hands. "Hey, about what happened back there. If it's any consolation—"

"It's not."

She closed the door just in time. As the panel slid into place, a bubble rose from her throat and burst free in a noisy sob. Another bubble followed, and then another. She pressed a hand to her mouth, but she couldn't stifle the sound. She kept thinking about her wedding day, and how she'd regretted not embracing her feelings for Kane. All the while he'd been exploring his feelings for someone else.

She was losing him in every possible way.

What followed over the next several minutes wasn't the sort of dignified weeping that befitted a queen. She drained heartbreak from her entire face. Her eyes leaked, her nose ran—even her chin had needed wiping at one point. When it was over and no more tears would come, she felt like someone had scooped out her insides and stuffed her with sawdust.

Still hiccuping, she shuffled to the adjoining bathroom, where she blew her nose and splashed cool water on her face. She riffled through a drawer of makeup and helped herself to a dab of skin-firming cream to lessen the puffiness beneath her eyes. With the help of a few other cosmetics, she made herself look human again.

Even if she didn't feel that way.

A peal of laughter rang out from the other end of the

compound and reminded her that she didn't have the luxury of hiding all day. It was time to put on her big-girl pants and do her job. First she would call General Jordan. Then she would scrape together the remnants of her dignity and face the crew.

She sat on the edge of the bed and issued a transmission request.

Jordan sat at his desk when he answered. The instant he spotted her, he flew up from his chair and asked, "What's wrong? Are you okay? Do you need troops?"

She touched the delicate area below her eyes. Maybe she could use some more skin cream. "I'm fine. No need to sound the alarm."

"But you've been crying."

"People cry. It happens."

"I've never seen you crack, not even in Marius's dungeon. So whatever made you cry, it must've been bad."

"Not really. It's just a new policy I enacted. Every now and then I'll shed a few tears to prove I'm not an android."

Jordan reluctantly took his seat. He rubbed the back of his neck and seemed to hesitate before he spoke. "Want to talk about it?"

"No, I don't."

He studied her for a few moments, moving his gaze across her face in a thoughtful way that made her stomach flutter again. This time she couldn't dismiss it as hunger. "Can I tell you something?"

She swallowed hard. "Can I stop you?"

"Only if you disconnect."

"Then go ahead."

"Princesses are born," he said. "Queens are made." He

paused to let that sink in as he leaned forward and rested both forearms on his knees. "Do you know the first time I saw you as a queen instead of a princess?"

She shook her head.

"On your wedding night, when I snuck through Marius's balcony and found you holding a laser blade to his throat." He delivered a serious look, until his cheeks darkened and he flashed a sheepish grin. "I saw what you were wearing and I said to myself: *Here's a girl who can do more in her underwear than most men can do in full-body armor.*"

That made her smile.

"You didn't wait for me to rescue you," he went on. "You used your wits and your resources to take control of the situation. You're tenacious, and that makes you unstoppable. That night I looked at a princess, but what I saw was a queen."

Without meaning to, she lifted a palm to her chest. No one had ever spoken to her like this, and from deep inside she felt her wounded heart beating a little stronger than before.

"You're destined for great things, Cassia Adelaide Rose," he said. "Don't lose sight of that. I know there are obstacles in your path, but I also know they won't stop you from reaching your destination. I believe in you." He smiled more tenderly this time. "I hope that counts for something."

The flutter in her stomach multiplied. "It does. More than you know."

"I'm glad to hear it."

They sat there grinning at each other for a while. Then Jordan clapped his palms and rubbed them together as if to get down to business.

Over the next fifteen minutes, he told her about a rebel raid on one of the royal fuel stations, and Cassia suggested adding barricades to block the station access. She also advised that he move the location of the royal armory to an abandoned grain silo to prevent weapons from falling into rebel hands.

When her turn came to give a report, she told Jordan everything she'd learned at the black market satellite, including the identity of Arabelle's former owner, Reegan "Necktie" Fleece. "From what Arabelle told me, it seems possible that the mob is involved—maybe with Fleece acting as the go-between for Marius and his backer."

Jordan tapped out a message at his workstation. "I'm sending his name to the tech team for an immediate search. Let's see what they turn up."

"He was traveling off world when we took Arabelle. I think he'll come for her."

"Agreed. If nothing else, he'll want to preserve his reputation." Jordan raised a brow as if remembering something. "Listen, I know this is a touchy subject, but we need to talk about your friend Kane. I think he might be feeding the rebels information."

She groaned. Kane was the last person she wanted to discuss. "He's a lot of things, but a rebel isn't one of them."

"That's not what I'm hearing."

"Hearsay isn't proof. You know that."

"Just be aware of what you tell him. That's all I'm asking."

That wouldn't be a problem. She had nothing to say to Kane.

A beep sounded from Jordan's workstation, and he glanced at his screen. "Well, that was fast. We've already got a hit." He leaned closer to the screen and blinked in shock. "No way."

"What?"

"The team was able to hack the transmissions between Fleece's ship and the black market satellite. They say he's on his way to New Haven—"

"That's not too far from here," she interrupted.

"That's not the interesting part," Jordan told her, still reading the screen. "Looks like there's an outbreak on New Haven identical to the one here."

"Maybe the mob is behind the contamination."

"It's possible. Assuming the mafia supplied Marius with weapons, they would have access to more of the same."

"And if the mob is using biological warfare against settlers, Fleece could have all the answers we need. Maybe even the antidote itself."

"We have to capture him," Jordan said.

Nodding, she thought for a moment. "Nobody outside Eturia knows Marius is imprisoned. As long as you keep jamming the interplanetary transmissions, nobody ever will. What if I contact the satellite and pretend I want to buy weapons from Fleece? Now that I'm Marius's wife, it shouldn't raise any suspicions if I act on his behalf."

"And then we grab Fleece when the deal goes down."

"Exactly. But we have to hurry or we could lose him."

Jordan stood from his desk and prepared to sign off. "I'll assemble a team and meet you on New Haven. We can work out a plan once I'm airborne."

The transmission ended, and Cassia rose from the bed feeling lighter and more hopeful than she had in weeks. Finally, she had a lead on a cure. Her call with Jordan had restored her sense of gravity, and she couldn't wait to set their plan in motion. She even found herself wearing a grin when she palmed the keypad and opened the bedroom door.

But her grin fell when she found Kane on the other side.

"Cassy, hear me out."

"Get out of my way. I have new coordinates for Renny."

He moved forward, crowding her until she had no choice but to back up while he came inside and shut the door behind him. "I know what you're thinking because I know how your mind works."

She imagined giving him the finger. "What am I thinking?"

"You want me to go screw myself."

"Close enough."

"You also think I want to be with Shanna."

Cassia's stomach tightened, but she faked a lazy shrug. "That's none of my business. I don't care what you do, or who you do it with."

"I hope you don't mean that. I care what you do."

For some reason that caused her anger to burst.

"Really?" she snapped. "Then take a wild guess what I was doing while you were hooking up with that girl. I was hobbled on the ground while a pair of bounty hunters took turns kicking the shit out of me and asking me where you were." She saw pain in his eyes and knew she was fighting dirty, but she couldn't stop herself. "I took a beating for you, Kane. I would have died to protect you. And if the Daeva had taken you instead of me, I would've come running. I wouldn't have let anything stop me."

"Do you think I stayed here by choice?"

"That's exactly what I think!"

"Damn it, Cassy," he yelled. "I *did* come running. I made it all the way to the air-lock in nothing but my swim trunks. When Doran and Gage tried to reason with me, I started throwing punches." He raked a hand through his hair until it stood on end. "Solara stunned me. I hated her for it, but she did the right thing. I knew it when you told me my survival was all you had to hold on to. If it weren't for her, I'd be dead."

Cassia turned her gaze to the floor. Hearing the truth only made her feel worse because she hadn't meant a word of what she'd said. She had never wanted Kane to come after her. She'd only told him that to cut him as deeply as he'd wounded her.

"The day of shore leave," he said, softer now, "we had a fight, remember? You said you didn't need me anymore. That really messed with my head. I was in a bad place when I met Shanna. She was nice to me, and that felt good. And yeah, maybe I let things go too far, but I shut it down right away because she wasn't the girl I wanted. She wasn't you."

Cassia heard everything he said, but what stuck in her mind and replayed on an endless loop was his admission that Shanna had made him feel good and he'd gone *too far* with her. What did that mean? How far was *too far*? Did he like kissing Shanna more than he liked kissing her?

He drew her back to the conversation by touching her arm. "I kept my promise. I told Gage to hold on to his money for now."

For now.

There it was: two words that reminded her of something she'd been fighting to ignore. Sooner or later, he would take the job Gage had offered him. And when that happened, their lives would follow different paths. He would move on with a new group of friends that didn't include her. Eventually, he would give his heart to another girl—if not Shanna, then someone else. It was just a matter of time.

She thought back to what Jordan had said about tenacity and how she'd rescued herself when no one had come for her. She had been stronger alone.

"Take the money," she said, looking him in the eyes so he would know she meant it. "We need all the resources we can get." She shifted her arm from beneath his hand and skirted around him toward the door. "Please tell Gage to be quick about it. I'm done with this place."

CHAPTER THIRTEEN

Kane had just lifted the lid to the breakfast porridge when Renny abruptly shouldered him aside and swiped the ladle from his hand to fill the first bowl. Ignoring Kane's grunts of offense, the captain reached into the spice cabinet for a pinch of nutmeg and asked, "Where do we keep the sugar?"

Kane rubbed his sore upper arm. He had at least ten pounds on Renny, not to mention a four-inch height advantage, but the captain packed a surprising wallop. "The same place we keep the unicorn meat and the mermaid tears. On the shelf of make-believe."

"We don't have any sugar?"

"What can I say? The captain's a cheapskate."

Before Kane could ask what was going on, Renny darted a glance at the stove's metallic hood, where Arabelle's reflection appeared from the opposite doorway. Her footsteps halted when she noticed him, but she recovered and sat alone at the table, folding her hands primly atop its surface and pretending to study a rust stain on the wall.

Now Kane understood about the sugar.

"What about honey?" Renny whispered.

Kane took pity on the captain and retrieved the secret stash of vanilla syrup he reserved for Cassia's coffee. He shook a few generous squirts into the bowl and watched with amusement as Renny bore the porridge toward Arabelle like a priest preparing a ritual sacrifice. After placing the bowl in front of her, Renny set a jasmine blossom beside it—a live flower that'd probably cost more than their entire galley budget for the week.

Kane shook his head. It was a good thing he'd locked up his signing bonus.

"I made it special for you," Renny told Arabelle, who refused to acknowledge him. "But if you're tired of porridge, I can have Kane fix something else."

Fix something else? Like what, beans?

By way of answer, Arabelle stirred her porridge and began eating in silence. Renny must've known better than to push his luck, because he patted the table and gradually backed out of the galley until he disappeared.

Poor guy.

At the same time, the rest of the crew made their way to the table—Solara jogging up the stairs from the engine room, Doran shuffling in with his hair still damp from the shower, Acorn scurrying into the galley with something thin and silvery between her teeth, and Cassia chasing after her. It seemed Acorn had stolen Cassia's com-bracelet, the one she used to chat with that asshole general of hers.

Two days had passed since they'd left Gage's compound, and Kane still felt the urge to vomit each time he remembered the snippets of conversation he'd overheard. Cassia had gobbled up her general's words like spiced cake at a harvest fair. But had she bothered to listen to her best friend for a few minutes afterward? No. And she hadn't spoken to him since.

Kane filled four bowls with porridge and snuck a glance at Cassia as she pried open Acorn's jaws. She barely looked at him anymore. His kiss with Shanna didn't mean anything to him, but it clearly meant a lot to Cassia. In a way he was glad for that, because it proved she thought of him as more than a friend. But he certainly couldn't say so, and another heartfelt apology would only blow up in his face.

That left one option: picking a fight with her.

After setting her bowl of porridge on the table, he returned to the stove and fixed a mug of coffee with three squirts of vanilla syrup and a pinch of cinnamon. To ensure she didn't leave the mug untouched as she'd done the last two mornings, he plunked it beside her bowl and then leaned down until their noses almost touched.

"We both know you want it," he said. "So quit punishing yourself. You can still be mad at me and drink your coffee."

Her lips thinned while color bloomed on her cheeks. Acorn must've sensed a storm brewing, because she took a nosedive into Cassia's pocket. "If I wanted to punish myself, I'd keep looking at your face."

"Isn't my face in half the pictures taped to your bunk wall?"

"Maybe I keep them there to scare away the devil."

"Just show him your feet," he said, going for her weak spot.

She had adorable toes, but she hated that her second one was longer than the first. "He'll run screaming back to hell with his forked tail between his legs."

"Keep talking and I'll send you there to meet him."

"I'll say hello to your demon-spawn mother while I'm there."

"Try not to wet yourself like you did at the palace."

"Hey!" He drew back an inch. That was hitting below the belt. "I was only four when that happened, and your mom was legitimately scary."

Doran laughed and pointed his spoon at them. "It's great to see you two fighting again." When Arabelle slid him a confused look, he told her, "It's their love language."

"Oh." Arabelle gave them a timid smile. "I speak that language sometimes, too."

"Enough games," Cassia snapped, though the tension had visibly unwound from her posture. She didn't even flinch when Kane sat down beside her. "We have bigger problems than your face," she told him, and then pointed at Doran. "Especially for you, Daro the Red."

"Me?" Doran touched his chest. "What'd I do?"

Cassia worked the com-bracelet over her wrist. She picked up her coffee mug and, after a moment's hesitation, paused to take a sip. "I just finished talking to my general. The pirate lord of sector two was found dead last night from garrote wounds."

"Garroting?" asked Solara.

"It's Necktie Fleece." Doran swore under his breath. "He's taking out the head of each sector. And he wants everyone to know it's him."

"That's what I think, too," Cassia said. "My guess is he's paving the way for the Zhang operation to move into pirate territory. This is war."

"But that's not how pirate law works," Solara argued. "You can't take a lord's territory unless you challenge him. The only reason Doran ended up in charge is because Demarkus insisted on a rematch."

"It doesn't matter," Doran said. "This isn't a lawful takeover. The mafia's trying to cause chaos by killing the Brethren leadership. And I'm next on the list."

Kane gave his friend a reassuring nudge across the table. "No one knows who you really are. Lay off the hair dye and the eyeliner, and Necktie won't recognize you if he passes you on the street."

"Stay off the streets anyway," Cassia told Doran. "New Haven is a big planet, but there's no reason to tempt fate."

Speaking of big planets, Kane wondered how they were going to find Necktie Fleece and capture him without earning permanent neckties of their own. Any man with the strength and skill to use a piece of wire to strangle a pirate lord was no one to underestimate. "How do we take him?"

"My soldiers are on the way," Cassia said. "General Jordan is tracking Fleece's ship. It's a passenger craft called the *Origin*. We'll know exactly when and where he lands, and as soon as his ship touches down, my troops will be there to hobble the landing gear and thrusters. Then we'll take him someplace secure for questioning and see if our hunch is right. With any luck, I'll have a cure to take back to Eturia, and the pirate lords can stop sleeping with one eye open."

"Two birds, one stone," Doran said. "Nice plan."

Kane agreed. He would die before saying so, but he had to admit this whole trip would be a bust without Jordan and his technical team.

"Hey, Kane," Renny called over the intercom. "There's an incoming transmission for you. Some guy who calls himself a badger."

"That's Norton, a friend of mine," he called back. He stuffed in one more bite of porridge as he stood from the table, then shouted with one cheek full, "Tell him I'm on my way."

He jogged up the stairs to the bridge, but by the time he reached the com center, the transmission had dropped. He was about to ping Badger back when Renny spoke to him from the pilothouse. "He couldn't wait. He asked me to deliver a message."

"What'd he say?"

"Come sit down."

Kane's stomach dipped. Everyone knew *sit down* was code for *bad news*. His mind raced with possibilities until it landed on the most likely outcome. "It's my mom, isn't it? Something happened to her."

"Come—"

"Don't make me sit down. Just say it."

But of course Renny didn't do that. First he set the autopilot; then he took the time to walk to the com center and settle a hand on Kane's shoulder. "She took a turn for the worse. She hasn't held anything down all week. Your friend doesn't think she'll last the night." Renny's eyes shone with so much sympathy it weakened Kane's knees. "He wants you to know so you can call home and talk to her before . . ."

"Before it's too late." Kane reached out to steady himself on the wall. Maybe he should've listened and sat down, because now his limbs seemed to have disconnected from his torso. "But she was okay when I talked to her the other day."

"I know. I'm sorry."

Kane nodded at the blur of dials and knobs. "Can you set the frequency?"

"Of course." Renny entered the code and delivered one final pat on the shoulder. "I'll give you some privacy. If you need me, just say the word. I'll be right downstairs."

Renny left the bridge, and it suddenly occurred to Kane that he wasn't ready for this. He wanted to stop the call—it was happening too fast—but he couldn't remember how to operate the equipment. He felt a sick sensation of spinning, as though he'd climbed aboard a carnival ride and couldn't get off.

The transmission connected, and a man's rough voice answered. Kane recognized it as the farmer's. The man sounded like he'd been crying, and that made Kane's throat squeeze.

"I want to talk to Rena. Tell her it's Ka—" He cut off and said instead, "Tell her it's Doodlebug."

* * *

Sometime later, he sat alone on the bottom bunk of the quarters he shared with Renny, slouched over with his head in his hands and staring blankly at the floor. He pulled in a breath and let it go. That was all he could do. His mind was as empty as a broken barrel. It seemed he should be crying or hurting or at least feeling guilty for leaving his mother behind, but more than anything, he felt numb.

His mom would be dead before morning.

He couldn't absorb it.

Cassia knocked on the door in three soft raps. He knew it was her because she always delivered two taps with a long rest before the third. He also knew he wouldn't have to tell her to come in. Her knocks were more of a warning than a request.

He didn't look up when she stepped inside, or when she shut the door and sat next to him on the cot. He felt the mattress sink and then the heat of her arm pressed against his. They sat that way for a while, just leaning on each other, until she dug in her pocket for something and held it in his line of vision. It was the prayer necklace he'd bought for her.

"I was thinking," she said, and brushed a thumb over the blue stone pendant. "I've had this necklace for months and I never really used it." She linked an arm through his. "Want to help me break it in?"

He watched her caress the marbled gem. He had never used a prayer stone, either. He wasn't religious. He'd only visited the temple when his mother had made him go, and he couldn't remember the last time he'd chanted a requiem. But despite that, he opened his palm and let Cassia sandwich the stone between their hands. Somehow, this felt like the right thing to do.

"Close your eyes," she said.

He did as she asked and visualized his mother, not the way she looked now, but with her cheeks full and smiling. That was how he wanted to remember her. Then he focused on channeling his energy into the stone and imagined that energy multiplying and reaching out to his mother while Cassia recited a traditional prayer for the dying.

"Spirits of our kin, greet your sister Rena and aid her in passing beyond the veil between our worlds. Take her in your arms and give her peace. Guide her into paradise and grant her rest from her labors. Comfort her until we meet again."

"Until we meet again," Kane dutifully repeated.

The prayer ended, and he released Cassia's hand. He couldn't say he felt any different. If anything, the hollowness within him had grown deeper—so deep he imagined he could swallow a pebble and never hear it hit the bottom of his stomach.

Cassia stroked his arm. "Talk to me."

"The way you talked to *me*?"

"That's fair," she admitted. "I shouldn't have shut you out because of Shanna. You didn't do anything wrong."

"You shut me out long before then."

"All right, I should have told you about my nightmares, too. I still have them sometimes, but not as often. I'm sleeping a lot better now."

"I know. The circles under your eyes are gone."

"Maybe they would have left sooner if I'd let you help me. Let me help you. Tell me what you're thinking."

He wanted to, but his head swirled with clouded thoughts that were hard to verbalize. Everything was changing so fast. His home didn't feel like home anymore. The only girl he'd ever loved was slipping away, and once his mother left him, he would lose his family.

"It's all going sideways." His voice sounded empty to his

own ears. "I want to stop it, but I can't. Nothing is the same as it used to be."

She made a noise of understanding and twirled a finger at the base of his head to comfort him, just like she'd done a thousand times in the past. But his hair was too short to wrap around her finger. That had changed, too.

"Look at me."

Slowly, he glanced her way.

She gazed at him with softness in her honey-brown eyes, but not pity, and he finally understood why she had wanted him to treat her normally after the kidnapping. The only thing that could make this situation worse was knowing she felt sorry for him. As she stroked his hair, she didn't fill the silence with platitudes like *Everything happens for a reason* or *It'll be all right.* She was simply present. That was more important than words, and she knew it. Somehow she always understood what he needed.

Maybe that was what prompted her to climb onto his lap.

Ducking beneath the top bunk, she straddled his thighs and scooted forward until their hips sat flush. His breath locked in anticipation of what might happen next. He knew from prior experience that things could end here, or they could go much further. A surge of blood rushed through his veins, and suddenly he didn't feel so numb anymore.

She watched him as she cupped his face and explored the length of stubble along his jaw. He looked back at her in silence, afraid to say or do anything to ruin the moment. The floral scent of her skin was more familiar to him than his own heartbeat, and he didn't think he could stand it if she pulled away now.

When she slid her arms over his shoulders and drew an inch

nearer, he took a chance and settled both hands on her lower back. Still holding her gaze, he slipped his thumbs beneath her shirt and brushed the slope of her spine—just a feather graze to test her mood, to see if she'd missed his touch as much as he'd missed hers. She rewarded him with a shiver, and soon her eyelids grew heavy. Though it nearly killed him, he stayed still and used nothing but his thumbs as he let her make the next move.

She strained the limits of his control by kissing a trail from his temple, down the side of his cheek, ending at the corner of his mouth. Chills rose along the back of his neck, and when her lips finally brushed his, all the empty spaces inside him filled with heat. He tried to hold himself in check, but then the tip of her tongue curled inside his mouth, and he was lost.

He tightened both arms around her, crushing their bodies so close there wasn't space to draw more than a gasp. He didn't care. Air didn't matter, only Cassia. It'd been so long since she'd let him hold her like this, and he would willingly suffocate if that was what it took to keep her in his arms. He tasted her mouth while squeezing her in a furious compulsion to pull her inside him. He wondered if he could ever feel close enough to her, even if they went all the way for once. Somehow he doubted it, but he desperately wanted to find out.

He kissed her hard, maybe too hard, because she broke away and panted against his lips. For a moment, he worried she might change her mind, but then she arched her hips and made a noise that said she didn't want this to end any more than he did.

She licked her lips and whispered, "Last time, okay?"

Kane nodded eagerly. Anything she said was fine with him. He repeated what he'd told her on a dozen breathless afternoons just like this, and what he hoped to keep telling her again and again for years to come.

"One more time."

* * *

The next morning was business as usual in every way that mattered.

Cassia wasn't cold to him. She didn't deliver the silent treatment. In fact, she'd woken up an hour early to take over his breakfast duty, which was a nice gesture for her. But when they sat down to eat and he finally caught her eye, there was nothing in her expression to reflect what they'd done the day before.

She simply smiled at him and asked, "Did you sleep all right?"

He blinked at her. How could she be so flippant about this? Okay, so maybe they hadn't gone all the way—she'd said no to that—but they'd done . . . other things. Things they hadn't tried before. "Like a stone," he said. But tonight's sleep wouldn't come as easily unless he could get certain *things* off his mind. "Thanks for making the porridge."

"No problem."

The conversation lulled after that, allowing dread to settle over him as he forced down his breakfast and wondered what was happening at home. Minutes later, Renny called his name through the overhead speaker.

"Report to the bridge for a video transmission," Renny said. "And hurry. You're going to want to see this."

Kane didn't have to ask Cassia to come with him. They both scrambled from the table and ran up the stairs to the pilothouse level. He paused at the threshold to brace himself for the worst. Only when he felt the warmth of Cassia's hand did he take a step inside the bridge.

He stopped short.

There at the com center, grinning at him in full holographic definition, was his mother, very much alive and sitting beside her farmer friend as though nothing had happened. Kane stared at her in confusion. Her eyes shone with happiness, no longer shrouded by dark circles. She didn't seem to be in pain. She wasn't even sweating or trembling.

"It's okay, Doodlebug," she told him, and for the first time since Kane turned eleven, he wasn't embarrassed by his nickname. "I feel better."

His tongue stuck to the roof of his mouth. It took a few tries to unglue it. "But how?"

"A miracle," the farmer said. "Last night she asked me to carry her outside so she could see the stars. We spent the night in the pasture, and when I woke up this morning, I thought she would be—" Emotion choked him, and he stopped to plant a kiss on her temple. He couldn't seem to stop touching her. He gripped her shoulders, stroked her hair, cupped the back of her neck.

Then Kane understood. The man was in love.

His mother pressed a hand to her heart. "The spirits heard my prayers and healed me. I can eat again, anything I want."

"It's true," the farmer said. "She's a bottomless pit today. Six eggs so far."

Kane shared a sideways glance with Cassia, who touched the Eturian prayer necklace tucked beneath her shirt. As grateful as he was for his mother's recovery, he didn't believe in miracles. There had to be a connection between the night air and her sudden revival.

"What about the others who are sick?" he asked. "Are they better, too?"

The farmer considered for a moment. "A few of my field hands look healthier today. Less shaky. I can't speak for anyone else, though."

"Spread the word that anyone with symptoms should spend the day outside," Kane said. "Let's see if that helps."

Cassia spoke up from beside him. "And tell them to keep track of where it's making a difference. I'd like to know if refugees in the city are seeing the same effects."

The farmer agreed to radio the next day with an update. Before they ended the transmission, Kane told the man, "Wait. I never asked your name."

"I'm Meichael," he said. "Meichael Stark."

Kane couldn't shake hands with a holograph, so he did his best to convey a look of respect. He didn't know whether his mother loved this man, but he knew she was in good hands. "Thank you, Meichael."

When the transmission ended, he turned to Cassia. "I want to talk to your general." His instincts warned that his mother's "miracle" was only temporary, and there would soon come a day when fresh air wouldn't revive her. "We need to go over the plan and make sure it's airtight."

"It is airtight."

"There might be an angle we missed. If Necktie slips through our fingers, we won't get another shot at him."

"But you and Jordan don't play nice."

"I'll be on my best behavior."

"Fine." She held up a warning finger. "But one snarky word and I'm cutting off the transmission."

"If anyone pokes the bear, it won't be me," Kane promised. As they made their way out of the bridge, he gave her a playful shoulder bump. "He's *our* general now."

CHAPTER FOURTEEN

"Our intelligence was right," Jordan said. "Fleece's ship requested permission to land this afternoon near a cattle ranch on New Haven. My troops will be in position before he touches down, so there's no reason for you to be there."

Cassia watched his boots while he spoke. Ever since her slipup with Kane last week, she didn't know how to act when she was together with both of them.

"I'll be there anyway," Kane said.

"I wasn't talking to you." The general's boots widened in stance, and Cassia could picture him with his arms folded, his head cocked, shooting daggers with his eyes. It was no secret that he still didn't trust the newest member of their strategy sessions. She peeked up and found she was right. "I would feel better if you stayed where you are. I'll radio you when we have Fleece in custody. You can join us during questioning."

She shook her head. "He thinks I'm buying weapons from him, remember? I don't want to give him any reason to doubt my story. I need to be there." And she *wanted* to be there. She had no intention of staying in the abandoned quarry where Renny had hidden the ship. When her troops brought Necktie Fleece to his knees, she would stand over him and make him feel like the cockroach he was. "Send the coordinates and I'll meet you."

Kane elbowed her.

"*We'll* meet you."

Jordan frowned but didn't argue. "If you insist."

As soon as his image vanished, Kane heaved a breath and slouched over as if two minutes of polite conversation had exhausted him. "Did the military issue the pole that's wedged up his ass, or was he born with it?"

Cassia turned on her heel and strode out of the common room. She would never say so, but Kane could take a lesson from Jordan. While Kane flirted his way through life with a perpetual wisecrack on his tongue, Jordan plotted a smooth and steady course guided by duty. There was something to be said for that.

Kane hurried after her. "Is Renny coming with us?"

"No, he won't leave Arabelle while Fleece is on the loose."

Kane made a noise of doubt. "Am I the only one who still thinks there's something off about her?"

"She's been through a lot. Besides, we scanned her twice and she came up clean."

"But the timing's suspicious, don't you think?"

"Maybe I thought so at first," Cassia admitted. "But the mafia kept her in the outer realm for two years, right? We made hundreds of deliveries all over the fringe during that time.

Renny was bound to cross her path sooner or later. I'm surprised it took this long."

"I guess that makes sense. I can't blame him for staying with her."

Neither could Cassia. She didn't want Fleece in the same time zone as Doran. For that reason she'd sent Doran and Solara halfway around the globe to investigate the settler outbreak. The only problem was they'd taken the shuttle and left her without a ride. "Let's ask Renny to drop us off south of the cattle ranch," she decided. That would give him plenty of time to return the *Banshee* to its hiding place before the arrival of Necktie's ship, and more than enough time for her to meet her troops in the field. "And wear your good boots. We'll be doing a lot of walking."

* * *

An hour later, she regretted those words.

"I shouldn't have worn my good boots." She grimaced when she stepped into another cow patty, her sole making a wet sucking noise as she pulled free. In such high grass, it was impossible to spot the land mines, and they were everywhere. So were the flies, drawn in by the hair-curling reek. She cupped a hand over her nose, but it didn't help. The stench clung to her sinuses.

Kane flashed a toothy grin as he passed by, paying no heed to where he stepped. "What's the matter? You don't like the smell of money?"

"Not this particular currency."

"It's just honest manure. It'll hose right off."

"Honest manure? As opposed to what, the devious kind?"

"I'd offer to carry you piggyback, but we're almost there."

"Uh-huh," she said. "Sure you would."

All of a sudden he froze and whipped his head toward the row of trees separating the grassy pasture from the wild underbrush beyond. He raised a hand, signaling for her to stop. "I think I found your troops."

She didn't see anything at first. But then movement in the distance caught her eye, and she was able to make out a tall, green-camouflaged body standing from a crouching position in the underbrush. She recognized the general's broad shoulders even before his voice called through her bracelet. "Take cover, Highness. We just got word that Fleece is arriving early. He won't expect you to be here yet."

As she glanced up at the noonday sky, thankful there was nothing in sight but a few wispy clouds, Kane took her hand and towed her toward the tangle of thorny bushes behind the trees. Once they were in the thick of it, someone tossed her a length of green mesh. She caught the netting and knelt on the ground with Kane, pulling it over both their heads.

From her new vantage point, she counted the soldiers around her. The squadron was smaller than she'd expected, no more than a dozen men, but each was armed, crouched, and ready, watching the skies with laser focus. Nearest to the pasture, two men sat in front of the group with a suitcase-size box she recognized as electronic hobbling equipment. Their job was to disable the ship from taking off once it'd landed. Beside them, about two yards away, another man gripped a set of hydraulic pliers, perfect for forcing open the boarding hatch. Then the rest of the soldiers would storm the ship to capture Fleece and his men.

She had every reason to be hopeful.

But the waiting was torture.

She had to keep wiping her sweaty palms on her pants. Kane passed the time by inspecting his pulse pistol, which only added to her stress because it forced her to picture him in the line of fire. Planning the raid had seemed simple, just a matter of applying the right strategy. She hadn't given much thought to the soldiers who would carry out her orders. But now, surrounded by all these men, it occurred to her that as their queen, she was responsible for the lives of every single one of them.

That turned her stomach.

A distant roar drew her attention skyward, where a passenger craft descended toward the pasture. At least twice the size of the *Banshee* with three times the thruster power, the ship was long and sleek, bearing the name ORIGIN in block lettering painted on its underside.

"Here we go," Kane said, holstering his pistol. He repositioned into a crouch, like a runner poised at the starting line.

Cassia felt the sensation of being watched. She glanced to the left and met Jordan's gaze, who pointed at her and then at the ground in a message to stay put. She nodded and tugged on Kane's sleeve. "Hey, let's hold back and let the soldiers do their jobs."

He opened his mouth and closed it again as a hot gust of wind from the ship's thrusters pelted them with dust and debris. The *Origin* had reached the pasture and was hovering above the ground about twenty yards from the tree line.

She shielded her eyes and watched its landing gear lower. Two camouflaged soldiers jogged onto the field with the hobbling equipment while the rest of the squadron crept cautiously out of the brush. The *Origin*'s landing gear had nearly touched the ground when suddenly something small and round dropped out of its waste chute, and the ship rose sharply into the air in takeoff.

There was a moment of confusion, followed by yells of panic. The soldiers dropped their hobbling gear and bolted toward the trees, shouting warnings that Cassia couldn't hear over the ship's roaring thrusters. Kane pivoted to face her. He must have understood what was wrong, because she'd never seen so much terror on his face. He mouthed the word *bomb* and then launched himself toward her, tackling her to the ground. His body landed on top of hers and knocked the air from her chest. The back of her skull connected with hard, packed dirt. There was barely enough time for the pain to register before a burst of scorching wind blew over her, followed by an explosion so violent it shook the ground.

Heat was everywhere. It tightened her skin and singed her clothes. Objects hit the ground all around her. She felt the impact of pebbles on her boots and sensed a staccato series of blows landing on Kane's body. She peeked out from below his arm and saw patches of flame through the smoke. Her mind's eye flashed to the soldiers she'd seen running for cover, but she quickly shut down that train of thought and focused on the ones who could be saved.

She squirmed out from beneath Kane and started with him. He had blood in his hair and patches of pink burns forming along both forearms, but otherwise he seemed all right. She helped him sit up and made sure he was lucid before scanning the area for more wounded. In their scorched, bloodied uniforms, the men were hard to distinguish from one another, but she identified General Jordan as he guided two limping soldiers toward the group he'd already assembled in the safe zone. If there was any control to be had in this situation, he'd found it.

Amid the chaos and the ringing in her ears, Cassia took a moment to process what had gone wrong. In such a large ship, there was no way Fleece could have seen any of them on the ground. He had to have known they were waiting for him, which meant someone had told him the plan.

Kane tapped her shoulder and pointed at the *Origin* as it shrank to a pinpoint on the horizon. She couldn't hear him, but she understood the concern on his face. Fleece was getting away. She nodded, but then a sudden realization turned her blood to ice. If someone had told Fleece the plan, then he knew where the rest of the crew were hiding. The bomb had only been part of the setup.

Fleece was going after Doran and Arabelle.

CHAPTER FIFTEEN

Powered by adrenaline and an army-issued jet pack, Kane rocketed two miles east of the pasture, where the Eturian squadron had docked their cruiser beneath a cloaking tarp. He loosened his grip on the throttle and scanned the ground, praying the ship's hiding place hadn't been leaked to the mafia. That cruiser was their only source of medical supplies, not to mention his only hope of reaching Doran in time. The jet pack was fast, but not powerful enough to propel him to the other side of the planet ahead of the *Origin*.

His earpiece beeped, and Renny's faint voice followed.

"Louder," Kane hollered while continuing to study the ground. "I can't hear you over these thrusters."

"I said," the captain shouted, "Doran knows Fleece is coming. I ordered him to report back to the quarry with Solara. I'm tracking the shuttle so I can meet them in the middle."

"What about Arabelle?" Kane asked. He'd assumed Renny's

first priority would be finding her a safer hiding place, not bringing her out into the open. "Fleece will try—"

"She's right beside me. Fleece will never touch her." There was a serrated edge in Renny's voice, sharp enough to cut steel. "Not her, or anyone else in our family. Not today—not ever. Is that understood?"

"Yes, Cap'n." Kane spotted the ship and dove toward it. "I found the cruiser. I'll report back once I deliver the med supplies."

He hit the ground running and wasted no time in yanking off the tarp until he found the boarding hatch. After entering the access code, he jogged up the entrance ramp and sprinted all the way through the ship to the pilothouse. There wasn't time to shed his jet pack, so he perched on the edge of the pilot's seat, prepared the cruiser for takeoff, and grasped the wheel.

But he'd never flown anything this large.

The ship lurched violently into the air. He overcompensated, which caused the cruiser to wobble as it gained altitude. There were too many switches and blinking lights. He scanned the control panel three times and still couldn't figure out how to retract the landing gear, so he left it in place and continued to the pasture.

The flight wasn't a smooth one, and neither was his landing. He touched down with a clatter that shook a few pieces of equipment loose. The cockpit alarms blared as he powered off the thrusters. Cringing, he backed out of the pilothouse. He supposed any landing he could walk away from was good enough. . . .

Good enough for anyone but Jordan, who was waiting at

the bottom of the exit ramp with his mouth hanging open. The general lifted a hand toward his ship, sputtering a series of incoherent words because he couldn't seem to find a curse strong enough.

"My ship!" he finally yelled. "You told me you could fly her!"

"She's here, isn't she?"

"Not all of her—I think you dropped the transmission during that sloppy free fall you call a landing!"

Kane was almost positive the general had exaggerated, but he darted a sideways glance beneath the cruiser to be sure.

Cassia came running over from the trees, what little was left of them. Most of the trunks had been reduced to charred stumps with jagged, protruding edges where the tops had blown off. It seemed she'd formed a triage among the wounded. Soldiers were separated into three groups based on the severity of their injuries. One group worked to repair weapons while another sat nearby cradling burnt or dislocated limbs. The third lay motionless on the ground.

"Any word from Doran?" she asked.

Kane repeated everything he knew. No sooner had he finished his recap than Renny pinged both their com-links. "Something's not right," he said. "I'm tracking Doran, and he's veering off course. He and Solara won't answer their coms. I wouldn't mind some backup. How fast is that Eturian ship you were telling me about?"

Jordan raised an index finger. "Don't even think about it."

Kane didn't want the cruiser. However, the brand-new shuttle nesting alongside the ship was another story. He thumbed at the craft. "Is that a Hypersonic Deluxe?"

"Yes." Jordan's eyes turned to slits. "And you're not touching that, either."

"If I'm not mistaken," Kane said, nodding at Cassia, "that ship, its shuttle, and everything on board are property of the Rose dynasty. Even your tighty-whities belong to the queen."

"Take it," Cassia told him. "I'll stay here and treat the wounded. Let me know what . . ."

Kane didn't hear the rest. He was already running back inside the ship to access the shuttle's docking station. "Stand by, Captain," he said through the link. "I'm on my way."

* * *

As Cassia watched the shuttle rise toward the clouds and launch into the distance, she felt a pulling sensation behind her ribs, as though her heart were made of taffy being stretched in opposite directions. She wanted to go to Doran and Solara, and to keep Kane in sight. She wanted to be with Renny. Her crew needed her; they were in trouble.

But so were her soldiers.

Jordan refocused her attention with a gentle touch. "Let's get the men inside. The cargo hold can double as an infirmary. It's not the cleanest room on the ship, but it'll do."

"All right."

"And at some point, we need to talk about him." Jordan didn't look at her, instead fixing his gaze on a shard of metal on the ground.

She could tell he meant Kane.

"There's something you should know," he continued, and

when he peeked up at her, his eyes seemed heavy, as if he understood the news would be hard to take. "Something I just learned, otherwise I would've told you sooner."

"What is it?"

"Later. First we'll see to the injured."

She nodded because he was right. The longer wounds were left untreated, the greater chance of infection setting in. Whatever he had to tell her could wait.

She helped haul the critically wounded on board using impromptu stretchers made from blankets. The ship stocked an impressive medical supply, even plasma and synthetic skin, which she put to use on two patients who'd suffered blood loss and extreme burns. Once the first group was stabilized, she began setting broken bones and administering Marrow Bond to accelerate the healing process. Finally she treated the minor wounds such as abrasions and light burns. She'd just set down her last tube of suture gel when she realized there was still a patient she hadn't seen—the general.

She peered around the cargo hold for him while stretching her lower back. She didn't know how many hours had passed, but the beam of sunlight shining through the open hatch had shifted to the opposite end of the room. She didn't spot Jordan in the cargo bay, and come to think of it, she couldn't remember the last time she'd seen him. After grabbing a med-kit, she wound her way through the maze of soldiers sleeping on the floor and continued to the corridor leading to the main part of the ship.

She eventually found him in the pilothouse, poring over transmission data. He didn't hear her approaching, so she stood in the doorway and watched him rub his eyes with one hand while bracing himself on the equipment with the other. His face seemed pale beneath the overhead lighting, pale enough to make her suspect he'd hidden an injury from her. Now that she paid attention, she noticed that unlike his pants, his jacket was clean and unburned.

He'd changed it.

"Where's your other coat?" she asked, causing him to flinch. "The one you were wearing earlier?"

He held a hand over his heart. Even startled, his skin didn't fill with color the way it should. "It was dirty, so I pitched it."

He was lying. Guys like him didn't mind grit on their clothes. She strode to the pilot's chair and swiveled it around to face the open portion of the bridge. "Sit down." When his boots failed to move, she added, "That's an order from your queen."

His lips slid into a sideways grin. Once he sat down and leaned against the seatback, she moved in front of him and began unfastening his jacket. As her fingers moved, she found her cheeks prickling with heat. She had imagined the general shirt-less a time or two—a girl would have to be dead not to wonder what he looked like under his snug-fitting fatigues—but in her daydreams he'd never been this close. The body heat radiating from his clothes and the sound of his deep, steady breathing made this a more intense experience than she'd bargained for. It was all she could do to keep her hands steady as she opened his jacket and pushed it over his shoulders.

Then she saw why he'd changed his coat.

"You should've come to me," she said, cringing at the dried blood that caked his T-shirt. He'd probably been cut by flying debris. Gently, she peeled the crusted fabric away from his skin and then tore his shirt in half to expose a six-inch gash on his lower belly.

Jordan sucked a painful breath through his teeth.

"You need sutures," she told him. "But first I have to clean you up. Sit tight while I find a sponge. And undo your trousers." She glanced down as her face warmed again. "It looks like that cut extends beneath your waistband."

She left the pilothouse and returned with a clean cloth and a bowl of warm water. Still seated, Jordan lowered his pants to midthigh and rolled down the waistband of his boxer briefs, exposing a set of V-shaped hip flexor muscles that were bound to make an appearance in her dreams tonight. She handed him the bowl and forced herself to study the contents of her med-kit instead of watching him sponge his bare torso.

When he was done, she knelt on the floor between his legs, but then quickly changed into a crouch. She'd vowed never to kneel before any man again after Marius, and she meant to keep that promise. She didn't talk as she sprayed antiseptic over the scrapes on Jordan's chest. When the time came to clean his deeper wound, she peeked up at him.

"Ready?"

Nodding, he gripped the chair's armrest. His grasp tightened as she sprayed the length of his gash, but he didn't make a sound.

"Now for the fun part," she said, holding up the suture gel. "This is going to burn like hellfire."

"And you wondered why I didn't come to you."

She carefully pinched his wound closed. Then, one slow inch at a time, she spread the gel in place and cringed in sympathy as its chemicals bubbled and sizzled over his flesh. He clenched his teeth and grunted. The pain wouldn't last long, but she knew from experience it was intense.

To ease the burn, she blew lightly on his abdomen. He gasped, and she immediately glanced up, expecting to find him hurt. But the heated expression in his eyes told her he wouldn't mind if she did it again.

She knew that look.

She had seen it a dozen times on Kane's face, most recently on the afternoon she'd spent with him in his bunk. The sobering thought jerked her to her senses. She felt a stab of guilt, but she couldn't tell for whom.

She cleared her throat and stood up. "You wanted to talk to me?"

Jordan raised both brows.

"You said it was important," she prompted.

"Oh." He seemed to catch on, straightening in his chair and swallowing hard. "Yes. It's about Kane Arric."

"What about him?"

"It's not hearsay anymore. I have evidence that he's assisting the rebels." Jordan arched against the seatback to pull up his pants. "He activated his old credit account on the day he returned to Eturia. The balance wasn't much, but it was enough to buy a large amount of ammonium nitrate. It's used for building bombs."

"And for fertilizing soil," she pointed out. "His mother lives on a farm. He probably bought it for her."

"Maybe. But remember when the rebels tried to raid our fuel station?"

"What about it?"

"They used nitrate bombs as a diversion. That's when we started tracking ammonium nitrate purchases. Kane's was the largest and most recent. That can't be a coincidence." Jordan lifted a hand as if anticipating her next words. "Before you defend him, let me finish. Yesterday my men found a rebel in our ranks. A soldier in the second battalion. He admitted during questioning that he asked Kane to gather information from you and report back with anything useful."

"Then he's lying, because Kane would never do that. Who's your source?"

"Norton Shalvis. His nickname is Badger."

The name put a hitch in her pulse. Kane had received at least two transmissions from Badger, and those were just the ones she knew about. But the calls had made sense. Badger was looking after Kane's mom. "All right, they've spoken to each other, but that doesn't prove anything."

"There's more," Jordan said. "The royal armory was looted. All the rifles we collected from the volunteers are gone."

She swore under her breath. More weapons in rebel hands— it was her worst nightmare. "I thought you moved the armory to the old grain silo."

"I did. I drove the weapons there and unloaded them myself. And I didn't tell a soul about it, not even my next-in-command. You and I were the only ones who knew." He raised a brow at her. "Did you mention anything about it to Kane?"

"No," she said. But as soon as the word left her lips, she recalled that Kane had been waiting right outside the door when she and Jordan had discussed moving the armory. He could've easily overheard the conversation and told someone the new location.

A chill rolled down her spine.

"Be careful what you share with him." Jordan pointed toward the cargo hold, where a distant groan of pain rang out. "I buried three good men today and I'll go home with nine injured, all because somebody talked to Fleece. I doubt Kane is the mafia's mole. He wants a cure as much as we do. But you might tell him something else, something related to the fight back home, and that might end up costing more lives."

Cassia nodded as a heavy weight shrouded her heart. She didn't want to lose any more men, and yet she hated herself for questioning her best friend. She busied her hands by reassembling the med-kit, but it didn't offer any distraction from her thoughts.

"Don't worry. I know who I can trust."

* * *

The Hypersonic Deluxe lived up to its reputation.

Kane reached speeds fast enough to strip him bald and peel the brown off his skin. The dashboard gauge indicated he could increase velocity by another twenty percent, but he stuck to his pace. Any faster and he might travel through time.

Besides, he was almost there.

He'd been listening to the exchange between Renny and Doran, whose com-link had come online about an hour ago. Someone must've placed a tracker on the *Banshee*'s shuttle, because no matter where Doran hid, the *Origin* followed.

That alone didn't pose a threat, but the half-ton pulse cannon mounted to its hull did. One direct shot at the shuttle and Fleece would succeed in dispatching another pirate lord.

Kane didn't have much of a plan, but he figured he'd start by piloting alongside Doran to see if he could find and dislodge the tracking beacon. Using his com-link, he locked on to the *Banshee*'s ever-moving position and followed it until he spotted the ship barrel-rolling to escape a blast of cannon fire.

"I see Renny, but not the shuttle," Kane said through the link. "Where are you hiding, Doran? Let's see if I can shake your tracker loose."

Solara's voice came through the link. "We're under an abandoned hangar at thirty-nine degrees north, eighty-four degrees west."

Kane set the coordinates and veered left. He glanced over his shoulder and noticed the *Origin* mirroring his flight pattern. It was like Fleece had overheard the conversation. "Never mind the beacon. I think Fleece is hacking our transmissions."

"That would explain a lot," Renny said. "Everyone go offline and change course. Let's see if that helps."

It didn't help.

The *Origin* continued its relentless pursuit of the shuttle, no matter how well Doran concealed it. Soon it became clear there was no hiding from the ship. Or running from it—not with that much thruster power.

"We need a new plan," Doran said. "I'm almost out of fuel."

Kane swore through the com-link. "What we need is a weapon."

"I'm fresh out of laser cannons," Renny told them, "but I've got a pistol for each hand. Maybe it's time to take this fight to the ground."

Kane thought back to the bomb the *Origin* had dropped out of its waste chute. Whether in the air or on the soil, they didn't stand a chance against the ship's firepower. He patted his chest to make sure the jet pack straps were still fastened. "Renny, let me try something first."

"Like what?"

Kane didn't want to say it aloud, in case Fleece was listening. "How many hits can the *Banshee* take?"

"Depends on where they land."

"Maneuver behind Doran and block as much pulse fire as you can. On my mark, we'll all shift due west." When nobody objected, he shouted, "Now!"

Three vessels simultaneously shifted to the west: the *Banshee*, its shuttle, and the *Origin*. All except for Kane, who veered east on a collision course with the largest ship. Maybe he didn't have a pulse cannon, but he had a missile in the form of a brand-new Hypersonic Deluxe.

"What're you doing?" Renny demanded. "Turn around!"

Kane fisted the wheel and watched the *Origin* grow larger as he approached it with blinding speed. He stayed above the line of fire until he was near enough to make out the mammoth bolts along the ship's hull, then he darted toward the cannon mounted at its underbelly.

"Stand down," Renny yelled. "Kane, that's an order!"

Kane wasn't listening. He was too busy mirroring the *Origin*'s final swerve as Fleece tried to avoid the collision. Kane aimed his shuttle directly at the pulse cannon at the exact moment its barrel swiveled toward him, glowing red and preparing to blast.

Locking the engine at full power, he punched the Eject button and closed his eyes as he flung backward into the air. Whiplash wrenched his neck, but he didn't hesitate to turn on his jet pack. Its thrusters roared, and he rocketed away from the ship as his shuttle struck the cannon with a deafening blast.

Heat nipped at the back of his neck. He glanced over one shoulder to find the belly of the ship engulfed in flames. There was only one way to extinguish a fire that large, and clearly Fleece knew it, because he pointed the *Origin*'s nose at the sky and took off like a shot. With full thrusters, it headed toward the atmosphere, where the lack of oxygen would choke the flames. Kane hadn't destroyed the ship, but he'd definitely put it out of commission for a while.

Once the crew had assembled on the ground, Renny smacked Kane upside the head and then pulled him into a hug. "You just earned two weeks' bathroom detail. Don't scare me like that again."

"Yes, Cap'n."

Doran glanced at a fragment of the shuttle's wing that had fallen in the grass. He let out a low whistle. "Was that a Hypersonic Deluxe?"

Kane saluted the wreckage. "May she rest in peace."

"More like pieces," Doran quipped. "How many shuttles have you wrecked now?"

"Two. Both times saving your pretty carcass."

"My pretty carcass thanks you."

"Me too." Solara strode around her boyfriend to give Kane a

peck on the cheek. "By the way, we have a lot to tell you. You're not going to believe what we found out at the settlement."

After the events of today, Kane would believe just about anything. But before they went any further, they had to figure out who was feeding information to Fleece. He noticed that Arabelle hadn't joined them. "Where's Arabelle?"

Renny glanced toward the *Banshee*. "She's lying down with a headache. I think coming close to Fleece really shook her up."

Right, Kane thought. *Or maybe she's the one who tipped him off.*

The look Doran delivered said he agreed.

"Now for the hard part," Renny said, eyes smiling behind his glasses. "Telling General Jordan you ruined one of his toys."

CHAPTER SIXTEEN

By the next morning, the scent of scorched earth had faded enough for Cassia to detect more pleasant notes in the air, like lemongrass and pine, but nothing could erase the ringing in her ears from the blast. She faced the rising sun and tried to focus instead on its warmth. She would miss this when the *Banshee* departed and her only source of heat came from a UV bulb designed to prevent transport madness.

"Ready to go?" Kane asked from the *Banshee*'s boarding ramp. He peered at her above the crate he carried, the last of the local cargo Renny had contracted to deliver. "After I strap this down, it's time for liftoff."

For the hundredth time, she searched his mannerisms for a hint of guilt or a trace of duplicity, anything to confirm that Jordan's accusations might be true. But he moved with the same easy gait as always.

"What?" he asked when he caught her staring.

"Nothing." She thumbed at the Eturian cruiser. "Give me a minute to say good-bye."

"Make it quick."

Turning her back to the sun, she faced the pasture where the crew had met last night to discuss what Doran and Solara had found at the settlement. The infected settlers had suffered identical symptoms to those on Eturia, and like Kane's mother, many of them had worsened and then abruptly bounced back. But in a strange twist, all of them had vanished on the same night—fifty men and women gone with no sign of a struggle. It was as though they'd teleported from their beds into an alternate dimension.

The group had decided the *Banshee* would continue to New Atlantia to investigate another outbreak while Jordan and his soldiers returned to Eturia to delve deeper into Marius's partnership with the mafia . . . or at least that was what Cassia had claimed. In truth, Jordan was returning home to plan a rebel sting. She'd chosen not to share that information with Kane for reasons she refused to examine too closely.

"There you are," Jordan called to her from the top of the boarding ramp. He descended the ramp and met her at the base. "I was about to come find you."

"How's the, uh . . ." She pointed at his lower abdomen, trying not to think about the tense moment that had passed between them when she'd bandaged it.

He lifted his shirt hem. All that remained of the gash was a thin pink scar. "Good as new. You're a queen of many talents."

"Hey, wrap it up," Kane hollered from the *Banshee*'s open cargo hold. He flashed both palms when Cassia glared at him. "Don't shoot the messenger. Renny said it's time to lift off." He gave Jordan a fake salute. "General, I can't tell you how sad I am to see you go. Sorry about your Hypersonic Deluxe. No hard feelings, right?"

Jordan groaned and muttered something under his breath.

"Sorry," Cassia whispered. "I know he can be grating, but—"

"But deep down he's a great guy?"

"Well, usually, yes."

Jordan backed up the ramp. He didn't say anything more, but he used his gaze to send a silent message that she should remember his warning.

She nodded in a silent reply.

As if she could forget.

*　*　*

Several hours later, she left her quarters to make a pot of coffee. She found it odd that she didn't pass anyone in the hallway, but she didn't think much about it until she reached the galley and glanced up at the wall's clock display. There were several throughout the ship, each showing the time, date, and current coordinates. According to this one, the ship was traveling away from New Atlantia instead of toward it.

She climbed the stairs to the pilothouse, expecting to find Renny, but she stopped short when she discovered the whole crew inside, even Arabelle, who seemed to have warmed up to the captain, judging by her position atop his knee. Kane occupied the copilot's chair, and Doran and Solara sat on the floor with their backs against the wall.

"Are you having a meeting without me?"

The dashboard lights told her Renny had already set the autopilot, but he pretended to set it again. "No, just talking."

"About?"

"Taking a small detour."

"That's why I came up here," she said. "We're going the wrong way."

"I need to make a quick stop." Renny slid his eyes toward her. "On Vega."

Vega?

Fear tightened her airway. She could almost hear the rustle of soybean leaves and the crack of breaking stems. She had never intended to go back there. She didn't know if she could stand to see that settlement again. Just thinking about the saltbox shops and the dusty streets made it hard to breathe.

"Why?" she asked.

"There was a problem with our last delivery payment."

"And you have to deal with it now?"

Kane stood up from the copilot's chair and stepped over an obstacle course of legs and feet until he reached her at the doorway. He took her elbow and guided her away from the group into the bridge. "You can stay on the ship," he said in her ear. "You don't even have to look out the window if you don't want to. The whole thing won't take more than an hour."

She released a quiet breath.

"Renny wants me with him at the warehouse, but I'll stay here if you need me." His thumb brushed the sensitive bend of her arm. "Just say the word."

"I'll be fine," she told him. As long as she didn't have to leave the ship, she could pretend she was anywhere.

"Arabelle's staying on board, too." Kane dropped his voice to a whisper. "She offered to scan the ship for trackers and bugs. Maybe you should help her. It's a big job for one person, know what I mean?"

She understood the subtext, but she didn't share his suspicion. Whatever means Fleece had used to spy on them, she doubted Arabelle was involved. Arabelle had no motive to help Fleece, and besides, she'd never asked the crew to bring her aboard. They'd literally snatched her and run. But to placate Kane, she told him, "Sure, I'll go charge the scanner."

* * *

Kane watched Cassia descend the stairs before he rejoined the crew and shut the pilothouse door. "She's gone."

"Okay," Renny continued in a low voice. "Like I said, I've been doing some digging into what happened the day Cassia was taken. The Daeva shouldn't have known we were coming, because I used an alias for the delivery. Cassia was right when she told Kane it was a setup."

"Someone tipped off the Daeva," Solara said. "For a finder's fee."

"Exactly, so I followed the money." Renny tapped the pilot seat's armrest. "Turns out one of the warehouse workers had a sudden windfall that week, and for an interesting amount of credits—exactly ten percent of Cassia's bounty. By all accounts the idiot couldn't find his ass with both hands, but he claims he won the money in an off-world survival contest."

"Who is he?" Kane asked.

"Jess Ranger. The hovercraft pilot."

Kane remembered that guy. He was tall and young, and not terrible-looking for a fringe yokel. Cassia had thrown a few glances his way, and the guy had flirted right back. He'd seemed a little too friendly, but Kane had dismissed his suspicion as jealousy.

"Looks like he used the money to buy a farm about a mile outside town," Renny said. "From what I hear, he has a cash crop ready to harvest."

Kane expelled a bitter laugh. "Not for long."

"You said it," Doran agreed. "We'll burn it to the ground."

"Wait." Solara seemed conflicted as she picked her cuticles and peered from one person to the next. "Are you sure he's the one?" she asked Renny. "There's no doubt in your mind?"

"Not one iota."

"Then I want in, too. But I don't think we should kill him."

"Oh, don't worry," Kane said. "Jess Ranger isn't getting off that easy."

* * *

If someone had stashed any surveillance bugs on the *Banshee*, Cassia couldn't find them. Since they'd landed on Vega, she'd been over every inch of the ship with a voltage scanner, and that was after shutting down the electrical systems and disconnecting the ship's battery supply to eliminate all current. Anything using the slightest trace of power should've shown up like a flashing billboard.

She blew a lock of hair out of her eyes and tossed her scanner onto the galley table.

How was Fleece doing it?

"No luck here," Arabelle said, approaching from the lower-level staircase. She strode into the galley and opened one hand to reveal a ball of auburn fur. "All I found was this delinquent trying to get inside a crate of dried apples."

Acorn spread her winged arms and glided to the table, where she scurried across its surface until she reached the hem of Cassia's T-shirt. Seconds later, the troublemaker found her favorite pocket and nuzzled her way inside it.

Arabelle tucked a scarlet curl behind one ear and opened the cooler to retrieve the iced tea she'd left to steep overnight. "Want some?"

"Sure." Cassia strode to the cabinet and stood on tiptoe to reach the cups. She wished Kane wouldn't put them up so high. When she noticed Arabelle watching, she laughed. "Short-people problems."

"Tell me about it." Arabelle flourished a hand at her own petite body.

"Do you ever feel like people don't notice you?" Cassia asked. "Whenever I make deliveries with the crew, the warehouse workers barely look at me. They glance at whoever's tallest, and then they start talking like I'm not even in the room."

"Yep." Arabelle nodded. "But that can actually be a good thing."

"How so?"

"You can learn a lot if you blend in and listen."

Intrigued, Cassia slid onto the bench.

"Fleece had a lot of shady people working for him," Arabelle said, pushing a cup of iced tea across the table as she took the opposite bench. "Shady but smart. A while ago, two of his tech guys were talking about how to hack transmissions—and how to keep from being hacked. They said all it took was tweaking the advanced system controls." She took a long pull of tea and smiled. "So I restored Fleece's transmitter to factory settings."

Cassia gasped. "That's how my team is hacking him."

Arabelle lifted a shoulder. "It felt good to get back at him in some small way."

"What about the *Banshee*'s settings?"

"Renny already asked me to check. They're secure. I don't know how Fleece was trailing us yesterday, but I don't think it had anything to do with our transmitter."

"Did Fleece ever say why he was in the fringe to begin with?" Cassia asked. "I mean, I assume the mafia's making a power grab outside their territory, but what's his role?"

Arabelle frowned as she nursed her tea. "I've been thinking about that ever since you said he was killing pirate lords. Fleece was always tight-lipped, but I heard him mention Daro the Red once or twice. He'd been planning the hits for months. I think that's why Ari Zhang sent him out here, to clear the way for some kind of expansion."

"But what can the mob do in the fringe that they can't do on Earth?" Cassia wondered aloud. It was true the outer realm had no laws, but Ari Zhang had successfully operated outside the law for decades, mostly because he had half the Solar League in his pocket. Expanding into the fringe didn't make sense from a business standpoint, either. Most of the galaxy's wealth was concentrated on Earth, so Zhang should fight to stay there, not leave. "Even if the mafia wins a foothold in pirate territory, they'll have to spend a fortune on security to keep it. What's the point when most of the fringe settlers are too poor to gamble or hire a hit man?"

"Desperate people can always find the money."

"But there has to be more to it than that. Maybe he's tired of paying off politicians and wants to move his business where there aren't any rules."

"Politicians . . ." Arabelle repeated. "I just remembered something. It happened so long ago that I almost forgot. The night Zhang sold me to Fleece, I heard him mention a bill that had failed. I guess he wanted a law passed, but he couldn't buy off enough politicians to do it. About a month later, Fleece and I were in the fringe."

Cassia wondered if the bill was a matter of public record. She doubted it.

"I didn't think much about it at the time," Arabelle continued, and gave a sad smile. "I had other things on my mind."

Cassia reached out and covered Arabelle's hand. "Of course you did. Living with Fleece must have been awful."

Arabelle stared into her tea, paling a shade. "It was."

"I can relate, at least a little bit," Cassia shared. "Renny probably told you about the bounty hunters who took me. It happened right here in this town, about half a mile away. That was the worst experience of my life, and it only lasted a few weeks. I can't imagine how you stayed sane." She squeezed Arabelle's hand. "How long were you with him?"

"I don't know. About a year, I guess."

"Who did you work for before then?"

"Before when? I've always belonged to Fleece."

Cassia wrinkled her forehead. Maybe she'd misunderstood. She thought Ari Zhang had taken Arabelle immediately after Renny had picked his pocket and left Earth. "You said Zhang came for you because he couldn't find Renny. He wanted revenge, and he knew that Renny loved you, so hurting you was the next best thing."

"Right."

"How long did he look for Renny?"

"A day or two. At first he wanted me to lure Renny out of hiding. Once he heard Renny was long gone, he sold me to Fleece."

"But that was more than two years ago."

"No, it's only been a year."

"Belle . . ." Cassia tentatively tried out the nickname and was rewarded by a soft smile from her bunkmate. "I've lived on this ship ever since I ran away from home. That was more than two years ago, and Renny was already here as the first mate."

"Are you sure?"

"Ask the crew if you don't believe me. Or check the ship's log."

"Huh." Arabelle stared ahead in confusion while wrapping a curl around one finger. "Maybe I lost track of time. That's easy to do in space, right?"

Cassia nodded, though a year was a lot of time to lose. More likely Arabelle had blocked out large chunks of memories that were too painful to relive. "So what's next for you?" she asked, changing the subject. "Do you have family on Earth?"

"A few cousins, but I can't go home and risk Zhang finding me. I think I'll stay here for a while." Belle peeked up, and her cheeks turned pink. "It's nice to have Renny back. I'm trying to take things slow, but it feels like a second chance for us."

"What changed your mind about him?"

"The way he fought for me yesterday," Arabelle said with pride. "He would've died before letting Fleece take me, or any of you. He's always been like that, completely devoted to the people he loves."

"You still love him." It wasn't a question. Words were easy to fake, but Cassia had never met anyone who could blush at will.

Belle propped both elbows on the table, leaning in as if to share a secret. "I never stopped. There's no one like Renny. He's the kind of man a girl can't forget."

Cassia agreed on all counts.

At that moment, the boarding ramp's motorized pulley whirred from the level below, followed by the clattering of boots against metal. Doran and Solara reached the galley, with Kane right behind them. They brought the scent of fire on their clothes.

"Why do you smell like smoke?" she asked, and then instantly forgot the question when she saw Kane's hands. They were swollen and streaked with blood from where the skin across his knuckles had split open. "What happened?"

He shrugged and peered longingly at her tea. "I fell."

"Uh-huh," she said, handing him her cup. "Fist-first into someone's face."

"No, really—"

"Save it." She could tell he'd been fighting. Physical evidence aside, he had that drowsy sheen in his eyes, the mark of someone coming down from an adrenaline high. "You need sutures. Whoever you hit had a sharp jaw."

"Yeah, well, it was worth it."

The loathing in his voice made it clear that this had been no ordinary brawl over a missed payment at the warehouse. This fight had been personal.

"Oh no." She began to see the real reason for this detour. "What did you do?"

He dodged the question by chugging her tea, and then Renny came power-walking through the galley like his boots were fueled by Infinium. Without a backward glance, he continued up the stairs to the pilothouse and called over one shoulder, "We ruffled a few feathers in town, so everyone hold tight and prepare for takeoff."

"Renny!" she hollered after him. "You didn't have to do this!"

"Priorities, Cassia." Before his voice faded into the distance, he left her with one last reply. "Now, quit arguing and strap in."

CHAPTER SEVENTEEN

*T*he next evening Kane returned to his quarters to change before dinner. He was so distracted by the tomato sauce he'd spilled down the front of his best shirt that by the time he noticed the sock tied to his door handle, it was too late. He flung open the hatch and caught a fleeting glimpse of Renny and Arabelle in all their glory.

He whipped around and darted into the hall, but not fast enough to stop the image from haunting his retinas. It reminded him of the time he'd caught his parents in the act during one of his father's rare visits, and he felt the overpowering urge to shampoo his eyeballs. Why couldn't Renny bolt the door like a normal guy?

Arabelle came out a minute later, her face nearly as red as her hair as she straightened her skirt and fled down the hallway.

It was going to be an awkward supper.

Kane knocked twice. "You decent, Captain?"

"Rarely so, but it's safe to come in."

Even though he'd watched Arabelle leave, Kane peeked around the room before stepping all the way inside. Thankfully, Renny was clothed and facing the rear wall. "Sorry," Kane said as he slipped the sock free and tossed it onto the top bunk. "I wasn't paying attention."

"No, it's all right," Renny told him, though the strain in his voice indicated otherwise. "I'm glad you're here. I've been meaning to talk to you."

Kane didn't really want to talk, not with the image of his captain's keister fresh in his mind. But as Renny blocked the path to the clean clothes, there wasn't much of a choice.

"I've made a lot of progress with Belle," Renny said.

"Yeah." Kane scratched the back of his neck. "I noticed."

"Things are going well."

Kane didn't like where this discussion was headed.

"*Really* well," Renny emphasized.

"Aw, come on, Captain. All I want is a clean shirt."

"What I'm trying to say is Belle and I are together now. So . . ." Renny trailed off, peering above his glasses as if the rest of the message should be clear. Finally, he blurted, "I need you to bunk somewhere else."

"Oh." Kane mentally smacked his own forehead. "Right, no problem."

"Maybe you can bunk with Cassia. You two are getting along again."

That was true, though the suggestion that he room with Cassia was like inviting an alcoholic to live in a distillery. But as his only alternative was the cold cargo-hold floor, he filled a box with his clothes and grabbed his pillow on the way out the door to his old quarters.

The room was vacant when he dropped off his box. He wondered if Arabelle was off somewhere breaking the news to Cassia. He hoped so, because he didn't want that job. After changing into a clean shirt and leaving the stained one to soak in the washroom, he returned to the galley and dished out six bowls of tomato soup with toasted chickpeas.

The crew gathered at the table, with Cassia and Arabelle bringing up the rear. As soon as he glanced at Cassia, he could tell she knew about the change in their sleeping arrangements. She wore the same look of concern that he felt inside.

Renny lifted his cup and motioned for everyone to do the same. "We officially have a new crew member. I think this calls for a toast—to Belle."

"To Belle," everyone repeated over the sound of clinking mugs.

Arabelle took Renny's hand and gazed at him with so much tenderness that Kane had to look away.

"Now that you're one of us, there's no avoiding it," Solara said. "You have to ask a question."

Arabelle smiled as if she'd been waiting for this moment. "I already thought of a good one. Would you rather have one wish granted today, or five wishes granted three years from now?"

"Neither," Renny said, and kissed the inside of her palm. "My wish already came true."

The whole crew groaned and threw their napkins at him.

Renny shrugged. "It did."

"I'd take mine today," Cassia said, retrieving her napkin.

"Me too," Kane agreed. "We're up against the mob. What's the point of five wishes if I don't live to spend them?"

Doran delivered a fist bump across the table. "You said it. I heard another pirate lord turned up dead—the same guy who took over sector two after the last chief died. I don't know how Fleece is picking them off so fast."

"I heard the same thing." Cassia frowned at her soup. "Yesterday he put his transmissions on lockdown. It's like he heard us talking about him and fixed his system settings."

Arabelle didn't say anything, but the cherubic grin left her face.

"Since all of you are taking your wishes now, I'll save mine," Solara said. "As much trouble as we get into, I'm sure they'll come in handy three years from now."

Kane didn't want the topic to drift back to the mafia, so he nudged Cassia's ankle with his boot. "It's your turn. Next question."

She alternated a few glances between her soup and his face, warning him that she had something on her mind. She couldn't seem to look at him when she asked, "Would you rather tell nothing but the truth, or nothing but lies?"

He hadn't expected such an easy question. "The first one. I always say what I'm thinking anyway."

"Always?" she asked. "Even when you close a deal?"

"Especially during a deal. I might present the truth in a way that benefits me, but I don't tell outright lies. Trust is too important for business."

"So you're saying you never lie?"

He paused and studied her for a moment. He sensed this was about him, but he didn't know what he'd done to upset her. "Is there anything you'd like to get off your chest?"

Everyone at the table grew still.

"Would you be honest with me if I did?"

"Enough, already. If you have something to say, come out with it."

"All right." She set down her spoon and folded both arms on the table. "Do you think I should abdicate the throne?"

Her question caught him off guard. Of course he wanted her to give up the throne—he always had. There was no other way for them to be together as equals. She had to know he wanted that more than anything.

"Do you agree with the rebels," she continued, "that I should step down and amend the charter so they can elect a new leader?"

"Ah," he said in understanding. Those were two very different questions. "Not exactly polite dinner conversation, is it?"

"You promised to be honest."

"I don't think you want the answer."

She sank an inch, peering at him with enough hurt in her eyes to make him wish he could take it back. "That's an answer in itself. You support the rebellion."

"No, I don't," he said, which was the truth. "Maybe I agree with what they want, but I don't support the way they're going about it."

"You wouldn't agree with them if you'd seen what the colony looked like before I took over. It was a black hole of chaos.

I accomplished so much by the time you came home. How can anyone say I'm not a good leader?"

"You're an amazing leader, Cassy. No one disputes that. But can you name the last monarch who cared as much or tried as hard as you do?"

She opened her mouth and closed it again.

"Neither can I," he said. "Because the royals never earned their power. They ruled by birthright. They were never accountable for anything, and that made them lazy and corrupt for so long that now no one trusts them—any of them. Not even you." He repeated what Badger had told him weeks ago. "You can be the best ruler in Eturian history, but that doesn't mean your children will be. Don't you think we should choose our leaders based on skills instead of bloodlines?"

She surprised him by saying, "Yes, I do."

"Then what's the problem?"

"The problem is the *chaos*. It's too soon for a change this big."

"Maybe now," he agreed. "But what about in the spring or the fall?"

"Still too soon. This needs to be a gradual transition."

"How gradual?"

"I don't know, but definitely during my lifetime."

"During your lifetime?" he repeated. "You're only eighteen. Your lifetime could span the next seventy years. What if something happens to you before you amend the charter? The other houses will take back their thrones. The people shouldn't have to wait another lifetime to choose. Hold an election."

"Like the elections on Earth? The ones that gave power to the same men who took bribes from Ari Zhang and then looked the other way when we needed protection from Marius?"

"Not all politicians are corrupt," Renny interjected.

"Enough of them are," Cassia said, looking only at Kane. "Enough that voters can't tell the difference anymore. I love Eturia. I'll devote my life to it. But if I let the colonists choose, they'll pick the candidate with the best promises and the smoothest lies. You know how they are."

Kane shook his head at her. For someone who claimed to love Eturia, she had a low opinion of its colonists.

"You're my best friend," she went on. "You of all people should have faith in me."

"Hey, you wanted honesty," he reminded her. "Don't be mad at me for giving you what you asked for. If what you really want is someone to smile and nod and say 'Yes, Your Highness,' then go talk to your general. I respect you too much to blow smoke up your ass. That's how you know I'm your friend."

They both fell silent after that, and for the first time since the argument began, they glanced around at the crew they'd neglected. Four pairs of eyes shifted uncomfortably from face to face while a layer of film dulled their untouched tomato soup.

Kane offered a self-deprecating grin and picked up his spoon. "Here's my vote: let's not talk politics at the dinner table."

"Or religion," she added with a stiff smile of her own.

"Still friends?" he asked her.

"Of course," she told him.

And then they didn't talk to each other for the rest of the night.

＊　＊　＊

They exchanged a few words the next day, but only as necessary, like when responding to a knock on the bedroom door with "Wait a minute, I'm not dressed," even though they'd seen it all before.

Unlike their previous fights, this time Kane didn't try to make peace. He didn't want to. He hadn't done anything wrong, and he resented Cassia for trying to make him feel like a traitor for having an opinion of his own. That didn't make him a bad friend; it meant he had a spine. Besides, loyalty was a two-way street, and she didn't seem willing to travel it. So until she was ready to apologize, he had nothing to say to her.

He'd grown used to the silent treatment—enjoyed it, even— when on the third night as he began drifting to sleep, she ended the stalemate by speaking from the bottom bunk.

"I want to ask you something."

He grumbled and rubbed his eyes. She'd picked a fine time to break the silence. "What?"

"Will you promise to tell me the truth?"

"If you promise you can handle it this time."

"It's about that day in Gage's compound," she said, "when I used his mom's bedroom to talk to Jordan and you waited outside the door. How much did you overhear?"

"Enough to sprain a muscle from rolling my eyes so hard."

"Did you hear us talk about moving the armory?"

"Yes," he admitted.

"Did you tell anyone?"

"No."

"Not even your friend Badger?"

"Not even him."

"Did the rebel commander ask you to spy on me?"

Kane's heart skipped a beat. How did she know about that? Her general must have caught on to Badger and tortured the information out of him. Or worse, used the truth extractor to learn the names of more rebels . . . like Kane's mom. The general wasn't supposed to use the extractor on citizens of the Rose kingdom, but who knew what rules he bent while Cassia was gone?

"Kane?" she prompted.

"Not directly, but yes. I said I wouldn't do it."

There was a long pause, followed by, "Why should I believe you?"

A sharp ache broke out in the hollow behind Kane's sternum, as if an arrow had struck him from the inside. He would think that after all these years, he'd learn to brace himself, but somehow her words always hit home.

"What did you say?" he asked.

"How do I know you're telling the truth?"

He huffed in disbelief. "I don't know, Cassia. Maybe because I gave you two years of my life without asking for anything in return. Or because I'd give you my next twenty years if I thought you wanted me." He didn't try to mask the pain in his voice. For once he wanted her to hear it. "But if you don't trust our friendship, I'll say this: I do hope the monarchy ends, but not enough to see people die for it. I wouldn't escalate the fighting with weapons. So you can either believe me or not. It makes no difference to me anymore."

When she didn't respond, he added, "Here's another dose of honesty for you. One of the reasons I'm taking Gage's job offer is *you.* You give me whiplash. One minute you're wrapped around me in my bunk, and as soon as I catch my breath, you stab me in the heart. I don't know if you like hurting me or if you can't help it. Either way, I'm ready to get off this ride."

He rolled over and punched his pillow a few times to fluff it. Nobody spoke after that, but sleep didn't come easily for either of them. He listened to her quiet sniffles from the bottom cot while he stared at the wall and tried not to think too hard about why she doubted him, about why he cared so much, about what would happen next.

About a future without her in it.

*   *   *

The alarm sounded too soon the next morning.

Kane's eyelids were lined with sandpaper when he blinked awake. The simple act of swinging his legs over the mattress drained his reserves. He peeked at the bottom bunk and found it empty, so he scraped together enough energy to hurry up and pull on his clothes before Cassia returned from the shower.

He didn't want to see her.

Their paths didn't cross in the washroom, and to keep it that way, he rushed through his morning routine. But when he reached for her pink laser blade, he froze with his fingers poised an inch from the handle. He could afford to buy his own blade now, maybe at the mercantile on New Atlantia. Until then, he would forgo shaving.

The scent of coffee reached him before he entered the galley, where breakfast was already made and the table set. A stack of neatly folded laundry rested on his spot at the bench, including the shirt he'd stained, which was now pristine and crisp. A week ago the offering would have thawed him, but now he saw it as another empty gesture, a strip of gauze on a knife wound. But as he wasn't stupid enough to refuse good food, he scooped himself a bowl of porridge and a mug of coffee, then sat down to eat alone.

He was halfway finished when Renny and Arabelle strode in, hand in hand, followed by Doran and Solara, who were linked at the elbows.

Kane lost his appetite. There was too much love on this ship.

"Hey," Renny called as Kane gathered his laundry and turned to leave. "About an hour until we touch down. Report to the bridge if you want a bird's-eye view of New Atlantia."

"Will do." Kane had always wanted to see the planet from the sky. Supposedly, it was dominated by turquoise water with only one small continent peeking above the surface. Every acre of land was used to grow crops and graze livestock, so the settlers lived in domed structures built above the sea, with clear fiberglass walls that offered a 360-degree view of the horizon.

For a fringe planet, it sounded like paradise.

Within the hour, he learned it looked like paradise, too. As the *Banshee* descended below the clouds of New Atlantia, he rested a knee on the copilot's seat and leaned forward, pressing his forehead against the glass for a better view.

All around him, there was only blue—a blanket of strikingly vivid cerulean that glittered beneath the light of two suns. The sea paled to azure in the more shallow waters leading to the continent, and there stretched a thousand miles of green-covered farmland and pasture that seemed to ripple as the wind tossed its crops to and fro. Dozens of structures bordered the shoreline, resembling massive bubbles resting on the water. As the ship flew nearer, he could make out three steel pillars supporting each dome and a horizontal tram chute connecting one building to the next. A single dome stood out from the rest. Set farthest from the land, it was surrounded by an aquatic fence that extended several hundred yards in each direction.

"That's the hatchery," Renny said, slowing as he passed over a school of silvery fish visible beneath the water. "They breed imported tuna from Earth. Beyond the gate, it's dead sea. Not so much as a shrimp lives out there."

"Dead sea," Kane echoed. Something about that turned him cold.

They continued to the merchant dome. Renny had scheduled their visit under the guise of picking up a shipment of dried fish, so he landed the *Banshee* on the adjoining docking pad and used the radio to check in with the warehouse foreman. The plan was for Renny and Arabelle to oversee the loading of the cargo while Kane and the crew found their way to the residential dome where the infected settlers were quarantined. By dividing and conquering, they hoped to make this a quick stop. Staying too long was risky without knowing Fleece's whereabouts.

"All hands report to the cargo hold," Renny said through the ship's com, "dressed to blend and prepared to disembark. You have two hours to find out what's making these people sick."

CHAPTER EIGHTEEN

Any illusions Kane had of New Atlantia as a resort planet died the moment he stepped inside the merchant dome. The fiberglass bubble offered more than a panoramic view; it also trapped the heat and stink of everything below it. Vendors, laborers, processed tuna—all baked in a rancid pie. The massive fans built into the ceiling were no match for two suns, and with a seafood packing plant so close, he felt like he was inhaling fish.

Which he was, really.

"What's the matter?" Cassia asked. She flashed a grin that didn't reach her eyes, which were bloodshot and puffy from crying. "You don't like the smell of money?"

He ignored the twinge of guilt in his stomach and instead peered above heads and storefront banners for the tram chute that would carry them to the residential domes. He spotted a station sign at the opposite end of the enclosure and began leading the way. By the time he reached the platform, the front of his shirt was glued to his chest. He peeled the fabric away from his skin, but the ventilation didn't help. It seemed sweating was a way of life here.

Doran used a sleeve to blot his forehead. "Maybe the tram is air-conditioned."

"Yeah," Solara said with a dry laugh. "And maybe the fish lay golden eggs."

When Cassia caught up, she brought the scent of a floral garden with her. Kane indulged in a whiff. The perfume microbes in her sweat glands didn't stop her from perspiring, but they kept her as fresh as a rose in June. The procedure had been excruciating. He still remembered how her parents had forced it on her when she'd turned eleven. Afterward, it had taken three days of his best jokes to make her smile again.

He shook the memory out of his head. He didn't want to think about that toothy grin, or how his insides had done backflips when she'd given it to him. He glanced at the station map, a series of bubbles connected by red and blue lines. "Where are we going?"

"The third one," she said, pointing. "It used to be the administration building, but the seals cracked last year and it flooded during a storm. It's still under renovation, so they're using it for quarantine."

"Will they let us inside?" Solara asked.

"It's all taken care of. I radioed the head nurse and told her why we're here. We can study the patients as long as we wear protective gear." Cassia gathered her hair in one hand and fanned the back of her neck, spreading her perfume through the air. "I told her it's biological warfare, not a contagion, but she didn't believe me. She said all the infected settlers came from the same apartment building."

Kane found that last bit interesting. "Maybe this isn't the same sickness."

"Or maybe the victims are being targeted," Cassia said. "The whole apartment complex was for hatchery workers, mostly young single guys who roomed together."

"Huh." Solara paused to blow down the front of her shirt. "Who would want to infect a bunch of bachelors?"

"A bunch of irritated bachelorettes?" Doran offered.

"What about the settlers who disappeared from New Haven?" Kane asked. "Did they have anything in common?"

Doran and Solara shared a long glance. "Actually, yes," Solara said. "Now that you mention it, they were all young, too. In their twenties, I think. But not just men. Almost half of them were women."

Kane wondered what it meant. At home the only common link among the sick was that they spent a lot of time outdoors. "Maybe these workers caught it from the hatchery instead of the apartment building."

"Maybe," Cassia said.

A whistling noise announced the arrival of the tram, which eased to a stop in front of the platform. Its doors parted to reveal several empty cars, cooled by nothing more than an oscillating fan. Kane chose to remain standing when he entered the car. If the commuters of New Atlantia were half as sweaty as he was, he didn't want to share their seats.

They continued through two more stations before stopping at the administration dome. A recorded voice from the tram speakers warned, "Construction zone, no admittance. All personnel must present credentials upon exiting the station."

The four of them stepped onto the platform, but there were no guards to check their identification. Kane didn't see anyone at all. Shielding his eyes from the blaring sunlight, he scanned the corridor leading toward the office park in the distance. Aside from a few piles of demolition materials, scattered tools, and the thick scent of mildew, nothing existed here.

The effect was eerie—an abandoned dome above a dead sea.

"This way," Cassia said, her boots crunching over pebbles of drywall as she strode ahead of him and brushed his shoulder. "They're using the governor's manor as an infirmary. It's supposed to be right behind the courthouse."

He absently rubbed his upper arm and followed along, watching the domed walls instead of the path ahead of him. It felt surreal to walk at sea level and listen to the water lapping steadily against the walls . . . especially now that he knew about the leaks. He couldn't shake the sensation of being trapped beneath a glass bowl. He tugged at his shirt collar and glanced at Doran, who was claustrophobic, to see if he felt the same way. But if Doran was anxious, he'd hidden it well, strolling by Solara's side and occasionally leaning down to blow on her flushed neck. Kane had just dismissed his fear as an overactive imagination when he saw something that stopped him cold.

On the floor about ten yards away, a pair of boot tips protruded from behind a stack of pallets. Each motionless sole tilted limply outward, indicating the owner was unconscious. Or worse. He hissed a command for the group to stop, and as they turned around, he pointed at the boots and whispered, "I think that's the station guard."

After glancing around to ensure they were alone, the four of them crept toward the pallets, silently picking their way around construction debris until they reached the boots. Kane was right—they were attached to a guard, a middle-aged man with a purple face and a wire garrote wrapped around his throat.

Cassia gasped and crouched by the man's side. While she felt for a pulse, Kane knelt down and untwisted the garrote. He checked over his shoulder as he discarded the wire. He was no expert, but the attack must've been recent, because the wire had drawn blood and none of it had dried.

"He's barely alive," Cassia whispered, and then drew a breath to inflate the man's lungs.

Kane stood up and shared a wide-eyed look with Doran and Solara. He knew they were all thinking the same thing: Necktie Fleece was somewhere in this dome, and none of them had brought a pulse pistol.

"The tram," Solara whispered.

Doran shook his head. "It won't be back for at least fifteen minutes."

"We can hide until then," Kane said, gesturing at the endless piles of demolition refuse. "There are plenty of places."

"What about him?" Doran asked with a nod at the guard.

Kane was about to suggest taking the man with them when an engine's roar drew his attention to the west end of the dome. A gust of warm air followed, smelling of salt and sea. It seemed someone had docked a ship outside and opened the landing pad portal.

"I'm losing him," Cassia panted, sweat trickling down the sides of her face as she pumped the guard's heart. "Help me."

Solara dropped to her knees and took over the chest compressions while Cassia probed the man's neck for a pulse.

Kane told Doran, "Stay here and keep watch. I'm going to check the landing pad."

"Not alone," Cassia said. "Take Doran with you. I'll keep watch."

Nodding, Kane jogged away with Doran's footsteps echoing behind him. Kane picked up the pace, choosing speed over stealth. There was no reason to quiet their boots now that the ship's engine drowned out the sound. They'd nearly reached the west exit when Kane noticed movement from outside the dome wall, and he ducked behind a massive waste receptacle, motioning for Doran to join him.

Together, they chanced a peek at the docking pad.

A small passenger-class vessel had landed so close to the entrance that its loading ramp almost touched the dome doors. Men of varying heights and builds had formed a line and were shuffling up the ramp into the ship. Judging by their matching uniforms, these were the quarantined hatchery workers. Though their feet dragged, the men didn't seem to be under duress. One of them stood out from the rest, dressed in gray. The ship's pilot, perhaps. He stood at the base of the ramp and handed something to each worker who passed.

"What's he giving out?" Kane asked.

"I don't know," Doran said. "But whatever it is, they seem

to want it. Money?" He craned his neck. "No, wait. It looks like they're eating it."

From this distance, Kane couldn't tell. "Let's get closer."

They zigzagged from one hiding place to the next until Kane didn't dare go any farther. He and Doran crouched behind a cleric's desk and took turns poking their heads above it. The view from here was perfect. Kane didn't recognize the ship, but there was no mistaking its pilot now that the man's scar was visible—thick and jagged in a horizontal line across his throat.

"It's Necktie Fleece," Kane murmured.

Doran leveled an index finger toward the ship's ramp, where the last two men were boarding. Necktie offered them a thin, palm-size cylinder, and they plucked it from his hands, eagerly bringing the device to their lips and huffing a series of deep breaths. "They're not eating it. They're breathing it."

"Inhalers?" Kane asked. "But why . . ." He trailed off as everything began to make sense. "The cure is airborne. That's why my mom felt better after she slept outside. There was something in the air that night." He thought back to the disappearing settlers on New Haven. There was no sign of a struggle because they'd left willingly. "Fleece is making people sick and giving them the cure if they'll come with him."

"Come with him where?"

That was what Kane didn't understand. Maybe Fleece had partnered with slave traders. That would explain why he wanted young men from the hatchery. Strong laborers fetched the highest price, followed by young women for the bordellos. He watched the last man enter the ship. As the boarding ramp retracted, it occurred to Kane that he should tell Renny what'd happened. He tapped the com-link fastened to his shirt. "Renny, we're not alone. Necktie Fleece is here."

"Copy that," the captain said. "Where are you?"

"In the quarantine dome. I just watched fifty guys board his ship. It's some passenger-class vessel, but I can't make out the name."

Just then Necktie Fleece paused on his way to the pilot hatch, snapping his gaze to Kane as if he'd overheard the entire conversation. Kane ducked below the desk, but it was too late. He hissed a curse and peeked up again. Fleece was climbing into his ship, but Kane knew better than to assume he was safe. The prickles along the back of his neck urged him to run.

He tugged on Doran's sleeve and they bolted east, darting around every obstacle in their path. Kane knew there was nowhere to go, but he pumped his legs harder toward the tram station in hopes that Cassia and Solara were still there. He tapped his com-link to warn them, but then caught himself and tapped it off just as quickly. The link wasn't secure. Whatever Arabelle had done to fix the system, it hadn't worked.

"Shut down your com," he hollered to Doran. "Fleece is listen—"

A tremor interrupted him, a light quaking that originated from somewhere deep below his feet. He kept running as the dome shook, causing everything inside it to clatter. He glanced out the fiberglass wall and wondered if a tsunami had struck. Fear choked him as he watched the ocean rise up, swallowing the dome and forcing jets of water though its leaky seals. He heard the unmistakable groan of metal giving way. The floor tilted, pitching him forward, and he scrambled to right himself as he finally understood what was happening. Fleece had detonated the support pillars.

The ocean wasn't rising—their dome was sinking.

"Cassy!" he shouted, barely able to hear his own voice above the clamor of toppling furniture. They had to find a way out before they sank too low. "Cassy! Solara!" he hollered, and nearly cried with relief when he saw them half stumbling, half skidding toward him, propelled by the floor's downward slope and dragging the unconscious guard between them.

Kane took one look at the guard's limp body and knew the man was a goner. His cheeks were no longer purple and he seemed to be breathing on his own, but what he needed to do was wake up and swim.

"We can't take him," Doran shouted. "It'll be a miracle if we make it out of here, and that's without towing a hundred and fifty pounds of deadweight through the water."

Solara cast an apologetic glance at Cassia. "He's right."

Though Kane agreed, he was glad someone else had said it first. He hated the idea of leaving an innocent man to die, but not enough to put his friends' lives at risk. "It's him or us. I don't like it, either."

"We have to try," Cassia argued. Water pooled around their boots, quickly rising to their ankles, and she lifted the man's torso to keep his head above the surface. "We can't leave him here to drown."

"Cassy, look." Kane pointed at the dome wall, now half submerged. There was no finding an exit point now—they were sinking too quickly. Water gushed in at a thousand gallons per second through every possible opening, which meant the dome would have to fill up before they could escape. "Feel how heavy he is. He'll weigh us down. If we try to save him, five people will die instead of one."

The water had reached their thighs now, and from all around, wooden chairs and planks began to float. Cassia grabbed the leg of an upside-down conference table as it swept by. She dragged it between them and then tried to lift the man onto it. "Let me rephrase," she said, each word strained by her efforts. "He's coming with us. So either help me or shut up."

Kane shared a glance with the others. Clearly, there was no arguing with her, so he hoisted the guard onto the table. "Fine, we'll do everything we can. But if it comes down to him or one of us, he stays. Understood?"

She dipped her chin.

"We need to plan a way out." He turned in a circle to get a feel for where the water was rushing in the fastest. Those breaks would provide an exit. He spotted a few fissures that weren't wide enough to squeeze through and then noticed a new torrent of water flowing in from the station platform. It flooded the space with so much force he was submerged to the waist before he could blink. "Looks like the tram tube snapped in half. Once the pressure's even, that's probably our best bet."

Cassia tried to speak, but she was already covered to the chin. Kane guided her hand to the edge of the table and yelled, "Everyone, hold on." He gripped the ledge at the exact moment his boots lost contact with the floor. The four of them held on tight as the table began to swirl in a tidal pool of current. Their floatation device had solved one problem and created another. Once the dome was fully submerged, they'd have to swim back down to reach the tram station.

The higher they floated, the more amplified sounds became in their shrinking pocket of air. Metal screamed and wood groaned against the steady churn of water. The crystal-blue sea was now a cold, dark soup littered with debris that crashed into him at every turn. Salt stung his eyes and blurred his vision. Soon light began to fade, casting them in a ghostly glow. He stretched his neck to peer at the fiberglass ceiling, and what he saw made his heart slam against his ribs. The horizon was barely visible as a streak of blue through bubbles of leaking air.

Then the sky slipped away.

He felt someone squeeze his hand, and he glanced over to find Cassia watching him with a question in her eyes. He knew her well enough to understand what she wanted, to make amends so that if they died today they would go as friends. But he shook his head, refusing to let her quit. If she wanted his forgiveness, she would have to survive and ask for it.

The ceiling rose up to meet them as the dome tanked underwater, sinking toward the ocean floor with alarming speed. Kane watched the pocket of air shrink. He shouted, "Dive for the tram chute. It'll get dark fast, so hold hands and stay together."

"I changed my mind," Solara hollered, clasping Doran's palm. "I want my wish now."

There wasn't time to laugh. Raising his face to the ceiling, Kane filled his lungs and then dipped below the water, dragging the unconscious guard with him.

At once, noises dulled, taking on a sinister tone as the dome continued to groan under pressure. Kane kicked his legs while blinking to acclimate his eyes to the salt. Soon he was able to squint well enough to see a dim path toward the tram station. He swam with his free arm, but each forward momentum was lost as the guard's body jerked him backward. Cassia caught up and helped tow the weight, which resulted in a clumsy tug-of-war that slowed them down even more. Panic rose in his chest, and she seemed to sense it because she shook a finger at him. She pointed at his hand and then at her own, communicating that they should work together. They tried again, this time syncing their movements, and before long they were able to make some headway.

Doran and Solara had overtaken them by so far that Kane could barely make out the shadowy outline of their legs. He swam harder, hoping Cassia would match his pace. His lungs made him buoyant, so he released half a breath to help him sink deeper. He hoped there was a pocket of air inside the tram station, because he wasn't even halfway there and already his chest burned.

When they made it into the station, everything turned black. Without sunlight he could no longer see Cassia to sync their breaststrokes. He didn't even know if they were swimming in the right direction. The sensory loss made his urge to breathe nearly unbearable. Pressure filled his face until his head felt ready to explode. His hope faded until he detected a new sound, different from creaks and groans. He heard voices shouting—and if they could shout, then they could breathe.

There was air in the station.

Drawing on all his strength, he kicked upward, pulling the

heavy body with him. He was so desperate to breathe that he would've let go if the anchor weren't his only link to Cassia. Just when he didn't think he could swim any farther, his face broke the surface and he drew the sweetest lungful of his life. He gulped it in, one breath after another, until his body was sated enough to notice the details around him. He heard Cassia surface and gasp, and then the echo of Doran and Solara speaking from somewhere farther away. Still blind, he felt below the water for the guard's neck and hauled him up. Kane scissored his legs to stay afloat, but he was tired, and keeping the man's head above water was hard without the leverage of something fixed to hold on to.

"Cass—" he said, cutting off as his mouth filled with water. He spat it out and spoke in a rush. "I can't."

"Let me help." She wriggled closer to relieve some of the burden, but she sputtered and coughed as the weight dragged her under.

"It's not enough. He's too heavy."

"Stay where you are," Doran called. "We'll come to you."

The sound of splashing carried through the darkness, growing nearer until an arm struck the top of Kane's head.

"Sorry," Solara exhaled into his ear. "I can't see my hand in front of my face."

After some awkward feeling around, the four of them were able to support the man's head. A loud crack from below reminded Kane that every yard the dome sank was another yard they'd have to swim before reaching the surface.

"We have to hurry," he said. "We're going down fast."

"Which way?" Cassia asked. "I'm all turned around."

Doran swore. "Me too. We need a—" He cut off and went quiet. The next thing Kane knew, brightness appeared from Doran's palm. He'd switched on his data tablet. "Not sure how much battery is left," he said, rotating the screen until its glow revealed a half-submerged tram sign, "so we'd better move."

They began a clumsy, unsynchronized swim until Cassia directed their movements by calling "Stroke" in two-second intervals. Once they found a rhythm, it didn't take long to reach the tram station, where the corridor ended in a T. Doran shone the tablet at each tunnel, revealing nothing but watery darkness. The tram's connective tubing had cracked in both directions, but which tunnel was shorter: the left or the right?

"Be back soon," Doran told them, then clamped his teeth around the tablet and disappeared beneath the water.

Darkness enveloped them once more, intensifying the sounds of the dome breaking and shifting. It was torture staying in one place, and even harder resisting the urge to call for help on the com-link. Kane reminded himself that if Necktie Fleece knew they were alive, he'd come back to finish the job.

A pinprick of light from beneath the water announced Doran's arrival. He heaved a breath that dislodged his tablet and then scrambled to catch the device. Holding the screen toward the left tunnel, he said, "It's our best bet. The break's not too far, but there's no more air after this."

Anxious to move, Kane hauled the guard toward the left tunnel, savoring the last pocket of air until his forehead bumped the ceiling. He readjusted his grip on the man's collar. "Everyone, grab a sleeve."

The group drew a collective breath and dipped underwater.

Kane used his boots to kick off the ceiling, propelling them forward into another synchronized swim. The light from Doran's tablet danced with each breaststroke, but it was enough to keep them on a straight path as they followed the tram tracks.

Doran was right—a break in the tube appeared. As Kane swam into open water, he glanced up where the hue transformed from deep indigo to vivid teal, finally leading to pale blue at the very top. His elation warred with panic. The goal was within view, but still so far away. As he clawed toward the sunbeams high above him, he created a mental game of it: everything would be fine if he could just touch the light.

The drag behind him increased suddenly, and he glanced down to find Cassia's hand had slipped from the guard's sleeve. She grabbed on to it again, only to slip once more. Kane tried to catch her eye, to tell her to let go, but she dodged his gaze. When his vision began to blur, he knew he was in trouble. He felt a tug at his shoulder and glanced at Doran, who pointed at the surface. Kane faced up and squinted at the captain swimming toward them with a metallic rope in one hand.

Through the haze of dizziness, Kane recognized the rope as the shuttle's tow cable. If one of the crew could reach that cable, it would pull them all to the surface. But he was only seconds from blacking out. They needed to form a longer chain and send one of them to the top.

Continuing to kick upward, Kane pried Doran's fingers from the guard's shirt and pointed from the tow cable to Solara's arm. Doran caught on quickly, and they created a human link with the guard at the bottom. Kane watched as Doran and Renny reached out to each other, and just as dark spots danced in his eyes, he saw their hands link.

At once, the drag eliminated, and then they were launching up through the water so fast he nearly lost his grip on the lifeline. But he held tight, and an instant later, his face met the blessed assault of two suns.

Kane sucked in a ragged lungful of oxygen before releasing Solara and dropping back into the water, where he bobbed to the surface again. Cassia appeared beside him, and while she caught her breath, he pulled the guard's head into the light. The man began to stir, eyes closed as he choked on the water he'd inhaled. Kane rotated the guard to the side and hammered his back, one fierce pound after another.

The crew swam close to lend a hand, each supporting the man's torso as he coughed and sputtered awake. No sooner had he opened his eyes than his chest lurched and he vomited all over the lot of them. For a moment, there was only stunned silence. Then peals of laughter broke out, chortles that were weak from exhaustion but filled with the purest kind of joy—that of being alive.

CHAPTER NINETEEN

From her bench seat inside the hyperbaric pressure chamber, Cassia held an oxygen mask over her face and peeked at Kane sitting on the opposite bench. He pretended to sleep with his head tilted back, arms folded, and legs crossed at the ankles, but his shallow breathing gave him away.

She wished they could talk. She hadn't thought anything could hurt worse than Kane's words from last night, but to watch him nearly die had shaken her to the core. Her heart was bursting with all the things she needed to say to him. But that wasn't a conversation to have in front of the crew, and at the moment Solara sat beside them trying to comfort Doran, who hated tight spaces and seemed to be fighting a panic attack with both eyes clenched shut.

"Just breathe," Solara murmured to him, her voice muffled by the mask.

He fisted his T-shirt and caused more water to pool on the floor. There hadn't been time to change out of wet clothes. The old-fashioned treatment for the bends—a side effect of diving deep and resurfacing too fast—worked best if administered quickly, so they'd kicked off their boots and taken whatever towels were tossed at them before crowding inside a small metal capsule resembling a submarine. As for the guard they'd rescued, he was in the infirmary having the water evaporated from his lungs.

Cassia felt a fullness in her eardrums, a sign that recompression had begun. She moved her lower jaw to clear her ears. Once they popped, she reached over and patted Doran's knee. "Almost done."

The treatment ended, and they ducked through the chamber door to find Renny on the other side, greeting them with a smile and a change of clothes from the ship. Cassia had never been so happy to see her boring canvas pants. Modesty forgotten, she stripped off her wet things and changed right there in the infirmary. The rest of the crew did the same.

"Where's Belle?" she asked after zipping up. Arabelle had piloted the shuttle and pulled them from the ocean, so a hug was in order.

Concern flitted across Renny's face. "She's lying down in her bunk."

"Another headache?"

He nodded while absently flexing his fingers. He did that sometimes when he was nervous and fighting the impulse to steal. "It's worse this time. She can barely see."

"Probably a heat migraine," Cassia said. It could happen quickly under two suns, especially to a light-skinned redhead like Arabelle. "I'll bet she was dehydrated, too."

"Yeah, that's probably it." Renny didn't sound convinced, but he waved the crew over. "Come on. I want you to meet someone."

He led them toward the wet lung station, where the guard they'd saved was lying in bed with a mask strapped over his face and a layer of bandages encircling his throat. An older man stood by his side, tall and rail-thin with a receding semicircle of gray hair clinging to his scalp. His weather-beaten skin marked him as a laborer, but he wore formal slacks and a dress shirt. He leaned down to shake the guard's hand, and a look of mutual respect passed between them. The guard's boss, perhaps.

As soon as Renny stopped at the guard's bedside table, he snagged a roll of medical tape and smoothly tucked it in his pocket. "This is Prime Minister Ahmad," he said, indicating the older man. "He wanted to thank you personally for what you did."

The prime minister shook all their hands. When it was Cassia's turn, she noticed his palm was callused, not what she expected from a politician.

"I can't tell you how grateful I am," Ahmad said in a voice even rougher than his hands. He glanced at the guard, and emotion welled in his eyes. "This man is like a son to me. We used to mine ore on Hephaestus before we immigrated here. He loaned me the credits so I could afford the transport fare."

The guard's face colored. He seemed uncomfortable with the attention, and clearly Ahmad knew it, because he shrugged and offered the crew a grin. "Anyway, look at me now. Prime minister of the fastest-growing settlement in the fringe. A few years ago we started with a hundred crates of imported eggs from Earth. Now we raise more tuna than they do. Who'd have guessed it?"

"Was the tuna your idea?" asked Kane.

Ahmad nodded. "They used to farm delicacies here—mostly lobster and crab—to freeze and ship to the tourist circle, but there wasn't enough of a market for it. After the investors pulled out and our old prime minister moved back to Earth, I took up a collection among the settlers who wanted to stay. We worked out a deal to transfer the charter and then ordered our first shipment of tuna eggs. The rest is history."

As Cassia listened, she glanced out the window at the merchant dome in the distance. She'd once considered it a fetid and disgusting place, but her memories turned sweeter now that she knew the whole story. She couldn't believe a group of settlers had accomplished so much in such a short time.

"You seem to be doing a great job," Kane said.

"Ah, well." Ahmed sheepishly tucked both hands in his pockets. "I try." A faint beep sounded, and he touched his earpiece as if receiving a message. "Duty calls," he told them, and delivered another round of handshakes before striding to the door. He paused and glanced at Renny. "Please keep me informed. I'll do whatever it takes to get my men back."

"I'll be in touch," Renny told him.

Cassia watched the prime minister leave. "Keep him informed? Does that mean you learned something?"

"Interesting that you should ask," Renny said, and patted the guard's shoulder. "This is Captain Forrester." By way of introduction, the guard raised a weak hand. "His vocal cords are out of commission, but while you guys were in the tank, we chatted with this." He lifted an electronic notepad from the table. "And he told me some interesting details about Fleece."

The guard poked Renny in the ribs and made a twirling motion with one hand.

"Oh," Renny said, nodding. "But first he wants me to say thank you. He knows it was a risk to bring him topside. He's not sure why you didn't leave him behind, but he's grateful all the same." After another prod, Renny added, "His wife thanks you, too. She's expecting again, baby number . . . five, I think."

The guard held up seven fingers.

"Wow," Renny muttered. "Now I know the national pastime here."

Kane moved closer to the bed and settled a brief hand on Cassia's shoulder. "You have Cassy to thank for that. We all pitched in, but she's the one who wouldn't leave your side. She resuscitated you, too."

The guard turned his gaze on her. Strangulation had burst his capillaries, but beyond the veil of redness shone an unmistakable gratitude reflected by his smile. He took the notepad from Renny and tapped a message, then held up the screen so Cassia and the crew could see it.

When the baby comes, we'll name him Cass.

An instant lump rose in her airway. No parent on Eturia would name a baby after her. It had been so long since she'd felt truly appreciated that she almost didn't recognize the emotion, but her greatest reward came when she shared a glance with Kane and noticed the admiration shining in his eyes, enough to tell her she'd earned back his respect.

She cleared her throat and said, "I'm honored."

Renny saved her from tears by changing the subject with no tact whatsoever. "Yes, yes. Very nice. Now back to the interesting part."

The guard slid Renny a glare, which he ignored.

"Right before Captain Forrester was attacked, he overheard a conversation outside the infirmary. You'll never guess where Fleece told the workers he was taking them."

"Bet it wasn't Narnia," Solara quipped.

"You're closer than you think," Renny said. "Both are mythical lands no one's seen."

"Middle Earth?"

"Better." Renny paused for dramatic effect. "Adel Vice."

It took a moment for Cassia to recall where she'd heard that name. Then it clicked. *Adel Vice* had been written on the scrap of paper the ferret had left behind on the black market satellite. "Then it's a location, not a flower?"

"So it would seem."

"Did the workers say anything else?" Kane asked. "Like what planet it's on? Or what they're supposed to do there?"

Renny shook his head. "That's the last thing Forrester heard before . . ." He trailed off with a glance at the guard's bandaged neck.

"Still, this is huge," Doran said. "Now that we know Adel Vice is a place, we can start putting out feelers."

Cassia agreed. This information changed everything. "I'll call Jordan and have him alert the tech team. Someone has to know where it is."

"And what the mafia wants with all those people," Renny added. "Speaking of which, we should head out soon. I don't want Fleece coming back to finish what he started."

The crew had no arguments there. They said their good-byes to Captain Forrester, who gave Cassia's hand an extra squeeze when he shook it. She kissed her index finger and gently touched it to the man's bandages, then left the infirmary with more spring in her step than she'd felt in at least a month.

She found the *Banshee* docked outside the merchant dome with its boarding ramp already lowered and ready for departure. Eager to tell Jordan what she'd learned, she jogged up the ramp but skidded to a halt the instant she reached the cargo hold and slammed into an invisible wall of fish.

She waved a hand in front of her nostrils and noticed Acorn scurrying from one storage crate to another, her tiny pink nose twitching furiously as she investigated the pungent new cargo. "Does the whole ship smell like this?"

The rest of the crew had the same reaction, each stopping short when they reached the top of the ramp.

"I didn't think anything could smell worse than Doran's burnt porridge," Solara said. "I stand corrected."

"Really?" Doran asked. "We're still talking about that?"

Renny strolled into the cargo bay, the only person not cringing. Either his nose had died or else he really loved tuna. "Relax. I already found a buyer."

"A *close* buyer?" Cassia asked.

"Very close. Only two days away." From behind his glasses, his blue eyes twinkled. "You might've heard of the place—a little colony by the name of Pesirus."

Cassia gasped. "Don't play with my heart, Captain." Pesirus was her mecca. Hellberry wine was made there from berries grown in bioluminescent bogs.

"It's no joke. I think we can afford an hour or two, provided you lie low"—he slid her a glance, chuckling—"and history doesn't repeat itself."

She felt the color rise in her face while Doran and Solara snorted with laughter. Much like the topic of Doran's burnt porridge, the crew loved regurgitating the tale of her infamous first visit to the hellberry festival, where she and Kane had overindulged on wine and woken up on the lawn of First Pesirus Presbyterian wearing nothing but grass clippings. That night had changed everything. They'd risked their friendship by sharing a first kiss. Maybe a grope, too. It was hard to remember.

But Kane didn't smile, or even blush, when he walked on board. Without a word, he strode past them and continued up the stairs, reminding Cassia there was something more important to discuss before her call with the general.

She followed him to the residential level but made a detour to the washroom to retrieve something special before joining him in their quarters. When she shut the door behind her, he glanced expectantly at her from his seat on the lower bunk.

"You know why I'm here," she said, lingering at the door because apologies never came easily. Especially not this one. "I'm sorry for doubting you. I didn't mean it."

"Are you sure? It sounded like you meant it."

"I'm sure. My brain might've lapsed, but in my heart I knew you would never spy on me." She left the safety of the door and took the spot beside him on the cot, facing him with one leg curled beneath her. "And I didn't mean to hurt you."

"I know." His voice carried an unspoken *but* . . .

"But I did anyway."

"Yeah."

"I can't take back what I said, but I can give you a token of my sincerity." She placed her pink laser blade on the cot between them. "If this doesn't prove I'm sorry, nothing will."

One corner of his mouth lifted. "Mine to keep?"

"It's all yours. Maybe let me borrow it on shower day?"

He lifted the blade and tipped it to and fro, inspecting its curved handle as though he hadn't used the device a thousand times. "I think that can be arranged."

"Am I forgiven?"

He pulled her into a loose, one-armed hug. "I guess so. Until next time, anyway."

She returned the hug and then wiped her dampening palms on her pants. *Now for the hard part.* "I want to tell you something else."

"Careful," he warned in a teasing voice. "Insult me again and you'll have to bribe me with something better than a laser blade."

"It's about what happened in Marius's palace."

All teasing ceased.

"On my wedding day," she went on. "There's a reason I never talked to you about that, and it's not what you think."

"You don't have to," he assured her.

She knew that, but she wanted to. So she paused to steel herself and then told him about the morning she'd awoken to find a bridal gown in her suite. "I was terrified. The wedding bought me some time, but I knew it wouldn't take long before Marius got bored with punishing me and ordered my execution."

Kane took her hand in both of his. "Cassy, I'm sorry you had to—"

"No, let me finish. This isn't easy."

He nodded, stroking her hand with his thumb.

"I didn't have a plan," she said, "and for a while I didn't have any hope. When I was at my lowest, the only person I wanted was you." Her pulse thumped, but she forced herself to keep going. "I had so many regrets for how I treated you. I kept putting distance between us because I knew my parents would promise me to someone else. I guess it was safer not to get too attached." She flicked a glance at him. "But it didn't work. All I did was hurt us both."

He didn't move, not even to breathe.

"I swore if I ever had a second chance, I would tell you all this. But then I took the throne, and there was so much to do. I told myself I was too busy with the colony to focus on anything else, but deep down I was afraid, just like before." She added softly, "So I gave you whiplash."

His hands tightened around hers and then abruptly loosened, as if he'd caught himself hoping too hard and then remembered to guard his feelings. She gripped his fingers and held on tight. She wouldn't let him down this time.

"Today I felt the same regret when I took my last breath inside that dome, only it was a hundred times stronger because

I already had a second chance with you, and I wasted it. I never thought we'd survive, but we did, and I'm done being a coward." To prove it, she looked him right in the eyes. "You said I could have your next twenty years if I wanted them. Did you mean that?"

His mouth worked in silence for a while, until he said, "Yes."

"Then I want them."

Hope lifted the edges of his mouth. "So you're ready to amend the charter?"

"The colony has to be stable first," she reminded him. "That could take years, maybe decades."

"Then we're right back where we started."

"No, we're not. I'm in charge now, not my parents."

"So we'll . . . what?" he asked. "Live in the palace together?"

"Why not? Half of Eturia thinks we're together anyway."

"I hate to mention this as we discuss shacking up, but you're married."

"In name only. It's temporary."

"But then you'll have to make another match. To unite the kingdoms and form a republic, you'll need money and alliances, right?"

"Yes." She couldn't argue with that. "But it won't change anything between us. Political marriages are different. The usual rules don't apply. My father had someone else, and so did my mother. Neither one cared."

"You want me to share you?"

"No, I would be yours in every way that counts. All I'd have to give my husband is a child, and that can be done in a lab. I'd make sure he was agreeable to the arrangement. No one would get hurt."

"So you'd be okay if I married someone, too?" He arched a blond brow. "Shanna, maybe? She and I get along pretty well. I could make children with her in a lab . . . cute little babies with my eyes and her chin."

The idea of Kane and Shanna linked in any way made Cassia want to punch a hole through the wall. And clearly he knew it or he wouldn't have asked.

"Would you be all right with that?" he pressed.

After huffing a breath and stewing in silence for a moment, she admitted, "Of course not."

"Then why is it fair to ask that of me?"

She took his face firmly between both hands to refocus his attention before the conversation derailed any further. "Listen to me. None of that matters. We can figure out the details later. All that matters is we finally want the same thing. Can't we just appreciate that and be happy for five minutes? Don't we deserve *five minutes* of happiness?"

With his face an inch from hers, she could feel his breath on her lips. Soon came the familiar stirring of awareness that always spread like honey through her veins when they were close like this. She knew the nearness had affected him, too, because she watched his resolve begin to falter. All of his unspoken arguments seemed to evaporate until he finally glanced at her mouth and murmured, "Let's make it ten. We're long overdue."

"How about twenty?"

With a hasty nod, he tilted back her head and kissed her,

soft and slow. The contact drew a whimper from her throat. He smelled so good, like sea and sand, and when she licked his upper lip, something within him seemed to break. He crushed her close and deepened the kiss. Before long, they were both panting for breath.

"On second thought," he gasped, "thirty."

"Thirty? Is that the best you can do?"

He chuckled and gave her a look that sent a southbound jolt of heat all the way from her navel to her toes. "How about you clear your schedule and we find out?"

She considered it done. All her days belonged to him now. Gazing into the eyes of her best friend, she saw so much joy that it strained the boundaries of her heart. She would never lose this feeling, never let him go again. As she reclined against her pillow, she trailed an index finger down the length of his chest and told him, "Go bolt the door."

* * *

Sometime later, they lay entwined beneath the covers, their heartbeats slow and their breathing steady, and closed their eyes to let the drone of the ship's engine lull them to sleep. The cot wasn't designed for two. Cassia's shoulder was pressed to the wall while Kane's elbow hung off the opposite side of the mattress, but neither cared. She liked the closeness and she knew he did, too. If this were a double bed, half of it would go to waste.

As she drifted into dreams, she felt a niggling at the back of her mind, a reminder of something she was supposed to do, but she couldn't make sense of it until a loud *beep* sounded from her wrist and made her jump. Beside her, Kane flinched so hard he rolled off the cot and landed on the floor.

"Jordan!" she said, clutching the sheet over her bare chest. "I forgot to call him!"

Kane started grabbing her clothes from the floor and handing them to her as the com-bracelet continued to beep. She turned them right side out and frantically pulled on her shirt and pants, then finger-combed her hair while Kane gathered his own clothes.

"Hurry," she urged.

He stood up, holding a ball of fabric between his hips as he thumbed at the door. "I can't exactly wait in the hall like this."

"Over there," she said with a wave toward the corner. "He won't see you." As soon as Kane had moved out of sight, she accepted the transmission.

In true form, Jordan leaned forward in his desk chair and inspected her image. "Are you all right? You look . . . frazzled."

"It's been a long day," she said, which wasn't a lie. "I meant to call you, but I nodded off as soon as I sat down." To change the subject, she launched into a story of the day's events, downplaying her near-death experience so he wouldn't panic and ask her to come home. She wanted to be the one who brought back the cure . . . and if she was being honest with herself, she wasn't ready to go home. "My captain's using his contacts to look for another outbreak. Now that we know Fleece is making people sick and using the cure as blackmail, maybe we can get ahead of him somehow."

Jordan nodded. "I'll tell the hackers to focus on Adel Vice."

"Any news on the bill that failed?" she asked. "If we can

figure out what Zhang tried to legalize on Earth, it might tell us what he's up to on Adel Vice."

"The team is still looking, but nothing so far."

"How are things on your end?"

"As well as can be expected," he said. "None of our sick have disappeared, and the refugees in the tent camp are holding steady. I found out that a few of the refugees never contracted the illness, so I sent them to the lab to see if we can find a reason for their immunity."

"Great thinking."

"I also talked to Councilor Markham. He's stalling the noble houses like you asked. So far they don't seem to know about the breakout." Jordan checked over both shoulders and lowered his voice. "And the rebel sting happens tonight."

On reflex, her breath caught and her eyes darted to Kane, who was now dressed and standing in the corner with his face concealed by shadows. She'd kept the raid a secret from him for so long that discussing it felt unnatural. She reminded herself that she trusted him and returned her attention to Jordan. "What's the bait?"

"Ammunition and imported fuel, like we discussed. I leaked the location to enough sources that the rebels are bound to find out. We'll have them in custody by morning and begin interrogations right away. One of them is sure to give up the commander. Once we cut the head off the beast and take out the secondary leadership, the rest will scatter."

"Good. Keep me posted."

CHAPTER TWENTY

From the galley stove, Kane absently stirred a pot of chili while checking the clock display on the wall behind him.

The rebel sting would take place soon, and he hadn't been able to send a warning transmission to his mother because Renny hadn't left the pilothouse a single time, not even to use the bathroom.

The man must have the bladder of a whale.

Kane couldn't stop hearing the words *take out the secondary leadership*. He didn't know his mother's role within the rebellion, but he did know that *take out* meant *execute*, and he couldn't risk that happening to her. If he had to physically drag the captain out of the bridge to make that call, he would do it.

Hopefully, an early dinner would accomplish the job.

He reached for his com-link, then caught himself and strode to the speaker embedded in the wall. He wanted to avoid using the link until he knew it was secure. While balancing a stack of bowls on one hand, he used the other to push the intercom button.

"Dinner's ready," he called.

Renny was the first to arrive. Kane held his breath and kept watch for Cassia while he set the table. More than anyone, he needed her to stay in the galley. Doran and Solara joined them from the lower level, followed by Arabelle and finally Cassia.

Kane met her at the threshold and handed her a ladle. "Serve the chili, will you? I have to run to the washroom."

Cassia gave him a searching look.

"I'm fine," he called, already climbing the stairs. "Don't wait for me."

To complete the ruse, he ducked inside the washroom, where he paused at the door until he heard the scrape of utensils. Once he knew the crew had begun eating, he tiptoed up another flight of stairs to the com-center in the bridge. Quickly, he entered the code and held a finger to his lips when the farmer answered.

"I need to talk to my mom," Kane whispered. "Hurry."

"She's not here," Meichael whispered back.

Kane's heart jumped. He was too late. "You have to find her and bring her home. The military's setting a trap. I don't know where, but they're using ammo to lure you in. The whole thing's going down tonight."

He hadn't expected the farmer to smile. "We know."

"What?"

"Badger wasn't our only informant. Don't worry about your mother. She won't be anywhere near the sting operation tonight."

Kane blew out a long breath.

"She's at a meeting to form a secondary co-op school. A

lot of teenagers dropped out when the war started, and most of them haven't gone back."

"That's nice," Kane said, not really listening anymore. His mother was safe. That was all he needed to know. "I have to go before anyone finds me here."

"I understand, and thank you. We appreciate the warning." Kane shut down the transmission and crept quietly out of the bridge to the stairs. He had just released the nervous tension from his shoulders when he rounded the corner and came face-to-face with Cassia waiting for him on the upper landing.

He froze.

His skin flushed hot and then cold. For an instant, they only stared at each other. He scanned her expression, hoping against all odds that she hadn't overheard anything, but when her eyes began to water and her chin trembled, he knew better.

"Cassy, no." He held a tentative hand toward her. "It's not what you think."

But she was already running down the stairs. He chased after her, following all the way to their quarters because he had to make her understand what he'd done—and more important, what he hadn't done. He hadn't spied on her. He hadn't lied.

She darted into their room and tried to shut the door. He wedged his boot in the jamb to hold it open. All that earned him was a pillow to the face.

"Take it," she shouted. Then she ripped his blanket off the top cot and threw that at him, too. "Take it all, because you don't bunk here anymore."

"Cassy, you have to listen to me. I told the truth when I"— he dodged a handful of clothes—"when I said I wasn't a spy.

This was the only time, I swear. People could've been killed. People I care about."

That seemed to enrage her even more. Her cheeks were wet and her eyes wild when she planted both palms on his chest and tried to shove him into the hall. He refused to budge. He had to make her listen. "I didn't have a choice."

"Get out!" she screamed.

"Just let me explain."

She clapped both palms over her ears. "Get out."

"Cassy, all I want is to talk—"

"I swear to god, Kane," she yelled, clenching her eyes shut so she didn't have to look at him, either. "I know where Solara keeps her stunner, and I *will* use it on you if you don't leave me alone!"

He could tell she meant it, so he staggered back a step, giving her enough leeway to slam the door in his face. The bolt slid into place immediately afterward. He slowly collected his clothes from the floor. Soon Renny appeared, offering a sock he'd picked up from farther down the hall. The captain didn't ask what had happened, and Kane didn't volunteer any details. The two of them gathered everything he owned and made their way to the common room, where they assembled a makeshift bed out of chair cushions and extra blankets.

After the captain returned to supper, Kane folded his clothes and stacked them on the billiard table. When there was nothing left to do, he sat cross-legged on the floor and waited to see if Cassia would calm down enough to leave her room.

She didn't.

CHAPTER TWENTY-ONE

When the *Banshee* touched down on Pesirus, Cassia felt more numb than angry, though not by choice. She preferred anger—to draw fuel from her fire—but she'd had no say in the matter. The change had come gradually, like a slow leak of emotions that her heart hadn't bothered to patch and fill. Now she was limp inside, empty and tired. She didn't even want to leave the ship for a mug of hellberry wine, and that was a damned shame.

"Cassia, report to the bridge," Renny called through the ship speakers. "You have a transmission."

A transmission? She sat up on her cot, then glanced at her naked wrist and realized she'd removed her com-bracelet before her shower that morning. She must've left it in the washroom, and Jordan had called the ship after failing to reach her.

Renny added, "Kane and the crew already left with the cargo."

In other words, it was safe to leave her quarters.

She tried not to look at Kane's pitiful bed as she crossed the common room, or at the laser blade she'd given him as she searched the shower stall for her bracelet, which wasn't there. Each reminder of him was a kick to the gut, the only time she didn't feel numb.

On her way to the bridge, she nearly collided with Belle, who was feeling her way blindly along the hallway with a scarf tied over her eyes to block the light. Cassia hadn't left her room much in the last two days, but it seemed Belle's headaches had intensified far beyond what was normal.

"You should see a doctor," Cassia said. "There's probably one in town."

"There is." Belle's cherry lips curved in a smile. "Renny called a specialist to come aboard. He negotiated it as payment for the tuna. He's always been clever like that."

"A man of many talents."

"I'm going to wait in my room. It's darker there."

"Need any help?"

"I can manage. Go and answer your call."

After watching to make sure Belle found her way to her quarters, Cassia continued up the stairs to the bridge. As predicted, she found Jordan's hologram there, seated at his desk with one booted ankle resting on his opposite knee. There was nowhere for her to sit in the small area, so she stood in front of him.

"Sorry," she said, holding up her bare wrist. "I thought I left my band in the shower, but Acorn must've run off with it again. I'm sure I'll find later it in my coat pocket. That's where she hides all her treasures."

Jordan tipped his head thoughtfully and watched her in the same warm, gentle way she'd grown to depend on. When he grinned, it carried more sympathy than amusement. "You're sad again. I can see it in your eyes. What's wrong, Cassia?"

He'd only used her name once before. Hearing it gave her an unexpected thrill that she tried to hide. "Nothing I can't handle."

His look said they both knew better, but he let it drop. "Should we talk about the sting? And what went wrong?"

"I know what went wrong. You have a mole in your ranks."

"Impossible."

"Oh, it's possible." She'd heard proof from a rebel, Meichael Stark, who happened to be the boyfriend of Kane's mom, another rebel. She still couldn't wrap her head around it.

"What about a mole in *your* ranks?" Jordan countered. "Did you say anything to Kane about the raid?"

"No," she said, and told herself it wasn't an outright lie. She didn't know why she kept protecting Kane. Or maybe she did know, but the truth hurt too much to admit.

Jordan seemed to sense her struggle. He stood up from his chair and inched toward her. When she didn't object, he took another step and reached out as if to cradle her face in his hand. Though it was only an illusion, the skin on her cheek flushed at the phantom contact. She was about to take a step backward when Renny strode in from the pilothouse and walked right through Jordan's hologram.

"Oops," Renny said, and then backed up and did it again. "I didn't hear anyone talking, so I thought the conversation was over."

Jordan awkwardly cleared his throat, cheeks coloring as he peered at her over the top of Renny's head. "Maybe you should call me when you find your band."

"I will," she agreed.

Then he vanished.

Cassia whirled on Renny. "What's your problem?"

The captain didn't apologize. Far from it. He wrinkled his nose and fanned a hand in the air as if to dispel any remnants the general had left behind. "I don't like that guy."

"You don't even know him."

"I know enough." Sabotage complete, Renny turned and made his way back to the pilothouse. "I know he's overstepping his bounds, and if you let him get away with it, you'll lose everything you've worked so hard to build."

"What?" She charged after Renny. "I'm not losing anything. We're friends. There's nothing wrong with that."

"There is when he stands to gain an entire planet by getting in your pants."

Getting in my pants? She was so thunderstruck by Renny's logic that she couldn't speak. She dropped into the copilot's chair and flung a hand toward the ceiling. Thankfully, her silent frustration was a language he seemed to comprehend.

"The way I understand it," he said, "Eturia was formed by four dynasties. Two of them surrendered to Marius during the war, leaving him in control of their lands. Then you married him and merged all those kingdoms into one." Renny glanced at her. "Am I right so far?"

She nodded.

"Okay. So now, if anything happens to Marius, which it probably will, control of the whole planet passes to you—until you share it by taking another husband."

"And you think Jordan's vying for the job?"

"I think that's his first choice. But if it doesn't work, he's in a perfect position to stage a military coup. It happens all the time."

"But you're missing a huge point. My parents abandoned the throne a long time ago. If Jordan wanted to take over, he could've done it already. But he didn't. He used his influence to put me in charge."

"And I promise he had an agenda. Men don't surrender their power for nothing."

Cassia knew the captain's heart was in the right place, but his conspiracy theory about Jordan was starting to feel like a personal attack. She'd made plenty of mistakes, but trusting Jordan wasn't one of them. Renny could criticize all he wanted. He hadn't been there when Marius had locked her in a dungeon cell. Jordan had been there. Renny hadn't whisked her away from Marius's suite and then helped her steal and dismantle a dozen enemy missiles. Jordan had done that. Since her return to Eturia, no one had supported her more fiercely than Jordan— not even her best friend.

She picked at a smudge of dried food on the console. "Is it that hard to believe he likes me for me?" She hadn't meant for her voice to sound broken. "Not everyone is working an angle."

Renny softened, turning to her with a gentle smile. "Of course not. You're an amazing girl, Cassia. You're strong and smart and incredibly brave. I'm only trying to open your eyes.

This general is shiny and new. He says all the right things and probably gives you butterflies in your stomach. But that's because you don't know his flaws. One day the glow will wear off, and I think you'll look back and regret letting go of the person you really loved." Renny reached out, covering her hand with his. "The one who was there for so long you stopped noticing his shine."

She pulled her hand free and tucked it beneath her thigh. Maybe she had taken Kane for granted once, but her kidnapping had changed all that. She would be with him right now if he hadn't betrayed her.

"It's not that," she admitted, because she needed to talk to someone, and the words flowed easier around Renny. She told him about all the times the rebels had learned information she'd shared only with Kane, and then about the transmission he'd sent two nights ago. "I caught him in the act. How am I supposed to ignore that?"

Renny didn't answer at first. He took the time to clean his glasses and then reposition them on his nose before he said, "Maybe you're not supposed to ignore it. Maybe you're supposed to understand it."

"Understand that he betrayed me?"

"Understand that you're not the center of the universe, Cassia," he corrected. Despite the gentle delivery, his message heated her cheeks. "There are other people in Kane's life, too. Did you expect him to put your feelings above the life of his own mother?"

"I wouldn't have let anything happen to Rena."

Renny slid her a disbelieving look.

"I wouldn't have!"

"How can you guarantee that when you're in another sector?"

She opened her mouth to reply, but Renny had stumped her. Even though she'd ordered her soldiers to arrest the rebels, not to kill them, she couldn't have prevented anything from going wrong. As much as it stung to know that Rena was part of the rebellion, Cassia couldn't bear the thought of Kane's mother shot down in the street.

"All right, fine," she admitted. "I can't blame him for not wanting to take that chance with his mom. But what about the other times he passed information to the rebels?"

"Are you sure that he did?"

"No, but the evidence points to him."

Renny shrugged. "I can't help you there because I don't know what happened. But I've seen the way Kane looks at you. I believe that boy would cut off his right arm if he thought it would make you happy." He nudged her. "And I think you'd do the same for him."

She stared at her hands. It wasn't that simple.

"I want you to realize what you have," Renny said. "The love of a good partner makes you stronger, not weaker."

"It doesn't always feel that way."

"That's because you mistake vulnerability for weakness. It doesn't make you powerful to hide your heart. Trust me; love heightens everything decent in life. Most people are lucky to find it once. What you have is even more special because loving your best friend is the cosmic jackpot. So don't let go of that without a fight. That's all I'm asking."

"That's *all* you're asking?"

"At least promise you'll think about it."

She hesitated. It felt like he'd dropped a boulder in her lap.

"I only pester because I care," he added. Then he went quiet for a few beats, and when he spoke again, he seemed to have gone misty. "I don't know if Belle and I will ever have children, or if we missed the boat on that. But if I had a daughter, I'd want her to be like you."

His words triggered her tear ducts, because in a secret place deep inside, buried beneath years of pain and abuse, existed the ghost of a little girl who wanted to make her parents proud. That girl had nearly starved from neglect, but now she beamed to know that someone as wonderful as Renny would want her for a child.

Cassia dabbed at her eyes. "You know how to twist a girl's arm."

"They say I'm a pretty slick thief, too." He reached into his pocket and pulled out her com-bracelet. "By the way, I took this from the washroom."

"You win," she said, and let him slip the bracelet over her hand. "I promise I'll think about it." She peered through a wall of tears at her captain: his long, gangly limbs; boyish hair six months overdue for a trim; glasses held together with medical tape. She was going to miss him something fierce. "And for what it's worth, I hope you haven't missed the boat. Any child would be lucky to have you for a father. *That* would be the cosmic jackpot."

* * *

Doran groaned and slumped against an empty pallet. "I never want to smell fish again."

"Again?" asked Solara. "I still smell it."

He scrubbed a hand over his nose. "Yeah, me too. It's like revenge of the tuna." He elbowed Kane. "Am I right?"

"Uh-huh," Kane said, only half listening. "Tuna." He gazed across a grassy field at the *Banshee*'s boarding ramp, which hadn't seen a boot in the hour since the neurologist had strolled onto the ship.

"Hey," Doran called.

Kane glanced at him.

"I don't think she's coming, man."

Neither did Kane, and that was what scared him. Cassia didn't just love hellberry wine; she lived for it. She must really hate his face if she would rather hide in her quarters than enjoy a mug served fresh from the barrel.

"I'll buy a bottle for her," he said, but then he wondered if she would drink it if she knew the wine was a gift from him. She might pour the whole bottle straight down the commode. "We'll tell her it's from you."

Solara looped an arm around his and led the way toward a small market beyond the warehouse. "How about this? You'll buy a bottle for her and save it until you two make up. Then you'll uncork it and celebrate."

"And end up naked on someone's lawn," Doran added from behind.

Kane chuckled. It felt good to laugh. "First I'll have to convince her to look at me."

"Maybe it'll take a while." Solara shrugged. "Wine gets better with age, right?"

"That's right," Doran agreed, and delivered an encouraging punch to Kane's shoulder. "She'll come around. Just unleash a dollop of that greasy charm of yours. You two'll be bickering again in no time."

They were halfway to the winery booth when their comlinks crackled with static and Cassia's frantic voice called, "Kane!"

He whipped his head toward the *Banshee* and saw the neurologist running—not walking, but actually running—down the boarding ramp. Before the man had even touched the ground, the ship's engines roared alive.

"We have to leave right now," Cassia told him.

He was already sprinting her way with Doran and Solara right behind him. "Copy that," he panted through the link. He passed the doctor and kept going without a backward glance. As soon as they crossed into the cargo hold, Kane retracted the boarding ramp and said, "Tell Renny he's clear for liftoff."

The words had barely left his lips when a sharp upward acceleration buckled his knees, and he landed on the floor. From there, he half walked, half crawled up the stairs until he found Cassia waiting for him in the galley. One look at her and he knew their personal problems would take a backseat to this emergency.

"What's wrong?" he asked.

"It's Fleece. We know how he's finding us and listening to our conversations."

She waved him up the stairs to the residential level, where they waited for Doran and Solara to catch up. Once they were together, she led the crew toward Arabelle's quarters and stopped outside her door. "She has a neuro-ocular implant," Cassia whispered. "The doctor said it's an old prototype that never made it to market because of brain damage. It collects everything Belle sees and hears, and transmits the data to an outside source."

"My god," Solara breathed. "Fleece has eyes and ears right on board the ship."

Kane glanced at Arabelle's door. "Did she know?"

Cassia shook her head. "The implant only holds so much data before it has to be purged. Each time Fleece reset it, he erased those memories. That's why she was confused about how long she's been with him. She lost more than a year's worth of awareness."

"What a bastard," Doran muttered. "That's why he sent her out on the food cart. She collected the names and faces of everyone who came and went from that hub."

"And then he erased the details before she could tell anyone," Kane added. "Now she's overdue for a purge, right? Hence the migraines."

"Exactly," Cassia said. "The specialist couldn't help, but he gave Renny the name of a guy who might be able to remove it." She gripped the door latch and warned, "Fleece might be listening, so don't say anything he can use against us."

The lights inside Arabelle's room were turned off, but the hallway's glow revealed her petite form curled up on the cot, a damp rag slung over her forehead. She was crying—not a faint sniffle, but the closed-mouthed sob of someone trying to muffle a great deal of pain. Sympathy swelled behind Kane's ribs. He'd shoveled his fair share of shit in life, but no one had ever fused a microchip to his optic nerve and used him as a human probe.

Solara sat on the edge of the cot and used her fingertips to massage Belle's temples. The act seemed to bring instant relief, because Belle unclenched her shoulders and went limp. She felt around blindly until her hand found Solara's knee.

"Thank you, 'Lara."

"How'd you know it was me?"

"You smell like engine grease."

Doran smiled. "Better than fish."

"Tell me about the wine," Belle said, her voice slurred from exhaustion but sincere, as though she wanted to live vicariously through the details. "Was it as delicious as I've heard?"

"Even better," Solara lied, having never tasted a drop.

"We wanted to bring back a few bottles, but there wasn't time," Kane said. "Now we have an excuse to go back someday."

Cassia glanced at him through her periphery. He searched for some sign as to what she was thinking, but her eyes gave nothing away and she looked quickly back at Belle.

Since there was nothing he could do, he decided to go.

He backed into the hall and headed toward the common room. A throat cleared from behind, and he turned to discover Cassia had followed him. She stood in the doorway of the quarters they used to share and gestured for him to come inside.

She didn't need to ask him twice.

In the span of a few heartbeats he had already joined her and shut the door. She faced away, making her intentions impossible to read, so he stood patiently by the door to give her space. He didn't want to lose ground by pushing her too hard.

"I was thinking," she finally began, and then her damned com-bracelet started beeping again. Kane gritted his teeth. He hated that thing. He wanted to flush it out the waste port and force Jordan to handle his own problems for a change.

"I'll give you some privacy," he said.

"No, you can stay."

But he didn't want to. He couldn't stand Jordan, and besides, he doubted Cassia trusted him enough to speak freely with her general. As she accepted the transmission, he reached for the door latch. But then he heard a man's nasally voice say "Hello, dear Cassy," and his blood turned colder than a butcher's heart.

Glowering at them from the center of the room was none other than Marius Durango's hologram. Kane glanced behind the image, but Jordan was nowhere in sight. He didn't recognize the furnishings in the background, but the rich wood tables and plush chairs indicated Marius had somehow returned to his palace.

Cassia froze with her mouth forming a perfect circle. The question *how?* was etched on her face, but she couldn't seem to force it past her throat.

"Yes, my dear, I promised I would find a way out of your prison, and I always keep my word." Marius drew out his final syllable in a clear attempt to remind them of his other promises, like *I'll have your eyes gouged out and every inch of your skin flayed from your bones.* "Your general was kind enough to link me to your band . . . after I threatened to drop poison capsules in your city's water supply."

"What do you want?" Cassia asked.

"My queen at home, where she belongs."

"And where's that? In the family crypt?"

Marius laughed coldly at her. "As if I would spend eternity rotting beside you. No, when I kill you, I'll bury your remains someplace more fitting. Like the landfill."

"You *are* as charming as they say," Kane quipped. "How could any girl resist an offer like that?"

Marius fixed his gaze on Cassia when he spoke. "She won't resist. Because now I know what's making your people sick." He flashed a razor-thin smile that transformed his face into something monstrous, like a wax statue with a slit where its mouth belonged. "My father earned quite the reputation for his neurological inventions, a reputation that reached all the way to Ari Zhang on Earth. It turns out the mafia commissioned my father for a delightful project before he died—a poison to subdue the masses."

"And let me guess," Cassia cut in. "In exchange for this poison, the mob agreed to supply him with weapons."

"A win-win deal." Marius's smile widened. "My father handed over his greatest invention, but he reserved plenty for himself. I just discovered it in his lab, along with his journal. It seems he wanted to study the long-term effects of the product before using it on our people, so he set his equipment to release small doses to a different kingdom. You'll never guess who he's been using as test subjects."

Kane clenched and unclenched his fists. If he could use one of his theoretical wishes right now, it would be the power to strangle a hologram.

"That's right," Marius said with barely contained glee. "Our neighbors to the south. And for each day my queen refuses to come home and face me, I'll allow my scientists free rein to find out exactly how lethal this product can be."

"But I'm nowhere near Eturia," Cassia argued. "It'll take weeks to get there."

"Then I suggest you don't make any stops, or you'll have no one but corpses to greet you. When you arrive, return all my missiles—deactivated, of course—on an open barge with no hiding places for your troops. Pilot the craft yourself and come alone. Anyone who follows you will die."

With that, his image vanished.

Cassia hissed a swear. "How did he escape?"

"Let's worry about that later." Kane verified that the link had closed, then pointed at Cassia's band. "Call your general. Tell him to spread the word that everyone should stay inside on days when the wind comes from the north. Whatever this sickness is, it's airborne. If we can limit their exposure, it'll buy us some time."

While she flew into action, he sat on the edge of the lower cot and tried to brainstorm a way out of this mess. Assuming Marius wasn't bluffing, he had three weapons at his disposal: water contaminants, a legion of troops unaffected by sickness, and his father's twisted science experiment. Jordan's men could reassemble the confiscated missiles and threaten to use them against Marius, but that would take time, and half the population might be dead by then. Somehow they had to find a cure for the sickness; otherwise Marius would hold it over their heads for generations to come.

Kane thought back to the inhalers Fleece had given the infected hatchery workers. If he could get his hands on one of those inhalers, the Rose lab could replicate its contents and distribute it throughout the colony.

An idea struck.

Kane bolted upright, hitting his head on the top bunk. He rubbed his skull and tapped the com-link pinned to his shirt. "Captain, I need a favor. Put your ear to the ground and find the nearest settlement outbreak. I want to take the shuttle there while you have Belle's implant removed."

The answer had been in front of him all along. To find the cure, all he had to do was embrace the sickness.

*   *   *

"This is the most pinheaded idea of your existence," Cassia snapped a few hours later as she stood beside him, seething at his reflection in the washroom mirror. "And that includes the time you licked a neutron battery to see if it had a charge."

He smiled at the memory. The battery *had* had a charge, something he'd discovered when it sent a surge of power through him and stopped his heart. Luckily, one of Cassia's tutors had already taught her cardiopulmonary resuscitation.

"This isn't funny, you idiot canker knob!"

"Who's laughing?" he asked, and turned his head from side to side in the mirror. The ancient bottle of black dye he'd scrounged from the depths of the storage closet had done its job better than he'd expected. Now if he could score a pair of cosmetic lenses, his own mother wouldn't recognize him, let alone Fleece. "Maybe I don't need the lenses," he mused.

Cassia growled and slugged his upper arm. He rubbed the spot while giving himself another once-over, and then decided he looked fine the way he was.

"Listen to me," she demanded. "You can't do this. It's too risky."

He shifted her a sideways glance. "Riskier than handing yourself over to Marius? What'll that solve? He'll just kill you and use his father's poison to control the whole planet. We have to find an antidote. There's no solution without it."

She glared at him while releasing a long breath through her nose. She had to know he was right. "Fine. Then I'm going with you."

Kane hid a smile. Sharp as the demand was, it hinted at progress between them. "Does that mean you trust me now?"

"To pull this off on your own? Hell no."

"That's not what I meant."

"Don't change the subject. I'm going, and that's final."

He didn't try to talk her out of it, partly because it was easier to change the weather than Cassia's mind, and in part because he needed her help. Someone would have to pilot the shuttle and pick him up after he snatched an inhaler from Fleece and made a run for it. But he couldn't tell her that. If she knew his whole "pinheaded idea" hinged on her involvement, she might not come with him.

"I'll let you come on one condition," he said, holding an index finger in front of her nose. "You have to promise—"

She cut him off by grabbing that finger and bending it backward, forcing him to his knees. It was a move she'd used a dozen times on him when they were kids, back before he'd learned better than to wave his finger in her face.

"You won't *let* me do anything." She released him and strode toward the exit. "I'll be waiting for you in the shuttle."

CHAPTER TWENTY-TWO

Cassia couldn't believe it had come to this.

"There's stupid, and then there's *stupid*," she told Kane as he landed the shuttle near the outskirts of a settlement so new she couldn't remember its name. "We're operating three levels below that. What's this place called again?"

"Batavion. They mine fuel ore here." He cut the engine and pulled a tarp from behind his seat. "And if you have a better idea, I'm all ears."

There was no plan B, and they both knew it. Batavion was the site of the only active outbreak they could find, which meant infiltrating the settlement was the most likely way to secure an inhaler. So while she helped Kane cover the shuttle, she mentally reviewed the details of his idiot scheme, making sure they hadn't overlooked any snags beyond the obvious.

The Batavion mine workers had recently begun to show symptoms. According to the pattern, that meant they would grow worse and disappear in about a week—plenty of time for Kane to join them and catch a potentially deadly lab-engineered disease that might or might not have a permanent cure. Meanwhile she would lie low in a town full of outcasts and convicts who'd probably never seen a lady outside of a brothel. Then, assuming Necktie Fleece actually showed up with the cure, Kane would pocket an inhaler, and in his weakened state, escape on foot from the galaxy's most infamous assassin. At which point Cassia would pick him up in the shuttle, and they'd evade a heavily armed ship and reunite with Renny somewhere in the void of space.

What could possibly go wrong?

"Did you bring the tracker?" Kane asked. "And the glue?"

She pulled them from her pocket and scanned his body for the right place to stick the pea-size beacon so it would stay put. *Belly button*, she decided. "Lift your shirt."

He chuckled, but for the first time since they'd left the ship, he seemed to lose some of his confidence. It showed in the wall that went up in his gaze. "While you feast your eyes, are we going to talk about our fight? Or are we still avoiding the subject?"

She hadn't expected him to bring that up. Glancing at his boots, she rolled the tracker between her fingers. "I think your navel's the best place for this. If anyone sees it, they'll assume it's a piercing."

"Still avoiding," he muttered under his breath.

He lifted his shirt to midchest and forced her to do a double take. The once-golden curls that encircled his navel were now a thick, inky black, making him seem older somehow. She hadn't realized he'd dyed his body hair, too, and she couldn't decide if she liked it. Her pulse seemed to, because it ticked to a new rhythm as she knelt in front of him and squeezed a bead of adhesive in his belly button.

When she inserted the tracker and held it in place, the hard press of dirt beneath her knees reminded her that she was kneeling, something she'd vowed never to do before any man. She started to shift to her feet but then relaxed into her original position. Kane didn't count. He would never try to make her feel small or degraded.

In that moment she knew the answer to the question that'd plagued her since the night of the rebel raid. No matter which direction the evidence pointed, Kane hadn't betrayed her in any way that mattered. He wouldn't do that to her. So she stayed on her knees until the glue dried, then tapped the device a few times to test it before standing up.

"Where's your com-link?" she asked.

He patted his pocket. "But it's muted, so you won't—"

"Be able to call," she finished. "I'll wait to hear from you."

"Do your best to—"

"Stay out of sight. I will."

"And stay close to—"

"The shuttle. I know."

He gripped both hips and stared her down. His brows were lowered and his mouth curved up, as if he was torn between irritation and amusement. "Since you can read my mind, go ahead and tell me what I'm about to say."

"Let's see," she said, and began ticking items on her fingers. "You want me to be careful, wear my pistol at all times, not talk to strangers, eat my vegetables, and say my prayers at night." She mirrored his pose. "Does that about cover it?"

"And don't tell Renny—"

"What we're really doing here. Or he'll jerk a knot in both our tails."

He nodded with exaggerated slowness, watching her for a few silent beats. Then the barrier in his gaze went up again. "I also want you to know—"

"That you didn't spy on me." She dipped her chin. "I know you were only protecting your mother. I wish you had told me instead of going behind my back, but now's not the time for that discussion, so let's keep avoiding it."

"So we're okay?"

"Until Fleece kills us, I guess."

"Well, be safe," he said.

"You too."

And then she watched him walk away, reminding herself as her feet twitched to run after him that there was no plan B.

＊　＊　＊

To his surprise, it took less than a day for Kane (or *Jude*, as he was known) to settle in among the miners in their camp outside the ore caves. No one questioned his story when he walked into the dorm and announced that his cousin's wife's best friend's brother—intentionally confusing so he wouldn't have to remember any names—had secured him a job. The miners didn't say a word, not even the foreman. They simply pointed their sooty fingers toward the empty bunks in the middle of the room and returned to their conversations and dice games.

While Kane rested in his upper bunk with one arm folded behind his head, he casually peered around the room to gauge the miners' health. Most of them seemed tired, but so would anyone after a ten-hour shift. The real clue was in the trembling of their hands and the sweat glistening on their foreheads. By his estimate, the temperature inside the dorm was a perfect seventy degrees. Knowing the disease was airborne, he inhaled through his nose to check for unusual scents. All he smelled was a crew in need of a shower.

A while later, he closed his eyes and drifted to sleep, thinking how backward it was that he hoped to wake up sick.

*   *   *

The next morning he awoke with the room alarm. Yawning, he blinked against the early rays of dawn filtering through the windows. He noticed right away the air smelled sweeter than last night, similar to the fragrance of candied almonds at the harvest fair. He checked himself for symptoms, but if anything, he felt better than the day before. His head was clear and alert, and his muscles practically coiled with energy when he jumped down from his bunk. He bounded toward the community washroom on springy toes, feeling like he could leap over the moon if he pushed hard enough.

And he wasn't the only one.

All around him, men chattered and laughed, high-fiving

each other with hands that were steady and strong. Their foreheads were dry, their eyes bright. The mood was more like a party than the beginning of a workday, and several of the miners who'd ignored Kane now ruffled his hair and delivered welcoming slaps on the back.

If this was the sickness, bring it on.

After a breakfast of protein biscuits, he spent the day hauling boulders of ore from the cave to pallets outside, where they were lifted by hovercraft and carried to a refinery about a mile away. His boots dragged by the end of his shift, but returning to the dorm to scrub his face and hands gave him an energy boost that carried him through a night of gambling and arm wrestling with the men.

The next morning he felt even stronger, so vigorous that he awoke before the alarm and decided to sneak outside and check in with Cassia. Once he'd reached a safe distance from the dorm, he pulled the com-button from his pocket and held it to his lips.

"Cassy? Are you up?"

A moment later, she replied with a groan. "It's the ass crack of dawn."

"I know! Isn't it awesome?" He faced east to watch the sky awake with smudges of crimson and marigold. "When was the last time you saw a sunrise?"

"I don't know, but it hasn't been long enough."

"Go outside. It's spectacular!"

"You're awfully peppy for someone who's not a morning person."

He smiled because it was true. "I only slept for two hours

last night, and I feel amazing. I don't know what these guys were complaining about. There's no outbreak here."

"Are you sure? The reports said—"

"Maybe they looked rough at first, but not anymore."

"Kane, that's part of the pattern." Her voice took on a note of concern. "People get better and worse, remember?"

He wanted to reassure her, to make Cassia feel as happy as he did. "I promise I'm fine. Just keep your head down for a few more days, and we'll have what we need." A carefree sensation swept over him, making his limbs go light and airy. He started to laugh because he knew everything would be okay. They would cure their people, Cassia would forgive him, and they'd live together in simple bliss. Their future was as clear to him as the hand at the end of his arm. "I love you, Cassy." He imagined the stunned look on her face and he laughed again, twice as hard. "I love you so much."

She didn't answer, but that was all right. She loved him, too.

"Talk to you soon," he said, and disconnected.

*   *   *

By the next sunrise, Kane was eating his words.

Metaphorically, of course. Because the thought of eating anything—even words—was enough to send him stumbling to the toilet, where he puked so hard his stomach nearly turned inside out. Then he did it again. When there was nothing left inside him, he groaned, hanging his head over the rim while every pore in his face opened up and oozed sweat. He couldn't tell if his skin was hot or cold, but he shivered and ached all over like he had a fever.

Had he actually wished this on himself?

He dragged over to the sink to rinse out his mouth, which left him with barely enough strength to return to his bunk. The lower cot was empty, so he collapsed there instead of climbing up to his bed. His muscles seemed to have decayed overnight. He knew he should replace the fluid he'd lost, but he didn't want to drink. Besides, he didn't think he could make it to the toilet if he threw up again.

The alarm sounded, and he gripped his head, cringing as the noise sliced a white-hot trail through his brain. No one's feet hit the floor, except those running to the washroom to lose the contents of their own stomachs.

From nearby, the foreman slurred, "Outta bed, men," while lying limp in his cot.

Kane didn't know why, but the order made his anger erupt. In the time it took for him to draw a breath, his head was hot with fury. "*You* get out of bed, asshole!"

"Shut your face!" came the response. "Or I'll feed you my fist, you little pissant!"

But neither of them moved. They were too weak to fight.

It went on like that for days.

Tempers flared; no one could sleep. Anything Kane managed to swallow came right back up again. He stopped urinating because there was no water left in his body. He wanted to call Cassia for help, but he didn't have the strength to reach inside his pocket, let alone find a private place to talk. The aches and fatigue were awful, but not half as crushing as the feeling of despair that settled over him by slow degrees, as if a pillow were descending from the upper bunk to suffocate him.

And he *was* suffocating.

Deep down, he knew nothing would be okay—not ever again.

Cassia would never forgive him. She didn't want a life with him, and she certainly didn't love him. All the times he'd kissed her, she'd probably been thinking about someone else, maybe General Jordan. That was who she really wanted.

Kane's eyes burned with tears that wouldn't come. His chest and stomach were sore from dry heaving. Everything hurt, even the hair on his head, and soon there came a point when he wanted nothing more than to die—anything to make the suffering stop.

Then one night a man wearing simple black fatigues and a gas mask that covered his entire face appeared inside the dormitory. He was tall and broad with a band of thick pink scar tissue across his throat.

Kane's spirits lifted. Necktie Fleece was here with the cure.

"Gentlemen," Fleece said in a dull voice distorted by his mask, "I understand you're in a lot of pain. I'm here to fix that—and to offer you a life beyond your wildest fantasies on a planet where there are no rules. It's called Adel Vice. If you go there with me, an honest day's work will buy anything you want." He raised his hands, priestlike, toward the ceiling vents. "Including this."

Kane glanced up.

He didn't see anything, but he heard a faint *hiss* and detected a familiar scent of sugared almonds. The smell was much stronger now, so thick it coated his tongue. He pulled in a lung-ful of air, and an instant jolt of euphoria rocked his body. The pain was gone, replaced by a pleasure so intense there wasn't a name for it. Nothing—no girl or drink—had ever made him feel this good. The ecstasy nearly crippled him. All he could do was arch his neck and give himself up to the rush.

But then the crash came, as swift and violent as striking the ground from a treetop. He cried out in panic, already empty and aching for more. In his desperation, he finally understood that this was no disease, at least not the infectious kind. He wasn't sick, and neither was his mother. They were addicts.

And he didn't give half a damn.

He would trade every cell inside his body for one more breath.

"This is just a taste," Fleece announced. "I have more on my ship—tanks and tanks of this sweet air—enough that you'll never feel sick again." He held up an inhaler that Kane recognized as his salvation. "Any man who comes with me can have it for free. All you need to do is line up at the door."

* * *

From inside the shuttle, Cassia leaned forward and peered through the windshield's telescopic panel at Fleece's ship, which was docked outside the mouth of the cave where Kane worked. Or where he used to work. He hadn't left his dormitory in days. No one had.

She didn't care what he'd said during their call—something was wrong. He'd acted too happy, almost manic, and that wasn't like him. Neither was his declaration of love. As guarded as he'd been with her since the fight, he never would've said it first. So instead of relying on him to tell her when Fleece arrived, she'd moved the shuttle to the ridge above his camp and had kept watch ever since.

Now she was ready.

She saw the dormitory's rear door swing open, followed by a line of men walking outside into the night. She could tell from Fleece's energetic stride that he led the way. The others shuffled along behind him, cupping their hands to their faces as they walked. That was a good sign. It meant they already had the inhalers with the cure.

She tapped the panel to zoom in, watching for Kane as she started the shuttle engine. Her heart lurched when she spotted him, an inhaler pressed to his lips. He stood at the very end of the line, the perfect distance from Fleece, who was now guiding the men onto the *Origin*'s boarding ramp without bothering to look behind him.

Cassia gripped the wheel and lifted off the ground, keeping Kane in sight as she descended toward the ship. When she noticed Fleece disappear inside the cargo bay, a prickle of hope stirred inside her. Without him standing guard at the ramp base, he might not even notice Kane was missing. Her fingers trembled with nervous energy.

So close now.

The glow of three moons helped her see well enough to maneuver the shuttle into position. She touched down behind an ore collection bin near the ship. A few of the miners glanced her way, but they stayed silent and plodded onward. Right before Kane reached the ramp, he turned his head and locked gazes with her. She waved him over while opening the passenger door. If he hurried, they might actually pull this off.

But he didn't move. He just stood there watching her.

"Come on," she yelled, pointing wildly at the door. "Hurry!"

He took a puff of his inhaler and leaned toward the shuttle. Just when it seemed he was about to come to her, he looked away and moved his feet in the wrong direction, going up the metal ramp instead of away from it. She watched in disbelief as he continued all the way inside the ship.

What was he doing?

Her pulse pounded. She kept waiting for him to come out, but he never did. The ramp retracted, and she leaned aside, peering into the cargo bay to see if he planned to jump through the hatch at the last moment. That didn't happen, either. The hatch sealed, and the *Origin* fired up its thrusters.

She shut the passenger door as gusts of dust and pebbles sandblasted the hull. The *Origin* lifted off, and she did the same, careful to stay in its blind spot. There had to be a reason for Kane to go inside. Maybe his inhaler was empty and he needed another. Or maybe Fleece had used threats to lure him on board. If Kane hadn't muted his com-link, she could ask him, but regardless, he would escape through the waste port as soon as he could, and she'd be there to catch him.

She kept pace until they reached the first orbiting moon. Then the ship opened up its thrusters and zoomed beyond the atmosphere. She punched the accelerator, but even at full power, the shuttle was no match for a ship of that size. With each minute, the distance between them seemed to double.

She used the telescopic panel to watch the *Origin*'s waste port, ready and waiting for Kane to appear. A quiet voice inside her head warned it wouldn't work, but she told the voice to shut up. Kane knew what he was doing.

"Come on," she whispered. "Where are you?"

As the miles stretched on, the *Origin*'s lead grew wider. Panic set in when the telescopic panel flashed an error message: TARGET NOT IN RANGE. The ship was so far away that if Kane expelled himself now, he would die before she reached him—assuming that had been his plan in the first place. She wasn't so sure anymore.

Her throat swelled and pressure built behind her eyes, but she refused to quit. She followed the ship until it was a pinpoint in the distance and, eventually, until she could no longer see its fuel trail. Even then, she cut the throttle and floated in black space, staring through the windshield for a full five minutes in case the ship reappeared.

Only when she couldn't avoid it any longer did she stop lying to herself.

He was gone.

She slouched in her seat as the dashboard lights bled into a wet blur of color. Numbly, she felt along the control panel until she found the radio switch.

"Captain," she said, and cleared the thickness from her throat. "I'm in the shuttle, and I don't know where I am. Can you run a track and intercept? I'm in trouble. I lost—" *Kane.* She broke down before she could say it. "Renny, I'm lost," she said in a hoarse whisper. "Please come and get me."

CHAPTER TWENTY-THREE

During the voyage, Kane learned to see Necktie Fleece in a new light.

The hangman became a deliverer, the tormentor a guardian of comfort. Kane both loved and hated the man because Fleece could administer pain with the crack of his knuckles and then take it away with a sweet breath of rapture.

From an expansive caged-in community room in the cargo bay, Kane and the others passed their days curled up on blanket pallets, listening for the cadence of Fleece's boots overhead. His steps were heavy and slightly uneven, a telltale *click-clomp-click-clomp* that warned when he was about to descend the stairs. Then, like dogs conditioned to salivate at the ringing of a bell, the men would turn their eyes to the ceiling with a mixture of fear and anticipation. Fleece was their savior, their patron saint of bliss, and they worshipped at the shrine of air tanks he kept mounted on the wall beyond their reach.

Fleece seemed to enjoy playing their pagan god. Each day, he punished and exalted them according to his will, bringing the flock to their knees with nothing but a lifted hand toward the release switch that would fill the bay with sugared air.

But he wasn't always merciful.

Sometimes he teased them simply because he could, reaching for the switch only to pull back his hand and walk away while they cried out and shook the wire cage in anguish. These power plays were rare, but sporadic enough to keep their heads low in humility when Fleece or his crew visited the miniature pit of hell they'd created.

Kane shivered and pulled both knees to his chest. He didn't remember how long it'd been since his last breath of relief, but his hands trembled and nausea twisted his stomach. As he rocked back and forth on the floor, his mind punctuated the pain by flashing images of people he'd left behind. Mostly he saw Cassia's face, though in vague, lightning glimpses that left him struggling to recall the exact shade of her eyes. He knew he should miss her—the others, too—but his emotions were fuzzy and distant. It wasn't that he'd stopped caring. He just didn't have the capacity to worry about them right now.

Click-clomp-click-clomp.

Kane gasped, cocking an ear toward the ceiling. He pushed to his knees and scurried on all fours to the front of the cage so he could be the first to fill his lungs if Fleece decided to feed them today. The other men did the same, a couple of them trying to shoulder him aside. But Kane was younger and stronger than the rest, and he used his fists to remind them of it.

Defending his position, he knelt with his torso pressed to

the chain link and craned his neck to peer at Fleece's boots coming down the stairway. He would know those boots anywhere. He even saw them in his dreams. Knee-high, distressed black leather, unpolished with a deep scrape along the back of the left calf. He kept his eyes fixed on their scuffed tips until they stopped in front of the cage and turned to face him.

"Gentlemen." Fleece greeted them as he always did, his voice dulled by the gas mask covering his entire face. "I have good news."

Kane didn't care. He wanted Fleece to shut up and flip the switch. But he peeked through his lashes and pretended to show interest.

"We're almost there," he continued. "Tomorrow you'll be on Adel Vice, your new home." He paused, spreading his arms wide. "Who's excited?"

Every man in that room wanted the same thing, and they all knew the best way to get it. They gave a chorus of cheers and whoops.

"Excellent," Fleece said, clapping his palms. "But before we arrive, it's important that you understand how Adel Vice works. It's a playground planet—an exclusive resort—and your job is to make our guests feel special. Some of you will do that in the kitchens or distilleries. Others will work in the casinos or lead tour excursions. But no matter what your role is, every one of you must abide by a single rule: you will say *yes* to anything a guest asks of you. The answer is always yes. Never no. Do you understand?"

Kane nodded vigorously. *Flip the switch. Please flip the switch.*

"Let's see how well you were listening." Fleece tapped an

ear. "If a guest asks for a cocktail delivered to the pool, what do you say?"

"Yes," the men chanted in unison.

"If a guest asks you to rub lotion on their shoulders, what do you say?"

"Yes."

"If a guest asks you for a dance, what do you say?"

"Yes."

"If a guest invites you to spend the night, what do you say?"

"Yes."

"That's right," Fleece murmured, though he still didn't seem satisfied. He clasped both hands behind his back and paced the area in front of the cage. When he stopped, it was right in front of Kane. Their eyes locked and held. Fleece sharpened his gaze as if to test Kane apart from the others. "If a guest asks you to fight one of the men beside you, and tells you not to stop fighting until that man is dead, what do you say?"

Kane didn't hesitate. "Yes!"

A thousand times, yes. Just flip the goddamned switch!

Fleece smiled. This time he was pleased. Kane could tell by the length of his strides as he made his way to the air tanks mounted on the wall. There was a collective exhale from all around, the sound of fifty men silently praying for release.

And then Fleece did it. He flipped the switch.

Kane was so elated he could cry. He squeezed his nose through an open square in the chain link and inhaled one eager gasp after another until he smelled that familiar aroma, the one that promised everything would be all right. And it was. The rush came like a thousand rays of sunlight trying to escape from his body. A blanket of pleasure wrapped around him, starting at his toes and electrifying every inch of him until he imagined his hair stood on end. With his lips parted, he threw back his head and rode the sensation for wave after intoxicating wave. Then slowly, it began to recede like the tide, farther and farther away until nothing remained.

When it was over, he found himself on the floor once again. Counting the hours until next time.

*   *   *

Adel Vice was a paradise in the making.

Most of the planet was still in basic terraformed mode, a blank slate of soil and sea. But the developed areas bloomed with lush, tropical greenery and crystal beaches made from the silkiest imported sands in the galaxy. A sprawling resort hugged the waterfront, stretching in a thin curve along the surf that ensured every room offered a stunning view. Behind the suites, construction was wrapping up for various restaurants, nightclubs, casinos, and a few buildings designated as VICE DENS. The clatter of nail guns filled the air, joined by the scents of plaster and wet paint as workers rushed to finish in time for next week's top secret grand opening. Supposedly, the first group of guests had been extended private invitations based on the absurdity of their wealth and their reputations for debauchery.

Whatever.

As long as Kane received his daily allowance, it was all good.

He'd only been here for three days, but he knew the routine. It wasn't exactly rocket science. The Zhang mafia ran the place. Ari Zhang was the head boss, but no one ever saw him. He'd brought in dozens of managers from Earth to take care of business. Those men wore red shirts to distinguish themselves from the workers, who wore white. As long as Kane did what he was told, he received an inhaler refill each morning at breakfast. The refill didn't give him the rush he craved—he had to work a whole week to earn that—but it made him strong enough to get through the day.

Obey the Redshirts. Breathe. Repeat. It was easy.

The first few days had covered basic orientation. Now Kane and the other newcomers were gathered outside the administration building to receive their work assignments. He peered at the dozen or so boxy dorms arranged in tidy rows behind the admin building and wondered which one would be his. According to rumors, workers were divided by occupation and bunked together in barracks similar to the mining camp on Batavion.

"All right, listen up," hollered a Redshirt at the front of the group. "When I call your name, report to the corresponding housing number. Your supervisor will meet you there and show you the ropes. Don't bother asking for a substitution, because that's not how it works here. You'll do the job you're assigned. Understood?"

Everyone nodded.

The Redshirt pointed at barracks number one and called the names of the maintenance workers. After those men strode away, he repeated the process for the service staff in barracks two, and then the cleaning crew in building number three. Somewhere around group six, he stopped mentioning what the occupations were. The seventh group consisted of all women. Their dorm was located off to the side, behind an electric fence. Kane dropped his gaze as the ladies padded quietly across the lawn. He didn't want to think about what their job was. He took a puff of his inhaler to chase away the sick feeling in his chest. As soon as that sweet flavor crossed his tongue, his shoulders lightened and he sighed in relief.

Sometime later, Kane heard his name, along with instructions to report to building number eleven. He waited to hear who else was assigned to that barracks, but the Redshirt moved on to the next group. With a shrug and another breath from his inhaler, he made his way to the last dorm at the end of the residential area. The door was propped open, so he leaned inside and peeked around, finding it vacant.

The room was laid out much as he'd expected, with two rows of bunks leading to a washroom at the other end. About half the mattresses were bare, telling him which beds were available—most of them upper bunks. No surprise there. What did pique his interest was the gym equipment lining the perimeter of the room. It looked like a training circuit.

Kane stepped inside for a closer look at the weights. If the Redshirts expected him to bulk up, maybe they'd increase his daily inhaler allowance. He would love that.

A toilet flushed in the washroom, and a beefy, middle-aged Redshirt strode into view. The man's legs were thick with muscle, forcing him into an awkward waddle that reminded Kane of the geese on Eturia. They were territorial birds, meaner than they looked, especially if you wandered too close to their hatchlings. That was how his friendship with Cassia had begun, when he'd rescued her from a rampaging goose by throwing his cookie to the bird. He would never forget the look she'd given him afterward, like he'd saved her from a burning building instead of a dull beak.

Kane felt a tug at his stomach. He shut down the memory and took another breath from his inhaler. One *hiss* later and the tugging was gone.

The noise caused the Redshirt to glance at him.

"I'm Jude," Kane said. "They told me to come here and meet my supervisor."

"That'd be me. Just call me boss." The man had an earthquake voice, low and rumbly. He pointed to a standing metal cabinet. "Sheets are in there. Pick a bunk."

Kane did as he was told, choosing an upper cot the farthest from the washroom. While making his bed, he thought of a question. "Hey, boss. Can I ask you something?"

The Redshirt grunted. "Shoot."

"I know I'm always supposed to say yes, but what if two guests want contradictory things? What if one person asks for lunch on the beach, but on my way to get it, someone else stops me and tells me to haul luggage?" The question might sound ridiculous, but he couldn't afford to make a mistake and lose his allowance. "Which guest do I listen to?"

For the first time, his boss grinned. "Don't worry about that, kid. You'll be working in the pit. Running errands isn't your job."

The pit? "What's that?"

"Live-action games and combat. It's part of the casino.

Guests lay odds on their favorite fighter, and you do your best to win. It's that simple."

Kane glanced at the weight rack. Now he understood the reason for the strength-training circuit. The men in this dorm were fighters. He wasn't sure how he felt about that. He was good with his fists, but not skilled enough to use them for a living. Then he remembered something Necktie Fleece had said on board the ship . . . something about fighting an opponent until the man was dead.

An icy finger traced his spine.

"Like gladiator games?" he asked.

"Yeah," his boss said, nodding. "Exactly like that."

The back door swung open, and a man in white walked inside, so tall he had to duck his head to avoid hitting it on the top frame. Clearly, he was a fighter, too. He hooked a left and disappeared inside the washroom, but not before Kane caught a glimpse of his battleship arms.

He wouldn't last five minutes against that guy.

"Look here, kid," his boss said. He must've seen the fear on Kane's face, because he reached in his pocket and produced a gold inhaler. "Do you know what this is?"

"The refill we earn at the end of the week?"

The Redshirt laughed. "Hell no. Better than that. Way better. Forget that garbage you breathed on the ship. This will make you feel so good you'll forget your own name."

Kane's heart raced with instant longing.

"This is a special kind of reward. Only two types of workers can have it—the lovers and the fighters." He gave the tube a light shake. "The best part is you won't have to wait a week to get your hands on it."

Kane licked his lips, too hypnotized to speak.

"The pit fighters are the real stars here," his boss said. "While the other schmucks haul luggage and fetch drinks, saving up for a weekly fix of diluted crap, you'll be breathing this golden air every time you compete."

A pang of need tore a jagged gash through Kane's insides. He sucked on his inhaler, pumping it again and again to stave off the craving, but it wasn't enough. He had to have what was inside that gold tube.

"Fight hard, and this'll be yours," the man promised. "Every single day of your life."

That was all Kane needed to hear.

He jerked his chin toward the weight rack. "When can I start?"

CHAPTER TWENTY-FOUR

Cassia's second homecoming was no better than the first. While she couldn't deny the accommodations were more luxurious—a private cruiser with Gage Spaulding as her escort—comfort wasn't everything. At least when the Daeva had dragged her home in chains, it'd been with the knowledge that Kane was safe. That peace of mind had given her the freedom to focus on her own needs.

Which wasn't the case right now.

She sat in the pilothouse, fidgeting in her seat, as she waited for Eturia to come into sight. During her last conversation with Jordan, she'd learned someone had cut the power to the entire prison block on the night of Marius's escape, so in addition to her murderous husband, every rebel her men had ever captured was now free to resume plotting against her. Then there was the issue of keeping her people safe, something she could only do by urging them to stay indoors.

But despite the mounting crises, her eyes kept wandering back to the transmission switch. Renny hadn't called today. Maybe she should radio the *Banshee* again to see if he and the crew had made any progress in tracking Kane.

"Land ho," Gage said in a mock sailor's voice while pointing beyond the pilot controls to a glowing marble in the distance. "There's your home."

Dread congealed in Cassia's stomach. She wasn't ready for this.

"Now, let's make like a null matrix element and vanish."

She slid him a glance. "A null-matrix-*what*?"

"Sorry," he mumbled, going a little red in the cheeks. "Science-nerd humor. I'm cloaking us so no one will pick up our signal."

With the press of a button, their ship became undetectable to satellites and radar. Gage's cruiser had all the latest gadgets, one of the reasons she had asked for his help. The other reason had to do with his constant science jokes. He had a brilliant mind. It was Gage who'd listened to her description of Kane's erratic behavior and theorized their plague was really an addiction. As soon as he'd suggested it, Cassia had known he was right. Half of her people were in withdrawal, Kane included, all of them in danger of losing their free will to Marius or to the mafia. But if anyone could find a way to break their dependency, it was the prodigy by her side.

"Thanks again for all this," she said, waving a hand to indicate the ship and beyond. She knew how busy Gage was with his start-up business. "I can't pay you right now, but I'll wire you the credits as soon as I can."

"Like I need your money," he dismissed with a grin. "You

see, I invented this super-fuel called Infinium. Maybe you've heard of it?"

She gave his arm a playful shove. "I think Solara had it backward when she called you the evil twin. Doran never flew me across two sectors in a private cruiser."

"*And* let you have the master quarters."

"And that."

"Well, don't count me out. I could be evil if I tried."

"It's too late. I already like you."

His smile warmed, but at the same time, defeat rounded his shoulders. "That goes both ways. Even though I know I don't stand a frosty chance in hell with you."

Because of Kane.

She had managed to forget about him for a fraction of a second. The reminder was a blow to the stomach.

Gage reached over and touched her hand. "They're going to find him."

"I know they will," she agreed. That wasn't the problem. What kept her awake most nights was wondering how much of the old Kane—*her* Kane—would be left after the crew tracked him down. She had no idea what was happening on Adel Vice, but if the mafia was involved, it couldn't be good. "Let's talk about something else."

Nodding, Gage gestured ahead, where Eturia loomed beneath a protective bubble of static. "How about we discuss that shield? I can disable it with a surge bomb if you want."

"No!"

He flinched. "You win. No surge bomb."

"I've seen your toys in action. No need for that." She pointed at the southernmost continent. "Once we're in range of the shield controls, I'll issue a ten-second override. That'll give us plenty of time to get through. Then we'll head straight for my security station before anyone sees us."

"Want to radio your people?"

"Not while there's a chance Marius might overhear." She didn't want him to know she was home until she knew how to handle him. "This'll be a surprise stop."

"You got it, boss."

Cassia smiled. At least she had great friends.

They continued ahead and made it past the shield without a hitch. Gage piloted the ship so swiftly toward the ground that her guards didn't notice the cruiser until it hovered above the landing pad. Then they came scrambling out of the station like ants under attack. As soon as Gage touched down and shut off the engines, Cassia used the external speaker to tell the surrounding troops to back away from the ramp.

"Lower your weapons," she called. "Your queen has returned."

She descended the ramp expecting to find General Jordan standing among his fellow officers, but he wasn't there. His second-in-command greeted her instead. The man didn't know where Jordan had gone, but his trembling hands, combined with the glistening of sweat on his forehead, told her Gage had just gotten his first patient. She ordered the officer to escort Gage to the lab, and then she strode inside the security station, where she stopped at Jordan's desk.

His chair looked odd without him in it. He'd sat there during so many of their talks that it almost seemed like a part of him. She picked up his data tablet and switched it on. They'd discussed arranging a meeting with the other noble houses to form an alliance against Marius, and she wanted to see if he'd made any notes. She scrolled through the recent entries until she read something that caught her eye. Jordan had already met with the heads of those houses—a week ago. Each family had agreed to fight against Marius on the condition that Cassia reinstated their lands and titles after her husband was executed.

Jordan had declined on her behalf. Without asking her.

Before she could stop it, Renny's warning echoed inside her head. *He's in a perfect position to stage a military coup. It happens all the time.*

"No," she whispered. That didn't make sense. Aside from the fact that she trusted Jordan, he was the one who'd put her on the throne to begin with. They were on the same team, and to prove it, she reached for her wrist to summon him.

Her fingers touched bare skin, reminding her that she'd left her bracelet on the ship. She jogged outside to the cruiser and made her way to the master quarters. As soon as she rolled the tension out of her neck, she sat on the edge of her bed and tapped her wristband.

Jordan accepted after the third ping instead of the first, but she tried not to let that worry her. He was probably in public and needed to find a quiet place to talk. Once his hologram appeared and their eyes met, his whole face lit up with joy. She let go of the breath she'd been holding. She never should've doubted him.

"This is a nice surprise," he said. He stood in front of a faded cream-colored wall that seemed to be part of a home, an old one judging by the scuff marks on the paint. "Are you all right? I didn't think we had a call scheduled today."

"We didn't. I'm touching base to see if there's anything new to report."

He peered around her, observing her surroundings inside the ship. He must have assumed she was still traveling. "How soon will you be here?"

"Oh, I'm al—" She cut short. "Almost on the ground. We should land in about five minutes." She didn't know what had prompted her to lie. Maybe it was because he hadn't mentioned the alliance meeting. Or maybe it had something to do with the niggling familiarity of the wall behind him. She could swear she'd seen it before. "Where are you?"

He scratched his chin and flicked his gaze to the side. "Just checking in on the families of the men we lost on New Haven. I'll wrap up soon and head back to the station."

Cassia felt a pinch in her chest. He was lying. "Good. Meet me in the cell block. I want to see for myself how Marius escaped."

"Be there in a few," he said, and disconnected.

Once his image vanished, she slouched over and rubbed her forehead while her heart sent a surge of panic through her veins. She didn't know what Jordan's intentions were, but regardless, Renny had been right. Jordan could dethrone her before lunch-time if he wanted to.

She bit the inside of her cheek and wondered what to do. She'd sacrificed so much for this colony—her family, her heart, even her best friend—and she refused to let it go without a fight.

She had a few minutes to figure out a strategy and take back what belonged to her.

*   *   *

She was waiting for her general when he walked into the security station.

If he had seemed glad to see her before, it was nothing compared to the brightness in his gaze as he locked eyes with her and crossed the floor in strides so long they threatened to split his pants. She stood at the doorway leading to the jail cells, leaning a shoulder against the wall and smiling at him. When he reached her, he guided her backward a few steps, out of sight of the lobby and offices. Then he scooped her into his arms in a hug that lifted both her boots off the floor.

She laughed, clinging to his neck for a moment before returning the embrace. "Well, hello to you, too."

"I'm sorry," he said, even as he squeezed her tighter. "I know this is completely out of line, but I missed you so much." He buried his nose at the base of her neck. "You have no idea how glad I am to have you home."

Once he set her down, she linked an arm through his. "We have a lot of catching up to do." She winked and led him toward the prison block. "Let's start in here. We'll have plenty of privacy."

"Anything for my queen," he said with a grin.

The jail was dark, which seemed to intensify the echo of their footsteps as they proceeded deeper into the room. All the cells were empty, as was the guard station. They strolled leisurely to the center cell, the one that used to belong to Marius, and then she untangled their arms and switched on a single light.

"How did the locks disengage?" she asked. The cell door was ajar, so she opened it further, inspecting the latch.

"Someone hacked the system and triggered the universal release switch. Then they cut the main power and the backup supply to keep the doors open."

She stepped inside the cell and peered at the door hinge. "But this cell had extra protection." She thumbed over her shoulder at the bed, still rumpled from Marius's final night there. "What about the charged floor panels?"

"All of it is electrical." Jordan crossed the threshold to join her. "It happened in the middle of the night during a shift change. The guards barely knew what hit them."

"Any suspects?"

"We think the rebels are behind it."

"Is the power restored now?"

"Yes."

"Good." In a flash of motion, she spun around to the other side of the door and slammed it shut. The lock engaged with a *buzz-click* and trapped Jordan inside. Then she held out a hand, nodding at the pistol holstered at his hip. "Give me your sidearm."

His lips curved in a hesitant smile, as if he didn't understand the joke. "What's this?"

"You and I are going to talk," she said, extending her palm. "After you give me your sidearm." When he didn't move, she added, "Your queen just gave you an order. I *am* still your queen, aren't I?"

By way of answer, he unfastened the safety strap, then removed his pistol and passed it through the bars, handle first.

"Your com-devices, too."

He handed those over as well.

After setting the items well beyond his reach, she stood in front of the cell door and folded both arms across her chest. "So, tell me. How is Kane's mother feeling these days?"

"How would I know?"

"Because you were just with her at the farmhouse where she lives. I recognized the walls from all the times she called Kane on the *Banshee*."

Jordan's face fell into the openmouthed stare of a man realizing he'd been busted.

"And that got me thinking," Cassia went on. "I was quick to blame Kane when the rebels raided our armory, but he said he didn't tell anyone the location. And Kane doesn't lie to me. His bluntness is the reason for half our fights. So I believe him. Two other people knew where those weapons were stored." She pointed back and forth between them. "I didn't tell anyone. That leaves you."

Jordan stayed quiet, his face pale.

"Which got me thinking again," she said. "What motivation could you possibly have to put weapons in rebel hands unless you were a rebel yourself?"

"Cassia," he breathed. "Let me—"

"Wait, I'm not finished." She laced her fingers behind her back. "Once I realized you were one of them, everything made sense—like the day you visited me in Marius's dungeon. You could've rescued me, but instead you suggested that I marry him. Then you waited until after the wedding"—she laughed without humor—"*long* after the wedding, to give me plenty of time to consummate the union so all of Marius's holdings would be mine. Then, to make sure I was the sole sovereign of Eturia, you turned down an alliance with the fallen kingdoms."

A ball of emotion rose in her throat. It hurt to put his betrayal into words, but she swallowed hard and kept going.

"The only thing I haven't figured out is your endgame." She studied him: the crooked slant of his nose, the eyes that had looked at her so tenderly, the man she'd considered a friend. "I know you planned to make me a widow so I could amend the charter, but what if I refused? Were you going to kill me? Or put me under house arrest? Exile me?"

In a barely discernible movement, Jordan shook his head. "No, I swear I wouldn't have hurt you."

But that wasn't true. He *had* hurt her. "You'll have to forgive me if I don't take your word for it."

"I'm telling the truth." He grabbed the bars, bringing his face closer to hers. "I knew you were different from your parents. I saw it that day when I came to visit you. A takeover was the last resort. I was going to persuade you to give Eturia to the people."

"By manipulating me?"

"Maybe this started as a mission, but I genuinely came to care for you. I never faked my feelings. They were"—he corrected himself—"they *are* real. If you don't believe anything else I say, please believe that."

Cassia stayed silent. She wasn't sure if it mattered. "Are you the rebel commander?"

He hesitated for a fraction too long. "Yes."

"You're lying." But she knew a way to change that. She glanced across the room at the truth extractor, the one she'd vowed never to use on her own people. Maybe she could make an exception in this case.

"Go ahead," he volunteered. "Bring it here and I'll hook it up myself. But learning the commander's name won't change anything. There are too many of us. We police the streets, we fund the schools, we rebuild homes and take care of each other. We're qualified to run this colony, and we won't give the nobles another chance to ruin it."

As he spoke, she delivered the necessary supplies. "Go ahead."

He narrowed his eyes.

"You did offer to hook it up yourself," she reminded him.

After a heavy sigh, he injected the serum and affixed half a dozen electrodes to his head. Ten minutes later, she began questioning him.

"Who are you?" she asked.

"Colter Alexander Jordan."

She faltered when she heard his full name. She hadn't known it until now, and she wondered why she'd never asked. "And what's your position?"

"My official title is director general of the Rose Colonial Army. But fifteen months ago, I joined the rebellion. I hated the way your parents and the other royals ran our colony into the ground. The people deserve to—"

"Did you orchestrate the jailbreak?"

He expelled a breath. "Yes."

"Did you let Marius go on purpose?"

"No. I meant to kill him, but I lost him in the chaos."

"Was manipulating me one of your orders?"

"No. My orders were to prepare for a takeover with minimal loss of life. It was my idea to try to influence you. I acted alone in that."

"What about Kane? Did you try to get him to spy on me?"

Jordan sucked his teeth before admitting, "Yes. And when he wouldn't do it, I tried to make you believe that he did."

"Why?"

"Because I needed you to trust me more than you trusted him." Jordan's ears turned pink at the tips. "And because I was jealous."

Her skin heated as she shared his embarrassment. She didn't ask him to reveal the commander's name because she had a good idea who it was. Besides, Jordan was right. There was no slaying this beast. The rebellion had become a hydra: for each head she cut off, two more would grow in its place. So instead she asked a question that shouldn't matter, but did.

"What if I'd never found out the truth? What would you have done?"

He gripped the cell bars and watched her with an intensity that made it difficult to hold his gaze. "I would've fought like a dog by your side. And after Marius was dead, I would've told you how I really felt. I would've given you the kind of kiss men write songs about. The kind that—"

"Got it, thanks," she interrupted. "Make your point."

His ears were fuchsia now. "I would have convinced you to form a republic. And if that failed, I would've kept you safe during the takeover." He raked his fingers through his hair, disrupting the electrodes. "More than anything, I would've cherished you, Cassia. Because I meant it when I said you were destined for great things. You're strong and resourceful, and I'm completely in love with you."

She looked away. The truth hurt more than the lies.

"I hope that counts for something," he said.

She nodded because she knew he'd meant it. "You know what's funny? You and Kane wanted the same thing all along. The difference is he was honest about it, even when it drove a wedge between us, and you lied to keep me complacent."

"I did what I had to do. If I'd told you the truth that day in Marius's dungeon, would you have agreed to amend the charter?"

"I don't know." She might have. She'd been awfully desperate at the time. "But either way, the choice should've been mine. You took that away from me, and I'll never be able to forget it."

"So what happens now?"

That was a good question. She didn't know what her next step would be, but she started by picking up his pistol and tucking it beneath her waistband. After some searching, she found a few bottles of water and set them within his reach, then she strode away and left him behind.

He wasn't her general anymore.

When she reached the doors leading to the main security station, she pulled them shut and waved over a guard. "Bolt these," she told the man. "There's an infestation in one of the cell blocks—mutated lice." She faked a shiver. "Jordan set off a fogger and went out the back. He said no one should go in for at least forty-eight hours. Understood?"

The man dug a nervous finger in his scalp. "Yes, Highness."

"Good," she said. "Now, assemble everyone who's not sick. I want to see what I'm working with."

CHAPTER TWENTY-FIVE

After finishing his last set of dumbbell curls, Kane pulled off his T-shirt and used it to wipe his sweaty face. His muscles ached from the workout, but it was a good burn, the kind of pain that led to something greater. As proof, he faced the mirror and flexed his right arm.

Damn.

Then he flexed the left one.

Double damn.

His biceps were off the leash. He had to hand it to his boss. The man was a total nut-buster, but he sure knew how to sculpt bodies. If Kane had known he could look like this, he would've bulked up years ago. He could almost bench three hundred pounds, not as much as some of the other guys, but enough that he stood a chance of winning his first fight tonight.

He took a swig of water and peered past dozens of fighters milling around the room until he found his boss demonstrating proper technique on the leg press. "Hey, boss," Kane shouted, then waited for the Redshirt to glance up. "Can I go for a run on the beach?"

The man's mouth pulled into a predictable frown. The first guests had arrived a couple of days ago, and for some reason the pit fighters weren't supposed to mingle with them.

"The sun's barely up," Kane added. "No one's out there."

"Yeah, all right." The boss pointed to a fighter walking out of the washroom, a mountain of a man who was yawning and rubbing the sleep from his eyes. Kane recognized him from his first day in the dorm. "Take Cutter with you."

Cutter shifted a glare at Kane, clearly uninterested in a pre-dawn run and resentful of being volunteered for the task. Kane offered the man a shrug. He wasn't happy about it, either. He didn't need a babysitter, but he knew better than to argue. When the boss was in a good mood, he was a lot more generous with the Gold.

"Can I have a bump to get me through?" Kane asked.

Cutter raised a hand. "Me too."

The Redshirt unhooked his golden inhaler from the cord around his neck. He handed it to Cutter, who took a puff and closed his eyes to bliss out for the rush. Cutter's neck went slack, and he tilted back his head, chanting nonsense at the ceiling. It was a common side effect to speak in tongues. The Gold was that good. None of them even bothered with the old inhalers anymore. Kane reached for the tube, already salivating for a taste, but his boss intercepted it and pointed it at Kane's bare stomach.

"What's that?"

Kane glanced down and noticed the tracker lodged in his belly button. He kept forgetting it was there. "Just a piercing."

"Take it out before your opponent does it for you."

Out of nowhere, a sudden rage erupted inside Kane's chest. He wanted the Gold now, not five minutes from now. He stared at the inhaler while batting down the urge to wrench it away from his boss. Then quickly he spun around to save himself from making a mistake he'd regret later.

He jogged to the washroom and made his way into a toilet stall, where he dug the tiny sphere from his navel and held it above the commode.

Kane paused.

It struck him that there was no turning back after this. The crew would never find him without his tracker. He wouldn't see Cassia again. His anger drained away, leaving behind an ache of guilt and longing. He wanted to be strong for Cassia, to fight for her.

But there was something else he wanted more.

His fingers separated as if acting on their own accord. The beacon dropped into the commode with a light *plink*. He stood transfixed, watching it swirl around and around in the water until finally it was gone. Then he backed out of the stall and returned to the training circuit.

"I'm ready," he said, speaking mostly to the inhaler. That tiny tube was the center of gravity holding his whole world in orbit. He would say he loved the Gold, but that would be an understatement. He loved his mother. He loved Cassia. What he felt for the Gold was beyond anything emotions could measure.

His boss offered the inhaler, and Kane made a special effort to take it slowly into his hands, not to snatch it like an animal. He brought the mouthpiece to his lips in the same deliberate way, one inch at a time. He'd created a game of it, seeing how long he could make the anticipation last before his brain shut down and his need took over.

One, one thousand. Two, one thousand. Three, one thou—

He pumped the cartridge, sealing his lips around the mouthpiece to capture every last molecule, and then sucked in a breath and held it.

The dorm flew away, taking with it the clinking of weights and the odor of sweat until he existed in a dimension all his own. Here he was a god. Energy coursed through him, so raw and pure that he clapped a hand to his chest to see if he'd grown a second heart. This rush was different from the old drug. It lasted. Even when he returned to the mortal world, his muscles hummed with power. He blinked the other fighters into focus and instinctively knew he could lay waste to every one of them. Nobody had better pick a fight with him today.

He was invincible.

Jogging in place, he pounded one fist into the opposite palm and glanced at Cutter. "Think you can keep up, old man?"

The giant bared his teeth in a smile. "Eat my sand, kid." Then he took off toward the back door, leaving Kane scrambling to catch up.

Cutter held the advantage as they darted in between the rows of dorms leading to the beach access. Once they reached the dunes, they flew up the deck steps and across the planks, their boots clattering loud enough to frighten a flock of newly imported seagulls into flight. The air was thicker at the shoreline, heavy with salt and humidity, but it didn't slow Kane's feet. He was powered by something supernatural. As he took the lead, he laughed and kicked up a storm of sand for Cutter to eat.

Kane sprinted along the water's frothy edge, speeding past the maintenance workers dragging clean lounge chairs onto the beach, continuing beyond the saltwater pool, all the way to the last block of suites, where something near the sand dunes caught his eye.

Dead bodies?

He slowed to a jog, squinting against the rising sun at three ladies in white crumpled on the ground in awkward positions. As he approached, he could see their clothes were torn and bloodied. Off to the side, a man in blue shorts sat in a relaxed pose, propped on his elbows with both legs crossed at the ankles. He was talking to a woman kneeling at his feet. She held something small and metallic in her left hand, but Kane couldn't tell what it was.

A breathless Cutter caught up, bracing his hands against his thighs as he panted and followed the direction of Kane's gaze.

"Those girls are hurt," Kane said, still trying to figure out what the fourth one was doing. She slid the metal object across the inside of her forearm, and a line of scarlet appeared. "I think she's cutting herself." And the guy in blue didn't seem to care. "What the hell?"

"Let it go," Cutter wheezed between breaths. "Guests can do what they want."

But what was the guest doing?

Kane strode closer, studying the pair. The man in blue muttered something to the woman in white, and she sliced a second line in her flesh. Then understanding dawned. The guy was telling her to mutilate herself, and she was actually doing it.

Because the answer is always yes, never no.

A bullet of rage struck Kane so hard he blacked out. When he came to, he was running toward the dunes with his hands curled in fists and a wild roar tearing from his lungs. The man jerked his gaze toward him and flinched, which enraged Kane even more. He craved violence more than air. All he wanted was to lay his hands on that man and rip the limbs from his sockets. He imagined the resistance of the man's flesh giving way, and his mouth watered. His muscles coiled with power as he flew toward his target, but just as he reached for the man's throat, an invisible force knocked him to the ground.

He spat out a mouthful of sand and clawed his way toward the man, who was now scuttling away on all fours to the other side of the dune. Kane fought harder to buck the weight holding him down. He didn't recognize the animal noises coming out of him, guttural snarls and howls of fury. His teeth ached in a primal need to sink into flesh. Someone was shouting, but he couldn't hear anything over the pounding of murder in his ears.

Then a sobering fist struck Kane's jaw.

". . . out of your mind?" Cutter yelled from above him. "You could've torn that guy's head off! The boss will have your ass when he finds out!"

At once, Kane's senses snapped into place.

Oh god. What had he done?

He'd attacked a guest! The Redshirts would punish him, maybe even change his work assignment. That would mean no more Gold. He didn't think he could survive going back to the old inhaler. He had to do something to make this right.

"We won't tell the boss what happened," Kane said, but then he remembered the guest in blue, who wouldn't stay quiet for long. He lifted his head and peered over the dunes for the man. "But first we have to kill that guy and hide his body."

No, wait. That was bad . . . or was it? He couldn't tell.

"Calm down," Cutter ordered. "We're not killing anyone."

"But what if they take me out of the pit?"

A new voice, almost too soft to carry over the crashing wave, said, "They won't take away your Gold."

Kane craned his neck and found the woman in white peering at him through pupils so wide her eyes looked more like onyx marbles than human tissue. She didn't seem to notice her guest had left, because she kept the blade suspended above her arm.

"You're allowed two strikes," she told him.

"How do you know?"

"Because I said no to this the first time." She had a faraway look on her face, as if she were talking in her sleep. "I thought my supervisors would take away my Gold, but they gave me more refills, not less. Then they said I could have another chance if I apologized to my guest."

Kane exhaled a long, hopeful breath. He could do that— apologize to the man in blue. And if the man forgave him, Kane would do better next time. He wouldn't ask to run on the beach, or anywhere else, ever again.

Freedom wasn't worth it.

✷   ✷   ✷

When the Zhangs heard about the attack, they sent a maintenance worker to Kane's dorm to install special bolts on all the doors and windows that locked from the outside. He didn't know what happened to the lady in white after her supervisor came to take her away, but she was right. The boss gave him a second chance.

"Now you know why pit fighters and guests don't mingle. I'm training you to be a warrior, not a socialite." The boss slapped Kane on the shoulder. "Shake it off, kid. I'm not mad at you."

"You're not?"

"You've got a big heart," the man said, shrugging. "That's not a crime. But try not to feel sorry for the ladies. They've got their own special brand of Gold. Yours makes you fierce; theirs makes them numb. I promise those girls didn't feel a thing. Besides, they're not dead. They just passed out from blood loss. They'll be good as new after a plasma shot."

Kane nodded, though he couldn't look his boss in the eyes.

"The whole resort's buzzing about the wild boy who charged Nicky Malone and made him piss his shorts. You even have a nickname. They call you the Wolf." His boss laughed while beaming with pride. "Did you really growl at Nicky?" Shaking his head, he murmured, "Damn, I wish I could've seen that."

"Nicky Malone," Kane repeated. That must be the man in blue. He'd offered to apologize, but the boss had forbidden it. He'd said it would make Kane look weak and hurt his reputation in the casino.

"He's a real monster," the boss confided behind his hand.

"The Enforcers tried popping him for a bunch of murders on Earth, but he's got the kind of money that makes evidence disappear. Know what I mean?"

Kane believed it.

"Anyway, it's gonna be a full house tonight. Most of the guests are betting on you, and they haven't even read the player profiles yet."

Kane had almost forgotten about the competition. He glanced around the dorm at the other guys. Only ten of them would compete tonight, including Cutter. A few men were working the circuit, but most of them sat on the floor or lay in their bunks, talking strategy and resting up for the games. Maybe he should do the same.

"What are my odds?"

"Thirteen to one. Everyone loves an underdog."

Kane crunched a few numbers in his head. If enough guests wagered on him at thirteen-to-one odds and he actually won, the casino would have to pay out a fortune. Which meant the Zhang mafia would lose money. He was no idiot. He knew what happened to people who stood between the mafia and their profits.

"Will Ari Zhang think I'm a liability if I win?"

His boss chuckled. "Hell no, kid. Zhang's a businessman. He's got a lot invested in you. Do you think he's going to waste a good fighter by rubbing him out after a win?" He ruffled Kane's hair. "Zhang wants you to fight hard. He's coming to see you play."

That surprised Kane. Ari Zhang still hadn't made an appearance here, so for him to attend the fight was a huge deal.

"You look tense." His boss offered the golden inhaler. "This'll help."

He was right. One breath later, Kane was invincible again.

"Don't sweat the numbers." His boss's voice seemed to come from above the ceiling, like a distant crack of thunder. It rumbled one last message and then faded into the clouds. "The house always wins in the end."

* * *

As promised, there wasn't an empty seat in the casino that night.

Kane peered up from the pit courtyard—which, ironically, stood at ground level—and scanned the rows of stadium seating that continued all the way to the ceiling. He hadn't expected so many spectators. At least five hundred guests of every nationality sat elbow-to-elbow, most of them laughing and talking in animated voices that hinted they'd sipped too much Crystalline with dinner. Their chatter created a steady din that Kane found annoying, but instead of retreating to the locker room, he continued his search until he found Ari Zhang in a private box in the middlemost aisle.

Zhang didn't exactly resemble his mug shot, but Kane had no trouble picking him out of the crowd. Dark-haired with a neatly trimmed beard accessorizing his face, he relaxed against his seatback and surveyed the arena with the kind of detached arrogance that came with power. Kane had seen that expression on the older generation of royals on Eturia. Tonight Zhang seemed almost bored, as though he couldn't decide whether the event was worth his time. Necktie Fleece and Nicky Malone flanked him on either side, though he paid them no attention. He must have sensed someone watching, because he met Kane's gaze and held the connection with cold, unsmiling eyes.

Kane had never challenged a shark to a staring contest, but this was how he imagined it would feel. He couldn't believe Renny had picked this guy's pocket. He gave the man a nod of respect and left the courtyard for the privacy of the locker room.

Inside the enclosure, the clamor of nine voices reverberated off the walls, each more frantic than the last. The men sat on long benches, sharing theories and rumors about what to expect in the main arena, which none of them had seen. They'd entered the pit through a pair of doors that led to a small courtyard and the locker room, where they were supposed to wait until their scheduled time to compete. What existed beyond those walls was a mystery.

"I know a guy on the construction crew," one man said. "He helped build this place, and he said the whole pit's a maze of death traps."

"Then who are we supposed to fight?" asked another man.

"The survivors, I guess."

Kane turned his face toward the glass panels along the ceiling, long windows that allowed them to see the audience's reactions during the games. He scanned the guests until he found a group of men pointing at the arena. He couldn't read their lips, but their eyebrows rose high enough to shrink their foreheads.

His palms began to sweat. He wiped them on the stretchy leggings his boss had made him wear, wishing he could take his Gold now instead of before game time. He was slated to compete dead last. He might actually crawl out of his skin by then.

When there were no more rumors to share, silence descended upon the room. Some men stood from the benches and paced the floor. Others closed their eyes and chanted prayers under their breath. Even Cutter seemed shaken, staring at his enormous hands without blinking. The group's fear struck Kane in an unexpected way. Until now he'd thought of these men as competitors and not real people. But that was what they were—brothers and sons with sweethearts they'd left behind, just like Kane.

They were all ordinary guys.

And he had to fight them? Maybe to the death?

"Listen up, men," called their boss as he entered through one of the doors leading to the arena. A few guys leaned aside to peer past him, Kane included, but there was nothing to see out there except another wall. "It's almost game time, and I know you're feeling the pressure. I'll give you something to take the edge off"—he shook his inhaler—"but first we need to go over your objective. The pit changes every day, so no two games are ever the same." He pointed at a different set of doors. "Tonight you'll compete in pairs. There are two different mazes, one for each of you. Your job is to make it to the battle platform on the other side, where you and your opponent will fight until the master of ceremonies tells you to stop."

So it was true. The pit was a maze.

The man with a buddy on the construction crew raised his hand. "What's inside the maze, boss?"

"I'm not allowed to say. All I can tell you is to be on your guard. The pit's interactive. There's a control panel on each seat, and the guests will try to sabotage the players they're betting against." He glanced at Kane. "The crowd's favorite will have the easiest maze, but don't let that fool you. These people didn't come here to watch an ordinary sport. They can do that at home. They came here to watch you bleed."

Kane's stomach lurched.

"Now, bump up, all of you."

The boss handed his inhaler to the first man, who took a breath and passed it down the line until it came to Kane. He pumped the cartridge two times before giving it to the next guy. Instantly, the Gold washed away all his fear and replaced it with energy. He shot up from the bench and jogged in place, wishing he could be the first player instead of the last. He was going to turn this maze over his knee and spank it.

A booming voice echoed through the speakers, welcoming the guests to the very first Adel Vice Bloodsport Tournament. The master of ceremonies introduced the first pair of fighters, and the men strode out of their respective doors to thunderous applause. When the applause died, a buzzer sounded, and at once, the crowd cheered.

Kane jumped up and down while glancing out the window. He couldn't see the maze, so he watched the spectators for a sense of what he was missing. Some guests leaned forward in their seats, yelling and pumping their arms into the air. Others punched buttons on their armrests. Every now and then, odd sounds would come from the pit—*thunks* and *thwacks*—and the guests would react by cringing and drawing their shoulders to their ears. One person shook his head and stood up to leave, but the rest seemed riveted, even the ones who hid their eyes and peeked through their fingers.

Kane listened for the MC to tell the players to stop fighting, but the announcement never came. There was another buzz, followed by a simultaneous moan of disappointment from the crowd, and then his boss told the next pair of players to step up to the doors.

The next round seemed shorter than the first, and so did the round after that. Each game ended with the same unsatisfied groan from the spectators. Kane was beginning to think the players weren't making it to the battle platform at all. Then his boss called the fourth-round players, and Cutter strode to the door.

"Good luck," Kane told him, but Cutter didn't look back.

The buzzer sounded, and Kane returned his attention to the guests, whose tolerance seemed to have waned. Now they watched the game while cringing and sucking air through their teeth. Even more of them hid their eyes. At one point, there was a scream from the pit, and one man in the stands clapped a palm over his mouth and lurched as if to vomit.

Their reactions broke down Kane's confidence. He peered at the doors to the maze while sweat slicked his body. The Gold in his system was no match for the adrenaline pumping a steady warning through his veins in time with his heartbeat: *Don't-go, don't-go, don't-go.*

The MC's voice called, "And our first champion—Brock Cutter!"

The crowd cheered. Kane was glad to hear Cutter had made

it to the other side, though it didn't escape his notice that the MC hadn't told the players to stop fighting. Either Cutter was the only man to survive the maze, or he'd killed his opponent.

"Last team, you're up."

Kane shared a terrified glance with the other player, a tall guy he vaguely recognized from the dorm. Both of their chests rose and fell too quickly as they made their way to the doors. Their boss clapped his meaty hands as if to motivate them, but then frowned at the sweat stains on Kane's bodysuit.

"Listen, you two," the boss said. "It's a horror show out there tonight, so I'm gonna break the rules and give you some pointers. Your ears are your best defense. Pay attention to the sounds inside the maze. If you hear a pop, get down. Same goes for a sizzle. If you hear a grinding noise, jump high and fast. Understood?"

Kane tried to say yes, but his mouth was too dry.

The door swung open before he was ready, revealing a short, walled-in passage that ended in a ninety-degree turn to the left. The floors and walls were painted glossy black, and here they were clean. He didn't expect that to last long.

The MC announced the tall man's name and then Kane's alias, Jude Warren. "But you might know Jude by another name," the MC said in a voice to build the crowd's excitement. "Let's give an extra-loud Vice Den welcome to our very own *Wooooolf!*"

Manic applause roared from the arena, and as much as Kane hated it, he was grateful for the crowd's favor. It meant less sabotage in the pit. A push from behind set his feet in motion, and the door slammed shut behind him. He kept his gaze fixed straight ahead as he strode to the end wall. He peeked around the corner and found a similar passageway, so he crossed that, too, and then darted a glance at the next leg of the maze.

A smear of blood on the floor warned him into a slow creep down the corridor. When he reached the crimson stain, he heard something grinding beneath the floor, and he leaped up barely in time to avoid a trio of whirling circular saws that rose through the floor and retracted just as quickly. Heart pounding, he took two steps and detected the scent of burnt hair. A fizz emitted from the left wall, and he dove for the floor, feeling the heat of open flames crackling above him. Pain seared the back of his neck, and he reached behind him to smother any live embers on his collar.

He stayed low after that, crawling on his belly and praying that the next threat would come from overhead. At the following stretch, a bubble popped, followed by a spray of pellets that burst into acid upon contact. They didn't strike Kane directly, but the acid dripping down the walls made his eyes burn, temporarily blinding him as he pushed to his feet and stumbled around the next corner to face an electrified grate.

Before long, he noticed a pattern in each corridor—one death trap from below and then two from above. He made it through three more stretches by repeating the same jump-dive-dive sequence, then he picked up the pace in the next passageway, hoping to outrun the spectators trying to kill him from the stands.

Their controls were faster than his boots. New horrors faced him around every turn, each designed for maximum gore. The fans cheered him on, and he hated them for it—for taking pleasure in his pain. He fantasized about forcing them through the maze and barricading the end so they could never escape. Then he would sit in the stands with the ladies in white and let them press as many torture buttons as they wanted.

The daydream was sweet, but it distracted Kane from the next *pop*. He dove too late, feeling a stab at the top of his right arm. When he hit the floor, he found six inches of razor protruding from his flesh. He glanced ahead and saw the battle platform at the end of the corridor, so he left the blade in place and half crawled, half ran toward the finish line.

He crossed it with a sob of relief, bracing himself for a riotous cheer. But the applause didn't come. Panting, he climbed the steps to the platform and raised his face to the stands, wondering why the crowd wasn't celebrating. His opponent hadn't emerged from the maze, and the sick twist in his gut told him that wouldn't change. He'd just won these sadists a lot of money.

Why weren't they clapping?

"Our very own Wolf has made it to the championship round!" called the MC. "Now one final battle will determine tonight's winner!"

One final battle?

Kane glanced around. There was no one to fight.

Two Redshirts appeared at the base of the stairs, holding a man between them who was so weak he couldn't support his own head. One side of his bodysuit was scorched, the other side crusted in blood. When the Redshirts reached the platform, they carried the man to center stage and dropped him there. Then he rolled onto his back, and Kane saw his face.

It was Cutter. Or what was left of him.

"Now for the final task," the master of ceremonies said in a dark tone Kane knew was intended for him. "Finish your opponent."

Kane couldn't move. He stared at Cutter and noticed two fingers were missing from his right hand. Fresh blood pooled beneath his thighs, but in a slow trickle that indicated how much he'd already lost. This man was broken. Even for the perverts in the stands, what enjoyment could they gain from a fight as unfair as this?

"Let's give our champion some encouragement," the MC said. A chant rose from the crowd, low at first, but quickly gaining momentum until their shouts of "Wolf! Wolf! Wolf! Wolf!" rang in Kane's ears.

He forced his feet across the planks until he reached Cutter. When he knelt beside the man, Cutter watched him beneath swollen lids. "Go ahead, kid." His breaths were wet and labored. "Make it quick, okay?"

Kane licked his lips. He didn't feel the same bloodlust that had fueled him on the beach earlier that day. Cutter hadn't done anything wrong. He didn't deserve to die.

"It's all right," he added. "I don't want to do this again."

But neither did Kane.

As he knelt on the platform, surrounded by hundreds of people chanting his name, he realized there was only one way to leave the arena and never come back. In that moment, he knew what he had to do. He gripped the blade protruding from his shoulder and yanked it free.

The stands went wild because they misinterpreted his intentions. He grinned at them. He looked forward to robbing them of their winnings. Slowly, he tipped back his head to expose his carotid artery. Cheers turned to gasps, but by then it was too late. Kane slid the steel across his throat, and the Wolf forfeited the game.

CHAPTER TWENTY-SIX

*T*he wind blew from the north that day, so Cassia fastened a gas mask over her face before exiting the shuttle. The walk from her landing pad to the research center was short enough that she could hold her breath, but Gage believed the drug, which he'd nicknamed Mist, could enter the body through the eyes as well as the lungs. His theory explained why all but twenty of her soldiers were in withdrawal, despite having worn smaller masks over their noses and mouths during outdoor drills.

She waited for the second set of interior doors to seal behind her before removing the mask and making her way to the chemistry lab to find Gage. She hoped he'd made a breakthrough last night, otherwise she might as well crash her shuttle into Marius's palace and save him the trouble of killing her.

She found Gage bent over a small boxy machine on the counter, one eye pressed against the scope. Though he couldn't possibly see her through the curtain of shaggy black hair around his face, he muttered, "Morning, Highness."

"How'd you know it was me?"

"Your footsteps are daintier than the average chemist's. By the way, you have a great team here. They could use an atom splitter, though. It'd make the work easier."

"Any progress?"

"Surprisingly, yes," he told her, still peering through the scope. "Addiction's a hard disease to treat. It changes brain function—right down to the chemical makeup—and it's nearly impossible to reverse. The good news is, because Mist is synthetic, I was able to create a nanoparticle to seek out that drug's particular pathway in the brain's reward center and deaden it." He reached out blindly for a vial of milky fluid, then held it up. "Once I inject this into your addicts, it'll kill the Mist pathway and mute the drug's effects."

"So we're going to cure them by causing brain damage?"

He lifted his head, grinning. "It sounds less impressive when you put it that way."

"But wait," she said as something occurred to her. "Why are some people immune? Like the farmer who lives with Kane's mom, and some of the tent city refugees. They spent a lot of time outside, and they never showed symptoms."

"I wouldn't call it immunity," Gage explained. "Some people are more resistant than others when it comes to forming chemical dependency."

"Okay, so if the good news is we can treat it, what's the bad?"

"It takes time to neutralize the pathways."

"How much time?"

"I won't know until I test it, but I'm guessing two weeks."

She couldn't wait that long. "Can my men fight while the injection is working?"

He lifted a shoulder. "Your soldiers will suffer withdrawals while their pathways are deconstructing. The symptoms won't be as severe as they are now, but I wouldn't trust anyone that cranky to wield a pistol."

Cassia chewed the inside of her cheek. She'd already stalled Marius for as long as she dared. At this point, her only hope was to raise a civilian militia. She didn't have money to pay anyone, but she could offer property ownership to those who volunteered to fight. However, that left her with the issue of training civilians for battle, and for that, she needed time and military leadership.

Which put her back at square one.

Her com-bracelet buzzed, and all thoughts of battle plans vanished while her heart leaped in anticipation of news from Renny. She tapped her band and found herself hyperfocused on Renny's hologram, searching his face for hints of grief or happiness. She detected a duo of lines wrinkling his forehead and immediately asked, "What's wrong?"

He didn't draw out the suspense or try to soothe her with small talk. "We found Adel Vice, and we have a lock on Kane's tracker. It's in the ocean, twenty miles offshore."

She lost her breath.

"His *tracker* is in the ocean," Gage stressed, boring his gaze into hers from across the room. "That doesn't mean he's with it."

"Exactly," Renny said. "There seems to be a sewage drain up-current. We're hoping he lost his tracker in the shower, or it ended up in a waste chute and got flushed out to sea."

Cassia nodded, blinking away the black spots dancing in her vision. "What do you mean, there *seems* to be a sewage drain? Can you get a visual?"

"That's the problem," Renny told her, and for the first time, she noticed the absence of natural light inside the *Banshee*. He was in space. "The whole planet is shielded. Right now we're staying out of range and hacking their transmissions to get a feel for where Kane might be. I can use a surge bomb on their shield, but the minute I do, the mafia will—"

"Shoot you out of the sky," Cassia finished, remembering the *Origin*'s firepower. And that was just one ship of many. "What have you learned so far?"

Renny's typically gentle gaze sharpened with enough anger to make the hair on Cassia's neck prickle. "It's a resort for savages and perverts. For enough money, you can come here and live out your most twisted fantasies. And I do mean twisted. It's hard to listen to some of what's going on down there. They even have men fighting to the death."

Those persistent black spots reconverged along her periphery. Now she knew what Ari Zhang had tried to legalize on Earth: a no-holds-barred carnival of bloodshed and depravity within the confines of his resort. "We have to get Kane off that planet."

"The other workers, too," Renny said. "After what I've heard, I can't leave any of those settlers behind."

Cassia agreed, but the real question was how. It wouldn't do any good to contact the Solar League. Even if the government wanted to help, Adel Vice existed in the outer realm, well beyond the League's domain. A private fighting force was an option, but paid soldiers would fight for the highest bidder, meaning Zhang could turn them.

There was no easy answer.

"Keep listening to their transmissions," Cassia said. She remembered the tricks Jordan had used to aid the rebels. "Find out when their security changes shifts and where their weapons are stored. Watch the shuttle schedule, and track where most of the activity happens. I'll see what kind of help I can put together, and I'll be in touch."

She disconnected.

Her heart was flying, but her mind was sharp. She knew she couldn't help Kane until she'd neutralized the problem at home, so her brain fixed on the quickest solution to taking down Marius. In an instant, she understood what she needed to do.

"Start the injections," she told Gage while striding out of the lab. "I'm going to the jail to visit my general."

With any luck, he would still be willing to fight like a dog by her side.

* * *

The afternoon sun cut through a gap near the barn ceiling, providing the only light for Cassia's meeting with the rebels. The glow was more than enough. From her position in the loft, she could see the resentment festering on the faces of everyone below. The men and women in attendance represented the two highest tiers of leadership, and there were more of them than she ever imagined. Their cutting looks and closed-off body language reminded her of what Kane had said weeks ago: that no matter how hard she worked or what she accomplished during her reign, the generations of royals who'd come before her had ruined the people's trust beyond repair.

She believed it now.

General Jordan stood by her side in a show of solidarity, but there was plenty of resentment radiating off him, too. His arms were folded and locked in place, forming a breastplate of muscle across his chest. His stomach growled, and he slanted her a glare. In retrospect, maybe she should have brought him more than one sandwich after locking him in a cell for twenty-four hours.

Jordan raised a hand to silence the group. "We don't have much time, so let's get down to business. The commander and I assembled you here because Miss Rose has made us an offer, and we'd like you to listen to what she has to say."

He took a half step back, giving her the floor.

Cassia didn't smile as she gazed down at the men and women filling the barn. She hadn't come here to win their hearts. "I know you don't like me, and I won't pretend to like what you've done, either. But Marius Durango is a threat to all of us, and as the saying goes, 'The enemy of my enemy is my friend.'"

A few low murmurs broke out, and she spoke over them. "I asked General Jordan to gather you here because I knew you wouldn't fight for me, that you're tired of risking your lives to defend my colony." She held up the data tablet she'd taken from Jordan's desk. "Which is why I'm offering to make it *your* colony. I had intended to give Eturia to the people—slowly, over time. I still believe a gradual transition is best, but if this is what it takes to save us, I'll make the change now."

The general joined her again. "Miss Rose has drafted an amendment to the charter that will dissolve the monarchy and establish an election to choose new leadership to govern the four previous kingdoms as one republic."

"And my name will be on that ballot," she said with a sharp look at Jordan.

"As will mine," he countered with a challenging gaze of his own.

A faint voice from below called, "Mine too," and the crowd parted to reveal Kane's mother sitting with her back against the barn wall, her face gray and streaked with sweat. "If I recover in time."

"You will," Cassia promised, then added, *"Commander."*

She knew she'd guessed correctly when Jordan stiffened by her side. Her main clue had been the activity surrounding the farm: meetings, transmissions, and the ammonium nitrate purchased with Kane's account. She'd briefly considered the farmer as the leader, but Rena had more inside knowledge of how the palace used to run, not to mention a natural charisma that was easily applied to politics. And given how the royals had left her unemployed and homeless after a lifetime of service to the monarchy, she would be plenty motivated to overturn the old system.

Cassia returned her attention to the rebels. "As for the rest of you, I'm prepared to sign this amendment into law as my last act as reigning queen, if you'll agree to join what's left of my soldiers in an attack on Marius tonight."

A man from the group shouted, "You don't have the authority to amend the charter."

"That's true," she admitted. "In order to make Eturia a free republic, either Marius has to cosign this amendment . . . or he has to die." She set her jaw. "If we work together, we can make one of those things happen by dawn. General Jordan and I have formed a strategy. All I need is your support to set it in motion."

"What do you say?" Jordan asked the rebels.

"How do we know she won't renege?" shouted the same man.

Cassia held up her finger, which she could prick and touch to the tablet for a legally binding DNA signature. "Say yes and I'll sign it right now."

But no one said yes.

Men and women glanced warily at one another while shifting on their feet. Cassia sensed that some of them agreed with her, but nobody seemed to want to be the first to say it. The silence continued until Kane's mother raised her hand and said, "Aye." Hers was the only confident face in the crowd. The farmer by her side nodded and echoed the vote. Then Jordan did the same. One group at a time, the others turned to Rena with a look of unmistakable respect, and the *ayes* carried around the barn in a sweeping vote until the majority's will became clear.

They would fight—not for the throne, but for themselves.

Cassia would take it.

*   *   *

That night she gave her husband exactly what he'd asked for: all twenty of his confiscated missiles, each disabled and strapped to a long, open barge that offered no hiding places for her troops. In keeping with his demands, she piloted the barge shuttle by herself, not bothering to conceal any weapons under her clothes. Marius wasn't an idiot. After what she'd pulled on their wedding night, he would have every crevice of her body scanned before coming anywhere near her.

When she reached the Durango border, she obediently stopped for inspection. The guards conducted a thorough search of the craft—not to mention her body—and discovered no traces of weaponry, so they radioed Marius and reported back with instructions for Cassia to land the barge at the armory, where a private shuttle would deliver her to the palace. She didn't delay. Within the hour, her barge and all its missiles rested on armory grounds.

As she climbed down from the pilot's seat, she scanned her surroundings by the light of the gathering moon. The Durango armory consisted of six metal sheds that led to underground bunkers, where weapons were stored safely out of range of enemy mortar. Several layers of fencing and shields surrounded the area, beyond which stood the soldiers' barracks and, about a mile beyond that, Marius's palace. She committed the layout to memory and strode alongside two armed escorts to a shuttle idling nearby.

"New destination," one of the guards told the pilot. "Take her to the lab."

Cassia's heart jumped. That wasn't part of the plan. "I want to see my husband," she demanded. "Deliver me to the palace first. Then we can go to the—"

The guard shoved her inside and slammed the door shut.

"Did you hear me?" she questioned the pilot, who ignored her and lifted the shuttle into the air. Moments later, they flew over the palace, then continued for at least another mile before descending.

Cassia rubbed the spot on her wrist where her bracelet belonged. The border guards had confiscated it during the inspection, and now she had no way to tell Jordan her new location. In half an hour, his mission would be complete, and he'd sneak inside the palace to retrieve her. How long would it take him to discover she wasn't there?

The shuttle landed behind a nondescript boxy building, unmarked and concealed on all sides by dense clusters of trees. Her palms turned cold as she exited the craft and met a new pair of armed escorts. Jordan would never find her here.

No one would.

At gunpoint, she walked through several sets of doors into the lab foyer, then followed the guards' instructions until she wound her way down several hallways to a small room containing two tall chairs, one with arm restraints and one without.

She didn't need to ask which chair was hers.

After a shove from behind, she sat down and rested both arms above the straps. One guard pointed his laser pistol at her face while his partner fastened restraints around her wrists and chest. Her legs were left free, but as short as she was, the tips of her boots barely skimmed the floor. She'd just begun scanning the room for anything she could use to her advantage when the door opened and Marius sauntered inside.

At the sight of him, she felt her stomach clench—not simply

out of fear and loathing, but because the grin on his face confirmed that she'd been outplayed. Then her gaze wandered to the box of syringes and electrodes in his hand, and she understood how fatally she'd underestimated him.

"Yes," he said, noticing the recognition in her eyes. "I know how your devious little mind works. The girl I married would have died before returning those missiles, so you're going to tell me what you're really up to." He handed the box to the guards, who divided its contents and approached her.

Cassia's heart slammed against her ribs. Jordan and his squad needed at least another twenty minutes before she betrayed their location. She had to find a way to stall the extraction process. When the first guard moved close enough, she kicked out and landed her boot between his legs. The other guards responded quickly, drawing their pistols.

"Go ahead and shoot me," she dared, knowing full well they wouldn't do it. They needed her alive to steal her thoughts.

Marius pointed at her shoulder. "Give the queen what she wants."

Before she knew what hit her, there was a flash of light, and the area below her left collarbone grew warm. She smelled scorched flesh, then felt a burning sensation that doubled by the second until she had to glance at her shoulder to make sure it wasn't on fire. The wound was deceptively tidy, just a coin-size red spot, but it burned like a live coal. She clamped her lips to keep from crying out, but her muffled sounds of agony were no more dignified than a scream, so finally she let one go.

"Laser wounds don't bleed," Marius said. "They're self-cauterizing. I can shoot you in a hundred different places and still keep you alive to tell me your secrets. Remember that the next time you feel the urge to fight."

She must've lost consciousness, because she blinked and noticed something new in her periphery. Electrodes were affixed to both sides of her temples, and when she glanced at the bend of her arm, she saw blood at the injection site. She whimpered in a mingling of pain and panic. How long before the serum kicked in?

Marius strode behind her. "Soon you're going to feel a warm tickle, right here." He ran a fingernail down the base of her skull, then bent to her ear and whispered, "I would know, wouldn't I? You put me through this so many times."

As badly as she wanted to slam her head into his face, the throbbing at her shoulder reminded her it wasn't worth it.

"And then you'll start telling me things," he whispered. "Dirty little secrets you wouldn't share with your closest friends. You'll hate yourself for it, but you won't be able to stop." His lips curved against her ear. "It's the highest form of personal violation, Cassy. I can't wait to show you."

"Cassy," she repeated as a bubbly sensation flowed over the back of her head. "I told you what would happen if you ever called me that again."

Marius stood up and circled around to face her, delight glowing behind his eyes. "What would you like to do to me?"

"Shoot you in the chest," she snapped. "It's not the death you deserve, but it's all I have time for." She wanted to stop there, but her mouth spoke without permission. "Kane needs me. Your mafia partners took him, and I don't know what they're doing to him, or if he's even alive. I have to hurry up and kill you so I can go to him."

Marius shared a laugh with his guards. "It's working. Leave me a pistol and wait in the hallway. I'll call if I need you." The men obeyed, and he settled in the opposite chair, well out of reach of Cassia's boots. "Too bad you're about to lose your head. Maybe you'll see your boyfriend in hell."

She tried telling herself that Marius hadn't asked a direct question, but it didn't make a difference. All her thoughts became words. "It doesn't matter if you kill me. Today I signed your death warrant." Then she told him everything about amending the charter and what the colonists had to do to make it legal. "Every rebel on Eturia knows that if you die, the monarchy dies with you. And trust me, they're highly motivated."

His smile flatlined. "My holdings won't pass to you, even in death. Our marriage is invalid. I never bedded you."

"Prove it."

All traces of amusement vanished from his face. "Playtime is over. You had a plan in coming here tonight. Tell me what it is, and don't leave anything out."

"I don't want to."

"Tell me now!"

Cassia held her breath to trap the secrets inside, anything to buy Jordan a few more moments. But the answer was like a sneeze, too far gone to repress. A groan built at the top of her lungs, then her chest heaved, and everything spilled out in a rush.

"Right now the rebels are in your armory, about to detonate a bomb that will destroy your entire store of weapons. At the same time, my men will infiltrate your military barracks and set off enough gas grenades to make your soldiers sleep for a week. Then General Jordan will steal an armed shuttle and fly to the palace because that's where he thinks I am. I don't know what he'll do when he doesn't find me. Probably tell his squadron to fan out and search the city for us. Their orders are to shoot you on sight."

Marius's eyes wandered over her face while he shook his head in denial. "No. That's not possible. My armory is impenetrable from every direction. Not even birds can fly over it."

"I know. So I hollowed out all twenty of your missiles and filled them with my fighters. The shells are so huge I was able to fit everyone inside. You let the rebels right through your gates, and now they're coming for you."

The floor trembled and a rumble sounded in the distance.

"There goes your armory," she said, and couldn't stop herself from jutting her chin at the door. "You should tell your guards what's happening so they can mobilize all the soldiers who aren't asleep in the barracks. It probably won't make a difference because the rebels are about to steal your armed ships, but it's worth a try."

Marius ran into the hall and shut the door behind him.

While he was gone, Cassia wiggled her wrists to loosen the restraints, but all she accomplished was a deeper throb in her left shoulder. She gritted her teeth and lurched forward in her seat. The chair moved an inch, so she did it again. She wasn't sure of her end goal, but she needed to do something besides dispense tactical advice to her enemy. Maybe if she jumped far enough, she could reach the laser pistol Marius had left on his seat.

He reentered the room and put a stop to her progress by shoving her wounded shoulder hard enough to make her chair tip backward. She screamed as white-hot pain exploded down the length of her arm. She must've blacked out again because she didn't remember hitting the floor. The next thing she knew, she was facing the ceiling with Marius looking down at her, a pistol in his fist.

She kicked with all her strength and connected with his wrist. The gun flew out of his hand, but it didn't take long for him to retrieve it. He returned to her with fury contorting his face, and in that moment she knew it was over for her.

"Remember what I told you?" he spat, leveling the gun barrel at her knee. "Here's one of the hundred places where a burn won't kill you." He sniffed a dry laugh. "Though you'll wish it had."

She moved her legs back and forth, forcing him to adjust his aim. Just when he'd grown frustrated enough to point the barrel at her shoulder, a series of pops rang out from the hallway, and he froze, glancing toward the sound. The door flew open so hard it crashed against the wall. Cassia couldn't see around her chair, but she heard three quick blasts, and then Marius stumbled back, clutching his chest. He still held his pistol in one hand, but he seemed too stunned to use it. He looked blankly from her to the smoke rising from his rib cage, as if she could explain to him how this had happened. Another blast fired, this time burning a tiny hole in his forehead, and then his eyes rolled back as he fell to the floor.

Cassia shifted left, peering around her chair leg, and spotted a familiar pair of boots striding into view. Then a pair of shrewd gray eyes peered down at her from above a twice-broken nose.

"Jordan," she breathed. "How did you find me?" She jerked her gaze toward the hallway. "Make sure you secure the building. Marius is trying to mobilize all the soldiers who weren't in the barracks."

"He *was* trying," Jordan corrected with a nod at the dead body. "Most of his men have already surrendered." He frowned and studied her laser wound. "Are you okay?"

Nodding, she repeated, "How did you find me?"

He lifted her chair upright and began unfastening her wrists. "By finding Marius. I had my men slip a tracking chip under his skin when he was imprisoned."

"He didn't know?"

"He had no idea." Jordan seemed to notice her electrodes for the first time. He frowned and peeled one free from her temple. "He hooked you up to the truth extractor. I didn't see that coming."

"Me neither. I hated it."

Jordan gave a dry laugh. "Well, at least you didn't profess your undying love to the person who locked you up. There's no living that down."

The mere thought of Jordan's feelings forced her to blurt, "I didn't love you back, but I was attracted to you." Her face flamed. She couldn't stop herself from pointing at his lower abdomen. "You have these amazing V-shaped muscles at the base of your hips. I used to daydream about them."

His lips curved in a smile. "They're all yours if you want."

"I only want Kane," she said, and it killed her that he might never know it. "He's more than a friend. I love him. He spent years making sacrifices for me, and now he's the one who needs help. I won't turn my back on him—not for you, or this colony, or anything else."

"I can respect that." Jordan offered his palm. "Friends, then? And I don't mean the enemy-of-my-enemy kind."

As she took his hand to shake it, his words sparked an idea. "Can you ping the *Banshee* for me? My com-band is gone, and I have to talk to Renny."

"Of course."

"And since we're friends now, I hope you'll do me a favor."

"Anything for my former queen."

"What's the fastest ship on this colony?"

He considered for a moment. "I noticed one of the Durango generals has a Hypersonic cruiser." His eyes flashed with understanding, and he added, "Which technically belongs to you, because we haven't filed the amendment with the Solar League yet."

"Perfect." She stood up slowly, favoring her shoulder. "While I look for a med-kit, I need you to bring me that ship. I'll meet you outside in ten minutes."

CHAPTER TWENTY-SEVEN

Kane awoke by layers, one slow sense at a time.

At first there was a vague awareness, the confusion of sliding out of dreams. Then came light. The brilliance pierced his closed eyelids, seeming to come from all around. No matter which way he turned his head, he couldn't escape it. With that motion came pain. His neck burned from the inside out, and as he stirred in bed, he found his muscles stiff and slow to respond. Finally, as he came around, he heard the sounds of angry male voices, slightly muffled by distance.

". . . not worth the risk," said one man. "He's already gone off twice."

"That's my fault," argued another voice Kane recognized as his boss. "I gave him too much. He built up a resistance, that's all."

"*That's all?*" repeated the first man. "There's nothing

stronger to give him! If he's grown tolerant to the Gold, then we might as well—"

A closer voice said, "Hey, kid," and Kane opened his eyes to find Cutter sitting on the edge of the bed.

Right away, he noticed they weren't in the dorm. This bed was tall with no upper bunk, situated in a bright, white-walled room. One of Cutter's massive arms was pinned to his chest by a sling, and two of the fingers on that same hand were paler than the rest. Judging by the scarlet line below the knuckles, it looked like they'd been reattached recently.

Because they had.

All of Kane's memories washed over him in a rush. "You're alive," he croaked in a dry throat. *And so am I.*

"Thanks to you," Cutter said. It sounded like an accusation.

"I couldn't do it. I'm sorry."

"Don't apologize. Not wanting to kill me is nothing to be sorry for." He pointed at Kane's throat. "By the way, you should've waited until the Redshirts were off the stage. Then you might've bled out before they treated you."

Kane tried to touch his neck, but both of his wrists were bound by his sides. "How long's it been?"

"A few days, maybe? I was out, too, so it's hard to say." Cutter glanced through the open window, barred from the outside. "They're sending me back to the dorm today. I don't think they'll make me fight tonight, though."

Kane didn't want to talk about the pit, so he changed the subject. "I see you have your fingers back."

"Yeah," Cutter said, tipping his head as if to admire them.

"It's a halfway decent patch job. But I'll probably lose them in the next game, so I'm not getting attached." He waggled his eyebrows. "Get it? *Attached?*"

The bad joke prompted Kane to study Cutter's pupils, which were wide enough to reveal how much Gold the medics had given him. He recalled the conversation he'd overheard about building up a resistance to the drug. What would happen when the inhalers didn't work on him anymore? How would he compete without the rush?

The door opened, and his boss walked inside. He jerked his head toward the hallway and told Cutter, "Back to the dorm."

Cutter patted one of Kane's legs through the blanket. "See you around, kid."

After he left and shut the door behind him, the boss gripped both hips and watched Kane as if he didn't know what to do with him.

"How much trouble am I in?" Kane asked.

His boss laughed without humor. "Almost as much as I'm in." He rubbed the back of his thick, beefy neck. "We really mucked up opening night for the casino."

"But I forfeited."

"That's not how it works. The last man alive is the champion. When you didn't finish Cutter, you threw a wrench in the system. Then I made it worse by interfering"—he pointed at Kane's neck—"and telling my men to seal off that wound. Now there's no clear winner, so the casino had to freeze the payouts while they decide how to break the tie."

"Cutter should be the winner."

"That's what some people think. Everyone else says it should be you, since Cutter was half-dead already. Either way, it makes Zhang look like he can't handle his business. That's bad for both of us. He's not the most forgiving guy."

A chill gripped Kane's stomach. If Ari Zhang had sold Renny's girlfriend into slavery as punishment for a picked pocket, what would he do to someone who'd humiliated him in front of an arena full of spectators? Could the mafia track down Cassia or his mom and make them pay for what he'd done?

His boss gave a sarcastic huff. "The only reason you're alive is because, for some ass-backward reason, the guests are still crazy about you. That stunt you pulled made you look even nuttier than when you attacked Nicky Malone. No one will shut up about it."

Based on that, Kane knew how the casino would break the tie. "They want a rematch."

His boss didn't say yes, but he didn't deny it, either. "Listen, I hate to do this to you, but I have to let you dry out. The Gold won't work until we lower your resistance, so as of today, you're cut off." His gaze moved to the floor. "I won't lie, kid. This is gonna hurt. The medic wants to keep you here so he can monitor your heart and restart it if it stops."

Kane's lips drifted apart. Was his addiction that bad?

"Hang in there," his boss said, then turned and strode toward the door. "I'll see you when it's over."

* * *

During the next week, Kane learned that hell wasn't a mythical place designed to scare sinners into good behavior. Hell was a state of survival in which suffering never ended. That was the real punishment—constant pain. His nerve endings screamed from one sunrise to the next with no interruption in torture. The only relief came when he died, though it didn't last long. The medic restarted his heart and apologized. He said he could sedate Kane during the withdrawal, but Ari Zhang had told him not to.

This was a lesson, and Kane learned it well.

He improved the following week, when his symptoms lessened to the same ones he'd felt on Batavion. It struck him as funny, how at the mining camp he'd wished for death to take away his agony. Back then he hadn't known the meaning of the word.

A few days later a team of workers came to haul his limp body out of bed and drag him to the washroom for a shower. As the men wrinkled their noses and scrubbed him down, he noticed they were Whiteshirts, not medics, which told him his lesson was meant to be shared. Rumor would spread about what he looked like after two weeks with no inhaler—gray-skinned and trembling, his once-bulging biceps now atrophied to half their size—and the workers would think twice before disobeying.

He certainly would.

When his boss came to see him, Kane could've hugged the man if his arms were strong enough. His boss's familiar face and duck-like waddle reminded him of how invincible he'd been in the dorm. He would give anything to feel that way again.

"How're you holding up, kid?"

Kane locked eyes on the golden tube strung around his boss's neck. A distant voice of reason whispered that the drug was the reason for all his suffering. If he used the Gold again, he would never be free of it. But that voice was quickly muffled by the screaming of every living cell within his body. He needed a breath of sweet air. He would do anything to have it.

"I'm ready," he said. "I'll fight harder this time."

"That's the right answer, kid." His boss pulled a chrome inhaler from his pocket. "We're gonna start you off slow and work up to the good stuff." He shook it while glancing at Kane's chest. "And beef you up again. You undid all my hard work."

Kane frowned at the silvery tube. What he really craved was the Gold, but he lifted his head from the pillow and strained forward, eager to take the mouthpiece between his lips. A few pumps later, energy flowed through his veins, charging his muscles and propelling him off the mattress into a long, arching stretch.

God, it felt good to move his body.

The drug didn't give him a rush, but the simple absence of pain filled him with so much euphoria that his breath hitched and his eyes welled with tears. "Thank you," he said, and meant it. His boss had delivered him from hell, and Kane would never let him down again.

"Sure, kid," the man muttered. "Now, come on. I want you back on the circuit in fifteen minutes."

* * *

The night of the rematch, Kane was ready.

More or less.

Three days wasn't long enough to replace all the bulk he'd lost, but the protein injections and circuit workouts had rounded his muscles and made them solid again. Most important, his boss had started giving him Gold—half strength at first, building gradually until a few hours ago, when he'd been allowed to bump up from the same inhaler as the other guys.

Drying out had given Kane an edge over the competition. He was still flying high from his last hit, punching the dorm bag as an outlet for his energy, while Cutter sat on the weight bench in the corner, grasping his knees and staring at the floor.

Kane looked away from his opponent and sank his fist into the bag. He had to focus on the equipment, to memorize its long, cylindrical shape and its cracked red surface, because that was what he would picture on the battle platform. Not a man. Just a bag.

"Time to suit up," hollered the boss, tossing white bodysuits at them. Kane caught his easily, but Cutter's reattached fingers hadn't fully healed, and he fumbled with the fabric before grasping it in his opposite hand.

Not a man, Kane reminded himself. Just a bag.

He purposefully avoided Cutter while changing into his outfit, and when the time came for the three of them to leave the dorm, Kane kept the pace by his boss's side, ahead of Cutter so he wouldn't have to look at him. During the walk to the Vice Den, Kane distracted himself by counting the distant crashes of waves and observing the play of moonlight over the sand dunes. But that reminded him of the morning Cutter saved him from killing a guest, and Kane had to break the silence to end those thoughts.

"Is there a new maze tonight?" he asked his boss. He hoped so. His reflexes were quicker than the competition's. If Cutter didn't make it out of the maze, Kane wouldn't have to kill him.

Guilt twisted his stomach. Had he really wished for Cutter to die?

"I need a bump," Kane blurted before the boss had a chance to answer his question.

"You can have one at game time. And there's no maze, just the final battle."

Sweat beaded on Kane's upper lip. "Please give me a hit now. All I need is—"

A rough slap to the face interrupted him. "Pull it together," his boss warned. "This is the last chance for both of us. I swear if you blow this for me, I'll make you dry out again before Zhang has you killed. Are we clear?"

Kane sobered at the memory of two weeks with no inhalers. "Yes, boss."

They continued in silence until they reached the pit doors at the far end of the arena. Kane heard the crowd long before he saw their faces, a rumble of excitement that added to the anxiety building behind his ribs. As soon as he strode through the entrance, the stands erupted in deafening cheers, and he shielded his face with one hand.

The crowd blurred into a mass of waving arms as he glanced around the pit, which had completely changed since his last competition. The locker room was gone, as was the maze. The floor stretched open now, with the battle platform situated in the middle. The distance to the ring was the same, but the crowd seemed closer somehow. Too close. All that separated him from the bottom row of seats was the exterior maze wall, nine feet high and stretching around the perimeter of the pit.

From somewhere out of sight, the master of ceremonies called over the speakers, "I present to you our champions: Brock Cutter . . . and the Wolf!" At the mention of Kane's nickname, the crowd lost their minds. He'd never hated them more than during that moment, as they howled for his opponent's blood. "Our champions are strong and rested up, and ready to battle to the death in your honor!"

Honor. What a joke. There was no honor here.

"Okay, you two," the boss shouted when they'd reached the platform steps. "I want you to give these people a show they'll never forget, so take these." He handed each of them a golden inhaler. "They're all yours."

"The whole thing?" Cutter asked.

"As many bumps as you want."

Even as Kane's fingers tightened protectively around his inhaler, he wished his boss hadn't given it to him. He didn't know if he had the will to stop after one breath, and he didn't want to end up drying out in the med-center again. "But what if we take too much? Won't we build up a tolerance?"

The boss licked his lips and took a sudden interest in his shoes. "Don't worry about that, kid. Just do what feels right, okay?"

Then he jogged away without a backward glance.

Kane shared a worried look with Cutter. He knew they'd both reached the same conclusion. If the boss didn't care about immunity, it meant the winner of tonight's fight wouldn't survive long enough to compete again. Ari Zhang wasn't a forgiving man. He only needed one of them to break the tie. Otherwise, they were expendable.

Kane scanned the arena for Zhang's private box, hoping to

read the man's intentions. He found the box in the same spot as before, situated in the middlemost aisle, about halfway to the top of the stands. But before his eyes made it to Zhang, they stopped on a familiar woman with a heart-shaped face and a riot of red curls spilling from a bun atop her head.

Kane did a double take. Was that Arabelle?

He almost didn't recognize her with a patch covering her left eye, but there was no mistaking the motherly curve of her face, or the intensity in her right eye, which was fixed on him and trying to convey a message he couldn't understand. He peered through the stands for the crew but didn't find them. Maybe the mafia had captured Arabelle. Glancing on either side of her, he noticed she sat in between her former owner, Necktie Fleece, and that bastard Nicky Malone, who wouldn't stop leering at her.

Kane felt sick.

He couldn't stand the idea of Belle as a lady in white—it hit too close to home. She was part of the *Banshee* crew, and that made her family. It might as well be his own mother sitting up there. As he watched her, he saw Nicky Malone trace an index finger along the length of her forearm, and his vision tunneled.

"Cutter?" he heard himself say.

"Yeah?"

Kane tore his gaze away from the private box and faced his opponent—who was a man, not a bag. Lifting his inhaler, he asked, "How powerful will a breath of this make you?"

"Not very," Cutter admitted.

"How about two breaths?"

"A little stronger than usual."

Kane nodded toward the middlemost aisle. "Strong enough to boost me over that wall?"

Cutter shifted a glance in that direction. Kane could practically see the wheels turning inside the man's head, weighing the act of helping him against the risk of what Ari Zhang would do to them when it was done.

"Yeah," Cutter said, grinning as he turned up his injured palm. "I'll probably lose these fingers again, but like I told you, I didn't get attached."

The master of ceremonies called out over the speakers, telling them to take their places on the battle platform, but Kane ignored him. He offered his hand and Cutter shook it.

"Godspeed, kid."

"Same to you."

Cutter jerked his chin toward the stands. "When you're up there, toss a few of those perverts my way. I'm not showing up alone in hell tonight."

Kane clinked his inhaler against Cutter's in a toast. "Here's to going out with a bang."

"I'll breathe to that."

They brought the mouthpieces to their lips. Kane pumped his tube twice and sucked in a deep breath, holding it while the layers of the mortal world peeled back and revealed a heaven of his own making. He was a god once more, his cells bursting with all the power of the cosmos, and tonight he would bring down his vengeance.

If the crowd wanted blood, they would have it.

Once his vision returned, he signaled to Cutter, who ran ahead to the wall and then bent low, lacing his fingers together in a stirrup. Kane sprinted toward the man and stepped onto his linked hands. In flawless unison, Kane jumped and Cutter heaved, launching his body to the top of the wall, where he grabbed on and climbed over the top into the stands.

Shouts broke out as the spectators in his path tried to run, but there was nowhere for them to go. As he scaled the rows with supernatural speed, he grabbed an occasional collar and gave its owner a headfirst journey into the pit. His eyes locked on his targets in the luxury box, and he growled in delight. His boss had told him *Do what feels right*, and nothing in his life had ever felt more natural than this.

For the first time, he saw fear on Ari Zhang's face, and it made his teeth ache to sink into the man's throat. Vaguely, he noticed Belle speaking into a button affixed to her shirt, but he paid her no mind. At least not until she pulled a thick metal hairpin from her bun and jabbed it into the base of Necktie Fleece's skull, dropping him instantly.

Kane stumbled in surprise, torn between admiration for the kill and anger that she'd stolen it from him. From behind he heard pistol fire, and then more screams from the spectators as they ducked to avoid being hit. He'd just reached the luxury box and hoisted himself inside when a laser pulse connected with his arm. He grinned. The pain didn't even register. He snagged Nicky Malone by the shirtsleeve and jerked him forward.

Kane paused to savor the fear in the man's eyes before grabbing him by the seat of his pants and throwing him like a rag doll into the pit. Then he stepped over the fallen body of Necktie Fleece and crept toward Zhang, who'd reached the far wall of the box and could go no farther. He was nearly within reach when, abruptly, every light inside the arena flickered and died. Blackness surrounded him.

"Kane," called a voice, and then gentle fingers probed his shoulder. He snatched the fingers and squeezed them, causing the voice to cry out in pain. "It's me, Belle."

He wanted to let go, but his hand didn't seem willing to obey. The need for violence pumped through his veins, urging him to crush her bones. It took a long moment before he was able to relax his grip enough for her to slip free.

"That's the signal," she told him, barely audible over the shouts of the crowd. "Renny blew the shield and took out the electrical grid. We have to find the exit and meet him outside. It's about to get ugly in here."

"I can't see."

Cautiously, she touched his elbow. "That's why I'm here. I lost an eye, but I gained an upgrade. Grab on to my shirt and follow me."

He allowed her to lead him blindly down the aisle, but then he remembered Cutter in the pit. "My friend's down there. I can't leave him."

"Don't worry. The pirates know not to touch anyone in white."

Pirates?

Kane glanced around, seeing nothing at first, until the guests seated near the exits opened the doors. Moonlight streamed inside as they shoved each other in a rush to escape. The dim lighting showed Cutter alive in the pit, surrounded by limp bodies. Kane waved at the man to get his attention, but it was no use. The arena was in chaos.

Frustrated, Kane returned his gaze to the exit. Energy coursed through him. He needed to move, needed to fight. He picked up Arabelle and swung her behind him, then growled as he plowed into the crowd of men ahead, throwing his fists and elbows and loving the contact of flesh against his knuckles. When the guests noticed who was behind them, they flung themselves out of his path, and he walked out the doors into the night.

He strode forward a few paces and froze.

If he'd thought the arena was in chaos, that was nothing compared with the havoc unfolding outside. Flames engulfed the long chain of suites hugging the coastline, forcing their guests into the open, where plainclothes men attacked them with stun grenades or bludgeoned them with clubs and pistol butts. Redshirts fired on the pirates, but it was no use. More of them kept coming as dozens of mismatched shuttles descended from the sky. In the center of the landing zone stood a tall, red-haired pirate with kohl-lined eyes, shouting orders to his men. Kane squinted and realized it was Doran, dressed like Daro the Red. Solara stood by his side, her face streaked with war paint and a rifle slung over her shoulder.

Arabelle tugged at Kane's sleeve. "Listen, I know the enemy of our enemy is our friend, and all that, but I don't like pirates. It's best if we round everyone up and go."

"Go?" he echoed, and then it struck him that the crew had come to take him away. That meant no more Gold. He would have to dry out again—for good this time. He shook her off and backed away. "No. I'm staying."

Arabelle gaped at him through mismatched eyes, one blue,

the other a prosthetic that glowed amber in the night. Then she tapped her com-link and muttered, "I need backup."

Renny's voice came from directly behind them. "I'll take it from here."

Before Kane could turn around, Renny grabbed him and pinned both his arms to his sides. Kane thrashed against the iron hold as his captain dragged him backward. He didn't want to hurt Renny, but panic took over his body. In a burst of strength, Kane curled forward and sent Renny somersaulting into the air. Before the captain landed on the ground, Kane turned and bolted toward the ocean like his ass was on fire.

His boots slid when they met the loose sand along the dunes, but he kept going, desperate to reach the water. He wasn't sure what he planned do there, maybe swim past the breakers and keep going until he reached the undeveloped side of the island. He could hide in the rough thicket of trees and underbrush until the crew left. He ran faster once he reached the packed, wet sand near the shoreline. The water was almost within diving distance when something tangled around his ankles and sent him pitching forward, and he landed hard on his stomach.

Coughing out a mouthful of sand, he rolled onto his back and found a hobbling cable wrapped around his boots. He sat up and jerked on the metallic ropes, but they wouldn't budge. Glancing at the waves, he wondered how far he could swim with his feet bound.

"Don't try it," a voice said. "I'll fish you out and drag you back."

He turned and saw Cassia's tiny silhouette in the moonlight. Even if she hadn't spoken, he would have known it was her.

The gentle curves of her body and the firm, unrelenting set of her shoulders were as familiar to him as his own flesh. But the warmth her presence gave him was no match for his longing to escape. He inched toward the waves. In a flash, she was there, hauling him back by his ankle restraints.

"Stop!" he yelled, and thrust a palm forward. He wished she would go away. He didn't want her to see him like this. "I don't want to hurt you."

"Keep waving that hand in my face and we'll see who gets hurt."

"I mean it. This drug makes me strong. I can't control what I do to people."

"I know." She dropped to her knees beside him. "That's why you have to come with us, so we can help you." When he shook his head, she added, "Gage found a cure. It's an injection that changes your brain chemistry. I've seen it work. In a couple of weeks, you'll feel like yourself."

"You don't understand." Fresh panic had him scooting away from her. He inched across the sand like a pathetic worm, hating what he'd become but unable to stop. "Two weeks was all it took last time. I can't go through that again."

"It won't be like that. I promise."

"How would you know?" he shouted. "You weren't here!"

She flinched back as pain flashed in her eyes, the kind born from guilt. He recognized it from all the times he'd looked in the mirror after the Daeva had taken her.

"I know I wasn't," she said. "But I never stopped fighting for you, and neither did the crew. They've been here for weeks, listening to the transmissions and waiting for the right time to attack." She thumbed toward the dunes. "These people can't hurt you anymore, but that doesn't mean you can stay. Doran made a deal with the pirates. If they don't hurt any of the workers, they get free rein over the planet when we're gone. After that, they'll ransom the guests. There's nothing for you here."

She was wrong. There *was* something for him here: the planet's entire supply of Gold. He even knew where to find it. If he was careful and stayed hidden, the pirates might never know he'd stayed behind.

As if reading his thoughts, Cassia glared at him and sharpened her voice. "Don't even think about it, you scum-eating son of a crotch smuggler! You're my best friend, and I'm not leaving without you."

"Just let me go," he pleaded with her. "You don't understand."

"Let me tell you what I understand." She fisted the front of his bodysuit, shaking it as her gaze shone with tears. "I want your next twenty years, and all the years after that. I gave Eturia to the people. I'm ready to go all in, but it doesn't mean anything unless you go all in, too. You have to choose me over the drug." She shook him again. "Do you hear me? I can't promise the treatment will be quick or easy, but I swear I'll be with you the whole time." A tear slid free, and she reached for his face. "I love you, Kane. Choose me."

His heart warred with his nerve endings, which were already screaming in protest against the withdrawal. He swallowed hard and gazed into her face. He'd dreamed of this moment for so long, but now he didn't know if he had the strength to tell her yes. As her hand drew nearer to his cheek, his resolve softened, but then he noticed something in his periphery—a black button concealed within her palm.

Except it wasn't a button. It was a handheld stunner.

Quick as a viper strike, he grabbed her wrist and rotated it for a better view. He realized with a stab of betrayal it was probably the same device Solara had used on him all those months ago in the underground compound.

"You tricked me."

Cassia didn't deny it. As she knelt there with her wrist trembling in his hand, he sensed the fragility of the tiny bones beneath her skin. The Gold urged him to squeeze; that was all it would take to snap her arm like a pretzel stick. But she returned him to his senses with nothing more than a look—the same sad, misty gaze that never failed to grip his heart and turn it inside out. With tears trailing down her face, she whispered, "Please, Kane. Choose me."

Before he had a chance to change his mind, he pulled her palm slowly toward his face until the stunner met his cheek. Neuro-inhibitors flooded his system, forcing his eyelids shut. As the world slid out from beneath him, he fought through the barrier of his own lips and the weight of his paralyzed tongue to mumble two final words to Cassia, his best friend and the girl he'd chosen, consequence be damned.

"All in."

CHAPTER TWENTY-EIGHT

"*T*his way for quadrants one and two," Cassia shouted, pointing at the *Origin*'s boarding ramp. She thumbed at a second vessel called the *Zephyr*. "Quadrants three and four, you're over here." With a wink at Belle, she added, "If you don't know which quad your settlement is in, ask the redhead with the sexy bionic eye. She'll point you in the right direction."

While Belle curtsied, Renny lifted a hand. "Remember, nothing leaves this planet except for you—not a single grain of sand. We *will* check your pockets when you board, so if you're carrying contraband, get rid of it now."

Activity stirred within the camp as several men and women tossed aside nutrient packets, shells, coins, and bits of broken jewelry the pirates had missed. Those weren't the items Cassia cared about. Aside from inhalers, she mostly wanted to keep weapons off the ships. The workers had received their injections, but they were still in the "edgy" phase of their recovery, and squabbles were bound to happen during the long journey home.

Renny waved the settlers forward, and they began lining up in front of their respective ships. Like everything else on Adel Vice, boarding was a team effort. Renny and Doran stood at the base of each ramp, patting down the settlers for contraband. Once clear, the men and women continued up the ramp to the cargo hold, where Arabelle and Solara greeted them with a knapsack of food and toiletries. After that, the hired pilots and crew, who'd been paid with the titles to both mafia ships, took over, directing the settlers to their group quarters.

Cassia's job was to stay in the camp with Gage and watch over those who weren't ready to leave—*the resistants*, as she called them. These were the worst cases, three workers who'd grown so dependent on the inhalers that she'd had to stun them before beginning treatment. Kane was one of the three, along with an enormous fighter from the pit and a woman with dozens of scars crisscrossing her forearms. It hadn't been easy, but Cassia had kept them sedated with tranquilizers she'd stolen at gunpoint from two pirates. Every second of the risk had been worth the reward of watching Kane recover in peace.

She entered the makeshift tent of blankets loosely tied to palm trees, and continued to the mattress in the far corner, where she'd positioned Kane for the best cross breeze. After taking a seat on the sandy ground, she started her daily ritual of sponging the sweat from his face with rainwater from the cisterns, making sure to clean the scar on his throat. To conserve the cistern supply, she used seawater to wash his chest and beneath his arms. All the freshwater on Adel Vice came from a well on the pirates' side of the resort, and she knew better than to ask them to share.

She noticed Kane's color had returned, and while she moved each of his limbs to exercise them, she debated whether she should stop his sedative. By the last arm stretch, she decided the time had come, and she removed his intravenous line.

"I can do that," Gage offered, poking his head inside the tent. "You should grab some lunch. There's still plenty of—"

"Let me guess. Eggplant Parmesan?" That was all they'd eaten since the night of the attack, when someone had rescued a giant vat of it from a burning restaurant. "Thanks, but I'll pass. I stopped Kane's meds, and I want to be here when he wakes up."

"I stopped theirs, too," Gage said, indicating the others. "It takes a while for the sedative to wear off. You've got time for a break."

"That's okay. I'm happy here." She liked to think that Kane sensed her presence, so she never strayed too far from his side. She brushed back his hair and grinned at the blond roots pushing up from his scalp. His head resembled a zebra, blond on the bottom, black at the tips. "You're getting a haircut when you wake up," she whispered in his ear.

Outside, engines rumbled to life, followed by blowing thrusters that rippled the walls of the blanket tent. The noise intensified as it rose above the trees and then faded slowly into the distance. Doran ducked inside the tent while attacking a heaping bowl of food. With one cheek stuffed full, he pointed his fork at Kane in a silent question.

"He's improving," Cassia said, then recoiled from the smell of eggplant. "How can you keep eating that?"

"Because it's damned delicious, that's how."

"Plus, it's not beans," Solara said, joining them. "No offense if you can hear me, Kane, but a girl can only take so much chili."

Doran nudged his girlfriend. "Hey, that gives me an idea. Let's load all the leftovers in the *Banshee*'s cooler before we leave."

Cassia made a face. "Or not."

"You'd better hurry," Renny's voice called from outside the tent. "Because your next job is loading our patients in the cargo bay. I want to be airborne by nightfall."

"Midday's even better," Cassia suggested. Even with Ari Zhang dead and a shaky truce between the crew and the pirates, it wouldn't be long before bounty hunters and hired mercenaries descended on Adel Vice to rescue the more influential guests trapped on the other side of the resort.

She sensed movement from the mattress, and all thoughts of pirates flew to her mind's periphery as Kane began to stir. She tried to remember what she'd learned about *grounding*, a technique that was supposed to help him adjust more quickly by stimulating his five senses.

To evoke touch and smell, she took his face in her hands and leaned down, exposing him to the perfume microbes beneath her skin. Then she whispered his name to give him sound, and gently kissed his mouth so he could taste the salt on her lips. All that remained was sight, so she held her breath and waited as his eyes moved beneath their lids.

Finally, he blinked awake, and she exhaled into a smile.

"Hey there, sleepyhead," she said softly. The stunner she'd used on him had probably worn off days ago, but to make sure, she asked, "Remember me?"

He narrowed his gaze for a moment as if trying to bring her into focus, and then a weak grin lifted the corners of his lips. "Cassy. I was just dreaming about you."

His response filled her with so much happiness it leaked from her eyes and turned him into a wet blur. She helped him into a semisitting position and lifted a cup of water to his lips. "Was it a good dream?"

He drained the cup in three eager gulps and then took a moment to catch his breath before answering. "Kind of. We were skinny-dipping in the hellberry bog. Just when things were getting steamy, you stopped and said I needed a haircut."

Her tears turned to laughter, and she ruffled his zebra hair. "Well, you do."

"Hey, go back to that 'steamy' part," Doran said, taking a knee beside the mattress. "That sounds interesting."

Kane's stomach grumbled, and he studied Doran's bowl. "What you got there?" When Doran showed him, Kane turned his face away. "Smells disgusting."

"More for me."

Kane glanced beyond Doran and noticed the giant man asleep in the middle of the tent. His eyes brightened. "Cutter made it out of the pit." He stretched his neck, peering farther, and smiled. "With his fingers. How about that."

"You missed a lot," Cassia said. Then she realized what day it was, and a nervous thrill passed through her. "In fact, the

Eturian election took place today." When his eyebrows rose, she filled him in on everything that'd happened back home, including the fact that his mother had been leading the rebellion. "I took the liberty of filling out your absentee ballot. I assumed your mom had your vote."

"Not necessarily."

That was sweet of him to say, but Cassia's royal heritage guaranteed that she stood no chance of winning. "It's pretty much a race between her and General Jordan."

Kane wrinkled his nose. "I sure as hell don't want his face on my currency." Then he froze as if something had just occurred to him. "Wait, what are you doing here on election day? You should be home. Voters won't trust you if you're off world during the campaign."

She shook her head.

"I mean it, Cassy. You should have gone back. I've been asleep this whole time anyway. I could've met you there."

She cut him off with a lifted hand and told him the surest truth in her world. "I'm exactly where I need to be." Then she planted a quick but firm kiss on his lips. "No more arguments."

Solara snorted. "Right. I give it five minutes."

Gage made his way to the mattress and crouched down, inspecting Kane's eyes with a handheld light. "Your pupils are responsive. Are you feeling okay?"

"I think so." Kane sat up all the way and experimented with his limbs, bending his knees and flexing his fingers. "I'm tired, but it's not that bad. I feel like I just got over the flu. The last time I dried out I was so weak I couldn't move."

"Any, uh . . . cravings?"

"Not that kind. The only thing I want is a shower." Kane's stomach growled. "And a bowl of chili." He smiled at Gage in thanks. "It looks like your injection worked."

Doran captured his twin in a playful headlock, scrubbing his knuckles over Gage's scalp. "Of course it worked. My brother's a genius."

Gage shoved him off and grinned as he straightened his hair. "A genius who doesn't trust pirates. Your captain's right. We should start packing." He glanced at the two other patients. "And load them on the ship before they wake up. I don't think they'll mind if the first thing they see is the inside of a cargo bay."

"Trust me," Kane said darkly. "They won't mind."

A beep sounded from Cassia's new com-bracelet. She knew without looking it was Kane's mother calling to check in on him. They'd discussed his progress every day. When she accepted the transmission, Rena's hologram appeared from within the farmhouse, where it seemed a party was in full swing. Several people milled about in the background making celebratory toasts, including Jordan, who wore a bittersweet expression that made clear the election's outcome. Cassia's heart sank an inch. She'd expected Rena to win, but it still stung.

"Doodlebug," Rena said with laughter in her eyes. No longer frail, she crouched down to Kane's level and reached out as if to touch him. "You look so much better, baby."

Kane's cheeks turned pink. "You too, Mom."

Cassia told her, "I take it congratulations are in order."

Rena offered an apologetic smile, clearly trying to be humble until Meichael appeared in the frame and covered the back of her neck with kisses. Then she ducked aside with a laugh. "I wanted you to hear it from me first."

"I appreciate that."

"You did the right thing, Cassia. I won't let us down."

Cassia smiled. Rena was well respected and would make a strong leader—she knew that now. Though the loss prickled, an invisible weight lifted from her shoulders. She would never again have to send soldiers into battle or sacrifice her happiness in service to the colony. She would never have to settle down or stop exploring. The rebels weren't the only ones who'd earned their independence today. For the first time in her life, she was free to choose her own destiny.

"I know you won't."

Kane took her hand, giving it a comforting squeeze. "Congratulations, Mom. I'm proud of you."

"That goes both ways, Doodlebug." She blew him a kiss and then let a group of well-wishers pull her out of the frame, at which point General Jordan strode forward to take her place.

"Arric," he said with a nod at Kane. "Glad to see you're okay."

Kane mumbled something resembling a thanks.

"Cassia, same to you." As Jordan shifted his focus to her, his gaze lingered in that old, familiar way. He seemed to catch himself and quickly added, "No rush on returning the Hypersonic cruiser you borrowed, just bring it back when you're ready. I can't wait to fly it. Is it as fast as they say?"

She cringed and glanced at the tent wall, beyond which lay the cruiser's skeletal remains. She'd landed it in a safe spot, but that hadn't stopped the pirates from stripping all of its useful parts before Doran had busted them and established the resort boundary.

Jordan's smile fell. "Please tell me you didn't wreck the cruiser."

"Got to go. We'll talk later." She tapped her bracelet to end the call, and Jordan vanished in a flash of irritation.

Kane scowled. "I can't stand that guy."

"Me neither, Doodlebug," called Renny from outside the tent.

Doran snorted and Solara giggled. Kane didn't bother glaring at them. He had to know a nickname that precious was bound to stick.

"Jordan's not so bad," Cassia said. "He came through for us in the end." At the irritated look Kane gave her, she added, "At least you won't have to see his face on your currency."

"Thank god for small favors."

She supposed the big question now was, *What next?* She'd been so preoccupied with Kane's recovery that she hadn't given much thought to what she would do if she lost the election. One option was to go home. Eturia was a free republic, so she and Kane were equals in every way. He could build a career in the clerk's office, and she could probably persuade Rena to give her a job within the government. But picturing that life made her feel more claustrophobic than excited.

She wanted more.

Gage broke into her thoughts when he spoke from the other end of the tent, where he was smoothing healing accelerant onto the arms of the woman in white. "For what it's worth, my job offer still stands—for all of you." He glanced at Cassia. "A former queen would make an amazing emissary advisor. I can't change the galaxy alone, you know."

Change the galaxy.

His choice of words struck her. Maybe Kane had been right all along and they should work with Gage. She couldn't imagine Renny would say no. They would change thousands of lives that way—just look at what they'd accomplished with Gage in the few months since they'd combined their skills.

"You know, that's not a bad idea," she said. "Since we started working together, we cured a disease, rescued hundreds of abducted settlers, took down Marius, and toppled an intergalactic mafia."

Kane chuckled. "Some of it in our sleep."

"So you'll consider it?" Gage asked, perking up and glancing all around. "Joining my team?"

"You know I'm in," Doran said as Solara threaded her arm through his and nodded in agreement. "On one condition," he added. "I won't work with Mom. I don't want anything to do with her."

"Not a problem," Gage told his brother. "She spends so much time lobbying for government contracts on Earth that she practically lives there."

Cassia worked a grain of sand between her fingers and tried to think of a way to broach the topic of Shanna without sounding jealous. "Maybe Kane could travel with us instead of with the third-sector sales team."

"Oh, with Shanna, you mean?" teased Kane right before he recycled her words about Jordan. "She's not so bad."

Cassia probed his upper arm. "Does it hurt here?"

"No. My laser wound's on the other side. Why?"

She made a fist and slugged him hard.

"Yes!" Solara pumped her arms in the air. "Five minutes! I was right!"

Kane grumbled to himself, rubbing the spot. "I can't believe I fell for that."

"Me neither." Cassia winked. "Want me to kiss it and make it better?"

A spark of mischief lit his gaze as he tapped his bottom lip. "This is where it hurts. Really bad. The pain is excruciating."

Doran and Solara shared a groan and made for the exit while Gage followed behind, mumbling something about packing supplies.

"I thought they'd never leave," Kane whispered. He cupped her face in one hand as his eyes turned soft. "I'm sorry you lost the election. Thank you for staying with me."

Cassia wasn't sorry. She'd meant what she'd said before—there was no place she'd rather be than inside this grubby tent with him. "Thank *you* for choosing me."

"Of course. Was there any doubt?"

Yes, there had been, on the beach before she'd stunned him. The struggle between the drug and his heart had played out so clearly on his features that she'd feared she had lost him forever. But she didn't want to think about that, so she kissed his forehead and held him close. "You know I love you, right?"

He murmured against her throat, "I love you, too, Cassy," and his words lit her up inside because the only other time he'd spoken them was under the influence of an inhaler. And that didn't count.

"Tell me again."

He did, over and over and over, until the other patients began to stir and she pulled away, not out of embarrassment, but to protect the moment and keep it private.

"So what now?" she said, brushing a thumb over his cheek. She hadn't thought to ask him whether he still wanted to work for Gage. Kane had spent most of his life following her from one crisis to the next, and she didn't want that for him anymore.

They were partners now—all in.

He made a show of thinking it over, then suggested, "How about a shower?"

Laughing, she gazed at her best friend, the boy whose shine had warmed her heart for so many years that she'd briefly gone blind to it. Now her eyes were open, and she saw him clearer than ever.

"That sounds like a good place to start."